TWIST THE KNIFE

Lost Kings MC #24

AUTUMN JONES LAKE

COPYRIGHT

DEDICATION

For my readers who are learning to love themselves: Never doubt your strength, your worth, or your right to ask for what you want.

ABOUT TWIST THE KNIFE

Jensen 'Jigsaw' Killgore, road captain of the Lost Kings Motorcycle Club, thrives on brotherhood, playing with knives, and dabbling in vigilante justice. An endless parade of willing women keeps his life uncomplicated, just the way he likes it.

But when Margot Cedarwood, a quirky, curvy mortician tied to his MC's business, enters the picture, his carefree existence is thrown off balance. Her dark sense of humor calls to Jigsaw's deepest inner demons, but it's her unexpected request for him to teach her a few things in the bedroom that ignites a spark he can't ignore. Despite his president's warning to keep his hands off Margot, Jigsaw finds himself captivated by the compassionate blonde who cares for the dead.

As the tension between them heats up, Jigsaw must decide if breaking all the rules is worth risking everything for the one woman who might be capable of doing the impossible—capturing his reluctant heart and soothing his scarred soul.

Twist the Knife is the 24th book in the popular Lost Kings MC series by *USA Today* bestselling author Autumn Jones Lake. This is Jigsaw's first book and *can* be read without reading other books in the series.

ALSO BY AUTUMN JONES LAKE

- SLOW BURN (LOST KINGS MC #1) – *free ebook!*
- CORRUPTING CINDERELLA (LOST KINGS MC #2)
- THREE KINGS, ONE NIGHT (LOST KINGS MC #2.5)
- STRENGTH FROM LOYALTY (LOST KINGS MC #3)
- TATTERED ON MY SLEEVE (LOST KINGS MC #4)
- WHITE HEAT (LOST KINGS MC #5)
- BETWEEN EMBERS (LOST KINGS MC #5.5)
- MORE THAN MILES (LOST KINGS MC #6)
- WHITE KNUCKLES (LOST KINGS MC #7)
- BEYOND RECKLESS (LOST KINGS MC #8)
- BEYOND REASON (LOST KINGS MC #9)
- ONE EMPIRE NIGHT (LOST KINGS MC #9.5)
- AFTER BURN (LOST KINGS MC #10)
- AFTER GLOW (LOST KINGS MC #11)
- ZERO HOUR (LOST KINGS MC #11.5) – *free ebook!*
- ZERO TOLERANCE (LOST KINGS MC #12)
- ZERO REGRET (LOST KINGS MC #13)
- ZERO APOLOGIES (LOST KINGS MC #14)
- SWAGGER & SASS (LOST KINGS MC #14.5) – *free ebook!*
- WHITE LIES (LOST KINGS MC #15)
- RHYTHM OF THE ROAD (LOST KINGS MC #16)
- LYRICS ON THE WIND (LOST KINGS MC #17)
- DIAMOND IN THE DUST (LOST KINGS MC #18)
- CROWN OF GHOSTS (LOST KINGS MC #19)
- THRONE OF SCARS (LOST KINGS MC #20)
- RECKLESS TRUTHS (LOST KINGS MC #21)
- DEEPER YOU DIG (LOST KINGS MC #21.5)
- RUST OR RIDE (LOST KINGS MC #22)
- AGONY TO ASHES (LOST KINGS MC #23)
- TWIST THE KNIFE (LOST KINGS MC #24)
- COLLECT THE PIECES (LOST KINGS MC #25)

OTHER BOOKS IN THE LOST KINGS MC WORLD

GLOSSARY OF CHARACTERS AND TERMINOLOGY

The Lost Kings MC™ World © Autumn Jones Lake

The following may contain spoilers if you are not caught up on the series or have skipped books.

Please note, this glossary only pertains to my romantic fictionalized motorcycle club world. It should not be construed as applicable to any other fictional club or a real-life motorcycle club.

THE LOST KINGS MC: UPSTATE, NY ("EMPIRE," NY)

President: Rochlan "Rock" North. Leader of the Upstate NY charter of the Lost Kings MC.

Sergeant-at-Arms: Wyatt "Wrath" Ramsey. Protector or enforcer for the club.

Vice President: Blake "Murphy" O'Callaghan. Murphy was the road captain up until *White Lies (Lost Kings MC #15)*

Treasurer: Marcel "Teller" Whelan. Handles the money and investments for the club. In After Glow (Lost Kings MC #11) Rock and Teller discovered they were father and son. In *Reckless Truths (Lost Kings MC #21)* they let the whole club in on their secret.

Road Captain: Dixon "Dex" Watts (newly appointed to the position in White Lies)

THE LOST KINGS MC: DOWNSTATE, NY ("UNION" NY)

President: Angus "Zero" or "Z" Frazier. As of *Zero Apologies* (*Lost Kings MC #14*), Z is the president of the Downstate, NY charter of the Lost Kings MC.

Vice President: Logan "Rooster" Randall: Rooster's story is told in *Swagger Sass* (*Lost Kings MC #14.5*), *Rhythm of the Road* (*Lost Kings MC #16*), *Lyrics on the Wind* (*Lost Kings MC #17*), and *Diamond in the Dust* (*Lost Kings MC #18*)

Sergeant-at-Arms: Grayson "Grinder" Lock as of *Throne of Scars* (*Lost Kings MC #20*)

Treasurer: Hustler

Road Captain: Jensen "Jigsaw" Kilgore; Jigsaw, Rooster's best friend from childhood.

THE LOST KINGS MC: PORT EVERHART, VA

President: Cypress "Ice" Caldwell

Vice President: Farmer

Sergeant-at-Arms: Pants

Treasurer: T-Bone

Road Captain: Boots

THE LOST KINGS MC: DEADBRANCH, TN

President: Squiggy

SAA: Steer from the Downstate NY charter moved to TN in *Throne of Scars.*

Retired President: Digger, we first met him in *Lyrics on the Wind.*

OTHER LOST KINGS MC MEMBERS

Thomas "Ravage" Kane: We've gotten to know Rav and his snarky humor a little bit better in each book. Ravage is a general member who helps out wherever he is needed.

Cronin "Sparky" Petek: Sparky is the mad genius/hippie stoner behind the Lost Kings MC's pot-growing business. He is rarely seen outside of the basement, as he prefers the company of his plants.

Elias "Bricks" Serrano: We have seen Bricks and his girlfriend Winter throughout the series. He's one of the few members who does not live at the clubhouse.

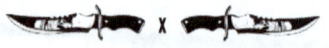

Sam "Stash" Black: Lives in the basement with Sparky and helps with the plants.

Hoot: We've seen glimpses of him since Slow Burn when he was a lowly prospect. He finally got his full patch, but still gets a lot of the grunt work.

Birch: We also met him as a prospect. He's been voted as a full-patch member but shares in a lot of the grunt work with Hoot.

Priest: The Lost Kings MC's national president. We first met him and his wife, Valentina, in After Burn.

Malik: Prospect for the Lost Kings MC. Helps out at Crystal Ball. Owns the Lucky Duck pawnshop in Ironworks.

Sway: Former president of the downstate charter of the Lost Kings MC. We've seen Sway and his wife Tawny off and on in the series since *Strength From Loyalty*, usually annoying Rock in some fashion. After some legal troubles in *Throne of Scars*, Sway disappeared to Florida and has not been seen or heard from since.

THE LADIES OF THE LOST KINGS MC

Hope Kendall North, Esq.: Nicknamed First Lady by Murphy in *Corrupting Cinderella (Lost Kings MC #2)*, Hope is the object of Rock's love and obsession. Their daughter is named Grace after Rock's mother.

Trinity Hurst Ramsey: Wrath's angel. Former caretaker of the club. She now has her own photography and graphic design business. She is married to Wrath, fiercely loyal to the club, and best friends with Hope. Although she loves her niblets, **Trinity and Wrath are happily childfree by choice and intend to *stay* that way**.

Heidi "Little Hammer" O'Callaghan: Murphy's wife and Teller's little sister. Heidi just graduated from college and works at Empire Med. Murphy officially adopted her daughter, Alexa Jade. In Reckless Truths, Heidi and Murphy had another daughter, Brittany, affectionately nicknamed "Bit-Bit" by her big sister.

Charlotte Clark, Esq: Teller's sunshine. Often credited with taming the brooding treasurer of the Lost Kings, Teller. As of *Reckless Truths*, she is pregnant with twins.

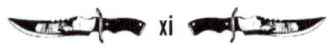

Lilly Frazier: Z's brave and devoted siren. The new queen of the Lost Kings MC's downstate charter. One of Hope's best friends. Z and Lilly's son is named Chance.

Shelby Morgan: Rooster's sassy little chickadee. Country music singer from Texas. We first met Shelby in *Swagger and Sass*.

Serena Cargill: Former downstate club girl. Abused by Shadow, the former VP of the downstate charter. Found love with her Grinder, her "murder daddy" in *Crown of Ghosts*. She is currently pregnant with their son Lincoln.

Emily C. Walker: Engaged to Dex. Serena's best friend. Introduced in *Throne of Scars*.

Margot Cedarwood: Daughter of the owner of the Cedarwood Family Funeral Home, a business the Lost Kings MC invested in as of *Reckless Truths*. Jigsaw has had his eye the pretty blonde mortician her since the day they met.

Liberty Isabel Walker: Libby is Emily's teenage sister. The Walker sisters have no other family. Grinder is protective of them.

Willow: Bartender at Crystal Ball, but once or twice we've caught her sneaking in or out of the basement with Sparky.

Swan: Lost Kings MC club girl and dancer at Crystal Ball. Swan has found a new calling as the yoga teacher for the old ladies of the Lost Kings MC and is slowly moving away from dancing at Crystal Ball.

OTHER RECURRING CHARACTERS IN THE LOST KINGS MC WORLD

Griffin "Stonewall" Royal: His story is in Fighting the Forbidden and Repairing the Wreckage. Remy's best friend and business partner. Helped Grinder out in *Crown of Ghosts*. In a relationship with Remy's little sister Molly.

Roman "Vapor" Hawkins: *Renegade Path* is his story. He is married to Dex's "niece" Juliet.

Remington "Ruthless" Holt: Owns "The Castle" with his best friend, Griff. An underground fighting ring Murphy used to participate in. We've seen him most recently helping out the club in

Crown of Ghosts. Guardian of his younger sister, Molly. Considering forming a support club for the Lost Kings MC with Griff, Eraser, and Vapor.

Dawson Roads: Famous (fictional) country music singer in the Lost Kings MC world. He's been mentioned here and there since *One Empire Night*, but we didn't officially "meet" him until *Rhythm of the Road* when Shelby was on tour with him.

Carter "Scribbles" Clark: Charlotte's goofy, often inappropriate, younger brother. Most recently rescued by the club in *Reckless Truths*. Given the road name *Scribbles* by Wrath.

Loco: Business associate of the Lost Kings MC. He covers the Ironworks area of the Lost Kings MC's territory. He has appeared throughout the series and become a strong LOKI ally.

Eraser: Owns Zips, a racetrack near the Lost Kings MC territory. Married to Ella. We first met him in *Renegade Path*, and again in *White Lies*.

Lynn Morgan: Shelby's mother. May or may not have hooked up with Jigsaw or Steer at some point.

Russell "Chaser" Adams: President of the Devil Demons MC in Western NY. (The Hollywood Demons series contains his story.)

Mallory "Little Dove" DeLova-Adams: Chaser's wife. Daughter of mafia boss Anatoly DeLova.

Angelina Adams: Mallory and Chaser's daughter

Linden "Stump" Adams: Chaser's father. Former president of the Devil Demons MC.

Sullivan Wallace: Jake's brother, and the owner of Strike Back Fitness. He's a significant character in *Bullets and Bonfires* and has his own book, *Warnings and Wildfires*.

Jake Wallace: One of Wrath's business partners in Furious Fitness. Jake has appeared off and on throughout the series since *Tattered on my Sleeve*. He sometimes holds self-defense classes for the ladies.

The mysterious "Quill" who we met in *Diamond in the Dust* and again in Crown of Ghosts. He is Chaser's newly discovered half-brother.

Anatoly DeLova: Mallory's father. Leader of the Russian mafia. Sometime business associate of the Lost Kings MC.

Stella: Pornographic film actress. The downstate charter is the sole investor in her production company. Ex-girlfriend of Z. Current… something of Sway. Her Sex in Every City series sometimes requires members of LOKI to work as bouncers on her film sets.

Inga March: Porn star, and former dancer at Crystal Ball. Sued the whole club for paternity of her son in After Burn (Lost Kings MC #10) Has not been seen since then.

Tawny: Sway's ol' lady. The former "Queen B" of the downstate charter of the Lost Kings MC.

Anya Regal: Porn princess of the Lost Kings MC, Virginia charter.

Shonda: Club girl from the Lost Kings, MC Virginia charter.

Lala: Club girl from Downstate NY.

Bonnie: Club girl from the Downstate club.

OTHER MCS: FRIENDLY CLUBS:

Devil Demons MC: Based in Western NY. Long-time friend of the Lost Kings MC. Their clubs are intertwined and share a lot of history. More of this is explored in the *Hollywood Demons* series.

Wolf Knights MC: Mostly an ally of the Lost Kings. They used to run Slater County but said they were dissolving their charter in White Lies and turning it over to the Lost Kings. As of *Reckless Truths*, Slater County is officially Lost Kings MC territory.

Iron Bulls MC: (From the Iron Bulls MC series by Phoenyx Slaughter): Southwestern outlaw club. Meets up and does business with LOKI once in a while.

Savage Dragons MC: (From the Iron Bulls MC series by Phoenyx Slaughter): Texas outlaw club.

ENEMY CLUBS:

Vipers MC: Used to run Ironworks until the Lost Kings took over that territory. Still active in other parts of the country.

South of Satan MC: Vermont MC who has stirred up trouble for LOKI in the past. Last disposed of in *Reckless Truths*.

LOST KINGS MC TERMINOLOGY

LOKI: Short for LOst KIngs. Only to be used by members of the Lost Kings MC.

War room: Where the Lost Kings hold "church."

Property patch: When a member takes a woman as his old lady (wife status), he gives her a vest with a property patch. In my series, the vest has a "Property of Lost Kings MC" patch and the member's road name on the back. The officers also place their patches on the ol' lady's vest as a sign that they always have her back. Her man's patch or club symbol is placed over the heart. Rock's patch is a crown. Wrath's is a star. Murphy's is a four-leaf clover. Teller's is a dollar sign. Z's is the letter Z. Rooster's patch is a rooster wearing a crown. As a joke, Wrath gave Rock and Hope a "product of" patch for baby Grace.

PLACES IN THE LOST KINGS MC WORLD

I use a mix of real and imaginary names to describe the places in my series. Again, I bend and shape geography to my needs as this is a fictional world that I have created.

Empire, NY: The territory run by the Lost Kings MC upstate charter. This is a fictional version of Albany, NY, the capital of New York State. Many of the Lost Kings MC's businesses are located in and around Empire.

Slater, NY: Loosely based on Schenectady County. Until recently it was the Wolf Knights MC's territory.

Ironworks, NY: Loosely based on Rensselaer County (Troy, NY). At the beginning of the series, it was run by the Vipers MC. It is now considered territory of the Lost Kings MC.

Union, NY: A fictional area two hours south of Empire, NY, where the "downstate" charter is located.

Crystal Ball: The strip club owned by the Lost Kings MC and one of their legitimate businesses. They often refer to it simply as "CB." Located in Empire County.

Furious Fitness: The gym Wrath owns with Murphy and Jake. Often just referred to as "Furious." Located not far from Crystal Ball.

Strike Back: Owned by Sullivan Wallace but members of the Lost Kings MC and Ruthless & Royal have worked and worked out there in the past.

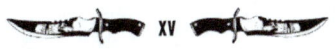

Johnson County/Johnsonville: Fictional area where Heidi grew up. About an hour west of "Empire." Where Strike Back Gym, The Castle, and Zips are located. Possibly the new home of a Lost Kings MC support club? We'll see!

Zips: Racetrack owned by Eraser where all the illegal gambling/racing in the area happens.

The Castle: Formerly a juvenile detention center. The building is now used to house the underground fighting ring run by Remy and Griff. Murphy used to fight here. Other LOKI members also blow off steam in the cage here from time to time. Located in the middle of nowhere, NY, it once-upon-a-time housed Griff, Vapor, Eraser, Sully, and possibly Teller during their "troubled youth" days.

Kodack, NY: Another fictional NY area located in Western New York. Somewhere near Buffalo, perhaps. This territory is run by the Devil Demons MC.

Empire Medical Center: Local hospital where all the Kings receive medical treatment. Heidi also works there now.

OTHER MC TERMINOLOGY

Most terminology was obtained through research. However, I have also used some artistic license in applying these terms to my romanticized, fictional version of an outlaw motorcycle club. This is not an exhaustive list.

Cage: A car, truck, van—basically anything other than a motorcycle.

Church: Club meetings all full-patch members must attend. Led by the president of the club, but officers will update the members on the areas they oversee. (Some clubs refer to the meeting room where they hold church as the "chapel." My club refers to it as their "war room."

Citizen/civilian: Anyone not a hardcore biker or belonging to an outlaw club. "Citizen wife" would refer to a spouse kept entirely separate from the club.

Cut: Leather vest worn by outlaw bikers and adorned with patches and artwork displaying the club's unique colors. The Lost Kings' colors are blue and gray. Their logo is a skull with a crown. The Respect Few, Fear None patch is earned by doing time for the club without snitching. Brother's Keeper patches are earned by killing for the club. Loyal Brother is for a brother who's spent more than five years with the club.

Colors: The "uniform" of an outlaw motorcycle gang. A leather vest, with the three-piece club patch on the back, and various other patches relating to their role in the club.

Fly colors: To ride on a motorcycle wearing colors.

Muffler bunny or "bunnies": A girl who hangs around to provide sexual favors to members. Old ladies in my series will sometimes refer to them as "friends of the club," depending on the girl in question. Some clubs refer to them as club whores, patch whores, or cut sluts. These terms are not regularly used in my series. Sometimes simply referred to as a "club girl."

Nomad: A club member who does not belong to any specific charter, yet has privileges in all charters.

Old lady/ol' lady: Wife or steady girlfriend of a club member.

Patched in: When a new member is approved for full membership.

Patch holder: A member who has been vetted through performing duties for the club as a prospect or probate and has earned his three-piece patch.

Road name: Nickname. Usually given by the other members.

Run: A club-sanctioned outing, sometimes with other chapters and/or clubs. Can also refer to a club business run.

I'm sure I'm forgetting something! But this should be enough to get you started!

CHAPTER ONE

Jigsaw

Jensen Killgore, 14 years old

Run!

Despite the chains tethering me to the wall, my mind keeps screaming at me to run. *Run.*

Instead, I remain frozen in place. "Sacred fire, guide my whip." My father's low prayer sends a shiver of dread down my spine. "Consume all that is impure in my son."

"I fear no evil," I chant, even though I'm supposed to remain silent. *You're the evil.*

One day, I'll be at the other end of that whip.

A subtle, high-pitched hiss slices through the air, building to a rapid crack.

Intense, searing pain sizzles from my shoulder to my ribcage. Fire races over my skin, leaving a throbbing ache radiating over my back. This isn't the first, second, or even third time I've been whipped. It never hurts any less.

Another trail of fire blazes across my back. I twist my hands in the chain. Something in my wrist pops. A groan drags out of my throat.

I won't give him the satisfaction of my screams or tears.

Relax. Relax. It hurts more if you tense.

Bullshit. Unbearable agony burns my skin no matter how I position my body.

A sting kisses my eyebrow and my body jolts with shock. My back's already a scarred mess. But my face?

I squeeze my eyes shut and drop my head. Wetness trails down my back. My body sags against the cold stone wall in front of me. The sharp tang of copper fills my nose.

Blackness blurs around the edges of my vision. Chaos and fear rule my brain. My thoughts jumble, focusing on the agony in my body. Red and black swirls in front of me, and I mentally toss myself into the swirl.

Pain claims every inch of my body while darkness mercifully claims my mind.

AGONY FLAMES OVER MY SKIN, straight down to my bones.

Cold, hard, filthy stone pushes against my cheek. I lift my head and blink into the darkness.

Infinite darkness.

I wait for my eyes to adjust. But still nothing.

No.

Despair wraps around my chest. The whipping wasn't punishment enough. He left me in the box—a small, narrow room with nothing but uneven, gritty stone to comfort my battered body.

I press my palms against the cold floor and try to push myself upright. Straight hellfire shoots up my arms. Every part of my body hurts so badly, I didn't realize my wrists are damaged from the chains. Carefully, I wrap my left hand around my right wrist, trying to assess the extent of the injury. Hot, swollen, rough skin. I press my thumb harder against the bone. Everything seems intact. I perform the same exploration on my left wrist.

I could be here for hours or days. Cataloging my injuries will make

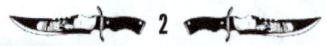

the time pass faster. Anything to keep my mind off the empty, dark, closet-sized room that locks from outside. Where my father always leaves me after my punishment.

Tears roll down my cheeks. How long will he leave me here this time? If I miss more school this semester, surely they'll send someone to check on me, right? The frequency and intensity of the punishments have escalated this year. No, not this year. Ever since my best friend's parents died and he was sent to live with his aunt and uncle. My father has it in his head that whatever demon possessed Logan's father to kill his wife, then turn the gun on himself, had somehow infected *me* with evil. Just because Logan was my friend? I never even got to say goodbye to Logan or mourn his mother—who I loved like she was my own. She was sweet, kind, and never quoted the bible.

My real mother's long gone. The harem of women my father replaced her with don't care what happens to me. My two older brothers left here as soon as they could, never bothering to return or check on me, even though they know what kind of damage our father likes to inflict. They don't even know how much worse it's gotten. How many more disciples my father's collected and has living on our family farm. How they spend every Sunday in the barn that's been converted into a "church" raging about sin and hellfire. How my father keeps threatening to take me out of school to save me from being "corrupted." Not that I love school, but at least it's something *normal* and gets me away from *here* for a few hours a day.

Logan's Aunt Em and Uncle Boone had always been nice to me. Could I call them? Would they let me stay with them if I confessed the true depths of my father's cruelty? Could I bare my scars to save myself?

One thing's becoming clearer and clearer with each "punishment" I receive.

If I stay, I'm going to die.

My neck aches and I rest my cheek against the cool stone floor again. After a few minutes of jumbled thoughts, I fall into another nightmarish sleep full of flaming demons.

A CREAK SPLITS THE AIR, bringing me back into my throbbing body.

The heavy door scrapes against the rough floor.

A faint beam of light stabs through my endless darkness.

My body stills. Breath catches in my lungs. Is he back? Will he kill me this time?

"Jensen?" a little voice calls out.

Jezebel—Jezzie, my baby sister.

No.

She can't see me like this. I don't want to be the cause of her nightmares. She's already patched me up in the past—something a kid her age shouldn't even know how to do.

I squint into the light and crane my neck, trying to see her. See if anyone's with her.

The door opens wider.

Jezzie's tiny shadow appears against the faint light of the basement. She's hope, comfort, and guilt in a long, pink flannel nightgown that sweeps over the tops of her bare feet.

"Go," I croak.

My father saves the harsh, physical punishments for his sons. But he's not above depriving her of food or some other twisted punishment just for checking on me.

"Jensen!" she whispers a little louder.

The door creaks closed. A few seconds later, a weak beam of light illuminates my cell.

"You're going to get in trouble," I mumble.

A soft white pillowcase stuffed with something other than a pillow lands in front of my face. Jezzie kneels next to me. A knife of shame that she has to see my body in this condition twists into my heart.

"I brought you something to eat," she whispers. "And water."

Another tear leaks from the corner of my eye. "Thank you."

I flick my gaze up and find her staring at my back, silent tears rolling down her own pale cheeks. No words to comfort her come to

mind and that crushes what's left of my soul. I'm her big brother. I'm supposed to protect her and reassure her. Not traumatize her.

For Jezzie, I bite through the pain in my wrists and force myself to my knees. My lips pull into a wobbly smile that probably looks more psychotic than comforting. She lets out a soft sob and quickly digs through the pillowcase.

"Here." She pulls out a wad of gauze, a bottle of antiseptic, and a tube of ointment.

I grit my teeth as she gently dabs at the wounds and carefully covers my back in the ointment. Finally, she lays strips of gauze over the worst parts. By the time she's finished, she's shaking.

"Why?" she sobs.

I don't have an answer.

"Father said you have bitterness in your heart, but I know that's not true."

It might not have been true before the whippings started, but I'm bubbling over with bitterness now. I don't waste what little energy I have correcting her, though.

My dry, cracked lips ache but I accept the mason jar of water when Jezzie pushes it into my hands. The tepid water slides down my throat, bringing little relief.

"Here." She unwraps a white cloth napkin and hands me two thick, rough-cut slices of homemade bread. An uneven layer of butter sticks out between the slices. Probably all she could get away with taking from the kitchen without anyone noticing.

"Thank you." I take a bite and chew slowly, savoring soft, squishy bread and the rich butter coating my tongue.

"It's fresh. Momma Ruth gave it to me," she whispers.

I lift an eyebrow, then wince as it pulls and stings.

"Jensen!" She gasps. "Your forehead."

"Is it bad?"

Instead of answering, she bites her lip and pulls out the gauze, antiseptic, and ointment again.

"It's okay, Jensen," she coos in her high-pitched, babyish voice. "Every scar tells a story."

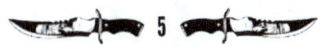

"Ah, the tongue of the wise brings healing," I whisper. I still my body as she cleans the cut over my eye.

"Momma Ruth give you the supplies too?" At least one of the wives doesn't hate me. Ruth isn't much older than I am. My father just brought her home one day and added her to his collection of disciples who live on our family compound.

"Yes," Jezzie says. "I like her. She lets me sleep in her room." Her voice falters. "The nights Father isn't in there."

"Good." Pain and exhaustion pull me down to the floor again. "Thank you, Jezzie."

She lets out a hiccup-sob and curls her small hand around my fingers. "I love you, Jensen. Please get better. I miss you."

A devil wraps its hand around my throat, leaving me incapable of making any promises. But I manage to whisper back, "Love you too."

Even if I don't survive, I want her to know that much.

A FEW DAYS LATER, I'm able to move without screaming. The door to my cell opens and I recoil. Fear races through my veins. But the long sweeping skirt all the women in the commune wear swishes across the stones.

Not my father.

I lift my gaze.

Ruth, her long red hair twisted into two complicated braids under a white bonnet, smiles down at me. Even in the weak light the freckles on her face and rounded cheeks suggest she should still be in school, not living as a slave to a religious fanatic who whips his children and locks them in small dark rooms for days as punishment.

She holds out a stack of clean clothing and a pair of shoes. "Your father says your confinement is over. You're to go to school and then come straight home."

School? Today, I can sit up without screaming. But I don't think I can tolerate an entire day riding the bus and sitting in the hard metal chairs in each classroom. And God help me if one of the morons who

enjoy mocking my clothes shoves me or even touches me. Instead of stabbing those bullies or cutting off one of their fingers—which I've decided I'll definitely do one day—I'll probably pass out from the pain.

Ruth crouches in front of me, her long dress pooling on the floor around her feet, and sets the clothes next to my hip. "Let me look at your back."

Instead of fresh bandages or ointment, she pushes an envelope into my hands. Confused, I frown and open it. A small blue paper rectangle flutters to the floor. *Social Security* is printed in red, curved letters at the top. My name and a long string of numbers.

Ruth stares at me with wide eyes, but I'm not sure what she's trying to tell me. I quickly pull out a piece of paper and unfold it. *Certificate of Birth.*

Documents. *My* documents.

I stare at her.

She bows her head and picks up a fresh roll of gauze and attends to my back. I bite my lip while she changes and cleans the wounds. Wadded up piles of rust-colored bandages drop on the floor while she works.

I stare at the envelope. A piece of green paper snags my attention.

A twenty-dollar bill.

Tears sting my eyes. Ruth barely knows me and she's risking her own safety to help me leave? That's what this is, right?

Or is this a test my father put her up to?

"Each punishment is worse than the one before. I'm afraid without...well you might not survive the next one," she whispers so low, I can barely make out the words.

"What about you?" I whisper back.

"I am with child. He will not hurt me."

Disgust churns my insides. "His?"

She sits back on her heels, shaking her head. "It does not matter."

How can I leave my little sister in this hellish place? "Jezzie—"

"I will take care of her." Her tone is a solemn oath. "You must save yourself, first."

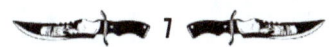

Running—leaving my little sister behind in this insanity—twists a knife of guilt deep into my chest.

Underneath my instinctive reaction, one thing becomes crystal clear.

I can't save my sister if I'm dead.

CHAPTER TWO

Jigsaw

THE DEMONS OF MY PAST ARE BRANDED INTO MY SKIN. NO MATTER HOW hard I twist the throttle, or how many miles of concrete I've put between my old life and my new one, those demons never give me peace.

On my back, the physical scars have been obscured with carefully placed ink, but they're still an ugly reminder of the brutality I was raised in. Of who I came from.

Now, I've made my home on the other side of the country, far from those memories. As road captain of the Lost Kings MC, the club that's been my family since I was twenty, I've found stability but I'm often still edgy and restless to *run*. My best friend, Logan—now known as Rooster—is the VP of our charter.

We've come a long way.

But the past never really rests.

Rooster's met the perfect woman and they'll be tying the knot soon. I love her like a sister and I'm happy for them.

I have way too much darkness in me to ever settle down with one woman. I don't even like to *sleep* next to one in case I wake up with nightmares. Love them and leave them smiling has served me well and I have no intention of ever changing that.

Soon I'll need to find my own place. Not that Rooster and Shelby have told me I have to move, but it's the right thing to do.

Today, I'm helping my little sister Jezzie move into *her* new apartment. I've been coughing up money for her college tuition for a few years. When she mentioned she wanted to switch to yet another school this semester, I finally convinced her to move to New York so we can be closer to each other.

Our relationship's awkward at best. Guilt's cemented onto my shoulders for leaving her behind. It doesn't matter that I was a kid myself. Or that I came back for her when I could. I chose myself over her and while I was living comfortably with Rooster and his aunt and uncle—finishing high school, going to keggers in the woods, and healing from the trauma my father inflicted—Jezzie was in hell.

At least my father will never harm another woman or child again. I made sure of that.

Now that we've finished clearing the load out of the truck she rented in Pennsylvania, I stop to fiddle with the locks on her front door. Dead bolt. I flick it in and out. Not bad. Frame's sturdy.

"Don't start, Jensen," my sister warns. "The locks are fine."

I glance up. She's standing in the hallway, hands on her hips, elbows pointing sideways, irritation all over her scrunched face.

I resist the urge to *boop* her on the nose.

The sweet kid who tended to my wounds turned into a young woman who's more like a hedgehog today—adorably unassuming to look at but when she's provoked, her sharp defenses prickle to life, keeping you at a distance.

"You're still too far away for my liking." This is guaranteed to piss her off, but I say it anyway. "You couldn't find a school closer to Empire at least?"

"Nooo," she answers slowly to punctuate her annoyance.

"All clear. No hidden cameras or anything weird that I can find." Rooster strides into the living room. "It's a nice place, Jezzie."

She beams at *him*. No attitude for ol' Uncle Rooster, she saves the snark for me. "Thank you, Logan."

"No problem."

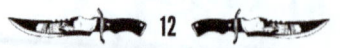

"Actually." Jezzie lunges at me and throws her arms around my neck so fast, I take a quick step back to balance myself. "Thank *you*. For finding this place, paying for it, moving me here." Emotion wells up in her eyes and she glances away, hugging me tighter and resting her cheek on my chest. "All of it."

Even though I'm not usually a hugger, I return the embrace, lifting her slightly off the ground. The scent of cotton candy tickles my nose. "Proud of you, Jezebel," I murmur against her hair.

She lets out a harsh laugh and pulls away. "Two colleges in the last three years. And I'm still mooching off you. What's to be proud of?"

"You could've gone to *no* colleges and spend your days milking goats and popping out babies." That's the life she *would've* had if our father'd had his way.

"Ugh." Her face screws into a disgusted pout. She pops her fist against my shoulder. "Why'd you have to ruin a nice moment by bringing up our freak show family?"

"Can't help it." I tug at a large chunk of her long, multi-colored hair. Pink, blue, and purple this month. "I like this. Reminds me of cotton candy." It also reminds me that she has choices now. Hair colors outside of nature would not have been permitted on the Killgore farm. Better to leave that unsaid, though.

"Is that your way of saying I look like a clown?" she asks, gathering all of her hair and twisting it into a bun, then letting it fall down her back.

I roll my eyes. "No."

"It's pretty," Rooster says.

"Thanks." Jezzie glances around the small, sparsely furnished space. Love seat. Desk. Bookshelf. Lots of boxes of books. *Heavy* boxes of books. Paying for her living expenses isn't difficult. She doesn't ask for much. The most expensive thing she owns is the neon purple fat tire ebike she asked for last Christmas. She swears that's all she needs to get around campus and the small college town.

"I'll get a job so I can take over some expenses," she says with a serious squint.

I snort. "Your cell phone and Spotify subscription aren't breaking my bank, Jezzie. Just worry about school."

"I think this is going to be a better fit for me. Almost all of my credits transferred. And once I get these summer classes done, I'll officially be a junior."

"I think you're going to do great here." I stuff my hands in my pockets and rock back on my heels. "And I like having you closer. I want you to come visit when you have time off."

"You can stay with us," Rooster adds.

Her eyes light up. "With you and Shelby?" She squees. "I still can't believe you're engaged to Shelby Morgan."

Rooster chuckles. "You and me both."

"Yeah, I can't believe anyone wants to marry his homely, bearded face, either." I shrug. "It really is true love." I cock my head. "Since when do you listen to country music, anyway?"

"Shelby's *more* than country music. She's a lyrical genius." She slaps my arm and grins. "I still can't believe you've been out on tour with her *and* Dawson Roads. I wish you'd let me ride along."

"Maybe next summer," Rooster says.

I had a different answer in mind.

"You sure you'd let me around all your MC brothers?" Jezzie flashes a wicked smirk at me.

Joke's on her. If she's going to date anyone, I *would* rather have her with a brother. I just can't think of one who's single and close enough to her age who I'd trust with my little sister. Jezebel's grown into such a contrary little pain in my ass, though. If I tell her I *want* her to date a Lost King, she'll be engaged to a fucking FBI agent or worse in no time.

"Yeah, they'll all know to keep their hands off you." That's sure to piss her off.

"Ugh."

There's a buzzing, and Rooster pulls his phone out of his pocket. He taps my arm and I nod.

"Biker business?" Jezzie asks with a hint of teasing.

"Something like that," Rooster says.

I hate leaving her this soon after she just moved into somewhere new.

"I'll be fine." She nods to the stack of boxes. "I'm looking forward to organizing all my books. And tomorrow I'm supposed to meet up with the girl I know who's in my program."

"Good."

"The guys for the truck are here," Rooster says. "I'm going to go meet them and check it over one more time."

"I got everything," Jezzie says. "I think."

"I'll check. No worries." Rooster pats her shoulder and walks out.

Once he's gone, Jezzie turns to me with a more serious expression. "I'll call Aunt Andrea later and let her know I'm all settled in."

"Good. She doing all right?" She's the only other member of our family either of us have had contact with in years. Since she extracted herself from our father's insane religious beliefs before he formed his fucked-up cult, she was the only person I trusted to raise Jezzie after I got her away from our father. She doesn't necessarily approve of me, so we keep our relationship minimal contact. But she was good to Jezzie and that's all I care about.

Rooster returns a few minutes later. "All done."

Jezzie hugs me again. Then Rooster.

Then we head out.

"All good?" Rooster asks as we exit the apartment building.

"I think so." I glance back at the tall, brick building. "Seems safe."

He stops at his bike, helmet in hand, and looks at me. "You two seem better. Like you're mending things. Being closer will be good."

Not in the mood to talk about it, I straddle my bike and grip the handlebars. "Yeah, I hope so."

The only way to mend our relationship is to let go of the guilt and pain of our past and start over. And I haven't figured out how to do that yet.

CHAPTER THREE

Margot

HEAVY, LILY-SCENTED AIR FRESHENER, ACCOMPANIED BY A SLIGHT undercurrent of vinegar, lingers in the air of my family's funeral home. Soft classical music hums from the speakers, maintaining the solemn, respectful atmosphere that's surrounded me since childhood.

My low heels snag on the worn hallway carpet. I stop outside the consultation room, take a long, slow breath, and smooth my dress over my hips. Quickly, I check the pins holding my hair back and nudge my glasses into place.

I can do this. He can't hurt me.

It's my job to help people through the worst time in their life. Sometimes, I take things too personally, absorb our clients' grief. Not today. I'm guarding my heart and mind.

I press my palm to the heavy oak door and push.

"Margot, just in time." My father stands from behind his desk and greets me.

Across from him, our client turns and smiles at me.

Daniel.

My ex.

He's not here to win me back.

I wouldn't take him back if he begged on all fours.

"You're as exciting in bed as a corpse."

Three years later and the final insult he hurled my way still haunts me. His tone so cold and unfeeling. The man I thought I loved was repulsed by me. I left my engagement ring on his kitchen counter and walked out. We've only run into each other a few times since that day. I was too embarrassed to even look at him.

I wasn't good enough to be Daniel's wife. But he trusts my family to arrange his grandmother's funeral. *Splendid.* It's my job to comfort people and handle all the small details, so all they have to worry about is mourning their loved one. *I can do this.*

Poor Mrs. O'Leary. I only met her a few times when Daniel and I were engaged, but she was always kind to me. I want to do my best for her. To give her a proper final viewing.

As I enter the office, Daniel stands and steps away from my father's desk. My heart squeezes, but dread coils in my stomach. He's still a good-looking man. Fine, chiseled jawline. Straight nose. Sincere brown eyes. Perfectly styled dirty blond hair.

Vicious, unkind mouth.

I stand straighter and dip my chin in greeting. "Daniel."

"Hi, Margot." He sweeps his gaze over me. Probably noting that I'm still too "plump" for his liking. I pull my shoulders back and resist the urge to suck in my stomach or fold in on myself to make my chest seem smaller. "It's good to see you again."

I force a tight smile, hanging onto my professional composure with my fingernails. "I'm so sorry for your loss."

"It had been coming for some time." His stoic demeanor cracks. "We're all thankful she's no longer in pain."

I nod once at the familiar sentiment. I've heard it a lot over the years, and I've probably said it a few times myself, but it never feels quite right.

My father clears his throat and tugs on his suit jacket. "I'll let you go over details of the viewing together."

Great. I handle consults with clients on my own sometimes, but I'd prefer my father stick around for this particular one. He's probably hoping Daniel and I will get back together. As I approach thirty, Dad's

18

started suggesting I "find a husband." He hasn't exactly given me any idea of where to look in the tiny hamlet of Pine Hollow. Nor do I have much free time to spend dating. Dad always liked Daniel, though. He's probably reading more into Daniel's choice to have his grandmother's funeral here than he should.

Obviously, I'd never told him *why* Daniel and I broke our engagement.

Once we're alone, I take the chair next to Daniel, turning it slightly to face him, but pushing it back so we're not too close.

"I want to do everything possible to honor your grandmother properly," I say. "Did she leave any instructions for her viewing?" This is never an easy subject to broach with clients, but with Daniel it's like clawing my way through a heavy curtain of grief *and* awkwardness.

A sad smile tugs at the corners of his mouth. "Did she ever." He pulls a thick peach-colored envelope from his inner jacket pocket. "Your father and I already went over the casket options. But maybe you could look at the one I chose and give me your opinion?"

Of course my father wanted to be the one to sell the most expensive part of the package. He knows every detail of every casket we have for sale in the selection room. He would've started with his top-down presentation, starting with the most expensive casket and working his way down until Daniel settled on something he was willing to pay for. Since he came from a family of investment bankers, I bet Dad didn't have to go too far down the line.

"Sure. I can do that. Will your mother be assisting you with any of this?" The one time I'd met her had been unpleasant. I'm not looking forward to a repeat.

He shakes his head quickly. "No. She won't be here until tomorrow. She wants it taken care of before her plane lands."

The glacier that took up residence in my chest the moment I laid eyes on Daniel melts a fraction. It's never easy on clients who have to make all these decisions themselves.

Daniel leans over and slides a large red-and-white shopping bag in front of him. "This is the dress she wanted." He unfolds a peach chiffon and sequined dress encased in a plastic bag, holding it up by the hanger for my inspection. Fancier than what most people request, but I've dressed clients in all sorts of outfits, even a clown costume once. A peach evening gown will hardly be the most unusual.

"She bought it for a cruise she was supposed to take next month." He swallows hard and his eyes shine. "I figured this is her final bon voyage, she should get to wear it."

"That's a lovely idea."

He returns the dress to the bag, then unfolds the peach-colored sheet of paper inside the envelope and lets out a heavy sigh. A photo slips out, falling on my father's desk. Daniel picks it up between two fingers and drops it in my lap.

"It's recent."

I stare at the photo of Mrs. O'Leary. She was a beautiful, elegant woman with a sleek cap of pale, shiny gold hair that she wore pulled back from her face with jeweled clips. My mind's already calculating the supplies I'll need to restore her to this version of herself.

"She still liked wearing makeup." A snide edge enters Daniel's tone as if it was silly for his grandmother to want to feel pretty at her age. "Never went without her coral lipstick." He plunks a heavy gold tube of lipstick on my father's desk.

I uncap it and unwind the stick of wax. The orange-y shade *is* a bit garish, but I should be able to blend something to look similar but suit her better. I reach over my father's desk and snag a pad of paper, pull a pencil from the cup next to his computer, and scratch out a few notes.

Coral lipstick.

Hair pins.

"Jewelry?" I ask.

"Her wedding rings." He extracts a white plastic container in the shape of a heart from his breast pocket, snaps it open and shakes out a simple solitaire diamond and gold band. "Oh, and coral nail polish. Of course."

"Of course." I jot that down too.

"Her earrings were simple gold hoops." He gestures to the bag at his feet. "They're in there too."

"Anything else you can think of?"

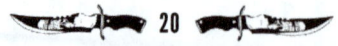

He tilts his head and frowns, as if panic that he's forgotten something is sinking in.

"Don't worry," I rush to assure him. "If you think of something later, you can always call or shoot me a text to let me know."

His frown deepens into a suspicious squint. "Margot, I'm with someone now."

Huh?

I blink and stare at him. "Okay?" My tone rises to an almost snotty-questioning lilt, unbecoming of my profession. He thinks I'm coming on to him?

Give him grace. He just lost his grandmother.

I wrangle my outrage and answer in the most cordial tone I can muster. "I tell *all our clients* to call me if they have any questions or remember something they want to add for their loved one."

"Oh. Right." He nods quickly. "I just don't want this to be weird. Since we…you know."

How dare he. "Daniel, that's ancient history." I flick my hand in the air as if our relationship is a distant—unpleasant—memory.

Never mind I'm so scarred from the experience I haven't wanted to go to bed with another man since we broke up. I won't let him know he hurt me so deeply. Or that I *still* question my desirability.

"Okay." His voice wobbles as if he doesn't trust me to control myself. I hate to break it to him, but he wasn't exactly Eros in the sack himself.

"Is there anything else?" I stand, hating how rude I'm being but unable to sit here any longer when he's acting like I'm about to jump in his lap and beg for his love sword to slay me. Whatever love or affection I had for him died when he compared me to a *corpse.*

"No, I went over music and flowers with your father." He stands and picks up the bag, holding it out to me.

"Good." Why does the room suddenly feel so small? "I'll get started on the preparations."

He reaches for me and shackles his hand around my wrist. My jaw drops at the sudden, desperate contact. "Just make sure she looks like herself. Like she's at peace."

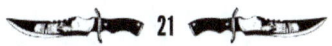

Mrs. O'Leary died in her sleep. There hadn't been a lot of restorative work that needed to be done. So, I feel confident answering, "Of course."

The office door creaks open and my father fills the doorway. Daniel releases me and I resist the urge to rub my sore wrist.

"Perfect timing." My father's gaze swings between Daniel and me. "Don't worry about a thing. Margot will take good care of Anne, Daniel."

"I know she will." Daniel flashes a quick smile at me, almost apologetic.

"I'll walk you out," my father offers.

Thank God. I mutter a few goodbyes, grab the bag of Mrs. O'Leary's things and excuse myself. My father stops me in the hallway, leaning in close and lowering his voice. "I have that other appointment coming in soon. I'll probably give them a quick tour."

"Not upstairs, though, right?" I'm not in the mood to have these shady investors my father's reeled in traipsing through my living quarters.

He scowls at the question. "Of course not."

"I'll be in the prep room if you need me." Remembering my manners, I turn toward Daniel and force a polite smile. "Don't hesitate to reach out of you think of anything else." I don't want to make the offer again, but my father will strangle me if I'm rude to a client.

Rubbing my wrist, I hurry down the hallway to the prep room.

HOURS LATER, I'm finishing what will be Mrs. O'Leary's final look. I glance at the reference photo, pleased I recreated the same hairstyle. The lip color is still bold but not as bright and I found a peach blush to complement it.

"Perfect," I whisper.

Footsteps in the hallway alert me to an incoming visitor. I continue working until it sounds like my father's entered the room.

"Dad, I'm almost finished with Mrs. O'Leary. I chose a slightly

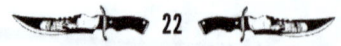

peachier blush. I think she'd like it if—" I glance up. Dad's not alone. The appointment. People who want to "invest" in our family funeral home. My father had been scant on details. Even though I have a lot of ideas on how to expand our business to make up for the general decline in our industry, the finances aren't *my* business.

I pull my mask down, snap off my gloves and step away from Mrs. O'Leary.

Four tall, muscular men in jeans, T-shirts, and black leather vests adorned with similar looking patches are with my father.

I recognize the tall, lean blond biker from previous visits—Marcel, I think. But the other three men are new. A red-headed, burly man with a full beard looks like he should be outside dropping trees with an ax, not touring a funeral home. The taller, broader blond biker must be related to Marcel—an older brother, maybe. The patch over his heart says he's the president.

Well la-di-da.

The fourth man leans down to whisper something in Marcel's ear. A bolt of frustration or annoyance creases Marcel's handsome features.

My father nods at me and holds out one hand. "This is my daughter, Margot. She's our mortuary cosmetologist." He doesn't bother giving me their names which is fine, I wouldn't remember them anyway. Not with the last one staring at me like he's trying to drill a hole through my skull with the power of his eyeballs.

My heart skips double-time.

In the sea of bikers invading my workspace, *he* stands out. Not just because of his height. All the men are well over six feet. It's not the leather vest with the patch that reads *Road Captain*, either—although that title is intriguing.

It's his eyes. The sharp way they dart around, observing and inspecting everything. Although, maybe it's fear, not interest in his surroundings. Few people are comfortable down here where we keep the bodies. A man like him, a biker who exudes raw masculinity, wouldn't admit to anyone that he's afraid of the dead. Or that he fears death.

The other three men seem keen, but their interest in my workspace is perfunctory. They're more focused on speaking with my father.

The road captain is focused on *me*.

Our eyes meet. His lips curl into a seductive smile. A jolt of electricity vibrates through my body—something I thought only happened in books or movies. He lifts an eyebrow, drawing attention to the scar running through it at an angle. He's so focused on me, heat burns over my skin like acid.

I whip around, forcing my attention back to my workstation. My heart pounds wildly, everything around me blurring into a shiny, metallic haze..

A few seconds later, the hairs on the nape of my neck prickle and a wave of warmth presses against my back.

"Margot." The deep baritone voice behind me resonates in my chest.

I twist to face him. He's so close, my shoulder brushes against his chest. My lips part as I stare up at him. *Brutal*—the only word that comes to mind. Brutal in the most handsome way. His eyes. So intense. He hasn't had an easy life. But he's confident. Cocky even.

My tongue ties itself into a knot.

He touches the fingers of his right hand to his chest. "Everyone calls me Jigsaw."

My eyebrows squinch into a frown. "Are you introducing yourself or inviting me to put together a puzzle?"

Did I really just say something so stupid to this man who looks like he probably throws knives as a hobby?

Sweat breaks out on my forehead and the strength seems to drain from my legs. I brace my hand against the smooth, cool counter. Dad told me this deal is important and here I am insulting one of the bikers within five seconds of meeting them.

One corner of Jigsaw's mouth quirks. "You're fun."

The memory of dealing with Daniel earlier still holds my emotions hostage. According to him, there's nothing *fun* about me. I'm no more exciting than dear old Mrs. O'Leary.

"You're the first person who's made that mistake." My voice comes out barely above a whisper.

He cocks his head and studies me, his gaze intense but without the disdain I felt from Daniel. Heat sears my skin. It's been a while since a man's taken an interest in me.

Not exactly a surprise since most of the men I meet are old enough to be my grandfather or *dead.*

I rarely have a chance to interact with men of the tall, terrifying, and handsome persuasion.

What is Jigsaw's real name? Am I allowed to ask? Can I ask him what it means to be the *Road Captain*?

Have I finally met a man who makes me feel *something*?

"Follow me, gentlemen." My father's imperious tone interrupts whatever Jigsaw was about to say. "Get back to work, Margot."

I scurry away from Jigsaw, all the way to the farthest cabinet where I stop to grab a fresh pair of latex gloves.

When I turn around, they're gone.

I'm alone again with Mrs. O'Leary.

But I can't stop thinking about the scarred biker...Jigsaw.

For the first time since Daniel cast me aside, I don't feel invisible.

CHAPTER FOUR

Jigsaw

FUCK ME. I BARELY PAID ATTENTION DURING THE REST OF THE MEETING. Although, I did manage to ask a question or two just to annoy Teller who obviously doesn't want me anywhere near his pet project. His attitude annoys me so much, I don't want to give him the satisfaction of telling him how fucking cool this is. Having a place to burn bodies whenever we need to will alleviate a lot of stress when the club's on a murder spree.

"Jiggy?" Rock's rough voice pulls me out of my thoughts. Has he said my name more than once?

He's waiting with an expectant expression. I glance at the house and press my hand to my chest. "You want *my* opinion?"

"You're standing here." Rock tilts his head and speaks with exaggerated slowness. "I assume there's a functional brain between your ears. Any thoughts?"

I glance at Teller. Is he going to jump down my throat if I answer? Probably. Too bad. "I thought it would be creepier but it's kinda homey. I get that the markups are high, but can the club really make enough bank to justify the hassle?"

"Eventually, yes," Teller answers with more patience than I

expected. "But having another place—besides a seedy titty bar—to wash cash is the real draw. And access to the crematorium."

Ah, yes. Our never-ending need for places to clean our dirty money. "Yeah, that part's cool."

I still didn't care for the way the old man spoke to his daughter. Margot. God damn, she's cute.

"Anyone else think his attitude toward the daughter is kinda shitty?" I ask, gesturing toward the home.

"I noticed." Teller shrugs. "Unless it interferes with the business, it's not our problem. We're not here to drag him into the twenty-first century."

I shrug. "Fair enough." It's not like our MC is all about equality, either.

Murphy doubles over laughing his big, bearded face off. "You got a thing for blondes, Jiggy? First Shelby's mom…"

Oh, hell no. He didn't bring Lynn into this. "First"—I shove a finger in Murphy's face— "Shelby's mom was most definitely *not* my first. Blonde or otherwise. And second"—I step back and smirk— "I appreciate females of all shapes, sizes, ages, and colors."

Teller groans. "You know women don't exist to be your dick sweaters, right?"

I can't help laughing. I'm so using *dick sweaters* in the future. "If they were, I'd prefer them warm and tight." I make a fist in front of Teller's face and shake it back and forth.

"Enough." Rock squeezes the bridge of his nose. "Yes, the old man's attitude is shitty, but Teller's right. It's not our problem. However, Margot seemed to like you, Jiggy. If it's all right with Z, I'd like you to help Teller with this project."

Hell yes. Rock knows what's up. He saw the spark between Margot and me.

With our Upstate president's blessing, I'll have plenty of time to return and get to know her better while I'm "helping" Teller fix up the place.

"Wait, what?" Teller stops and stares at Rock. "You heard him. He'll be asking her to try his dick on for size."

"How crass." I let out a big, fake yawn and shake my head. "You're the one who came up with dick sweaters, not me."

"He's…available." Rock turns my way and smirks. "Women seem to find him charming."

"They really do," I agree.

"Fine. You're right." Teller glances at the funeral home. "It'll be helpful for Jigsaw to keep her occupied and away from me."

Fuck yeah, sign me up. I'll occupy the fuck out of Margot. I salute Teller with two fingers instead of the one I really want to fly in his face.

Despite what any of them think, it's not Margot's pretty face and perfect, curvy little figure that interests me the most. Nope. When I looked in her eyes, I glimpsed something dark that I recognized all too well. Maybe it's her ease at working with the dead. But I sense it's more than that and I'm eager to find out everything I can about Margot Cedarwood.

CHAPTER FIVE

Margot

THE O'LEARY FAMILY IS SMALL, BUT ANN O'LEARY HAD A LOT OF friends. The viewing room is packed. Even the hallways are crowded. During the viewing, I walk a continuous loop from the front door to check on Henry, who greets people, hands them a pen, and asks them to sign the register book, to the viewing room where my cousin Paul is stationed a discreet distance from the casket in case there are any issues—like the one time we had a son try to climb *into* his mother's casket and almost knocked it off the catafalque.

I ran into Daniel briefly this morning but haven't seen him since.

My father's out back preparing things for the trip to the cemetery, while I continue observing and fixing any issues that arise.

On one of my rounds, Paul signals to me that there's an issue in the back of the room. It doesn't take long for my gaze to land on pieces of a broken vase. I hurry over to pick it up before someone gets hurt.

Holding the large chunks of broken porcelain in my hands, I stand and turn quickly—only to freeze when I find myself face to face with Daniel.

"Hi," I squeak. "How is everything?" I add in a slightly less startled, more professional tone.

"Wonderful. Truly. Thank you for everything." While his words are appreciative, he seems rigid.

My gaze slips past him and I realize, we're not alone. A tall, slender blonde stands slightly behind him, holding one of his hands.

"Everything's lovely," she says. "Thank you for taking such good care of his nana."

Nana? I've never heard Daniel refer to his grandmother so informally, but okay.

"Uh, this is Danielle." Daniel pulls her forward.

Thank God I have years of experience maintaining a blank expression. Daniel and Danielle? *Lordy.*

"Hi, it's so nice to meet you," I say, lifting my hand with the broken pieces of vase as an excuse for not shaking her hand. "I'm Margot."

She wrinkles her nose, then glances toward the front of the room at the casket. "I love what you did with Nana's makeup. That coral lipstick she always wore." She lifts her shoulders to her ears and scrunches her face in a full-body cringe. "Just awful."

I blink and fight the urge to point out her own red lipstick isn't doing her any favors. Speaking ill of the deceased at their own service happens more often than my tolerance can handle, so I shouldn't be surprised. But it tells me all I need to know about Danielle.

"Well, we all have our own unique style." I run my gaze over Danielle's plain black dress. "Beauty truly is in the eye of the beholder, as they say."

Daniel frowns at his girlfriend, then me.

I force a sweet smile. "Well, I need to throw this out."

"Just add it to my tab." Daniel laughs awkwardly.

Oh, I will.

"Please let me know if you need something," I say. "Paul is also around, and my father is preparing things for—"

"I know. I spoke to him." Daniel cuts me off. "You'll be there too, right?"

"Ah, no. I usually stay here to tidy up and help direct anyone who comes late."

"Babe, let her do her job." Danielle pats Daniel's chest and fusses with his tie.

"I am. Margot has a way with the dead." Daniel lets out an awkward chuckle.

My stomach clenches tight. Is he…making fun of me? *Margot has a way with the dead, because she's practically a corpse herself, har, har.*

Get a grip. It's his weird way of complimenting me.

Compliment or not, it feels crummy.

"Nice to meet you." I nod at Danielle, then turn and hurry away from them.

I exit the viewing room and speed down the hallway into the kitchen. It's empty for now. I dump the broken pieces of the vase in the trash, then lean against the counter. Hot tears well up in my eyes and I blink them away.

Why am I crying over him?

We're over. I don't even have feelings for him anymore. Not romantic ones, anyway. Bitter ones, I have plenty.

But he's moved on. Danielle probably rides him like a rodeo queen and screams through every orgasm and I'm…stuck. Afraid to get intimate with anyone again.

What if there's something wrong with me? I'll be the freaky girl who lives in a funeral home forever.

What kind of person thinks about these things at a viewing? Shame slides through my chest. I should keep my thoughts focused on Mrs. O'Leary.

So that's what I try to do for the rest of the afternoon.

CHAPTER SIX

Margot

Buzz. Buzz. Buzz.

"Noo. Dad. Why can't you text like a normal person?" I groan and bury my head under my pillow.

Buzzzz.

Damn, maybe he needs me to go on a pick-up with him. We get calls all times of the day and night to pick up bodies. It's my least favorite part of the business.

I roll out of bed, my feet tangling in the sheet. I fight my way free and hurry to the front door of my apartment on the top floor of the funeral home. I skid to a stop in front of the intercom and stab my thumb against the button.

"What's up, Dad?" I ask.

"The bikers are on their way. Open up the crematorium for them, show them how to use it—"

"Wait, what?" I practically screech. Everything about his deal with the bikers seems shady. But I assumed they were using our business to launder their dirty money. Using our crematorium in the middle of the night points to something much more sinister.

Dark curiosity twists through me. I take a breath and pretend to be more concerned than intrigued. "Are you sure that's a good idea, Dad?"

"Just do it." He hesitates and the intercom clicks off, then on again. "Don't ask them questions and don't get involved in…whatever it is. Just show them how it works. Don't stray far though, in case they need something. And when they're done, go through the cleanup with them. Make sure they take the ashes and…anything else when they go."

How exactly am I supposed to force a bunch of bikers to do anything? But the time for questioning my father has long passed. "Okay, I can do that."

"Thank you, Margot." He sighs and the intercom goes dead again.

No warnings to be careful from my loving father. Either he trusts the bikers not to hurt me or he doesn't care if they do.

Confused, nervous, and more excited than a prudent woman should be, I hurry into my bedroom. In my cavernous closet, that's really more like a long, narrow bedroom, I study my options. A wig seems silly. There's no reason to disguise myself. I settle on thick black leggings, a black, long-sleeved T-shirt, and black sweatshirt. Finally, I twist my blonde hair into a loose bun and tuck it under a black knit cap.

The full-length mirror on the back of my closet door says I look like an amateur cat burglar.

No time to change. My father didn't give me a timeframe for when the bikers are going to rumble in here and make me an accessory to whatever crimes they've committed tonight.

I slip my feet into a pair of black sneakers and head down the wide, carpeted staircase to the first floor. Small motion lights pop on to brighten my way. Something necessary when I get calls in the middle of the night. The second floor is dark. My cousin's either asleep or out. On the first floor, I stop in the main kitchen and grab a bottle of water out of the fridge. Who knows how long I'll be waiting outside.

Darkness surrounds the parking lot behind the house. I shut off the motion-sensor lights that flood the parking lot whenever a car pulls in. It's not a populated area and it's not like we don't use the crematorium at night sometimes, but I'd rather not call attention to our activities. There's enough moonlight and lights spilling from the house to see what we're doing.

I glance over at my father's house, beyond the home's multi-car garage. All the windows are dark. Sure, my father probably went home and to sleep after he woke me up.

How much time do I have before the bikers get here?

I open the door to the crematorium and flip the lights on inside the low, brick building. The tools they'll need are lined up neatly against the opposite wall.

Now that it's ready. I return to the back porch, sit on the bottom step and stare up at the inky-blue sky.

Will Jigsaw be with the bikers tonight?

Three or four different vehicles roar along the main street out front. That has to be them.

A few seconds later, a dark, lifted truck pulls into the parking lot. A loud, rumbling diesel pickup follows, then another truck, and finally three or four motorcycles roar over the blacktop.

What the hell? It's like Mad Max and all his furious buddies just invaded my peaceful home.

Dark, shadowy figures step out of the trucks. I stand, clutching my water bottle tight in my hands.

What am I going to do if they attack—soak them with my spring water? They're bikers, not vampires. And this isn't holy water.

One of the dark figures moves to the tailgate of the first truck but he's stopped from opening it by the driver.

Four men move toward the house, and I hurry to meet them in the middle of the parking lot. As I get closer, I recognize the men who came to meet with my father, including Jigsaw.

My heart beats faster but I keep my expression blank. Should I say hello or just nod in greeting?

He's not here to flirt. He's here to burn a body.

Shaking that off, I focus on Marcel who seems to be limping and… bleeding? "Are you hurt?" I gasp when he stops in front of me.

So much for not asking any questions. But I can't help it. I didn't expect them to show up injured. Should I offer to get him a first aid kit or something?

Marcel flashes a faint smile. "I'll be all right." He tilts his head toward the crematorium building. "I'm not sure what information your father gave you..."

"He said to give you whatever you need." My gaze sweeps over the other men. No one else seems injured, but they all look weary and on edge.

"Show us how it works." Marcel nods to the building. "That's all we need."

It's almost like he wants me to hand over the keys and go away. "Oh. All right. I can do that."

I sneak a quick look at Jigsaw, but he's focused on one of the other trucks that pulled into the parking lot.

The man who tried to open the tailgate joins us. He's—surprise, surprise—another tall, muscled man with hair as black as midnight and piercing blue eyes. Every bit as good-looking as the other men. Maybe "sexy underwear model look" is a requirement to join their motorcycle club. Handsome as he is, his expression is as grim as the other four. He doesn't bother to introduce himself and I don't ask.

"I'll get it started." I turn. "Follow me."

I'm uncomfortably aware of the five bikers looming behind me as we cross the parking lot to the low, brick building that houses the cremation chamber. Good God, they could do anything to me and no one would ever know. Well, my father would but what would he do about it?

Absolute terror grips me as I unlock the door and step inside. I hurry to the giant metal box and pull out the rollers. Then I move to the side panel and fire up the chamber.

"Uh, usually you'd have a container or..." What am I saying. None of this is normal. "Without it, a, uh, body can clench and appear stiff... sometimes it freaks people out..." My voice trails off again. I doubt these men will get freaked out by a pugilistic stance. "You'll put...your, um, *item* in the retort. Close the door and..."

"Okay," Marcel says. "How long?"

How many bodies do they have? "The whole process takes two to three hours, depending on the size."

Jigsaw whistles and Murphy elbows him in the side.

"Then you'll scrape the bone fragments out through the bottom," I continue. "You can put them through the processor, that will grind them into ash." I point to the metal machine in the opposite corner. "I can get you a container for that."

Please take all evidence of tonight with you when you go.

I glance at the five men. Their expressions are blank.

Utterly terrifying.

"Do you want me to get you a cot?" I ask no one in particular.

Rock glances at the black-haired man who shrugs.

"No, that's fine," Rock says. "Thanks, Margot."

My gaze slides to the door. "Any artificial parts like medical devices, or pacemakers, knee or hip replacements and jewelry should be removed..." Why am I bothering? Dad said not to ask questions and here I am coming dangerously close to asking yet another question.

What has my father gotten us into?

The bikers exchange a few glances. They're going to end up tossing me in the chamber with whoever else is in the back of that pickup truck, aren't they?

I squirm in my shoes. Sweat collects along the band of my knit hat. Why'd I bother to dress like a cat burglar anyway?

"Hypothetically," the tall dark-haired one says. "If some of those things end up in there, what happens?" He jerks his thumb toward the chamber.

"Well, metal can withstand the heat of cremation. It'll be with the ashes and bone fragments. We use a magnet to collect the pieces to dispose of them separately. Sometimes the metal can be recycled but we don't usually do that." I'm rambling now, so unnerved by their intense interest in every word coming out of my mouth. I hurry to finish with the most important part. "But pacemakers or anything with a battery can explode, make noise or possibly damage the chamber."

Rock and Marcel exchange glances. Then Rock lifts his chin at me. "All right. Thank you, Margot."

That sounds like a *get lost* dismissal to me. But I can't just leave them here with the crematorium at full blast. What if they need something? Or break something? Or hurt themselves? Obviously, my father has no intention of disturbing his sleep to attend to the bikers' body burning needs.

Let's face it, they're not here to dispose of some financial records. There are definitely bodies in the back of that truck.

Don't be so judgmental, hypocrite.

But now that they don't seem as threatening, I'm not scared. I'm not disgusted either.

I'm enthralled. Fascinated.

What did they do tonight? Who did they kill? Was it someone who deserved to meet their maker? Or was it just some petty turf war dispute? According to all the research I'd done since I met Jigsaw, motorcycle clubs fight over territory and perceived insults all the time. Enemies of clubs—this one in particular—have a habit of "disappearing" according to the *Empire Times*.

"We're all set, Margot," Marcel says. "We don't need the cot."

Of course they don't need help transporting the bodies. They're men. Tall, muscular men who can easily protect themselves and carry a dead body when they're done doling out vigilante justice. They don't have to resort to creative methods for body removal. How freeing it must be to know you can handle the dirtiest jobs.

Marcel walks outside with the dark-haired one. Jigsaw follows him.

"Margot?" Rock prompts.

"Oh. I'll leave you be." I glance at the chamber that's roaring now. "I'll be close by if you need help with anything—"

"No reason for you to get cold out there." He jerks his thumb over his shoulder. "Give Jigsaw your number. We'll text you if we need something."

I blink rapidly. He wants me to walk up to Jigsaw and give him my number? What if he laughs in my face? Or thinks I'm coming onto him?

Hardly the time for that.

"Sure, uh, okay." I force a shaky smile. "Can't I give it to you?"

The corners of his mouth slide up and his eyes crinkle at the corners. The smile of a man whose patience is running thin. "Left my phone in the truck."

"Right. Okay."

I hurry out into the cool night.

And run smack into a hard, warm, very tall male body.

"Easy, little one." Firm hands grip my shoulders, gently holding me steady. "Where's the fire?" A harsh crack of laughter follows the question.

I peer up into Jigsaw's cheerful face.

My lips twist with amusement. "Right in there."

He releases my shoulders but continues staring at me. "Where you going in such a hurry?"

"I got the feeling Rock didn't want me to stick around." I swallow hard and stare at his muddy boots. Where exactly were they tonight? "He, uh, wanted me to give you my number. So you can, uh, text or call me if you need something."

I finally meet his intense eyes again.

"That right?" His voice is low, almost teasing. The corners of his mouth hike up and he flicks his gaze toward the door. "Yeah, follow me."

He turns and walks toward the row of vehicles in the parking lot. Such a confident, casual swagger. As if he's not up to something nefarious in the middle of the night.

"Uh, where?" I hurry to keep up with his long stride.

He slows his steps. "My phone's in the truck."

"So is Rock's apparently," I mutter.

A tall, bearded man's leaning against the tailgate of the big diesel truck that pulled in earlier. He stiffly pulls away, standing straighter as we approach.

"You all right, motherclucker?" Jigsaw asks.

The man heaves out a long, annoyed breath. "How are you still this chipper?"

"I didn't get stabbed," Jigsaw answers in a cheerful tone. "Margot, this is my best friend, Rooster."

The first introduction of the night.

Rooster sucks in a pained breath and holds out his hand. "How are you, Margot?" He grips my hand in a quick firm shake. "Sorry we got you up in the middle of the night. Appreciate your help, though."

"Of course." I blink and drop my gaze to his side. "Are you okay? Did you really get stabbed?"

He flicks an annoyed glance at Jigsaw. "I'll be fine." He dips his chin and casts a friendly look my way. "Thank you, darlin'."

"I can get you gauze or we should at least clean it," I insist.

His expression doesn't change. "I'm okay."

I stare at Jigsaw, maybe he'll talk some sense into his friend.

As if he understands the questions in my eyes, Jigsaw smirks. "He's a stubborn one." He rests his hand on my elbow and steers me toward the passenger side door. "Let me grab my phone."

Phone. Right. I'm supposed to give Jigsaw my number and then get lost.

Jigsaw turns toward me, standing in the open door of the truck. Faint light from the interior glows over Jigsaw's tall, imposing frame, making him look both sinister and sexy. "Got your phone?" he asks.

"What?" I shove my hand in my front pocket. "Yes, but—"

"I want you to take my number." He meets my eyes and one corner of his mouth curves. "In case you ever need anything."

Ever?

"Okay." I step closer until we're almost touching.

He leans in, his arm pressing against my shoulder, his heat folding over my skin. The scent of woods and earth surrounds me, and I fight the urge to lean my head on his chest.

"Here." He tugs my phone out of my hands and works his thumbs over the screen. His phone buzzes a second later, the screen lighting up with the words *Last Responder.*

I break into wild laughter. It's a common joke in the mortuary business and I'm impressed he came up with it. "I have a T-shirt of the grim reaper driving a hearse with *Last Responder* on it." I nod at the phone.

He chuckles and hands me back my phone. "I need to see you in that."

Pleasure rolls through my body, perking up parts I thought were dormant. Are we flirting? Or is he pretending to be interested in order to distract me, so I don't ask questions about what his brothers are doing here tonight?

The thought steals any joy that'd been bubbling inside me.

"Everyone gets a nickname," he says, throwing another breath-stealing grin at me.

"Huh?" I blink at him.

He holds out his phone and shimmies it from side to side in his hand. "Well, everyone important to the club gets a nickname."

Important to the club.

Wait a minute. *I'm important to his club?*

Duh, of course I am. His club wants after-hours access to my family's crematorium.

I need sleep.

"Is it okay if I save your number under *Jigsaw*?" I peer up at him and hold out my phone.

"Sure. It sounds better than 'random dipshit.'"

I explode with laughter. Twice in five minutes, he's made me laugh. This must be a record.

"Do you want something to drink?" I gesture toward the house. "For you and the guys?" I hurry to add so I don't sound desperate.

He lifts his head, staring over me in the direction of the crematorium. "Yeah. Appreciate it."

"Follow me." I hurry toward the house.

Behind me, there's murmuring and a harsh laugh. I stop and glance over my shoulder. Rooster and Jigsaw are scowling at each other. "Rooster, do you want to come in for a minute?" I ask.

"Nah, I'm all right. Thanks."

Jigsaw slaps his friend's shoulder and strides toward me, his long legs covering the pavement faster than mine.

At the back steps, he stops and waits for me to go first, then hurries to open the screen door for me.

"Thank you," I whisper in a breathless rush. It's not the brisk walk across the parking lot stealing the air from my lungs, it's *him*.

I push the door open and turn to the right, leading to the large, but outdated, main kitchen. "We keep refreshments and things here for... guests." It's been years since we used it as our family kitchen, but we keep it well stocked.

Jigsaw stands in the center, his head swiveling to take in the dated room. I throw a glance around, trying to see it through fresh eyes. Dark wood, mustard yellow countertops, and rust-colored appliances. An earthy color palette that probably brought warmth to the space at one point but now looks like it belongs in a museum.

"Do you cook in here?" Jigsaw asks.

Why does he want to know? "Uh, sometimes. When we have a viewing, I'll bake cookies or something."

He nods thoughtfully.

"Are you hungry?"

He slides his gaze over me. "A little but there's no time right now."

Right. Stupid question. I swallow down my sudden jangle of nerves. He's not going to hurt me. He can't stay long. They've had a rough night. He's only here to obtain some refreshments for his brothers.

"At least it's a nice night." I rub my hands over my pants a few times, then open the refrigerator. "Not raining or something." Am I really yammering about the weather?

I grab two bottles of water and close the refrigerator.

When I turn, Jigsaw's resting his back against the counter with his arms crossed over his chest. I hold out both bottles of water to him and he takes them. He sets one on the counter, uncaps the other, and takes a long sip without his eyes ever leaving my face.

"I have more water under here." I turn and bend down, opening

44

one of the lower cabinets and pulling out a case of bottled water. Nothing fancy. Plain, generic spring water.

"Don't worry about it." The plastic bottle crinkles and pops.

"It's no trouble." I heft the case into the air.

"Margot." Jigsaw's at my side, taking the case from my hands and setting it on the counter. "You're going to hurt yourself."

"I'm stronger than I look." I flex my arm, not that it shows off anything since I'm wearing a sweatshirt. "I pick up bodies, remember?"

Instead of laughing, he tilts his head and studies me as if I'm the most fascinating thing he's encountered. "You do that by yourself?"

"No. Goodness. No. We go in teams of two, sometimes three people, if necessary."

Something buzzes. Jigsaw slips his hand into his pocket and the buzzing stops. "I need to get out there and help."

"Sure. Oh! Let me get you a first aid kit for Rooster."

I raise on tiptoes and fling one of the top cabinets open. Instead of a first aid kit, I find a package of gauze. "I can run upstairs and grab—"

"This will work." He plucks the package from my hands. "You saw how stubborn he is. Thanks."

He glances at the case of water again. "You sure you don't need it?"

"I have more down there." I gesture toward the cabinet. "We go through a lot whenever there's a service."

Nodding, he hefts the case under one arm, carrying it as if it weighs nothing. I scurry ahead to open the door for him.

"I'll, uh, be around if you need something," I say.

"We'll try not to bother you." His lips quirk. "Pretend we're not even here."

Is he being funny or was that a warning to mind my own business?

In the doorway, he kicks his foot out, holding it open. "Lock up behind me."

Before I have a chance to tell him I always lock the doors, he leans down, his face close to mine. For some reason my body thinks he's going in for a friendly kiss on the cheek and I turn my head slightly.

But he pivots and captures my lips instead. A soft warm brush of his lips with a slight scratch of stubble.

It's over before I have a chance to react.

Or kiss him back.

"Night, Margot."

Stunned, I stare up at him. *He kissed me.*

He's not smirking or laughing. No, he's staring at me like he wants to eat me alive.

"See you soon." His low, warm voice sounds like a promise or a threat.

I lock the door behind him, hurry upstairs, and don't look back.

CHAPTER SEVEN

Jigsaw

AM I SMILING? MY MOUTH'S PULLED INTO A WEIRD, NON-SARCASTIC, upward sensation I'm not used to as I cross the parking lot back to Rooster's truck.

I didn't want to leave Margot. Her cute, flustered expression when I gave in to the impulse to kiss her almost stopped me from walking out the door. I usually relish the corpse-disposal portion of our nocturnal mayhem activities, but I haven't been all that helpful to my brothers tonight.

Talking to Margot was more fun than murder clean-up. Watching her round little ass as she bent over to grab the case of water almost made me lose my mind.

"Are you okay?" Rooster huffs a laugh.

I yank the goofy smile off my face and scowl at him. "I'm fine, why?"

"You look like a puppy who just had his tummy rubbed."

"I *wish* she'd rubbed my tummy." I glance back at the funeral home. A few low lights flicker beyond the windows, but not enough to see anything in the house. Is Margot watching us from inside? Or did she go upstairs and back to bed like she said she would? How can she rest knowing bodies are being burned so close to where she sleeps?

I can't fake indifference a minute longer, and it's not like I'm fooling my oldest and closest friend one bit.

"Isn't she adorable?" I gush like an eleven-year-old girl who just got an invitation to a school dance.

Rooster rumbles with laughter, then winces and touches his side. "Yeah, she's cute. Not freaked out about us all showing up in the middle of the night, either." His gaze strays to the house. "Real nice of her to be worried about me, since we've never met."

"Don't let it go to your head." I throw the wad of gauze at him. "She wanted to patch Teller up too."

He rolls his eyes. "You better tread carefully, brother. You fuck around with her and screw this business relationship up, whole club will want your head on a stick."

He's got a point, not that I'd ever admit it. It's my duty to keep Rooster's ego in check. Can't do that if he thinks he's right all the time. "How insulting." I pull an indignant, hurt face as I set the case of bottled water on the back seat.

I slide my hunting knife out of its sheath, slice through the plastic cover, wriggle a bottle out of the tight package, and hand it to Rooster. "What if I really like her? Maybe she's *the one*."

A pleasurable shiver, like a premonition of good fortune, runs up my spine.

I shouldn't say shit like that out loud just to fuck with Rooster. It's probably bad karma or something since I don't believe in soulmates. Or at least not that there's a soulmate out there for *me*. Rooster, on the other hand, found his soulmate. That's great for him, and I love Shelby, but their cutesy, lovey-dovey life isn't for me.

"The fuck you doing, Jigsaw?" Z calls in a hushed whisper. "We could use your help."

"Making sure the big, bearded pin cushion doesn't keel over." I jerk my thumb at Rooster, who snorts.

"You all right, Rooster?" Z asks, genuine concern in his voice.

"I'll live." He tilts his head toward me. "Jiggy ain't looking after me as much as he's been busy flirting with Margot."

Z shoots a glare at me, and I hold my hands up in an appeasement gesture. "Hey, Rock wanted me to keep an eye on her. He sent her out here to talk to *me* specifically."

Z stares at me. Awww, did I really leave my president speechless?

"Yeah, all right. Guess it's good to keep her out of our business." He glances around the parking lot. "Where is she?"

"She went inside. I told her I'd text if something comes up."

"Smart." Z jerks his thumb over his shoulder. "Fucking taking forever but we're almost ready for the next contestant."

I hold up one hand. "Don't forget, I need a pinky or two for my collection."

Z does a slow eyeroll, head-tilt thing that's not as funny as he thinks it is. "Are you fucking serious?"

I cross my arms over my chest, holding his gaze.

Z leans in close and whispers, "You realize if someone ever finds your 'collection' it can be used against you as evidence, right?" He lifts his brows to punctuate his words.

"No one's finding my stash."

Z turns to Rooster. "Is he fucking serious?"

Ever my protector, Rooster shrugs. "Everyone needs a hobby."

"Jesus Christ." Z plows his fingers through his hair. "The bone fragments are still pretty big once the burning's over. We have to put them through the grinder to turn 'em into ash. Can't you just take a bone chunk?"

That actually would make things easier than what I normally do, but I'm enjoying fucking with Z. "But how will I know it's the pinky?"

Z clenches his jaw and snarls—something I've rarely seen him do. Maybe it's time to dial it back a bit.

"Bone chunk will be fine," I concede before his head explodes.

"Great," Z claps his hands together, "now that we've sorted out *souvenirs for the insane,* can we move things along?"

Rooster lifts his chin toward the brick building. "Want me to move my truck closer?"

"That'd be preferable." Z barely controls his sarcasm. Out of respect for Rooster's injury, no doubt.

"I'll do it." I hold out my hand for Rooster's keys, but he shakes his head.

"Let me do something," the stubborn fucker insists.

"You got stabbed, brother," Z points out. "Wasn't that enough?"

Rooster grunts and shuffles into the truck, holding his side. He lets out a barely audible groan as he hoists his big ass into the cab.

Z turns his stern, presidential glare on me. "In between sifting through bone fragments, will you please keep an eye on him? I'm trying to reach Doc. See if he'll meet us at Upstate's clubhouse. No way he's driving all the way downstate in that condition."

"You know I will." I tilt my head toward the house. "Margot offered to help, but you know how stubborn he is."

Z's lips curl into a slight sneer. "Or he was concerned since she usually spends her time sucking blood *out* of bodies, not trying to keep it in."

A violent urge to defend Margot washes over me, even though I barely know the woman, and technically Z isn't wrong. He's also my president and I respect him. So I keep my lips zipped. Even in the weak moonlight, my irritation must show on my face, though.

"Easy." Z holds out his hands in a "calm yourself" gesture. "She's a nice woman. I'm just saying, she usually attends to the dead, not the living."

"I hear you, Prez."

Rooster's loud, diesel engine rumbles and chugs to life. He slaps the driver's side door and sticks his head out of the open window. "You two wanna get the fuck outta my way, or should I use you to fill in the potholes?" he shouts.

"So much for not waking up the neighborhood," Z grumbles as we move toward the brick building.

"What neighborhood?" I ask. "There's barely any houses out here."

Z grunts in response as he turns to wave and guide Rooster closer to the crematorium.

Rooster turns the truck off. Z jogs over and presses his hand to the door. "Stay put. We'll handle this."

"He won't sit there for long," I warn Z when he meets me at the back of the truck.

"No shit." He circles one hand in the air. "Let's hurry the fuck up, then."

I grab the handle and lower the tailgate. Two freshly killed corpses, neatly rolled into dirty sheets, wait for us. *Bye-bye, final members of the South of Satan MC.*

The hinges creak and the tailgate drops open with a hard thud that sounds like the door to night ripping itself open.

The sound of retribution's clean-up is music to my demented ears.

CHAPTER EIGHT

Margot

FOUR FUNERALS AND A WEDDING THIS WEEK.

My social calendar really needs an overhaul.

And I'm attending Teller's wedding with my father. Like a twelve-year-old. Although my father didn't have to work hard to convince me to go with him.

I haven't stopped thinking about Jigsaw since the night he was at our house. He'll be at the wedding, right? He has to be. Of course, I didn't tell my father Jigsaw was the reason I said I'd go to the biker's wedding. If he's ever going to let me take over the family business, I have to prove to him I'm willing to nurture business relationships.

Not that I'm sure I actually *want* to take over the family business. I'm the obvious choice, since both of my brothers decided to opt out. I wanted to be a cosmetologist. But as soon as I finished cosmetology school, I enrolled in the Mortuary Science program at the local college. I passed my national and state board exams. Although Cousin Paul sure has made it known he's open to taking on the burden of the family business.

Ugh. I don't even *want* to compete with Paul. When we were younger, I was closer to him than my brothers since they're both so much older than me.

But one day, I might end up fighting my cousin for the family business.

Stop it. Today's a day to celebrate life and love.

What does someone even wear to a biker wedding? It's warm, so I choose a dress I've wanted to wear but didn't have the proper occasion. Now I do. It's a sleeveless mint green with bright pink flowers. The skirt falls to my shins. I'll pair it with a wide pink belt and bubble-gum pink, patent leather open-toed heels. Everyone assumes I sleep in a coffin and surround myself in black, but I love color. For work, I have to present myself as bland and toned-down as possible. Dark colors, low-key makeup. It's just not appropriate to greet a grieving family in something as bright and cheerful as a mint green and hot-pink dress.

It's perfect for an outdoor wedding, though.

I carry my heels down the three flights of stairs to the main floor of our home and meet my father in the parlor where he's leaving Paul instructions for the afternoon. Death doesn't care about plans or weddings. The grim reaper loves to show up at the most inconvenient times. I'll be surprised if we even make it to the wedding and are able to stay through the whole event.

Paul smiles when he sees me. "You look pretty."

"Thanks."

My father gives me a more critical once-over, as if there's a slim chance he might ask me to go upstairs and change.

"That's lovely, Margot," he finally says.

"Thank you." If I had a mom or an aunt to gush about clothing with, I'd show off that the dress has pockets. But I don't, so I have to be content with patting my right pocket, holding a tube of lip balm, and the left one with a tiny tin of mints.

"Let's go. I'm not quite sure where the place is, and I don't want to get lost in Empire County."

I already pulled up the map on my phone earlier. It is way out of the city limits. At Teller's house.

AN HOUR LATER, I spot dozens of teal and silver balloons sticking out in the lush, green foliage.

I point ahead and to the left. "I think that's it, Dad."

He slows the Cadillac. "Thank you."

I squint at the giant black iron rooster-shaped mailbox the balloons are attached to. Two stone pillars on either side of the driveway look like they were recently installed.

The long, wide gravel driveway is flanked by neatly trimmed grass and trees. Cars, trucks, and motorcycles are parked on either side of the driveway. It looks like they tried to keep the parking orderly for a while but then people just started leaving vehicles wherever they wanted. A white chicken squawks and flaps its wings, running in front of the car.

A tall, slender man in one of the black vests identifying him as a Lost King holds out a hand to slow us.

My father rolls down his window and the man sticks his head in, searching the car like he's looking for a bomb. "Name?"

"Cedarwood."

"Welcome, Mr. Cedarwood." The man flicks his gaze to me and beams. "You must be Margot?"

Surprised, my cheeks warm and I fiddle with my dress. "That's me."

"My name's Sparky." He flashes a lazy smile. "If you need *refreshments*, I'm your guy."

Refreshments? Right now, he seems to be directing traffic.

"Where can I park in case I get a call and need to leave early?" my father asks.

Sparky nods solemnly. "Death waits for no man, right?"

My father's head jerks in surprise, but he nods slowly, appreciating Sparky's understanding. "Unfortunately."

Sparky taps his hand on the roof. "Let's put you near the exit. You can park in front of my bike. I'm not leaving any time soon."

"Thank you."

Through a series of hand waves, gestures and shouts, Sparky guides my father into a spot right next to one of the stone pillars marking the driveway. There's no way for anyone to block us in unless they block the entire driveway.

We step out and my father tries to hand Sparky a tip.

Sparky chuckles and holds his hand in front of him like a crossing guard slowing traffic. "No, I'm the one giving out favors." He hands us two cellophane bags that appear to have a small brownie in each. "My gift to Teller and Charlotte's guests."

"Thank you," I say, smiling brightly to make up for my father's hesitation to take his bag.

We're a few steps away from Sparky when my father hands me his brownie. "Take mine. You know I can't eat that."

"Sure." Dad may need to avoid sugar, but I love brownies. I stick both bags in my purse for later.

"Are you okay to walk in those?" My father points to my shoes.

I glance at the gravel driveway and sigh. We just had to park as far away as possible. "I'll be fine."

I end up walking in the grass when I can. The closer we get to the house, the louder things are. Different groups of people are milling around the yard. Anxiety snakes its way through my chest as we follow the path between the side of the old farmhouse and several barn-like outbuildings to the backyard.

Days' worth of decorating must've been done to transform the backyard into a wedding wonderland. Rows of chairs are lined up in front of a beautiful floral arch. Behind that, the natural landscape of forest stretching up the side of a long, steep hill creates a beautiful backdrop.

I scan the crowd, searching for Jigsaw, trying not to be obvious about it. He's probably here with someone. Or even worse, what if he's married?

My father and I take seats in the last row. We don't actually know anyone here. At least I don't.

The ceremony starts and the maid of honor walks down the short aisle with a young man and takes her place at the front. "That woman looks like Mayor Concord's daughter," my father whispers. "And that's Judge Oak officiating."

As the face of the business, my father's always been the one to socialize with community leaders and to lobby politicians. It's not something I've ever been included in. Nor do I want to be. I prefer to help the families and clients who come to us.

"Oh." What else does he expect me to say? Besides, I'm still busy searching for Jigsaw.

There. Near the front left. Wearing a worried frown while he helps a heavily pregnant blonde woman stand.

Well, damn. He *is* married.

And about to be a father.

Then an older man with a sinfully perfect silver beard scowls and elbows Jigsaw out of the way, taking the blonde's hand. He was there the night all the bikers showed up to borrow the crematorium, but I didn't say more than a couple of words to him. Is he Jigsaw's father-in-law?

I'm so distracted by the scene, and trying to figure out everyone's roles, I miss most of the ceremony. Until a baby starts wailing.

My stomach rumbles and I quietly unwrap one of the brownies, careful not to get any crumbs on my dress. I pop a small piece in my mouth.

Then the ceremony's over and Teller kisses his bride. They're so passionate and intense it's almost uncomfortable to watch. Well, for me. Everyone else seems to whoop and cheer for them. Even my father gives a half smile and claps.

That's probably what he wants for me, isn't it? Not only did my brothers decide the family business wasn't their destiny, neither of them has married or had children, yet. No grandchildren to carry on the Cedarwood legacy.

According to my ex, I'll have to get better at sex if I plan to marry and have kids one day. Although, I'm sure women throughout history have had to bear children even if they didn't enjoy sex. That's too depressing to contemplate at such a happy occasion.

Just focus on these two beautiful people I barely know celebrating their love.

Everyone stands as the bride and groom run down the aisle

holding hands. It's hard to believe this is the same man who showed up after hours covered in blood, casually tossing bodies into the fire.

How fascinating.

After the ceremony people mingle, something my father excels at and I don't. Unsure of what to do, I follow him around like a well-trained puppy.

I'm standing slightly behind him and to his left when a taller, curvy woman with long auburn hair approaches with a warm smile stretched across her pretty face.

"You must be Margot?"

"Uh, yes." I step out of my father's shadow and shake her hand.

"I'm Hope." She hesitates, frowns, then smiles. "The, uh, stepmother of the groom. Thank you for coming."

"Oh, yes. Of course. Thank you for inviting me. I've only had a chance to meet Teller a few times..." And the last time he was splattered with blood.

Nope, better not say that out loud.

Rock, the president, steps up next to Hope, placing his arm around her waist and resting his hand on her hip. *Oh, God. Hope's the president's wife.* She may look nice and inviting but her curious green eyes seem to be quietly assessing me. She's probably trying to figure out how much I know about what her husband and the other men did the night they "borrowed" our crematorium. Thank God I never actually saw anything incriminating.

What's a polite way to express that all of her stepson's and husband's secrets are safe with me?

"Hello, Margot." Rock dips his chin in greeting. "Nice to see you again."

"Nice to see you too, Mr. North."

"Rock," he corrects.

"Rock," I repeat. Neither of them look old enough to be Teller's parents but that seems rude to say, so I bite my tongue.

Teller and his bride join us. Hope beams at them and Teller leans down to kiss her cheek and whisper something in her ear. Her lips curve and she gives him a playful slap. They're all so…casual and loving toward each other.

"Thanks for coming," Teller says to me. "Margot, this is my *wife*," he unleashes an utterly charming grin like he's thrilled to finally use that word, "Charlotte. Char, this is Margot."

Charlotte smiles wide and doesn't seem to be annoyed she's wasting time talking to a stranger on her wedding day. She stretches out her arms and pulls me into a hug. "Thank you for coming," she says softly against my hair. "It's so nice to finally meet you."

So, everyone knows I'm the body disappearing service lady?

My father turns and Teller makes the introductions again. Charlotte shakes his hand politely, but he doesn't get a hug. I guess I'm special.

Eventually, I gravitate toward the table of food, picking up a can of soda. I pull the brownie out of my purse and pop the rest in my mouth, then wash it down with Sprite.

I'm staring off into the woods, wondering if I can hide until it's time to go home when a shadow falls over me.

"Look who it is, our little last responder." Jigsaw's rich, low voice slides over my skin like velvet. "What are you doing over here?"

I glance up into his amused eyes, my breath stuttering in my lungs. My heart pitter-patters faster and heat races over my skin. This is ridiculous. I've never responded to any man this way before.

"Thirsty." I hold up the half-empty can.

His lips quirk. "Sprite?" He chuckles. "You want wine or something? There's a table over there." He lifts his chin toward one of the barns.

Is he making fun of me? "I don't drink."

"Ever?"

"Not when you've had as many results of DWI on your table as I have."

"Shit." He runs his hand through his hair. "Yeah. Makes sense."

"Where's your wife?" I sip my soda casually while watching his face.

"My *what?*" His eyebrows draw down and he rears back. "Why would you think I'm married?"

"Or girlfriend."

"You're misinformed." He snorts. "I don't do relationships, sweetheart."

I turn, scanning the backyard, but it's so crowded now, it's hard to search. "The pretty blonde." I curve my hand in front of my stomach. "Who looks ready to give birth any day."

"Serena?" He laughs, then quickly looks around. "Jesus. She's my SAA's ol' lady."

"She wasn't old."

He shakes his head quickly. "That's just what we…never mind. Serena's my friend. She's Grinder's fiancée. Christ." He casts another quick glance around our immediate area. "He hears you say that, the grumpy old goat might gut me."

I can't tell if he's joking or actually afraid of one of his brothers sticking him with a knife.

"Wait." I clap my hand over my mouth and giggle. "I thought he was her dad," I whisper.

His mouth flattens. "Whatever you do, don't say that to him. Please."

I nod quickly, unsure of why that seemed so funny. "Of course not."

Jigsaw tilts his head. "Are you okay?"

Suddenly, my legs feel kinda rubbery. "I think so." I clutch my stomach, willing the swirly sensation to go away.

"You get too much sun?" he asks.

Burning shame pulses over my cheeks. Is he making fun of me the way people have my whole life? "Just because I live in a funeral home doesn't mean I'm a ghoul who never sees the sun." Why did that sound sad rather than the angry I was going for?

He stares at me with comically round eyes. I'd laugh if I wasn't so itchy with embarrassment.

"No. It's hot." He waves his hand toward the chairs we sat in for the ceremony. "That's why Serena said she didn't feel well."

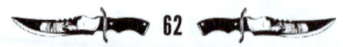

"Well, I'm not pregnant."

He rakes his gaze over me. "No, but you *are* pretty."

When he drags his eyes back to my face, they're heartbreakingly sincere.

Heat bursts over my skin. "Thank you." My legs wobble. I've been fine in my heels all day. Why are they now a problem?

Jigsaw frowns again. "Are you sure you're okay? Have you eaten anything today?"

"Just one of the brownies the guy who helped us park handed out...Sparky?"

"Nooo." Jigsaw squeezes his eyes shut. "Fuck."

"What? He was very nice."

"Come here." He clasps my elbow and steers me toward a small, round picnic bench set up under an old maple tree, even farther away from the guests.

"Their yard is so pretty." I carefully slip my leg over the bench and sit as ladylike as possible, tucking my full skirt around my legs. "It's like they have their own park or something."

"Teller's a country boy. He's always doing one project or another around here." Jigsaw settles onto the bench next to me. "Sometimes he ropes us into helping."

"That's nice of you."

"Not that nice. I don't do it often." He laughs. "Rooster keeps me busy enough at his place."

"You live together?" I gasp and lean in, lowering my voice. "Are you a couple?"

He scowls. "Couple of *what*? Bikers? Friends since elementary school? Yes and yes."

"Sorry, that was rude." I press my hand to my forehead. "I feel so fuzzy."

"When'd you eat that brownie?"

I shrug. "I dunno. During the ceremony. After."

"Shit," he mutters.

"What."

"You said you don't drink." His lips quirk into a teasing grin. "I'm guessing you don't indulge in the devil's lettuce, either?"

I lean in closer. "You mean *smoke weed?*" I half whisper, half gasp. "Never."

"Satan's balls." He laughs and shakes his head. "Seriously?"

The pieces of whatever puzzle he's offering aren't clicking into place fast enough for me.

"You ate a pot brownie, Margot." He lifts an eyebrow. "You're going to be flying high for a while."

Horror and indignation battle inside me, but indignation wins. "Don't give me the eyebrow raise of judgment." I lift my head in a haughty manner. "I didn't know the brownie was laced with," I pause and cast a shifty gaze from side to side. "Laced with *pot*," I finish in a hushed whisper.

Jigsaw chokes, then snorts with laughter. "Eyebrow raise of judgment?" He raises his eyebrows higher.

Oh God. No. What if he thinks I'm making fun of his scar? "I didn't mean..." Now I'm fixated on the faint jagged line running across his forehead through his eyebrow. Did he get in an accident? A fight? I can't ask. That's rude.

He doesn't seem to notice my inappropriate staring. "It'll take a bit to fully kick in and it's gonna last for a few hours." His voice is nothing but sympathy and concern. Not a trace of contempt for how dumb I am for eating something a stranger gave me.

Hot tears sting my eyeballs. "My father will kill me if I embarrass him here."

"I'm going to kill Sparky for not warning you." He lifts his head, his intense gaze scanning the party.

"I still have one if you want it." I reach into my purse and pull out the crinkly cellophane-wrapped evil brownie.

He takes it from me and smirks, then turns it to show me the iridescent green sticker on the back in the shape of a marijuana leaf.

"Oh." Damn, why didn't I notice that? Would it have mattered if I did? "You can have it."

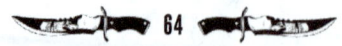

"Nah." He hands it back to me. "I think I better stay clear-headed to watch over you."

"Watch over me?"

"You said you've never done it before."

"Oh, I've *done* it." I clap my hand over my mouth and giggle.

Why are you brining up sex when there's nothing to brag about? My brain is truly scrambled.

His lips twitch with amusement.

"Jiggy! There ya are!" A short, pretty blonde runs up behind Jigsaw and wraps her arms around his neck, halting whatever he was about to say. "Where ya been hiding?"

He reaches up and pats her arm. "I'm hardly hiding, songbird." He tips his head back and smiles at her. "What're *you* up to?"

"I *was* watching Grace, but she wanted her momma, so Hope took her inside for a nap."

A nap. Maybe that's what I need.

"Shelby." Jigsaw reaches over and taps my arm. "Have you met Margot?"

"Sorry, I'm being rude." Shelby steps closer, holding out her hand. "Hi, Margot."

"Margot's a friend of the club." Jigsaw tilts his head at me. "Shelby's Rooster's fiancée."

"Oh!" Recognition flits through my fuzzy brain. "I met Rooster."

Shelby's eyes narrow slightly.

"Hey, Margot," Rooster's deep rumbling voice interrupts. He wraps his arms around Shelby's waist and leans down to kiss her cheek.

"Hi." I wiggle my fingers. "How are you?"

Jigsaw stands and pulls Rooster aside, whispering something in his ear. Rooster snorts and glances at me, then nods.

Great, is Jigsaw telling everyone I'm a dope who ate a dope-laced brownie?

"We're gonna grab food," Rooster says, taking Shelby's hand. "You want us to bring you back a plate?" he asks.

I clutch my stomach and shake my head.

"Nice to meet ya, Margot," Shelby says. "I'm sure I'll see you again before the night's over."

When they're out of earshot, I lean over to Jigsaw. "Did you have to tell him?"

"I tell Rooster everything." He doesn't even bother denying it and he doesn't look embarrassed.

"Everything?"

The corner of his mouth lifts. "Almost everything." His expression flattens into something more serious. "I wanted to let him know so he can ask Sparky to stop handing out those damn brownies."

"Don't get Sparky in trouble. He was so nice to us."

He ducks his head and laughs. "Fuckin' Sparky."

"Margot! There you are." My father's frazzled voice rushes up behind me.

Another wave of dizziness sloshes around my stomach.

I brace myself against the table and turn. As my father gets closer, I straighten my spine and try to erase all evidence that I'm high from my face.

"Hi, Dad! What's up?" I ask in a cartoonishly chipper tone.

Jigsaw cough-laughs into his fist.

I'd kick him if I didn't think I'd fall off the bench.

When I don't immediately jump up, my father frowns. "I received a call for a pick-up. I have to go but—"

"I can take her home, Mr. Cedarwood. No problem," Jigsaw offers.

My father seems...relieved? He tilts his head and stares at Jigsaw. "It's a long drive. Are you sure?"

Jigsaw nods. "I remember how to get there."

Dad frowns, his gaze sliding between us. "Is that okay with you, Margot?"

"Yes," I answer a little too fast.

He stares at Jigsaw for a few beats. "If you're sure..."

"I haven't been drinking, sir," Jigsaw answers like the most responsible college boy in the dorm. "I'm good to take her home whenever she says she's ready to go."

Surprisingly, my father seems satisfied. "Well, I hate to make you

leave early." He glances at Jigsaw again. "If you're sure you don't mind."

"It's really not a problem." Jigsaw lifts his chin. "I promised Teller I'd be available to give rides to any guest who needed one tonight."

"Well, that's very nice of you." My father holds out his hand and Jigsaw shakes it quickly. "Thank you, Jensen."

Jensen. That's his name. *Jensen.* I like that.

"All right." My father nods at me. "I'll see you later."

"Do you need me to help?" Please let the answer be no. I don't think I could stand up straight for two minutes let alone prep a body right now.

"No. Paul's meeting me there. And I called Rudy in. You enjoy a night off."

I nod quickly. "Okay."

I lazily track my father's movements as he stops to speak to Rock, then Teller and Charlotte.

"You okay?" Jigsaw asks.

"No, I feel really spinny." I loop my fingers through the air next to my head a few times.

"You want to go inside and take a nap?"

I slide my gaze to the big farmhouse that suddenly looks miles away. Nap in someone's house during their wedding? That seems like poor guest etiquette. "No."

He pulls out his phone and taps the screen several times.

A few minutes later, Sparky shows up, looking sheepish. He thrusts a thick, folded, shiny blue blanket at Jigsaw.

"Thanks," Jigsaw growls.

"I'm sorry, Margot," Sparky says. "I thought you knew."

He looks so sad, I can't be mad. *Ha! I rhymed.* "It's okay. I've just never done it before."

"I'll stay with you and walk you—"

"Nope. I'm staying with her." Jigsaw stands, and even though he's only a few inches taller than Sparky, he seems to tower over him. "You've done enough."

Sparky fidgets and shifts back and forth on his feet. "I'll bring some snacks."

My stomach lurches. "I feel too queasy to eat."

Concern draws Sparky's eyebrows down. "Queasy? That's—"

"She'll be fine." A bit gentler, Jigsaw adds, "Some water and food would be good. She might be hungry later."

"Got it." Sparky salutes Jigsaw and hurries away.

Jigsaw unfolds the blanket and spreads it out under the maple tree next to us. It's slick, and shiny, made of a sleeping bag-like material meant to keep us dry from the damp grass.

"Come on." Jigsaw holds out his hand to me.

"You want me to just nap on a blanket?"

"You don't have to sleep. Just close your eyes until the queasiness passes."

Thank God for his strong, steady presence. I need his assistance more than I expected. I clutch his hand and use it as leverage to lift myself off the bench. My head might be in the clouds, but my body feels like concrete blocks in human form.

At the edge of the blanket, I toe off my heels and touch my feet to the cool, soft ground.

"Ahhh." I close my eyes, enjoying the bliss of tiny blades of grass tickling my toes.

A low rough chuckle comes from below me.

My eyes pop open.

Jigsaw's sitting on the blanket with his back against the tree.

I sway on my feet a little. Even relaxed and in bright daylight, he looks utterly lethal.

He pats the blanket next to him.

Exhausted and dizzy, I drop down and slide over the slick material until I'm kneeling next to him.

"Are you okay?" he asks.

I nod slowly, jostling all sorts of inappropriate thoughts and questions around inside my skull.

He pats his thigh. "Use me as your pillow."

I blink and frown at him. "Are you serious?"

"Or fold the edge of the blanket up if you want. It's big enough."

I drag my gaze to where the blue meets green grass. It looks so far away. And Jigsaw looks so inviting. I slide my body down, the fabric of my dress making a *zzzzzzp* sound against the slick blanket.

I curl on my side, my cheek resting against his rock-hard thigh. "You're very hard," I murmur.

He chokes and sputters. "What?"

Slowly, the words that came out of my mouth trickle into my brain. "Uh, not like that." I squeeze his thigh. "You're all muscle."

He chuckles. "Thank you." His body shifts.

"Are you sure you're comfortable like this?" I ask.

"I'm fine." He shifts again and something glides over my cheek, pushing my hair over my shoulder. His heavy arm settles along my side, his hand resting on my hip. "I got you. Just relax. Try to enjoy the high."

"Relax," I murmur. The calm and safety absorbing me into another world.

CHAPTER NINE

Margot

FLOAT.

That's all I do for the next few...*hours?*

When I finally claw myself out of the soft, mushy feeling, I'm on my back with my hands folded over my stomach like I'm about to be placed in a coffin. The heavy weight of one of Jigsaw's arms still rests protectively over me with his hand over mine.

I blink and stare into the branches of the tree above us. Green leaves and darkening sky beyond.

What time is it? I gasp and sit up, jostling Jigsaw's arm. "How long have I been out?"

"Hmm?" He stares at me groggily. "A little while. Hungry?"

He reaches for a big blue-and-gray cooler on his other side. "When Sparky says he's bringing snacks, he doesn't mess around." My stomach feels rumbly now instead of queasy, so that's an improvement.

But as I sit up, my brain swims and sloshes around. "Has the pot altered me forever?" I blurt.

"What?" Jigsaw laughs. "No, I don't think so."

"It wasn't laced with anything else?"

"No. Sparky's a purist. He wouldn't dare mess with nature's

harvest." He passes me a cold can of Sprite and a blue can koozie with a crown, dollar sign, and sun with today's date on the bottom.

"Wedding favor?" I ask, staring at the design.

Jigsaw taps the crown image. "For Lost Kings." He moves to the dollar sign. "Teller's symbol for the club." Finally, he lands on the sun. "Charlotte's nickname is 'sunshine.'"

"Ah, clever."

"We're all about the symbolism, baby." He gives me a cocky wink and smile.

Laughing, I take a sip of the soda, sighing as the cool, sweet liquid eases my dry throat. "I didn't snore, did I?"

"No." He hands me a plate stacked with cold cuts and a fresh, squishy roll.

I wave the condiment packages he offers away and slap a few pieces of ham and a slice of cheese on a roll. "How embarrassing. Everyone knows I got high and passed out like a nerd?"

He drills me with a hard stare. "It's not your fault, Margot."

"I made you miss the whole party."

"You didn't *make me* do anything." His lips quirk. "Few people have that ability."

"Why does it seem so much...quieter?" I glance toward the backyard but it's only a few couples in lawn chairs talking now.

"A lot of folks went up to the clubhouse." He lifts his chin toward the long hill stretching behind the house. "Or down to Crystal Ball and our other clubhouse."

"Crystal Ball? The strip club?"

He lifts his eyebrows. "You know it?"

I shift my gaze to the side. "I knew someone who danced there in college."

"Really?"

"Yeah, she didn't stay long. It wasn't for her."

He nods slowly. "I'm sure a lot of girls figure out real quick it's not just glitter and dollar bills."

"That's what she said."

"Margot, be honest," he says in a teasing voice, gaze drilling into me. "Are *you* the friend?"

"Me?" I gasp. "No one wants to see that."

A frown draws his eyebrows together. "See what?" His tone's sharp, disapproving.

"Me…like that." I run my hands through the air in an outline of my body. "Naked," I whisper.

He leans forward. "You're mistaken," he whispers back. "What about your boyfriend?"

"What boyfriend? I came with my *dad* today."

"I figured that was just a business thing." He shrugs. "You're not seeing anyone?"

"I'm too broken for a boyfriend." I giggle and clap my hand over my mouth. "That sounds like a song."

He freezes and stares at me. "What did you say?"

"Broken in the s-e-x department." I quickly look around to make sure no one overhears me. "One star, do not recommend. Boring in bed." Is it the pot making me admit this to a guy I barely know? "Maybe I can be fixed?" I mumble the last word, as I lose my nerve. "Who knows."

Jigsaw continues staring at me.

A hot flush of embarrassment creeps up my chest, chasing away a good portion of the pot-brownie high.

"You're not broken, Margot," he says through clenched teeth. "Who told you that?"

"It doesn't matter."

"You just need to meet the right person who appreciates you."

"But I'll only disappoint them." A truly awful and wonderful idea takes shape in my mind. Jigsaw's been so kind to sit with me today. He's patient. He said he's not in a relationship. I'm attracted to him but we're so opposite, there's no chance of an attachment forming…

"Maybe you could be my tutor? You know, teach me," I blurt out.

He sets his plate down and sits forward. "Teach you *what*?" His voice is low and raspy. Interested or disgusted by the idea—I can't tell.

Realization at how stupid it was to even ask sets in, but I continue digging my awkward grave anyway. "You *know*..."

Jigsaw's eyebrows crawl up his forehead. "Teach you *sex?*"

I wince at the outraged disbelief darkening his words and expression. I'm probably not as pretty as the kind of girls he's used to but I'm not a complete toad, either.

"Well, yes." This was dumb. Why did I think this was a good idea again? Can I even blame this on the pot brownie?

"How old are you?"

Is he actually considering my request?

Heat burns the tip of my nose, and spreads over my cheeks. My face must be pink enough to match my shoes by now.

"Never mind." I pick up my plate and tear off little pieces of my roll. I'm too disgusted with myself to eat any of it, so I just end up sprinkling crumbs all over my dress.

How am I ever going to look at Jigsaw again? Maybe I'll call Teller and ask him to send a different brother to help out from now on? The MC's supposed to be our partner. It won't be weird if I reach out, will it? I could start by thanking him for letting me come to his wedding. That's normal, right?

No. I can't do that. What if that gets Jigsaw in trouble with his boss or president or whatever. It's not fair to get him in trouble because I embarrassed myself.

"Why me?" he finally asks.

I risk meeting his eyes. They're round with curiosity and... interest? "I, uh, like you."

"You don't even *know* me."

I know him well enough. I shrug. "I feel safe around you."

"You shouldn't," he mutters.

"I felt safe enough to sleep on you." All my pride travels south. This isn't going well. "You don't seem to judge me. Well, at least up until now."

"Judge you how?"

I shrug. "You know, for 'playing with dead people.'"

He winces. Maybe I'm wrong. Does he think I'm a weirdo? And he's only being nice to me because he has to?

"You make an honest living and you help people through a rough time," he finally says. "Why would I judge you for that?"

"You'd be surprised the things people say."

"People are assholes."

I huff a sad laugh. "No arguments there."

Jigsaw

Why does considering Margot's proposal rocket my heart rate into the red zone? She's an absolutely fascinating puzzle. Shy but brave. Smart and compassionate, but somehow sheltered too. So innocent she's never been high in her life but bold enough to ask me to teach her about sex.

I want to collect and study every piece of this woman.

She slides her tongue against her bottom lip and my cock reacts as if the gesture was an invitation, hardening behind my zipper. I shift on the slippery blanket and force the images of all the places I'd like her pretty pink tongue to visit aside.

"You're a good guy," she whispers. "I knew it the second we met. I guess that's why."

Good guy my ass. If she knew all the wicked things I'm picturing doing to her, she wouldn't think there's an ounce of goodness in me. And if she knew all the horrors that lurk in my mind, or all the violent deeds I've been part of—and enjoyed—she'd probably run screaming all the way back to Pine Hollow.

"If you say so." Man, I was not expecting this today. First, having her fall asleep on my leg. Now asking me to teach her to fuck.

She always looks so prim and proper, comes from a prominent family, yet she had no problem being around the club today. She likes Sparky, even though he accidentally got her high.

High...fuck! *That's* why she made that ridiculous request. It's Sparky's latest strain talking.

"You were nice enough to sit here with me while I slept. You must've been so bored. You missed the party because of me."

I've been to enough parties in my life. And once Z heard what happened to Margot, he was more than fine with me sitting this one out.

More importantly, I'm almost *never* able to settle down and be still. Even when I sleep, it's violent and fitful. But with Margot, sitting here and watching her, it was so easy.

"That's not a reason to have sex with someone," I point out.

She shrugs. "Why not?"

This is insane. She can't possibly be serious. "It doesn't bother you that I'm a biker?"

"Why does that matter?" Her gaze shifts toward a row of bikes backed up against the side of Teller's house. "As long as I don't have to ride, it's fine."

"You've never been on a motorcycle?"

Her steady, sincere gaze drills into me. In the low afternoon sunlight, it's hard to make out the color of her eyes. An interesting blend of blue and green with gold flecks.

What the fuck. I've never studied the color of a woman's eyes with this much curiosity before.

"No. Unfortunately, I've seen one too many results of motorcycle accidents." Her tone's so solemn. So serious. Almost like she's about to cry.

Normally, if some citizen pointed out the dangers of motorcycles, I might look them dead in the eye and say something like, "Yeah and if I stab you in the face with a pencil right now, for the rest of your life you can tell people how dangerous pencils are." Or if I'm not feeling stabby, something trite like, "I'm not here for a long time, I'm here for a good time." A good, hard fuck-off stare and, "Not as dangerous as not minding your own business" always works too.

But Margot? Damn, I bet she's seen some gnarly shit. I don't want to make light of that. Besides, she's not trying to convince *me* that I shouldn't ride. Just telling me that *she* doesn't want to. I can respect that.

"What, you're not going to try and convince me that it's perfectly safe?" she asks.

"No, I know it's dangerous," I answer. "But I'm not distracted by my phone or fucking with the radio when I ride. I keep my eyes peeled for hazards, like other drivers, which is usually the biggest threat to bikers. I wear a helmet and I never ride impaired."

"Minimizing risk."

"Yeah."

An odd sensation simmers along my spine. Margot's acceptance, her kindness, makes her even prettier. Anxious eyes looking anywhere but at me. Dark lashes fluttering. Pink lips, just the perfect amount of pouty. None of that poison filler injected into her lips until they look like they're ready to burst like so many women I encounter lately.

A vivid image of turning her around, sweeping her hair aside, and unzipping her dress won't stop flashing in my mind. I'd ask her to keep those cute Barbie-pink heels on while I bent her over the nearest object and admired every inch of her.

"You're impaired." I need to hit the brakes on this sex tutor idea of hers now. I finish the last bite of my sandwich and start picking up the garbage. "You don't know what you're asking."

"Sure." She sounds so sad, I want to yank my words back.

She takes a bite of her sandwich and chews slowly. Good God, now I can't stop thinking about having her mouth on me.

I jump up and almost fall right back down, my butt's so numb from sitting on the ground for so long.

"I'm going to toss this." I hold out the paper plate and wrappers in my hands. "There's, uh, wedding cake in the cooler. I'll be right back. Want anything?"

"Another can of Sprite?" She holds up her almost-empty can.

"There's one in there." I point to the cooler, then haul ass to the house.

The garbage cans on the other side of the house are overflowing with trash. "The fuck?" I grumble, stuffing my trash inside the closest one.

I need a minute to get control of myself.

As I head for the side door leading into the kitchen, I bump into Murphy. Figures he and Heidi didn't leave yet.

"Where've you been?" he asks.

"Around."

He tilts his head and frowns. "Why do you look so stressed?"

"I'm not." I blow out a breath. "Hey, you got a truck or something I can borrow?"

His eyes widen, and his big, red beard shifts as his jaw drops slightly. "Since when do you want to sit in a cage?"

"I told Margot's dad I'd drive her home, and she's not dressed to ride." I'm not telling Murphy what Margot shared with me. It feels too personal.

"Yeah, I'll get you something." He runs his hand over his beard. "Actually, Heidi's car is still parked down here." He tilts his head toward one of Teller's garages.

"The Hellcat?" I ask hopefully.

He snorts. "No. Nice try, though. Her SUV."

"Aw, shit. That thing barely qualifies as an SUV. It's tiny."

He shakes his head. "You want it or not?"

"Yeah, I'll take it. Thanks, bro." I slap his shoulder.

"I'll get the keys." He turns toward the house.

"I'll go with you. The garbage cans are overflowing, I was going to ask Teller for some bags and clean that up before I go." Playing with a day's worth of trash should get my mind off of Margot's request to be her sex...coach...tutor...whatever the fuck arrangement she proposed.

"You want to be garbage man instead of hanging with Margot?"

"I'm trying to be a polite guest."

"I don't think Charlotte wants her guests on garbage detail."

He pulls the latch for the side door, and I follow behind him. Heidi and Charlotte's friend Mercy are in the kitchen. Heidi glances up and beams at Murphy as if she hasn't seen him in ten hours instead of ten minutes. So disgustingly, adorably domestic, these two.

"Hey, Little Hammer," I say to Heidi. "Murphy said I can borrow your SUV for a couple hours. That okay with you?"

"Wow," Mercy drawls. "You're actually *asking* her permission, even though your bro said it was okay?" Her mocking tone isn't as cute as the sass Shelby always throws my way. Or the witty banter I like to engage in with any of the club's ol' ladies. Maybe it's because Mercy's *not* an ol' lady that I find her so fucking annoying.

Ignoring her, I keep my focus on Heidi.

"Of course you can borrow it," she says. "How's Margot feeling?"

"Better."

Murphy hands me a set of keys. "Tank should be full. It hasn't been run for a little while, though. If it gives you any trouble, let me know."

"I will. Thanks."

Outside, Dex is at the garbage cans. Apparently, he decided to play garbage man whether Charlotte likes it or not. I stuff the keys in my pocket and hurry to help him.

"Give it to me." I wiggle my fingers for one of the industrial sized trash bags in his hands.

"Thanks," he says, handing it over.

I give the bag a few good shakes to unfold it and hold it open while Dex tosses stuff inside.

"You talk to Emily?" I ask. Brother's been pining for that cute redhead for months, everyone knows it. Since she's Serena's best friend, Dex has ample opportunities to run into her.

"Jesus Christ, why is everyone up in my business today? We're supposed to be celebrating Teller and Charlotte finally gettin' hitched, not worrying about who I do or don't talk to."

Someone's touchy. "Uh, bro, I've barely talked to you since this morning."

He waves his hand through the air in annoyance. "Grinder was annoying me with his rust or ride bullshit earlier."

I snort-laugh. Sounds like Grinder. "He's like a grumpy old papa bear, huh?" I didn't know Grinder before he went to prison, but from the stories Z tells, Grinder's always been a wise old owl, handing out advice to the baby owls in his flock. Now that he's out of prison, assumed the role of Downstate's sergeant-at-arms, back on his feet, and about to have a baby, he's returning to his normal, meddlesome, advice-giving self, according to Z.

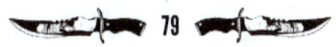

"Papa bear, my ass," he grumbles. "I already got Rock for that."

"Yeah, but Rock won't give advice unless you ask for it."

"As it should be."

Once the bag's full, he tugs it from my hands. "I got this. My gift to Teller was I'd haul all this down to throw out at CB."

"Gee, and all I brought was a cash envelope." I slap his shoulder. "I'll catch you later."

I nod and say a quick hello to other guests as I pass them, but the *stay the fuck away* face I'm wearing seems to keep my path clear.

I round the corner of the house and my gaze immediately lands on Margot.

Fuck, she's pretty. Who the hell would judge her about anything? Or make her doubt herself so much, she'd ask someone like *me* for sex tips?

Then my gaze lands on the man sitting next to her on the blanket now. Eazy—a brother from downstate. Fucker's on the road more than he's at home but of course he's *here* today.

Talking to my girl.

No.

Not my girl.

My student?

No.

Fuck this. Eazy's road name is the predictable result of him easily talking girls into bed. I don't need Margot to decide she should ask *him* for help instead.

"Hey, fucker." I kick his boot. "Dex is looking for you to help him out."

He slowly turns his head and stares up at me with irritation written all over his pretty-boy face. "For what?"

"Don't know." I pull the keys out of my pocket and dangle them above Margot's head. "You ready to go, babe?"

She flashes an apologetic smile at Eazy. "Jigsaw promised to drive me home."

Eazy frowns at *drive*. I rarely willingly put myself in a cage and all my brothers know it.

"You mean ride, darlin'," he says.

"She's not dressed for it, dumbass," I snarl. I won't embarrass Margot by telling him she doesn't ride. It seemed like a personal reason she might not want to share with random people.

I hold out my hand to Margot and help her off the blanket. Still a bit high or maybe her butt's numb like mine was, she tumbles forward, landing hard against me.

She braces herself with two hands on my chest and looks up at me with the sweetest expression.

"You've got frosting on your nose." I swipe it off with my thumb, then pop it in my mouth.

"It was good cake," she whispers. "Did you eat any?"

Suddenly, I can think of a very *different* kind of cake I want to eat.

"Well, then. I better get going." Eazy springs up. "Nice meetin' you, Margaret."

Margot frowns but doesn't bother correcting him.

Looks like I'm still in the lead for the position of sex coach.

Eazy slaps my shoulder and lets out a dirty chuckle. "Have fun with that ride."

I sneer at him and he laughs harder. *Asshole.*

Margot's hands are still on my chest, calling up the wildest urge to strip down and have her hands on my bare skin.

"Sorry I left you alone for so long," I say.

"That's all right."

"Eazy didn't...he wasn't rude to you, was he?"

"Not at all."

"Good."

I'd hate to ruin Teller's wedding by maiming one of my brothers today.

MARGOT'S quiet for the first half of our drive to Pine Hollow. I keep glancing over to see if she's asleep, but she's always staring out the window.

"How do you feel?" I ask when I can't stand the silence another second.

"Stupid."

"What? Why?"

"I'm sorry I asked you." She takes a deep breath and continues, "What I asked you back there. Please forget about it."

"What if I don't want to forget it?"

Her dress rustles as she shifts her body to look at me. "What does that mean?"

"It means we should talk about it more."

"I briefly considered asking your friend Griff." She waves her hand in the air.

A pulse of jealousy slows my racing heart. "Say that again?"

She curls her fingers in her dress, bunching up the skirt, then releases it and smooths the fabric over her legs. Her long, elegant fingers move quickly but gracefully. With one word I could finally have her hands on me. I don't even care that I wasn't her first choice.

"My mechanic, Griff. I saw him at the wedding."

"Yeah, what about him?"

"I'm not usually interested in younger guys," she continues, "but he's quite handsome and he's always so kind to me at the shop." Her lips pull into a frown. "But then I learned he has a girlfriend, so I never asked..." Her voice trails off as if her brain just processed the words coming out of her mouth.

Griff *doesn't* have a girlfriend, yet. He's obsessed with his best friend's little sister Molly. Everyone, except her brother, knows it. Did Margot already ask Griff and he told her he has a girlfriend? Or did she see them hanging out at the wedding and assume they were a couple?

Doesn't matter.

I won't correct Margot's wrong assumption.

No, I'll have to thank Molly. Apparently, she's the only thing stopping Griff from being Margot's sex tutor instead of me.

Because I'm definitely accepting the job.

CHAPTER TEN

Margot

Silence rules the rest of the ride to my house.

Why did I say that about Griff? To make Jigsaw jealous so that he'd say yes to my proposal?

It's like I've been on a downward doom spiral ever since I saw Daniel. *You're like a corpse in bed* just keeps replaying in my head on an endless loop. If I could just find someone to learn or practice with, so that when I meet the right guy, I won't be a disappointment to him maybe I wouldn't feel so damn awful.

"You know there are dating apps," Jigsaw says.

Spoken like someone who hasn't been on a dating app recently. "I don't want to *date.*"

"There are escorts. Male escorts."

"I couldn't be so...intimate with a stranger. I'd be too self-conscious to actually learn anything."

He lets out a strangled groan. "What makes you think *I'd* be a good teacher?"

Now he's just irritating me. "Well, you're a good-looking man in a motorcycle club that surrounds itself with beautiful women. I assume you're experienced. But if you're not, just say that."

"Oh, I'm experienced, baby." He casts a dark look my way that sends a thrill to each of my erogenous zones. "How many men have you slept with?"

"That seems personal."

"You wanna use me as your sex coach. *That's* kinda personal."

"I don't want to *use* you." Okay, maybe I do. "It's not like you get *nothing* out of it."

"As you so sweetly pointed out, I can go bust a nut in any random woman hanging around my club."

"Gross," I mutter.

We're finally cruising down my street, and I sit up. The house is dark. Dad isn't back yet. Jigsaw pulls into the parking lot and stops the car right in front of the porch stairs.

"Will you come in and let me make you coffee?" I offer. "It's a long drive back."

His lips twist into a wry grin. "Is that your way of saying you don't want me to stay over?"

My hand's on the door latch but I turn and stare at him. "You...you want to start tonight?"

He stares at me for a few beats. "No, probably not. We should discuss a few things, first."

"Uh, that doesn't sound pleasant."

The solemn look on his face sends my stomach into my shoes. He's not having sex with me. I made an ass out of myself at the wedding. Blubbering that I'm bad in bed and need tutoring. What grown man wants to deal with that? He probably only humored me because I was high.

High or not, we had a bit of a connection, right? I didn't hallucinate the interest sparking in his eyes.

I'm keenly aware of him at my back as we approach the porch steps.

Bright, golden light floods the immediate area around the porch.

"Christ, those are blinding." Jigsaw throws his arm up to cover his eyes. "Glad you have them, though."

"Sometimes we get people creeping around, thinking we have drugs or valuables they can steal," I explain.

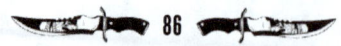

I grip the handrail and carefully pull myself up the steps, still feeling a bit unsteady in my heels.

"Seriously?" he asks. "Trying to rob a funeral home? Feels like bad karma."

"You'd think." I sigh. "I hate to sound like my father, but people don't have a lot of respect for the dead or those who tend to them anymore."

"People don't fear being punched in the face as much as they should anymore, either."

I chuckle at his blunt, violent observation. "That's a colorful way to put it."

I slip my key into the lock and push the door open. Inside, I hurry to the alarm panel and punch in the code.

The door closes behind Jigsaw with a heavy *thunk*.

I toe off my heels and stack them neatly on the first step of the staircase leading upstairs.

"What's up there?" Jigsaw asks.

"Well, the second floor used to be the family living quarters when I was a kid. Now, there's a parlor we use sometimes for overflow guests and a room for kiddos who are having a hard time with the solemn nature of events down here. My cousin's suite is at the end of the hall. My apartment is on the third floor."

"Where does your dad live?"

"Next door."

"Ahhh." He nods slowly. "So you're in this big house all by yourself most of the time?"

He seems to be asking out of concern for my safety, not because he wants to stay the night without my family knowing. Maybe I should be insulted, but for some reason that makes me like him even more.

And makes me feel worse that I tried to treat him like my own personal sex worker.

"Paul lives here. He's on call too. But we both kind of do our own thing in our down-time."

"When will your dad be back from the call?" he asks.

I shrug. "It's hard to say. Depends on where it was and the

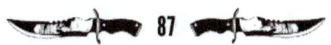

paperwork involved. It could be hours before he returns here with the body, or any minute."

He throws a glance at the back door. "You ever have a problem with someone trying to break in, you know you can call us, right?" He tilts his head toward the parking lot. "Protection is part of the arrangement with my club."

"But you all live so far away." My lips curve into a small smile. "Although the Slater County sheriff would probably take just as long to get here."

He frowns slightly. "I have a couple friends over in Johnsonville who'd get here quicker if you need help."

"Griff? Remy?" I ask. Obviously, they're close enough to the club that they were invited to Teller's wedding.

"Yeah," he growls. "And another couple of guys."

I wish I'd never admitted that I thought about asking Griff to help me with my problem. It was only a fleeting thought, and I only said it because Jigsaw's inevitable rejection hurt my feelings.

"Let me make that coffee," I say, hurrying into the kitchen. The old, white linoleum under my feet, though spotless, squeaks in familiar spots—an audible reminder of how long it's been since we've updated this part of the house.

He follows behind me, seeming to take up an unusual amount of space even in the large kitchen. He hovers close while I measure the coffee and hit Brew.

"How do you like it?" I face the dark wood cabinet, my hand lingering near the handle.

"Black with sugar."

I turn, glancing at him over my shoulder. "No cream?"

"Nah." He swivels his head around, checking out the kitchen in a more leisurely manner than the last time he was here.

A wave of self-consciousness follows me to the refrigerator. I pull out a carton of half-and-half, check that it's still in date, and set it on the counter, then find some stray sugar packets in a drawer.

Once we have our coffee, I cup my steaming mug in my chilled hands. "Let's move into the parlor, it's more comfortable."

"Lead the way." He grabs his mug and waves his hand in a flourish that's almost mocking.

Instead of returning to the main hallway, I push through a swinging door into a long, rectangular room that looks more like a museum than a living room. I perch at the edge of a bouncy cushion on the long gold velvet settee with wood-carved armrests and legs.

"Comfortable or time capsule?" Jigsaw quips, a half smirk playing over his lips as he examines the faded marigold wallpaper.

I bristle, not appreciating the critique of my family's home. But even I have to admit the heavy drapes, floral patterns, and ornate velvet furniture make it look like the set of a seventies murder-mystery show that takes place in a, well, funeral home.

"The death business is rather…conservative." I hate the note of apology in my voice. If I had my way, I'd redecorate the whole house. My own space upstairs is much more modern.

"It's charming." The couch dips as Jigsaw sits on the cushion next to me. Closer than polite company. So close, his thigh brushes mine and our elbows touch.

Oh, boy. An elbow touch. How racy!

"Well." I clear my throat and lean forward to set my mug on a coaster on the coffee table. "My dad could have sold out to one of the big national death services companies a few years ago when they were buying up family funeral homes like ours. But he's stubborn."

"Sounds complicated." Jigsaw sips his coffee. "But you're a necessary business, right? Death is inevitable."

"Sure. But more people are using cremation now. Or choosing to have smaller, more personal services." I huff a quick laugh. "The death business is *dying*."

His lips twitch.

"It's one job market where there is little to no growth." Why am I babbling about death when I'd rather talk about something extremely *life*-affirming?

"What would you do if you weren't doing this?" he asks.

"Makeup." There's something I haven't admitted to anyone in a long time. "I went to cosmetology school before I obtained my Mortuary Science degree."

He nods slowly and a flush of embarrassment licks at my cheeks. He probably thinks that's a low-effort, girly career.

"Strange I ended up here instead, right?"

"Not really." He tilts his head, pinning me with a playful stare. "The woman you thought was my wife, Serena, is a makeup artist. Well, she was a physical therapist, but she makes more with her YouTube channel now and it's more flexible with the baby coming and all."

"Really?" I squeal. "Which channel?"

His eyes widen, like he's surprised I'm so interested. Or maybe he's embarrassed he brought it up. What kind of biker wants to admit he knows anything about makeup?

"Tranquil Sparkle."

"I know that one! Oh my God, I'm surprised I didn't recognize her."

A wary look creeps over his expression. Almost…protective? "She's been posting older videos as she gets closer to her due date."

"Wow, you seem to know an awful lot about it."

He glances at his cup and shakes his head. "I do some of the admin for her channel and monitor her socials and stuff."

"No way, really?"

"Yeah, Rooster does a lot of the tech stuff for some of the club's other…businesses." He pauses and clears his throat. "So, I got into helping him with that."

"Is that what you do for work?"

He stops as if he really needs to think about the answer. "I do whatever the club needs me to do."

"So you have a bunch of bosses, not just one?"

"Not at all." He leans forward and pulls a coaster off the top of a stack in the center of the coffee table. "I'm a biker. We make our own rules. Follow our own laws."

I lift a brow at the coaster under his coffee cup. "And yet you just used a coaster."

His lips twitch with amusement. "I'm a biker. Not a heathen." He twists his body so he's facing me. "And I'm a guest in the space of someone I like."

He means me. "Oh," I whisper.

"So, I don't punch a time card or work a normal nine-to-five. But yes, I do answer to my club."

"And don't do relationships." I remind him of his earlier statement.

"Right. I'm free to do what I want—"

"Do *who* you want?" I arch a brow.

His lips curl into a knowing smirk. "That too."

Perfect segue to return to why he's really here. "Well, if it eases your concerns, I like you too. But I don't want to *date* you, Jigsaw."

His face pinches into a warning scowl but I continue anyway.

"I want you to teach me how to...*fuck.*" My voice falters on the curse. *Damn.* Lost my grip on my big girl panties there.

Ignoring my embarrassment, I lift my chin and stare him in the eyes.

His *trying to scare me away* face softens. "Little lady death," he murmurs. Reaching out, he traces one finger against the curve of my cheek. "So brave and fierce."

"Me?" My voice rises to a squeak.

"This could be dangerous. You have no idea what you're asking." That sly smile curls his lips again. "What if I'm into some sick, kinky shit?"

Why hadn't *that* occurred to me? Everything about him screams unconventional. What if that also applies to the bedroom? My friend April has told me more than a few horror stories about some of the guys she's gone out with and the weird things they wanted to do to her.

"I...uh...I just want to learn the basics." I flick my gaze to the ceiling. "I mean, I *know* what to do. Just help me improve my...skills. Teach me about what men like." I narrow my eyes. "And who are you calling little lady death?"

"I don't want to mess up our arrangement." He gestures to our surroundings. "This is a business deal for my club."

"So?"

"You need me to spell it out for you?" He blows out an annoyed breath and shifts to the other side of the cushion. His hard gaze continues to drill into my face. "If you catch...feelings, it's gonna make things awkward."

"Catch feelings?" I cross my arms over my chest and shoot him my sharpest glare. As if he's *so* irresistible. "What if you're the one who *catches feelings?*"

He snorts. "Not possible."

"I'm that repulsive?"

His cocky expression fades. "Not at all." He rakes his gaze over my body and lowers his voice to an obscene lion-like purr. "Not. At. All."

Jigsaw

Flustered Margot is even more fun than high-as-fuck Margot. But not quite as hot as teach-me-to-fuck Margot. This woman's ten different personalities inside one small package and I'm loving each one.

Liking. Not loving.

Never that.

"How much *education* do you think you need?" I ask just to see her scandalized eyes widen. "Hand jobs 101? Advanced blow job technique? A seminar on reverse cowgirl? A master class on anal? What skills are you looking to improve?"

Her eyes bug and she dry heaves at *anal.* Guess that's not a skill she wants to learn. I take a sip of my coffee to hide my laughter while I wait for her answer.

"The basics. I want to start from the ground up. Give me an idea of what men today expect." She frowns. "No master classes. Nothing in my butt."

I choke on my laughter. "You realize, what *men* expect and what *I* expect might be different. I'm not really in the habit of running around asking every man I meet how he likes to fuck."

"But you...your club brothers, you never talk about sex?"

"Uh, if you didn't notice, the brothers with ol' ladies are hyper-protective of them. No, they don't give details. Ever. I had to share living quarters with Rooster and Shelby when she was on tour and all I can tell you is that they're a loud and *often* kind of couple. I covered my head with my pillow and prayed for Rooster to be cursed with erectile dysfunction. I didn't stand by and take notes."

"I just want to learn to be good at it."

Something vulnerable in her voice tugs at my conscience. Forgot I had one for a decade.

I grab my coffee and take a quick sip. It's cool now. Bitter. I set the mug on its coaster again. "What are you doing Friday?"

She blinks a few times, then frowns. "Uh, I'm going to this car show thing in downtown Johnsonville. Why?"

"Car show? Really?" Interest colors my question. The way she shifts her gaze away, I think she assumes I'm making fun of her.

An awful idea forces me to ask something I shouldn't. "Are you going to the car show to troll for a sex coach?"

"What?" Her brow wrinkles with an indignant frown. "No! It's the first show this season. I go to them all the time."

"By yourself?"

"Well, sometimes my friend April comes with me. Or my cousin Paul goes but it's rare we both have a night off."

"What do you do?"

Her eyes light up, then her mouth turns down, wiping the joy off her face. "Nothing exciting. I'm usually the youngest person there. They close off a section of Main Street. Everyone parks facing the street instead of parallel to the curb." She makes a series of hand gestures to demonstrate. "It's rather informal. You just walk up and down, checking out everyone's classic. If you go often enough, you get to see the different stages of restoration for some of the vehicles. A lot of people work on their own cars. I take mine to—"

"Griff?"

"Well, Jerry's Garage, but yes, Griff's done a lot of the work on it. But Jerry knows my dad from the Chamber of Commerce, so he always helps me out."

Chamber of Commerce. What the fuck am I thinking? I can't get involved with this woman. Even if it's only for a few fuck lessons.

Demons help me. Forbidden fruit really is the sweetest.

"Are you allowed to bring a guest?"

"Y-yes," she stammers. "Of course. You drive up, pay five bucks, park and put a card with some info about your car on the dash, then walk around if you want to. Some people stay with their cars because they don't trust people. But I like to walk around."

"You're not worried about someone damaging your car?"

"Not really. The people who go to this are mostly local and pretty respectful. The diner stays open late and some of the businesses have sales and stuff. It's a nice way to support the community."

"You don't support Pine Hollow?" I tease. "The actual community where you live and have your business?

"Business comes to us from Johnsonville too." She lifts her chin. "Pine Hollow only does one car show a year and I go to that one too, smarty pants."

A rough chuckle rumbles out of me. Can't remember the last time someone as cute as Margot called me *that.*

"Can we go together?" I ask.

She throws me a surprised side-eye. "Like a *date?*"

"I don't do that," I remind her, shuddering at the thought.

No matter how much she says she likes me or trusts me, I don't peg Margot for a woman who's comfortable jumping into bed with someone she barely knows. What's the point of giving her "lessons" if we start off on a rocky foundation? All my hands-on training will be wasted.

"Let's hang out one on one," I suggest. "When you're not under the influence of pot brownies. And we'll see how things go."

Pink spreads over her cheeks and she ducks her head. "Sure. I'd like that."

"Good. What time do you want me here?"

"Um, six. Is that okay?"

"I'll be here." I slap my hands on my thighs and stand. "I better get going."

She stands, an uncertain expression playing over her face. I sure as fuck *want* to stay. Take her to her room, strip her down, and teach her all the ways our bodies can work together.

"Sure." She nods quickly. "It's a long drive."

Maybe she *doesn't* want me to stay. A few charming words and I could easily convince her.

But that's not what I want.

"I'm sorry, I never asked," she says in an apologetic tone. "Where do you live? Near Teller's place?"

"No, between our downstate charter near Union and the upstate charter."

"Oh. That is a long drive then. I'm sorry I kept you."

"It's fine. I'll crash at Upstate's clubhouse tonight. Z and Rock will probably call us to a joint church since everyone was here for the wedding."

"Church?" she asks over her shoulder as she returns to the kitchen.

Why didn't I just use an easier to understand civilian word? "Not what you're thinking." I follow her into the kitchen and set my mug on the counter. "It's our mandatory meeting where we all sit down and touch base about club business, discuss problems, see if anyone needs anything, plan future road trips, stuff like that."

A slight smirk plays at the corners of her kissable lips. "How very corporate of you."

She pushes through the door that leads to the hallway. My gaze strays to her pink shoes neatly lined up on the bottom step, then higher.

No. I'm not walking her upstairs or asking to see her place. No matter how sober she seems now, it's not the right time. I've never slept with a woman who wasn't one hundred percent with it and I'm not starting now. No matter how much I want her.

Nothing I "teach" her would probably stick, anyway.

Keep telling yourself it's all about the lessons, buddy.

The hint of amusement on her face fades. She puts her back to the door leading outside and stares up at me. "You won't discuss...*this*... you know, what I asked you to teach me with your club, right?"

"What? No. What kind of guy do you think I am?"

"Well, you pointed out that your deal with my father is a business relationship and you said church is for discussing business..." She shrugs.

"Gotcha." I nod quickly. "No, I won't say anything." *Unless it becomes a problem.* Z doesn't tell anyone else where to stick their dicks. In fact, he was fuckin' Stella, our most valuable porn star, before he married Lilly. So it'd be real hypocritical of him to say something about me "educating" Margot. Hell, even Rooster has only *suggested* I not fuck his mother-in-law to be.

No, wait. Those threats probably weren't suggestions.

This deal is Upstate's action. But there's no fuckin' way I'm asking Teller for his, what, permission? *Fuck that.* Besides, Rock told me to keep Margot occupied, so I'm following orders. The daughter of our business partner has a problem and I'm going to help her solve it. Simple as that.

That's the excuse I'll use if the club finds out and questions me. I can say it with a straight face—probably.

"I won't say anything about us unless I have to," I promise.

"Why would you *have* to?"

I open my mouth but the answer I'm about to give negates everything else I told her tonight.

If our relationship becomes more than a few fuck lessons.

If it turns into something real.

If I want to introduce you to the club as my ol' lady and give you my patch.

Which absolutely isn't going to happen.

CHAPTER ELEVEN

Jigsaw

I was right about Z and Rock calling everyone for church the next morning. Good thing I stayed at the main Upstate clubhouse instead of going to the new one down in Empire. All I had to do was get dressed and walk downstairs. I don't even have to bother with my boots.

The clubhouse is quiet as I jog down the hardwood stairs. In the living room, the large flat-screen TV on the wall is on at a low volume. Cartoons play across the screen, but it's not some of the club's kids busy watching. Sparky's giddy, childlike giggles and Stash's harsh guffaws break the silence. They're sprawled on the couches in the same exact spots they were last night when I came in. Their dedication to laziness could make a sloth jealous.

I eyeball the twin two-liter bottles of Mountain Dew on the floor with suspicion.

Sparky flips his gaze to me and sits up. "You stay here last night?" He yawns and stretches his arms high, lifting his shirt to show off his pasty white belly. He slowly eases himself off the couch and yawns again.

"I literally talked to you two clowns when I came in," I remind them, amusement and a hint of exasperation coloring my tone.

"Remember I asked if Murphy's room was free and you said, 'nothing in life is free' then fell off the couch giggling?"

Sparky glances at Stash who shrugs and rolls off the couch, landing on his feet.

"Why are you walking around barefoot?" Sparky approaches while staring at my feet like he finds them personally offensive.

I wiggle my toes. "What? I have nice feet. After church I'm going to go outside and touch some grass." I glance down at his big, woolly socks. "You should give it a try sometime."

He giggles like a five-year-old. "I *touch grass* all the time. I'm one with the grass."

"You're one with something, all right," I growl.

"Great comeback," Stash sneers.

"Give me time. I just got up." I reach out and smack the ends of his unruly hair. "You ever bother to brush that shit? Looks like a squirrel-tail hat my pappy had when I was a kid."

"The fuck it does." He brushes my hands away and slaps his wild hair into place. "Girls love running their fingers through my hair."

Several bikes pull into the parking lot out front, interrupting our insult ping-pong. Sounds like at least one or two from my charter. I lift my chin at Stash. "What'd everyone do, stay at the other clubhouse last night?"

"Most of the single dudes did. Dex actually went in to work at CB. Grinder and Serena stayed with Wrath and Trinity. Z and Lilly are at Rock and Hope's."

"Rock must be loving that." I snicker into my hand. Rock's always making sly threats about Z showing up to his house unannounced.

Sparky shrugs. "I think Alexa stayed there too so the littles all had a sleepover."

"Cute." Glad I wasn't anywhere near *that*.

Upstairs, doors slam and sleepy voices increase in volume.

"I can't believe we're the first ones up," Sparky says to Stash. "This must be a sign of good moon energy."

I squint at Sparky. "Did you even go to sleep last night, moonbeam?"

"Is that Jiggy I hear?" Shelby's soft southern twang drifts down the stairs.

I lift my head, the corners of my mouth instantly lifting. "It's me, songbird."

She comes into view, hurrying down the last few steps, dressed in a matching teal workout set and her blonde waves piled in a messy bun on top of her head.

A big grin spreads over her face when her gaze lands on me. "Where'd you run off to last night?" She hurries over and quickly wraps her arms around my middle, giving me a squeeze hello.

Shelby's one of the very few people whose hugs don't instantly make me recoil. Or she does it so often, I've been desensitized. We've been through some shit, and I care for her like she was my own sister.

"You're chipper this morning," I say, returning the hug.

She casts a quick smile at Sparky. "I suspect I'm feeling a lot better than some of y'all gonna be feelin' today."

Shit, is Margot okay this morning?

I give Shelby another quick squeeze. "I'll be right back."

Where the fuck can I go to find some peace and quiet in this clubhouse? I should've checked on Margot before I left the bedroom.

I head down the hallway, passing the bathrooms. The door to the yoga studio—what used to be Upstate's champagne room—is wide open, and beyond it it's shadowy. Perfect.

I slip inside and close the door behind me, then pull out my phone. Text or call? Does anyone make phone calls anymore? What if she's still asleep? *Text it is.*

Me: How are you feeling today?

I stare at my screen until the message shows delivered. Fucking shitty, slow cell service up here.

"Jigsaw?"

So intent on my damn phone, I didn't hear the door swing open. I startle and turn. Swan's slight frame stands in the doorway. She reaches out and flips on the light switch. "Are you joining us for yoga today?"

I blink rapidly, adjusting to the sudden flood of bright light. "Ha. Nice try." I stuff my phone in my pocket. "Got church."

"I'll rope you in one of these days," she teases.

Sit and watch my brothers' wives and ol' ladies moving through sensual poses? Not fucking likely. "I'm sure you will."

As I step into the hallway, the chatter coming from the living room has increased. I cock my head, listening for Z. Nope. My prez isn't here yet. I still have time to hit the dining room. After church, we'll all sit down for breakfast together with the ol' ladies, kids, and whoever else is up here. But before church, the girls usually make sure we have coffee and some other snacks.

Bright light streams in through the huge windows in the large, cafeteria-style dining room. Tables and chairs are still stacked to one side of the room. To my right, the bar counter's overflowing with morning drink options. Coffee, hot water, and this week someone stuck a cooler full of bottles of orange and cranberry juices out too.

Instead of coffee, I grab a bottle of orange juice, twist the cap and take a deep sip.

"Do you want a muffin to go with it?" someone asks from behind me.

I turn and find Lala holding a tray of fat, freshly baked muffins. The rich scent of citrus and cinnamon tempts me into snatching the biggest one from the tray.

"They're cranberry orange." She sets the tray on the last clear space on the counter.

"Looks good." I search the area for a plate or napkin.

Bonnie, another club girl from Downstate, steps up to the counter and sets out plates, napkins, a tub of butter, and a tub of cream cheese.

"How'd you know that's what I was lookin' for, darlin'?" I tease.

She beams at me. "Where'd you go last night? Thought I'd see you down at the other clubhouse."

"Nope." I slice my muffin in half, dig into the cream cheese and smear it all over one side.

"That's how I like them too," Lala says, gently bumping Bonnie aside to grab a muffin of her own. Bonnie shoulder checks Lala.

I lift my gaze to the ceiling. *Can't a man eat a muffin in peace?*

"Ladies, there is more than enough of me to go around," I warn them, hoping that if I identify the elephant in the room, it will deflate it. "But I'm not looking for company today."

Behind me someone snorts. "Since when?"

Lala giggles but Bonnie glares at me. I sneer at her and she hurries with Lala back into the kitchen.

Still laughing, Dex grabs a cup and fills it with coffee. "You eat too many pot brownies last night?"

"Not a single one."

I cast a quick glance around the still mostly empty dining room. That could change any minute, though. After church, Dex will probably head into Crystal Ball and I won't be able to get him alone. "Can I ask you something?"

Caught mid-sip, Dex raises his eyebrows at me.

"Don't you dare laugh," I warn. "I'd ask Rooster, but I already know the answer and it won't be helpful."

"Well, don't keep me in suspense," Dex answers in a dry tone. "Now I'm dying to know."

Fuck. Am I really doing this? I roll my eyes and jam my hands into my pockets. I can't believe I started this conversation. It's not like Google isn't free.

Tucking my juice bottle under my arm and holding my muffin, I grab his elbow with my free hand and move us into the far corner of the dining room.

Dex stares at where I'm holding onto him. "Can I at least get a muffin before you inflict whatever insanity's going on in your head today?"

"Here." I thrust my remaining half at him.

He stares at it like I tried to force a dead fish down his throat. "Thanks, I'm good." Irritation's clear in his voice.

Just ask and get this over with.

"When's the last time you were with a virgin?" I end up whispering the last word like I'm eleven years old again, waiting for my father to pop out of the shadows and crack his whip across my back.

A line forms between Dex's eyes, like he's trying to decide if I'm serious or clowning him. He sucks in a breath like he's preparing to rattle off a long, scolding speech.

"I'm serious." Hopefully that helps skip the lecture and get to the advice part.

He blows out a breath and runs his hand over the back of his neck. "What kind of question is that?" His eyes narrow. "What poor, unfortunate virgin are you planning to bed?"

I don't need him putting two and two together and calculating it's Margot. I realize she's *not* a virgin but she's definitely inexperienced, so this seemed like the simplest way to phrase it without sharing too many personal details. "No one you know."

He opens his mouth and I hold up my hand to stop the question I know is about to come out. "Yes, she's legal and then some. Come on. You're always preaching all that sex positivity shit. Help your brother out. Have you ever been with a virgin?"

He stares at me for a few more seconds. "Uh, my wife when we were in high school." He lets out a heavy sigh. "What exactly is your question?"

What the fuck *is* my question? Or am I looking for Papa Dex to talk some sense into me?

"How'd you make it good for her...and how'd you help her, I don't know, gain confidence that she was doing things right?"

He tilts his head and shifts his gaze to the window for a second. Not like he's judging me, more like he's pondering the question. I knew once Dex got over his initial shock, he'd come through for me.

"Fuck, I don't know if I thought about it quite that way. We were *both* virgins, so it was a lot of awkward fumbling around together until things felt good."

An almost fond smile tilts the corners of his mouth, not the sad frown he usually gets when he mentions his wife—which is almost never.

"But, unless you've been lying all those times you've bragged about your...conquests," he rolls his eyes, "you *know* what you're doing."

My lips curve into a cocky smirk. "So I've been told. Many, many times. By an infinite variety of—"

"Good Christ." He cuts me off. "Whoever she is, let the poor girl find someone else."

I open my mouth to say something snarky but stop. *Should* I tell Margot to find someone else? Someone she actually has stuff in common with?

No, she's not looking for a relationship.

And she specifically asked for *my* help.

"She doesn't want anyone else," I say.

He heaves out a heavy, annoyed sigh. "Does she masturbate?"

"I don't know."

"Well, let her show you what she likes. Or help her figure out what she likes. Every woman's a little different." He casts a stink eye toward the kitchen. "Since I assume you've only been fucking bunnies for the last decade—"

"With the occasional civilian MILF thrown in for variety."

"Great." He shakes his head and bites down his laughter. "Older women usually already know what they like."

"*Yesss*, they do." I let out a dirty laugh.

He rolls his eyes. "Right. And muffler bunnies will tell you whatever they think you want to hear—" His eyes widen as if he stumbled upon the answer to a great mystery. "You care about whoever this is. A lot."

"Care is a bit strong." *Lie.* "I like her and want to teach her some skills for her future." I wave my hand in the air like it's nothing.

"Is she running away from a convent or something?"

I snort-laugh. "No."

"I don't know what else to tell you." He sighs. "Make her comfortable. Go slow. Pretend you know what foreplay is."

"Oh, I know *all* about foreplay, brother."

He rolls his eyes again. "Don't assume she's into everything you're doing to her. Realize she might be too nervous to tell you *no*. Pay attention to her body's signals." He lifts his shoulders, scrunches his face into an unpleasant cringe, and holds his hands out like he's pushing someone away. "*This* isn't a sign to fuck her harder."

When I nod but don't offer my usual snarky comment, he drops his hands and continues, "Don't jam your dick down her throat. Be patient with her. Show her what *you* like. Communicate. That's the biggest thing. Make her put into words what she actually likes and wants you to do."

I absorb each suggestion, especially that last one. All things that should've been obvious. Did I really need Dex's advice?

Or was I just hoping he'd try harder to talk me out of it?

"Thanks, brother." I slap his shoulder.

"Does this mean you're not going to help me out at CB anymore?" he asks.

I curl my lip. Why the fuck would he assume that? "No, why?"

"Figured someone that innocent might not like her man working in a strip club."

"Whoa, whoa, whoa. I'm *not* her man. I'm no one's man."

He narrows his eyes, then shakes his head. "You know what? It's not my business. Just be nice and be clear with her that it's not a relationship."

"Already covered that part."

"Well, give her a refresher course before you get down to business. Don't be a dick. But be clear."

"I will."

He stares at me a few seconds longer. "Wow, I really woke up in the Twilight Zone this morning."

I slap his shoulder. "Buckle up, cupcake, shit's only going to get stranger."

CHAPTER TWELVE

Margot

JIGSAW: HOW ARE YOU FEELING TODAY?

I whimper and drop my phone back on the nightstand. My head's full of soggy cotton. A weird, unpleasant buzz bounces around my skull.

Slowly, the events of last night return to me.

I asked Jigsaw to be my sex coach.

We're going out on Friday night.

And then probably having sex afterward?

We never actually said *what* we'd do after the car show. A slow tingle of anticipation throbs below. It's been a couple of years since Daniel. Am I even ready for this? What if my girly bits have sealed shut from lack of use?

That was the whole point of asking for his help.

Sighing, I throw the covers back and roll myself upright. Barely any hint of daylight peeks through my blackout curtains and shade. I stand, stretch and slide my curtains open, then pull up the blinds, letting the morning sunshine wash over me.

My gaze shifts to my phone. Jigsaw's concern cuts through my embarrassment. I send him a quick response.

Me: A bit fuzzy headed. But ok.

Maybe he'll think I forgot about our Friday night plans. That would probably be for the best. I set my phone down and run to the bathroom.

A few minutes later, with a freshly scrubbed face and empty bladder, I wander into the kitchen. My stomach recoils at the thought of food. I thought pot was supposed to give you the munchies?

I unwrap a cheese stick and chew on it while I brew a pot of coffee.

Did Jigsaw text back?

While the coffee's brewing, I hurry into my bedroom and scoop up my phone.

There's a message waiting on the screen.

Jigsaw: Can't wait to see you Friday night.

He remembered. And he wants *me* to remember.

I type out *me too*, then erase it. What if he thinks I'm too eager and breaks the date?

My phone buzzes. I'm holding it so tight, I jump.

Dad: Could use your help this morning.

Nothing like prepping a dead body to take the romance out of the air.

Me: Be down in a few minutes.

I change into long black pants and a long-sleeved black T-shirt. We might have family members stopping by later. I walk into my long closet all the way to the end where I set up a vanity station. I tap a button on the large rectangular vanity mirror taking up a good portion of the wall and sit at the glossy, white table. My eyes are a little puffy but at least I don't look like I spent most of the night high and sleeping on a stranger's lawn.

I twist my hair into a neat bun, line my lips with neutral mauve, and dab on a creamy lipstick. With my face and hair presentable, I cross the room to the ornate cherry wood jewelry chest that once belonged to my mother. From the top drawer, I choose a pair of small gold love knot earrings.

AS I'M LEAVING, I absently reach up and flick one of the round ornaments hanging from the bar above the chest.

Who am I kidding? Even if Jigsaw can somehow manage to teach me to fuck like a goddess, the only man I'll ever attract is bound to be in the death business too. Or he'll be a freaky weirdo who wants me to give him access to bodies to play with like my first boyfriend.

My schedule isn't really family friendly, either. Do I even want to raise kids in this house? My brothers and I all grew up here. And I was exposed to some terrifying stuff at an early age.

One thing at a time.

Improve bedroom skills.

Try dating.

Then worry about the rest of it.

I finish a few other morning chores, then head downstairs.

"Morning, Dad," I say, stepping into the prep room.

He's wearing all the protective equipment today. A stench that even the state-of-the-art ventilation system and action powder can't contain assaults my nose. I find a stick of odor blocker and dab it under my nose, then slip into my own gear.

"How was the rest of the party?" Dad asks, the respirator making him sound like a sci-fi villain.

"Fun." At least the parts I remember were pleasant.

"Jensen brought you home with no issues?"

"Yes, he was very nice." *He didn't even flinch when I propositioned him.*

"Good."

I gesture to the table. "What do we have here?"

My father casts a sad look at the black body bag on the table. "Unattended death. He'd been there a few days. Too decomposed to embalm."

"How sad." Unattended death. No family to find him for days.

That's what's going to happen to you if you don't figure yourself out and get better at sex.

"We're going to need to use a pouch and have the service as quickly as possible," Dad continues. "Can you start on the arrangements for me? The family should be here shortly. It's a mother and her daughter.

Be gentle with the mother, she's very emotionally fragile. He was her last sibling."

I haven't met them yet, but the weight of their grief is already pressing down on me. "Yes, of course." I'll have to think of a nice way to let them know we'll be placing him in a disaster pouch inside his coffin to contain all the fluids and that there is no chance of an open casket.

"The daughter identified the body, so she's aware of the condition," my father adds.

"Poor woman." How awful to have that be the last memory of her uncle. But how kind of her to spare her mother the pain.

Who will do that for me one day?

Probably no one.

CHAPTER THIRTEEN

Jigsaw

THE LONG RIDE TO MARGOT'S PLACE SOOTHES MY EAGER SOUL. Twisting the throttle gives my hands something to do other than burn to touch Margot's skin. Paying attention to the road and surroundings keeps thoughts of peeling off her clothes at bay.

That all goes to shit the second I see her.

Prim and pretty, Margot steps off the porch and onto the asphalt of the parking lot behind the funeral home. Last time I saw her she was wearing teal and pink. Now she's dressed in a light-pink, short-sleeved cardigan, with a thin matching pink shirt underneath, and a full, pink swing skirt with layers of ruffled lace swirling underneath.

I rest my helmet on the seat of my bike and tug my gloves off.

She approaches slowly, as if she's afraid to get too close to the bike.

"All right to leave it here?" I parked close to the house, so hopefully it's out of the way—and out of sight of her father—unless he specifically walks around this side for some reason.

"Sure." She squeezes the small pink purse in her hands and twists the strap around her fingers.

I shouldn't find a woman her age so fucking adorable but damn, every time I see Margot she makes my mouth do weird shit like smile.

Underneath all my desire to teach her everything about sex, I've been looking forward to just seeing and talking to her.

I squint at the skirt—are those tiny gray, black, and white poodles printed all over it? "Are you wearing an actual poodle skirt with poodles on it?"

She grins wide and it transforms her from pretty to blindingly beautiful.

"Yes." She grabs the sides of the skirt and swings it from side to side. "I wish I could've found it in yellow to match my car."

"The pink's nice." *Good green goblins, since when do I care about things like the color pink?*

Everything about Margot seems to fascinate me. I can't stop staring at her as we cross the parking lot to the multi-car garage. Three little shiny pins on her collar catch my attention but I can't quite make out what they say while we're walking. One looks like a red crab crawling out of a pot. Another is in the shape of a tiny pink dumpster? The third one's the smallest, a black, red, and white square.

We stop in front of the garage and she hands me a car key on a ring with a yellow daisy ornament dangling from one end. I hesitate before accepting it. "You want me to drive?"

"I assume you know how." She arches an eyebrow. "Since you drove me home the other night."

"Funny girl." The garage door in front of us rattles and starts rolling up, revealing the pristine yellow Thunderbird waiting in the bay. "I mean, you trust me to drive your fancy classic car? It's in mint condition."

She turns and tilts her head, staring up at me with a solemn expression that almost makes me wish I'd kept my mouth shut. "I'm planning to trust you with my body, so why wouldn't I trust you with my car?"

Excellent point.

I'm not sure how to answer. Instead, I drop my gaze to the pins.

The little crab on one pin is holding up a *say no to pot* sign. I burst out laughing. "Clever. Did you already have the pot pin before the wedding?"

She lets out an endearing giggle. "No, I saw it after my experience with Sparky's magic brownies, and thought it was perfect for my collection." She tilts her head to the side and lowers her lashes. "I knew you'd be the only one who got the joke, so I had to wear it tonight."

We already have inside jokes on our first date.

No. Not a date.

Moving on. The dumpster pin. *Unsolicited Opinions from Random People.* I let out a snort. "Amen to that."

"You'd be surprised how many men at the car shows come up to lecture me about what I should or shouldn't do with my car."

"No, I wouldn't be surprised at all." I scoff, "The kinds of men who do that aren't going to get the joke, though. Or they won't realize it's for them. They're going to use reading the pin as an excuse to stare at your tits."

She slaps her hand over her pins. "Ewww."

Don't worry. I'll handle anyone who stares at you for too long tonight. I shrug, then lift my chin. "What's the last one?"

She slowly removes her hand to reveal a tiny juice box with a poison apple on the front.

"I just thought it was cute." She shrugs and shifts her gaze to the house. "My father asked me not to wear my *hex the patriarchy* and *slay all day* grim reaper pins since they might offend people who could be potential customers."

"Your dad still approves your outfits?"

She tilts her head. "I took it as a suggestion. Not an order."

All right then. As much as it rubs against all my personal instincts, I see the man's point. Margot said the business is conservative. A grim reaper on the funeral director's daughter—while funny as hell to someone like me—might be bad for business.

"Ready to go?" she asks.

"Let's do it." I don't want to do anything to damage Margot's pristine yellow convertible, but she asked me to drive, so I get behind the wheel and fire it up.

The Thunderbird purrs beneath my hands as I ease it out of the

garage and onto the road. Margot's quiet at first. I'm concentrating on not fucking up her car, so I don't have much to offer.

"Thank you for coming with me," she finally says. "I know motorcycles are more your thing."

"I like cars. Well, classic cars. Interesting cars. Not the generic shit boxes everyone drives."

She titters with laughter. "That's why I always wanted *this* car. Something different. And the yellow is so sunny and pretty." Her voice drops. "Opposite of the hearse."

A laugh pops out and I cover it with a cough. "Yeah, you could say that."

I find my way to Main Street; only a portion of it is blocked off for the car show.

"Drive right up to the cones." Margot leans forward and points. "They'll let us in."

I slow the car as I approach. Two old men with reflective vests and clipboards wave us closer. I roll down my window.

A worried frown creases the forehead of the guy who approaches us.

He ducks down to peer in the window. "Margot, is that you?"

"Hi, Fred!" She leans forward and waves.

"Hey there." He stares at me like I'm holding Margot at gunpoint in her own car.

I rest one arm on the sill and leave the other on the steering wheel. "Evening."

"Are you rolling in to show tonight, Margot?" he asks.

The fuck else does he think we brought the car for?

"Sure am." She beams at him and reaches for her purse.

"That'll be five dollars…" He looks at me expectantly as if he's waiting for me to give my name.

I'd stashed cash in my pocket earlier and pull out the five just as Margot's unzipping her wallet.

"I've got it, Jigsaw," she mutters.

Ignoring her, I hand the money to Fred. He dips his chin and nods, the older generation's version of "good boy," I suppose.

He hands me a blue ticket with the number sixty-nine on it. My lips curl into a smirk. It must be the universe's way of telling me *that* should be Margot's first lesson.

"Thank you, sir. Anywhere in particular I should park?"

He points straight ahead. "Front of the diner might be a good spot. There's no official areas designated, though."

"All right." I ease the car forward and crawl toward the diner, careful not to hit any of the folks walking in the middle of the street.

I back into a space next to a glistening seventies Ford F-100 pickup. The light blue metallic paint glitters under the late afternoon sun. "Now, that's my kind of classic," I say to Margot.

Her eyes widen and she does this little bounce thing in her seat that's cute as hell. "I love this truck! Wait 'til you see the interior, it's immaculate."

Her enthusiasm is contagious. My usual scorn for events that require civilian interaction fades to a dull disdain as I step out of the car.

Margot sets the blue tag on the dashboard, then pulls a small mirror and brush out of her purse. She runs the brush through her hair and by the time she's finished dabbing on some lipstick, I'm opening her door.

"Oh." She stares up at me in surprise.

"Ready?" I hold out my hand.

She blinks, then slowly sets her hand in mine. I gently tug her out of the car, pulling her flush against the front of my body. She stares up at me with questions in her eyes.

Kiss her. "You look really pretty tonight."

Her lips part.

"I should've said so sooner," I continue. "But I got distracted by the pins on your sweater, and the poodles on your skirt."

"Thank you," she whispers.

I'm unable to resist the magnetic pull of her lips for another second. I lean down and brush my lips against hers. A soft kiss. A fraction of what I actually want to do—absolutely devour her.

She presses her hands against my chest. Is she pushing me away?

No. The fabric of my T-shirt tickles against my skin as she curls her fingers in the material. She's trying to pull me closer.

The sharp bleat of a horn tears us apart.

She pushes her glasses into place and fusses with her dress. "Sorry. I'm not very good at public displays of affection."

What do I say to that? Half my brothers downstate would include fucking on a pool table in front of everyone in the clubhouse as a "display of affection." A little kiss in the street is nothing. But it's obviously a big deal to Margot.

"I'm, uh…" She blushes and stammers as she pulls away.

I grab her hip, stopping her from moving farther.

"You said this wasn't a date…" She flicks her gaze to mine. "What are you doing?"

A note of confusion or hurt lingers in her question. What *am* I doing? "Lesson one. Getting comfortable with being affectionate in public."

Her eyebrows scrunch together in a frown of concentration.

"Any man you're with should want to claim you in public. Let other men know you're taken."

"How very primal."

I lean down and whisper in her ear, "Deep down, we're all just animals, Margot."

Margot

My heart's thudding so hard, Jigsaw can probably hear it over the hum and roar of engines.

He kissed me in the middle of Main Street. Daniel never even wanted to hold my hand in public. I kissed him on the cheek once and he spent the next half hour lecturing me on my inappropriate behavior.

This isn't supposed to be a date, though. How do I handle this? Treat tonight like a date where I'm gaining experience? A dress rehearsal of sorts? That doesn't seem fair to Jigsaw, but he did agree to our…arrangement. And he's the one who kissed *me*.

 120

"Yes, I guess we are all animals," I finally say. I can't tear my eyes away from him. He has to be the most brutally handsome man I've ever had in my presence. Having his attention so intensely focused on me is addicting.

"What year is this?" someone shouts, shattering the moment.

Jigsaw growls and puts his arm protectively around my shoulders. A guy, probably a few years older than me, stands by the driver's side of my car, waving at us.

"Sixty-five," I answer.

"It's really nice." He skims his hand over the hood without quite touching the paint and leaving fingerprints. "You do the work yourself?" He nods to Jigsaw.

"No," I answer. "Jerry's Garage does the maintenance for me."

His eyes spark with interest. "Yeah? Are they local?"

"Yup. Actually." I open my purse and pull out one of the cards with Griff's name on it. "Jerry used to do all the work himself. He does all sorts of classics." I circle around to meet him at the front of the car. "But Griff's done the more recent work."

The guy accepts the card, glances at it and nods. "Thanks. I'll have to check them out. I just moved to the area. I have '67 Mustang Fastback I need someone to take a look at."

"Oh, I love the design of those. Does it have the in-line six or a V8?"

He lifts his eyebrows. "V8." His gaze shifts to something behind me. He taps the card in his hand. "I'll definitely check this place out. What's your name so I can tell them you sent me?"

"Margot."

He flicks his gaze over my shoulder again, then sticks out his hand. "Noah."

His hand's warm, his grip firm. "Nice to meet you."

"Likewise."

Instead of walking past us, he turns around and strides away from us. Quickly.

I turn and collide with Jigsaw. "Have you been standing there the whole time?"

The harsh lines of his face soften, and he stops glaring twin holes into Noah's back. "Yup."

"Why didn't you say something?"

"He kept things polite, so there was no reason to interrupt you." He lifts one shoulder. "And I didn't have anything to add to the conversation."

What am I supposed to do with that? I probably should've made more effort to draw him into the conversation instead of being rude.

I nod to the Ford pickup truck he'd shown some interest in. "I'm ready to check this one out."

"Me too." He captures my hand.

We approach the truck slowly. Jigsaw stands back to admire the paint. "It's very glittery." He wiggles his fingers in the air over the hood.

"It's a special paint with holographic glitter in it."

He nods and slowly walks around the truck. The owner's sitting in a chair near the tailgate, and he waves hello to me.

The look on Jigsaw's face is almost wistful as he peers inside and checks out the blue-and-white leather seats. "Damn, it *is* immaculate."

"The seats are all custom too."

He takes a step back. "Is picture-taking allowed?"

"It's encouraged."

He pulls out his phone and snaps a picture of the truck from the front, then taps at the screen a few more times before tucking the phone away.

"My friend's uncle had a truck like this when we were kids. Well, year and model. Nowhere near this condition." He chuckles. "It was good ol' seventies bronze and orange. I think Rooster's aunt would've preferred glittery blue."

"Did his uncle show it?"

"No, it was a grocery getter." An almost affectionate smile brightens his expression then twists with sadness. "He used to joke that he wanted to be buried in that truck."

By the change in tone, it sounds like his friend's aunt and uncle are no longer with us. I'm not sure how to ask that, so I wait for him to continue.

He shakes his head like he's tucking away a bittersweet memory for safekeeping. "Anyway, you don't see a lot of them anymore. And definitely not in this condition. I sent the pic to Rooster."

"That was sweet."

He shrugs.

We walk all the way around the truck. The owner grins at me.

"How you doing, Margot?" He stands and nods at Jigsaw. "You going to introduce me to your fella?"

I let out an awkward chuckle. Should I correct him? No, he probably saw us kiss earlier, that'll be weird if I say he's just a friend.

While I'm debating it, Jigsaw introduces himself and compliments the truck.

Burt eyes Jigsaw up and down. "You're a big fella, aren't ya?"

Jigsaw's eyes widen and he quickly stares down at his boots. "Damn, I guess so."

Burt grins wide and laughs, then winks at me as if giving me his approval.

"I'll keep an eye on your car, Margot," Burt says to me. "You two go look around."

"Thanks."

Jigsaw takes my hand again and we move on to the next car—a purple Corvette. "I love these. If I ever decide to get another classic, it'll be a Corvette."

And then I can't stop rambling about engines, bodywork, and restoration. Jigsaw's quiet but keeps his head cocked my way the whole time. Almost like he doesn't want to miss a word.

"Sorry," I finally say. "I didn't mean to keep talking."

"I'm listening to everything you say." He squeezes my hand. "How'd you get into classic cars?"

"The T-bird was my grandmother's."

He stops and stares at me. "Really? It's been in your family *that* long?"

I nod quickly. "Yup. Dad was convinced he'd sell it after she passed." A slight smile tugs at my lips as I recall the way his jaw dropped when we sat down at the lawyer's office for the reading of her will. "But she left it to me."

"Was he mad?"

"No. Just surprised." I glance around at the line of classic cars rolling down the street, searching for places to park. "Speaking of surprises, there seem to be way more cars tonight than I anticipated."

His gaze follows mine, and he nods. "Seems that way. That's a good thing, though, right?" He gestures to the shops lined along either side of the street. "More business for the locals?"

"Yes. More variety in vehicles too."

The corners of his mouth lift. "You thirsty? I could use a drink."

"A little." I point to the diner. "Their lemonade is really good."

"I'll grab it." He lifts his chin to the line of cars in front of us. "While I'm gone, make a plan for what other cars you want to see." He circles one finger in the air, his relaxed smile making it clear he's game for whatever I choose.

"That's easy. All of them."

Jigsaw

Laughing, I hurry into the diner. Of course she wants to see all of them. I do too, honestly. It's fun listening to her get so animated about cars.

I don't want to leave her alone for too long, so I don't bother checking out the menu and just order two lemonades.

The gray-haired man behind the counter nods to my cut. "What'd you roll in with tonight, sir?"

"Nothing." I swipe my card through the reader without looking at the total. "My girlfriend's got a yellow Thunderbird."

What the fuck just came out of my mouth?

It was just easier to say girlfriend, instead of *friend who's a girl.* That's it. Nothing more.

The man frowns. "Yellow Thunderbird? Are you talking about little Margot Cedarwood?"

I narrow my eyes and pull my shoulders back. "Yeah, why?" My tone hovers between *keep her name out of your mouth* and *fuck off*.

"No reason. Didn't know she was seeing someone. That's all. You two have a good time." He passes me the two cups of lemonade.

Shit. Does he know Margot's dad? That'll be fun if it gets back to the old man that she's "dating" some sketchy, scarred biker.

Fuck it. What's the old man going to do about it?

I grab two straws from the counter and head outside, scanning the area for Margot.

A flash of pink sweater and blonde hair grabs my attention. *There she is.* Across the street, near a 1980s silver Corvette, deep in conversation with an older, pot-bellied man in a goofy hat, too-small T-shirt, shorts, sandals, and ankle socks. Even from where I'm standing, his posture and the way he leans in close to her sends a possessive fiery streak through my veins.

For someone who seems so shy at times, she sure talks to a lot of people.

Margot's too sweet to realize this old creep's coming on to her. Like that guy Noah, earlier. I could tell he was debating whether he should ask for her number by the way he kept checking me out. At least he didn't seem like a perv.

But this guy? It's almost painful to watch her talk to the empty potato sack who's so obviously attempting to flirt with her. He leers and smiles too wide. Laughs too loud. Keeps trying to touch her upper arm so he can graze his thumb against the side of her breast.

Satan take the wheel.

Eyes on Margot, I march across the street. Just as I called it earlier, he leans down and practically shoves his chin in her cleavage to "read" her pins.

Please curse this fool with the urge to fuck a blender.

Time to put an end to this.

I shift both cups into one hand, walk up behind Margot, and rest my free—but cold—hand on the small of her back. She startles, then leans into me, as if she knows I'm here to put a boot up this guy's ass. She turns and stares up at me with wide, surprised eyes.

"Hey, darlin', everything okay?" I hand her one of the lemonades and ignore the man who's suddenly standing telephone pole straight and staring anywhere but at Margot's tits.

"Yes, thank you." She waves one hand in the air. "This is Glen. Glen, this is my friend, Jensen."

Friend.

I guess introducing me as her "sex tutor" would've required a few minutes of uncomfortable explanation. But "friend" doesn't sit right with me.

Glen slides his slimy gaze over my cut. His head swivels back and forth, as if he's trying to figure out how the hell the biker and the poodle-skirted princess met each other.

"Lost Kings...I know Bricks. He's done some work on my bike," Glen says. "Good guy."

At least he's not dropping names just to hear himself talk. If he really is a customer at Rock's custom bike shop, I don't want to be a total dick. "Yeah, he is," I agree. "You ride?"

"Nothing like the miles you put on your bikes." He laughs and sweeps his hand toward the car parked next to the Corvette—a black-and-gold eighties Trans Am. "My first love."

I nod, even though a Trans Am is nothing I'd brag about.

"Nice ride," I say, trying to keep the sarcasm out of my voice. "You come to these shows often?"

"Every chance I get," Glen replies, his tone dripping with an attempt at casualness that feels anything but. "It's a great way to meet like-minded enthusiasts." He smirks, his gaze lingering on Margot a moment too long. "But we know each other from Jerry's Garage, right, Margot?"

The corners of her mouth hitch into a patient smile. "We do."

Glen grins like an idiot. "The car world is small, small, small."

I step closer, wrap my arm around Margot's waist and subtly pull her against my side. "Yeah, it's a small world," I say, my voice lowering. "Never know *who* you'll run into. Or *where.*"

Glen chuckles, a nervous edge to his voice. "True, true. Well, I should probably get back to my car. Don't want anyone touching it," he says, casting a final lingering look at Margot. "It was good seeing you again, Margot. Nice meeting you, Jensen."

"Likewise," I reply, my tone flat. I wait until he's on the other side of his car, talking to someone else, to pull a few inches away from Margot. I still keep my hand on her back, though. "You okay?"

She nods, but a bit of pink dusts her cheeks. "I'm fine. Glen's alway…chatty."

"Too chatty," I mutter, handing her one of the straws. "Let's keep walking."

She pokes the straw into her cup and takes a sip. Fucking hell. Her lips would look so much better wrapped around something else.

"Thanks." She hesitates, then looks up at me, her eyes searching mine. "Are you mad at me?"

"What? No," I say quickly. "Why would I be mad at you?"

"You seem tense." She stops walking and faces me. "Edgy." She waves her hand in front of my body.

"Edgy, huh? I've been called worse." The street's full of more people now, so I move us to the sidewalk, out of the flow of traffic. "I didn't like the way Glen was leering at you. That's all. I was worried about you."

"Oh!" Her face brightens. "Nah, Glen's a big blowhard. But he's harmless. You were right, though." She brushes her fingers against her pins. "He stared at my chest for so long—either he can't read, needs glasses, or he was trying to guess my cup size."

"He can read fine," I grumble.

She tips her head down and plays with her straw. "It's nice having you with me." She takes a quick sip of lemonade.

"Just think of me as your attack Doberman."

She blinks. "Oh, I hope that's not why…that's not the only reason—"

"*I'm* the one who asked if I could come with you, remember?"

Her apologetic expression softens. "Oh, right. You did." She stares at the cup in her hand, then fiddles with her purse. "Let me pay you for the lemonade."

"Are you kidding?" I tap the hand holding the purse. "Knock it off."

"You know, if you keep paying for everything, then this is kind of like a date," she points out in a low, amused whisper.

I definitely don't need her thinking that. "Can't we do things my way without slapping a label on it?"

Margot opens her mouth.

"Jigsaw!" a high voice squeals, cutting off whatever Margot was about to say. Then another screech splits the air. Dozens of people turn to stare at us.

Two barely dressed dancers I recognize from Crystal Ball slide off the hood of a purple hot rod and clomp over the pavement in their heavy, platform boots.

What the motherfuck did I do to deserve this?

Johnsonville is far enough outside of Empire, I didn't expect to run into anyone I know here. It's a small, local car show that still advertises in the local *Pennysaver* for fuck's sake.

"Hi, Jiggy!" Stacia lunges like she's going to hug me, then must remember I'm not Ravage—who'll use any excuse to let the strippers rub themselves all over him. She stops short and rests her hand on her hip, striking an unnatural pose to show off her tiny purple string bikini and shiny, black platform boots.

Kyla, mousy girl that she is, maintains a respectful distance, her hands anxiously twisting in front of her red, orange, and yellow bikini top. "Please don't tell Dex we're moonlighting."

"I doubt Dex gives a fuck what you do in your off time." I glance at Kyla, then Stacia. "As long as you're not missing a shift to do *this*, he won't care."

"Oh, good!" Kyla leans up on her tiptoes like she wants to whisper in my ear, but I don't bother leaning down. "We're letting guys know they can come see us dance at CB too."

"Good." I shrug, not really giving a fuck. I cover shifts there once in a while to help out the MC when Dex is short on bouncers. But other than that, I don't have anything to do with running the place. Dex has infinitely more patience to deal with all the bullshit that comes with running a strip club than I do. He's a fuck of a lot nicer to the dancers than I'd be too.

Stacia's gaze keeps bouncing from Margot to me, as if she finally noticed I'm not alone. "Oh." She wrinkles her little button nose into a sneer. "Who are *you*?"

I wrap my arm around Margot. "None of your business."

Margot hasn't said a word, but she glances up and frowns. *Time to go.* I don't need these little twits interfering in my life or being rude to Margot.

I steer her away from the girls. "Have fun, ladies."

"See you at the club, Jiggy!" they shout, as loud and obnoxiously as possible.

"Friends?" Margot asks in a tight voice.

"No." Shit, is that embarrassment snaking over my chest? It's been so long, it's hard to identify the uncomfortable feeling. I don't owe Margot an explanation.

Or do I?

"I'm sure they'll just think I'm your sister or something," she mutters.

"I doubt that."

Margot starts walking faster, heading straight for her car. I'm on her like a sweater, using my arm around her shoulders to slow her steps.

"Margot, stop."

Girl's stronger than she looks, she keeps powerwalking as if I'm not hanging on her like a bag of concrete. "Can we go?"

At the car, I force her to face me. "Stop. They're just girls who work at the club the MC owns. That's it. I didn't want to give them your name because then they'd run back and gossip about us to everyone." I cock my head. "I assume you don't want it to get back to your dad about our arrangement?"

The pink on her cheeks deepens. "Oh. I guess not." She presses her hand to her mouth and giggles. "That might be awkward."

"Right."

"So that means you didn't tell anyone in your club?"

"No. I told you I wouldn't."

"Only because of the arrangement between your club and my dad,

though, right?" She lowers her gaze. "Not because you're embarrassed to be with me?"

I really need to find whoever gave this woman such a low opinion of herself and beat them senseless. "Not at all. I'm not in the habit of telling my brothers anything about who I spend time with."

Shit, that sounded a fuck of a lot worse than I meant.

But Margot doesn't seem too bothered. She nods. "I'm still ready to go, though."

"Are we allowed to?" I whisper, casting an overly dramatic wide-eyed glance at the barricades blocking off the end of the street. "I feel like a hostage," I joke to lighten things up.

She sighs. "Everyone usually rolls out together at the end, but we can leave whenever we want."

As if on cue, the blue Ford next to us rumbles to life. The old man throws a wave at Margot and slowly pulls out of his spot.

"Let's follow him," Margot suggests.

"All right."

We hustle into her car. I start the engine and slide the Thunderbird behind the truck, keeping some distance between us.

It seems to take forever to roll down the quarter mile of city street, but we finally pass the barricade. The truck turns right at the first intersection, and I finally stomp on the gas and speed away.

Margot

This was never a date.

What was that insane surge of jealousy that shot through me when those girls screamed out his name? He knows those women. Has probably seen them naked. I mean, *I* practically saw them naked, they were wearing so little. And I'm supposed to let him see *me* naked sometime tonight?

No way.

"You okay?" he asks.

"I'm fine." I'm being ridiculous. Everything I've read about motorcycle clubs focused on salacious details. Why am I surprised he's on a first-name basis with exotic dancers? "Was it more fun than you expected?"

"Yeah. The club goes to bike rallies and shows all the time. The participants here were just older and more tame, but otherwise it's kinda the same thing."

"Bike shows? That sounds like fun."

"It can be. They're crowded, though, sometimes."

"You don't like crowds?"

He waits a beat or two before answering, "Depends on the crowd."

I let out a light chuckle and smooth out the wrinkles in my skirt. "I can relate."

He glances over. "You seemed fine. People wanted to talk to you."

"I told you it's a small area."

"I guess so."

"Where'd you grow up? Union?"

His hands tighten on the steering wheel. "Oregon. Then Washington State. And eventually I ended up in New York."

"That's a big move," I say, intrigued by such a massive change. "What brought you to New York?"

He hesitates, a slight frown creasing his brow. "We patched into the Washington charter first. And after a few years, it was time to find a new home."

"*We*, as in you and Rooster?"

"Yeah." He casts a quick sideways glance my way. "And I wanted to get my sister as far away from our father's side of the family as possible."

A protective edge to his explanation touches me. "How old is she?"

"Twenty-two. Just got her to transfer to a college in New York so I can see her more often."

"That's nice. You're close?"

"Not really...it's—"

"I get it. Families are complicated." I hate that I've made him uncomfortable with all my questions.

"What about you?" His posture relaxes to the easygoing driver he'd been earlier. "You've never wanted to leave Pine Hollow?"

"Never had the chance." I stare straight ahead at the dark road, my gaze sweeping left and right, checking for deer. "The family business is here." My voice falters. That didn't stop my brothers from pursuing other careers. "Since my brothers decided not to help out, I feel... obligated, I guess?"

Jigsaw's voice lowers, almost to a whisper. "That's not a way to live, Margot."

"I like what I do." I cross my arms over my chest. "I think I help people."

"You do." He glances over at me, his gaze piercing through me. "I see how much care you take with everything you touch."

"Sometimes, I see my life in two paths." I draw in a shaky breath. Do I really want to reveal the gnawing doubt that eats at me? "I could go this way." I slowly extend my left arm, curving to the left. "And do anything I want. Move somewhere new. Start over someplace where no one knows me as that weird girl who grew up in a funeral home."

Jigsaw's grip tightens on the steering wheel, his jaw clenched. "Who said that to you?"

"Uh, everyone throughout school."

"Kids are assholes."

"Please." I try to deflect with a shaky laugh. I glance sideways at him, taking in his strong profile and muscular arms. "You were probably captain of your football team and dated all the cheerleaders."

He snorts a laugh. "No, that was Rooster." The smile quickly fades. "I was the kid from the wacko religious commune who wore strange clothes and freaked people out by quoting fiery lines from the bible."

"Oh." That was probably the last thing I expected him to say about his background. "What religion?"

"One of those aggressive branches of 'Christianity' that breaks away and forms a smaller group of nutjobs who all follow the orders of the supreme nutjob leading them."

"Like a cult?"

"Yup." His voice is tight, like he isn't going to discuss this much longer.

I'm sorry doesn't seem right but I'm not sure what else to say. "But you…made it out?"

"I did."

"And saved your sister from it?"

He glances over again. "Yeah, I did."

My house comes into view. Large, yellow, and imposing on the quiet street. Jigsaw pulls into the parking lot and heads for the garage bays.

He turns the car off and hands me the keys.

Disappointment and nerves swirl through me. I wanted to keep talking. To find out more about him. But I think the conversation part of the evening is over.

What if I'm not ready for what comes next?

CHAPTER FOURTEEN

Jigsaw

FOR THE SECOND TIME THIS WEEK, I FIND MYSELF IN THE HALLWAY OF the funeral home. Tonight, Margot doesn't lead me into the kitchen. She turns toward the stairs, resting her hand on the thick, dark, hardwood banister.

"Do you want to come up and see my place?" she asks over her shoulder.

That's why I'm here. "Sure."

A thrill of anticipation builds as I follow her up three long flights of stairs. I'm always excited to sleep with a woman but something about *this* feels different. That Margot trusts me to teach her everything she wants to know elevates this into something more than a simple hookup. The pressure to get things right, to give her the best experience, has me tied in knots that I'm looking forward to unraveling with her.

We finally reach the top. It's a small landing. Barely big enough for the two of us to stand on comfortably. The door reminds me of something you'd find on the outside of a house and it's purple. Margot presses her finger to a pad over the latch and the door clicks open.

The "apartment" isn't what I expected at all. No faded yellow wallpaper or gold carpet up here. No black walls, coffin, or goth decorations, either. It's an open space. Dark hardwood floors gleam under bright, white light fixtures. A living area with built-in bookcases. The walls and bookcases are painted a deep spring green. A large, over-stuffed royal blue lounge chair, the size of a twin bed, is tucked into a corner by the bookcases. It has a low table in front of it and a small round table next to it. Books are scattered over the tops of both. No sign of a television. Nothing to indicate she has guests on a regular basis, or ever.

The green ends in the kitchen, where everything is stark white and stainless steel. Two high-backed chairs are tucked under a counter that extends from the kitchen. A basket of red apples, bananas, and oranges sits in the center.

"This is nice." When she said she lived on the third floor of the funeral home, part of me worried she was trapped up here like Cinderella in the attic with the mice.

"Not what you expected?" she asks.

"No."

"After I graduated, passed my exams, and received my license, my father gave me the money to remodel the top floor," she explains. "It was a bunch of old, dark, twisty rooms before that."

"Nice graduation present." Kinda feels like she built her own— really nice—prison. She lives at her job, *with dead people downstairs!*— but I keep those thoughts to myself.

Two doors are on my left and Margot slides them open, revealing a long, narrow coat closet. She shrugs off her sweater and hangs it on a hook inside.

Past the closet, and farther left, there's a closed door that I assume is her bedroom. But the hallway continues, leading to two other closed doors.

She holds out her hand.

I stare at her.

She drops her hand. "You can hang that up in there if you want?" Her voice falters and she glances away.

I like Margot but I don't know her well enough to allow her to handle my cut. "Thanks." I slide it off, and hang it in the closet.

"Do you want something to drink?" She kicks off her shoes off and nudges them into a straight line next to several other pairs of sneakers and boots.

"Sure."

She glides soundlessly into the kitchen. Almost like a little kid skating across the polished floors. Cute.

I lean down and unlace my boots, toe them off and line them on the other side of the closet doors.

Something in the refrigerator clinks as she opens the double doors and stares inside. "I don't have beer or alcohol."

Without my boots, I slide silently into the kitchen until I'm right behind her. "That's okay."

She jumps and turns. "You're quick." Her interested gaze runs over me. "And quiet."

"For now."

She blushes and turns toward the fridge again.

"The Saratoga water's fine." I nod at one of the blue glass bottles lined up in the door.

She turns and stares at me with wide, shocked eyes, like my request doesn't compute. "Bikers drink mineral water?"

I snort. "I can't speak for all bikers. But *this* biker does whatever the fuck he wants." I reach past her and pluck one of the bottles free.

"Sorry, I didn't mean…" She grabs a bottle of lime juice and another mineral water.

"Yeah, you did. It's fine. You think we're all beer-swilling cavemen, I get it."

Her cheeks turn even redder. I should dial it back. Margot doesn't seem to recognize when I'm teasing her.

She'll learn.

I set the bottle on the counter and walk over to the sink. Pink hand soap that smells like flowers flows out of the dispenser. Better than nothing. I wash my hands quickly and grab a paper towel to dry them.

Margot watches intently, and pulls out a large, sliding drawer to reveal a garbage can.

"Grimy from touching all the cars." I tap my fingers together in front of her face.

She laughs softly.

I ease into one of the chairs at the kitchen counter and uncap my water. Margot stands across from me, keeping the counter between us.

"Does your father come up here often?" I ask.

"Almost never." She leans sideways and gestures toward the door where there's a small box in the wall. "He buzzes if he needs me." A slight smile curves her lips. "I'm finally getting him to text instead, though. It's been a slow process."

Yeah, I'll bet Cedarwood doesn't like change.

I won't ask how often she has guests overnight. Or if he gives her a hard time about it. Does she ever spend a night *out*?

The seating options are limited. I'd like her closer, but I want to go at her pace. I turn, in case there's a couch I missed somewhere. But no, it's just the jumbo-sized blue lounge chair. It's roomy enough for two people if you don't mind snuggling. Looks like a better spot to get comfortable with each other instead of heading straight for her bedroom.

"You don't have people over often?"

"A select few." Her already anxious smile wobbles slightly. "Not a lot of people want to hang out at a funeral home." She rolls her eyes. "And the ones who are *too* eager to come over are usually walking red flags."

I snort and nod. That doesn't surprise me.

"You were the appropriate amount of interested and cautious," she adds.

"My interest is purely in *you*. Not the environment." In Margot's serene and modern apartment it's easy to forget there might be corpses downstairs.

"Do you mind if I change?" She tugs at the sides of her skirt.

But I've been aching to push that skirt up around your waist, bend you over something, and fuck you all night. "No, go ahead."

No coy invitation to follow her into the bedroom passes her lips. She doesn't even give me a second glance.

Maybe I need to recalibrate my expectations for tonight.

I take another sip of water and set it on the counter, then move over to the lounge chair to test it out. It's low to the ground and the arms are so wide, I basically have to crawl into it.

I'm situated with my back to the fluffy cushions when Margot returns. Part of me hoped she'd return in some sexy underwear but she's wearing loose gray pajama pants and a gray long-sleeved V-neck T-shirt with black flowers printed all over it. Simple, but still sexy as fuck on her.

"Oh, you moved." She stops and stares.

I pat the space next to my hip. "Come join me."

A shy smile curves her lips. She hesitates for a second, then hurries over and quickly climbs in.

"This is some chair." I turn on my side to face her. "It's big enough to be a bed."

"I *do* fall asleep reading here sometimes." She nods to the stack of books on the table next to me. "I work such odd hours that I want to unwind for a few minutes before bed but end up nodding off. It's comfy enough that I don't mind."

"Come closer," I urge.

She rolls onto her hip, so she's facing me.

"Closer." I grab her thigh and guide it over mine. "That's better." I slide my arm under her body, pulling her against me. "Much better."

"Oh." She rests her hand over my heart and stares at it for the longest time before finally lifting her gaze. "Can we kiss a little?" She raises two hopeful eyebrows.

That's more like it.

"We can kiss a lot," I answer.

A faint smile ghosts her lips. "I liked when you kissed me the other night."

"I'm surprised you *remember* me kissing you the other night."

Pink floods her cheeks and she shakes with nervous laughter. "I wasn't that bad."

"Nah, you were cute."

"Will you teach me how to be a good kisser?"

There's a subject I'm not sure I'm equipped to teach. An unfamiliar oily sensation slides through my chest. Shame? I don't spend a lot of time kissing, usually too eager to get straight to the fucking. And I don't want to admit that to Margot.

I trace my finger along her bottom lip. "I bet you're already a good kisser. Your lips were made for kissing."

She ducks her head, nuzzling against my chin like a shy kitten. I twist and kiss her cheek. Her lips press against my neck, not kissing or even sucking, more like she's checking my pulse.

Finally, she brushes her lips along my jaw. I cup the back of her head, turning her so our lips meet. A simple mouth to mouth touch. She hums a soft sound that seems encouraging. Jolts of satisfaction prickle my chest. I slide the tip of my tongue along the seam of her lips but no more.

I bet she thinks she's bad at kissing because some asshole slobbered all over her face. Who the fuck wants to deal with that? She's so hesitant, almost innocent, with the soft, long brushes of her lips against mine.

After a few teasing licks, she pushes closer, her body almost fully resting on mine. An encouraging groan works out of my throat. I slide my hand down and grip her ass, holding her against me. She buries her fingers in my hair, teasing her nails against my scalp. A deeper groan of satisfaction eases out of me. Nothing tickles my pleasure center like a woman's nails against my scalp.

Her lips part and I lightly stroke my tongue against hers. A quick taste and then I retreat.

"Mmm." She hums and presses her hands to my cheeks, trying to hold me still. "Tell me what to do."

I circle her wrist with my fingers and drag it back to my chest. "Put your hands on me."

She hums another happy sound and gently squeezes my pec, then my shoulder and down my arm. She pulls away, breaking our kiss and squeezes my biceps again. "God, your arms are amazing. Like granite."

Shaking with laughter I lean in and kiss her again. "Thank you."

She fiddles with the sleeve of my shirt. As bad as I want her hands on my skin, I'm not ready to take it off. I need her writhing and too desperate for my cock to ask any questions about all the scars on my back. And right now she's still in an exploratory, inquisitive mood.

She hitches her leg higher, her thigh accidentally grazing my hard dick desperately trying to make his presence known behind the fly of my jeans.

"Oh." Her eyes widen and she drops her gaze to my crotch, which does nothing but make my dick even more eager to show off.

"We've barely touched." Her voice holds a note of wonder— as if a hard dick is a novelty. "We were just kissing."

"Your sweet body's pressed against mine." I trace my fingers against her T-shirt, along the length of her spine, until I'm cupping her ass cheek through very thin pants. Not much else seems to be blocking our skin from touching. Maybe a thin pair of underwear or a thong? "You told me where you want the night to go. So, yeah, my dick's so hard it hurts."

"For me?"

I stretch my neck and pretend to search the room. "You see anyone else here?"

She laughs softly. "I feel like I tricked you into this."

Few women have ever worried about *my* feelings. I'm more like a carnival ride to most women I've encountered. Something wild and scary they enjoy for a few minutes. Then they have a fun story to share for the rest of their lives—all about how the mean, scarred biker who likes to play with knives gave them a few orgasms and sent them on their way.

"You didn't trick me into anything." How can she think I don't want to be here when I'm desperately trying to balance my need to go slow with her and my desire to fuck her to pieces?

I touch my lips to hers again. "I want to be here with you. We should talk about—"

"*Meeerow.*" Something bumps against my shin.

"What the fuck?" I yank my legs up, jostling Margot off of me. My gaze lands on a sleek black cat with bright, curious green eyes sitting on the edge of the chair.

"Meeerow." The little fucker jumps on *me*, and casually strolls up my body like I'm his personal balance beam. *"Mrrp."* It dips its head and butts my chin to rub its soft silky fur against my face.

"Um, hi there." I carefully lower my hand and pat the cat's head.

Margot stares at us with wide eyes. She knows this cat, right? He didn't just wander in off the streets or come in with its owner's body?

"Mwrrawr." The cat purrs like a motorboat and keeps rubbing my chin.

"Gretel, what are you doing?" Margot scoops the cat into her arms. "Sorry, I hope you don't mind cats. I didn't say anything because she never comes out of hiding when there's someone here."

Gretel's freakishly bright eyes are still focused on me. Her motorboat purr in full throttle, her little toes flexing and retracting like she's reaching for me.

"I like cats," I answer slowly. "Their *give no fucks* attitude speaks to my soul."

"That's Gretel," Margot laughs.

"I had farm cats when I was a kid. They weren't this friendly, though."

Margot sets Gretel down and the cat returns to rub herself all over my chest. I sit up and scratch behind her ears.

"She's never this friendly with people." The open-mouthed stare Margot's watching us with highlights this is a rare occasion. "Ever."

If my brothers were around, I'd make a crack like, "See, females of every species love me," but that seems like a weird thing to say to the woman I want to fuck about the cat who's currently *drooling* on my hand.

Gretel flops on the end of the chair and rolls to her back, kicking her paws in the air. I reach over to rub her belly and she playfully grabs my hand and swipes her scratchy tongue over my knuckles.

"Even her little toes are black," I say, playing with her paws.

Margot nods. "She was a shelter kitty, there on borrowed time. I saw her sweet face in a post someone shared and couldn't stop thinking about her." Her eyes water. "I always wanted a pet and Dad wouldn't let us because, you know, too much chance for it to get out and run downstairs during a service or something."

"But he let you have one now?"

"Well." Her lips stretch into a secret smile. "I didn't *ask*. Black cats have a hard time getting adopted and the shelter couldn't keep her much longer. So, I just brought her home."

"He doesn't even know she's *here*?"

"No, he knows." She scratches behind Gretel's ears and that cat *"mrrrps"* at her again. "She's leash trained, so I take her for walks around the property sometimes. He just..." Margot shrugs. "Made peace with it, I guess."

Margot's a little badass in her own way.

Like her welcoming switch has been flipped off, Gretel rolls to her feet, hops off the chair and strolls away. She turns a corner and disappears.

"She's not going to come back and watch us, is she?" I ask.

Margot lifts one shoulder. "She's never shown interest in anyone else before, so anything is possible." She turns toward me. "Where were we?"

I curl a finger, inviting her closer. "You were earning an A-plus in kissing."

"Ooo, an A, huh? I never got those before."

"A-*plus* and really? You strike me as very studious."

She settles into the chair again, lining herself flush to me, so we're touching almost everywhere, relaxed and easy. "No, I was more the 'Cs get degrees' kind of girl, until senior year. I need to *really* enjoy the subject matter to excel at it."

A deep rumble of laughter pours out of me. She blinks, then blushes. "Oh, I just realized what that sounded like." She presses her finger to my cheekbone, tracing to my chin. "It's true, though. I enjoy being in your presence."

Something in my chest *thunks*. What's this woman doing to me? My entire soul wants to leap into her hands for safekeeping.

"I've never felt like this before." She frowns, so adorably confused at...enjoying some light kissing?

This has been bugging me since the wedding and I have to ask before we go further.

I push her hair off her cheek and rest my finger under her chin, applying enough pressure so she'll look at me. "Who said you weren't good at sex?"

An edge creeps into my tone I didn't intend. I can't help it. Someone made her feel so bad about herself, she asked a biker she's got nothing in common with to teach her how to fuck, and now she seems shocked that I'm praising her kissing skills. Worse, she's surprised she likes kissing.

"It doesn't matter."

Who was it? Why did it bother her so damn much and where can I find him? Instead of a finger, I'll cut out his tongue. Then he'll never be able to hurt someone as sweet and vulnerable as Margot again.

"Yes, it matters. Tell me." I use my sternest tone.

She stares at me with pained eyes. "My ex."

"Well, I figured it was an ex. But he's an ex for a reason, right? Why do you care? People say all sorts of shitty things when they break up." Not that I'd ever broken up with anyone, but I've witnessed the horrible shit people are capable of when love twists into hate.

"I really don't want to talk about it," she says.

Fury shoots through my veins. Not at Margot. At whoever bruised her self-esteem. "Please?"

She shakes her head. "Not before we...Maybe after."

Whatever it is, she must think it's so awful, she doesn't want it in my head while I'm fucking her. She doesn't want me judging if her ex was right or not. Normally, the pushy asshole in me would keep badgering her until she told me everything I want to know.

But I just can't do that to Margot.

"Okay." I lean in and kiss her forehead. "I hope you trust me enough to tell me one day."

She bites her bottom lip. "I trust you or you wouldn't be here."

"Show me then." Usually, I'm not a fan of lots of physical contact.

Unless it's for a specific—and damn good—reason. But I'm dying for Margot's touch. Eager to have her curious hands all over me again. "Touch me like you were before."

"People don't usually like me touching them," she whispers, sliding her hand over my shoulder and down my arm. "They think of what I do…"

I curl my hand around hers and bring it to my lips, kissing each of her fingertips. "I'm not afraid of anything, Margot."

Liar. I'm terrified of falling in love with this woman.

CHAPTER FIFTEEN

Margot

JIGSAW MIGHT NOT BE AFRAID OF ANYTHING, BUT I AM. I REALLY LIKE him. His kisses. His voice. His body. The gentle way he petted Gretel, even though she'd rudely interrupted us.

But telling him my ex had compared me to a *corpse*—cold, immobile, and boring—in bed was something I can't bring myself to share with him. What if we're in the middle of an intimate moment and he's thinking, "Damn, that guy was right, she sucks at this?" He wouldn't be able to hide his disgust, and I'd die of shame.

Thankfully, he dropped it for now. To further move him away from that topic, I return to our kissing lesson. "Maybe you can give me a report card to let me know how I'm performing," I suggest, like it's the best idea ever and totally normal.

He stares at me with the strangest expression. "You want me to *grade* you? At sex?"

"Well, guide me, maybe? 'Improvement needed,' 'satisfactory,' that kind of thing."

"Margot, you don't have to keep reminding me I'm only here for one purpose. I got it."

Oh my God. Is that what he thinks? Why does he seem so *hurt*?

"That's not what I meant." I drop my gaze. "I'm sorry."

He grips my chin, forcing me to look at him. "It's fine."

The relentless pounding of my heart won't stop. We've barely started and I'm already messing this up.

"Tell me what to do?" I ask.

He settles back against the cushions again. "Come here." He pats his thigh.

Eager, but a little on edge now, I scoot closer to him. "How do you want me?"

A flash of animalistic desire lights up his eyes. "Every single way I can have you."

Ohhh. That might be more than I can handle. My entire body flushes and tingles with wild desire for the unknown.

"But for now, turn around and put your back against me."

That doesn't seem like we'll get a lot of kissing done but I'm eager to try anything with him.

He guides me with his hands on my hips and even arranges my body where he wants it over his lap. My butt resting on his thigh, his arm around my waist, and if I tip my head back, I can kiss along his jaw. He grips my chin, angling my head. A long, contented breath flows out of me. He seals his mouth over mine, and gently slides his tongue inside. I moan into the kiss as jolts of electricity shoot straight between my legs. The hand at my waist slips under my shirt, tickling my stomach. His thumb grazes the edge of my bra. Higher and he cups my breast, lazily circling my nipple with one finger.

The desperate pulsing between my legs increases and I whimper from needing something I can't name. He breaks our kiss and stares down at me with approval in his eyes.

"That feels so good," I whisper.

"What?"

"Everything you're doing. The way you're holding me."

He releases a groaning sound of approval and nuzzles against my neck, sucking at a sensitive spot I didn't know I have. "I like the way you fit against my body." His hand squeezes my hip.

"You make me feel secure." Both body and mind.

"Good." He tugs the cup of my bra down and my body jerks when his fingers brush against my hardened nipple. Underneath me, his body shakes with restraint.

His other hand moves lower, sliding under the waistband of my sweatpants. My breath catches in my lungs as he slides his fingers over my sheer panties.

I gasp and jerk my hips up.

"Like that?" he whispers against my ear.

I exhale a shaky breath and nod.

"Say it." He strokes over the damp material right along the seam of my lips and groans. "Your panties are soaking wet."

"Sorry."

His movements stop. "What do you mean *sorry?*"

I try to shrug but he has me held so tight, my shoulders have nowhere to go.

He kisses my cheek. "It's a good thing." His voice drops to a low, sensual rasp as his fingers slide over my lips and up to my clit. "Your body likes what we're doing."

It's almost a question.

"I do. A lot," I whisper. Especially the way he says, "What *we're* doing" instead of "What I'm doing to you." Somehow that makes a big difference.

"Good." Another kiss on my cheek. I could drown in his kisses alone.

"Tell me what you like better." He rubs up and down over my clit, circles it, then settles two fingers on either side.

I take a gulp of air and wiggle my hips, spreading my legs wider.

"You like that?" he asks.

"Yes, please do it again."

"With pleasure." He takes his time sliding and rubbing, never pressing for more or even trying to move my underwear out of his way.

My breath stutters. "That feels really, really good," I whimper.

I'm so close to *something*. My body straining but not quite reaching what it needs. A whine of frustration slips out of me.

"There's no hurry. I've got you." He presses more kisses to my neck and cheek. "Relax and close your eyes. Just let your body feel. Stop thinking so much."

I never stop thinking.

But for him, I want to try.

Why can't I stop wondering how I measure up to every other woman he's ever held?

"You're so pretty stretched out like this for me," he whispers in my ear. His strokes increase in pressure. "I could touch you here all night. Just like this."

I rest my head against his shoulder. Endless moans and high whimpers scrape against my throat.

"Love those sexy little sounds you're making."

The whole point of this was to teach *me* how to please a man. How can he be so focused on my pleasure?

My hips buck against his hand. I try to hold still but he breathes out, "Fuck yes" like he's in awe of my body's every movement. "Do that again. Again. Keep going."

"Oh!" Little stars burst behind my eyelids and a loud buzzing in my ears drowns out everything. After a few heartbeats, I blink my eyes open and find him staring at me. I curl my hand against his cheek, pulling him closer. Our lips meet. "Thank you," I whisper. "That was really nice."

"Nice?" He lifts two teasing eyebrows.

Did I just insult him again?

He dips his finger under my panties. I hiss as he touches me with nothing between us, except all my hair down there.

"I didn't...Guys usually prefer no hair, right? I wasn't sure...it's usually a little tidier." My entire body floods with heat. Why did I let time get away from me today and forget to shave?

"Stop." He spreads his hand, cupping me, and lets out a long, satisfied groan that vibrates against my ear. "You feel perfect." He inhales a sharp breath. "I love that you're so fucking wet," he hisses as he glides one finger between my lips, heading lower.

Fear grabs me and jerks my body to a stop.

His fingers stop exploring but stay where they are. "Why are you tensing up?" he asks, his breath warm against my cheek. "Hmm? Tell me."

"I don't really like *that.*"

"Don't like *what*? Be specific."

The hand under my panties remains still. Like a car with the emergency brake pulled up, not going anywhere. But the hand anchoring me to his body shifts under my shirt and cups one breast, lightly teasing my nipple.

"What don't you like?" he asks again.

God, this is mortifying. Why couldn't I keep my mouth shut.

I *did* ask him to help me, though. "I don't like, you know, fingers rammed inside me." I jab my finger in the air like I'm stabbing at an elevator button.

His body jerks, like maybe he's trying to swallow laughter. "Did someone do that to you?" he asks in a tight voice.

He's not laughing. He's angry.

I pull a shoulder forward in a half shrug.

He rests his forehead against my temple. "Were you wet like this?" He slides his fingers against me, then trails them along my inner thigh.

No, never. "I don't think so."

"I won't put anything inside you unless you ask me to," he promises with an aching sincerity that I actually believe.

A little overwhelmed, I turn my head and kiss him. That teasing tongue of his sweeps against mine at the same time his fingers begin rubbing directly against my skin, no material between us this time.

Breathing hard, I pull away. "When will you teach me how to make *you* feel good?"

His lips, reddened from all our kissing, curve. "I'm having fun with you right now." His eyebrows draw down into a teasing imitation of a sad face. "You don't want to deny me my fun, do you?"

I open my mouth to answer but his finger slides directly against my clit. My entire body jerks. Gibberish comes out of my mouth instead of words.

If he wasn't doing such wickedly wonderful things to my body, I'd say the laugh he lets out is pure evil.

He continues the sensual dance of his fingers.

My skin's on fire. Heat and pressure consume me. Another wave builds and bliss quickly crashes over me. My hips roll and I inch my legs farther apart.

He glides his fingers between my lips again, resting the heel of his palm against me. This time, I want him inside me, but I can't form the words. I slide my hand down, under my sweatpants, resting it over his.

He growls against my throat. "What do you want?"

"Make me come again, please?"

"How?"

"With your fingers." I press down on his knuckles.

We share a breath as he slowly pushes a finger inside me. I tilt my head back and our eyes lock. My breath catches as he slides deeper, then withdraws. The heel of his palm grinds against my clit as he continues the steady in and out rhythm. He slowly works in a second finger, the gentle stretching sensation unlike anything I've tried before.

I dig my feet into the chair cushion and lift my hips, pushing into the penetration.

"Yes," he murmurs. "Good girl. Fuck my fingers. Show me what you like."

I shudder with pleasure from the filthy words and the intensity in his voice.

He continues with deep, slow thrusts. The needy ache expands. My breath catches and I curl my body forward as he hits the perfect spot.

"Right there. That's so good," I chant. Sounds I've never made before tear out of my throat.

If tonight is only lesson one, I don't know how I'm going to survive the rest.

CHAPTER SIXTEEN

Jigsaw

PRIDE AND FURY HAVE TAKEN UP RESIDENCE IN MY CHEST.

Pride—that I've set Margot off three times now—without even getting her naked.

Fury—that some asshole in the past hurt her. Was it the same piece of shit who told her she was bad in bed? Did he degrade her to cover up for how little he understood about female anatomy?

Breathing hard and with a dazed smile on her face, Margot whispers, "Thank you."

"You're very welcome." Reluctantly, I pull my hand out of her underwear.

"You can call me little lady death, now." She flashes a goofy smile. "I feel like I've died and gone to heaven thanks to you."

Shaking with laughter, I cup her cheek and kiss her. "There's a saying about orgasms being a little death."

"La petite mort," she whispers. "I thought it was just a literary euphemism until now."

Those sweet, softly spoken compliments she keeps handing me will be my undoing.

Slowly she sits up, taking her weight off me for a few seconds while she rearranges herself. Then she straddles my lap and rests her hands on my shoulders. "Now, teach me how to do that for *you*."

I widen my eyes but can't stop laughing. "You want to kill me?"

"Only in the good way." She purses her lips. "Please?"

Fuck, I want to teach her so many things. I could stay up all night long demonstrating my favorite positions, and it still wouldn't be enough.

"Show me." I slide down in the chair, jostling her in my lap.

Confusion furrows her brow. "How?"

I glance down at the bulge in my jeans. "Show me that you want to please me." I keep my voice low but firm.

She swallows hard, like this is becoming too real for her. Her lips part as if she's going to ask another question but then she attacks my belt buckle.

A little grunt of frustration pushes past her lips. "Help me."

Chuckling, I undo the belt and the fly of my jeans, then tuck my hands behind my head.

"Much better." Her eyes sparkle with excitement—she really does want to learn and I'm more than happy to teach. Without hesitating, she tugs my briefs down, freeing my erection.

She blinks and stares. "Wow."

One corner of my mouth curls. "That's always nice to hear."

An anxious expression ripples over her face. Tentatively, she wraps one hand around me. Christ, her soft, warm little fingers feel so good. I hiss a harsh breath of pleasure. She flicks her gaze to my face, worry in her eyes.

"You feel good on me," I whisper. "Keep touching. Use both hands."

"I *need* both hands," she mutters, gripping me firmly.

I'm caught between laughing and groaning with pleasure. Fuck, she's fun.

The tip of her tongue traces her top lip as she concentrates on exploring my length. I circle my fingers around one wrist and pry her off me. "Wet your hand."

She catches my eye and slowly licks from her palm to her fingertips, then resumes her soft exploration.

"Fuuuck." I grab her other hand and bring it to her waistband. "Touch yourself. Get your hand wet for me."

Her eyes widen at first, but she quickly dips her fingers under her sweatpants. Her breath catches as she touches herself.

"Like this?" She pulls her hand out, showing me her glistening fingers.

"Just like that."

She wraps her hand around me again. Thank fuck I'm sitting in the chair. My legs twitch and my eyes roll back as she wraps both wet fists around me.

"Keep going," I encourage.

She glides her hands down to the base, tightening her grip, then back to the crown.

"That's good."

My hips jerk as she runs her thumb through the pre-cum gathering at the tip, swirling it in a tight circle. I suck in a shaky breath.

"Is that okay?" she asks.

"Yes," I breathe out. "Sensitive there."

A bit of her tentativeness fades. She slides her hands over me again and again, growing more confident with each stroke.

Lesson. I'm supposed to be teaching her...*something.* Feels too fucking good. Hanging onto my control by a thread, I inhale and exhale a few rapid breaths while trying to rub my brain cells together.

"Every man will be different," I say, hating the thought of her ever touching anyone else. "Experiment. See what he likes. Don't be afraid to ask."

Worry creases her brow. "What do *you* like?"

Everything and anything as long as you're the one doing it to me.

"You can use more pressure." My mind blanks as she immediately squeezes harder, adding a twist of her wrist at the base. "Fuuuck, that's really good." I flex into her hands.

Her teeth sink into her lower lip, and she mimics the same movement over and over.

"That's good, baby. You're doing so good." My words come out choppy, but a smile spreads across her face.

My skin prickles as she pumps harder. Christ, I want my cock pushing between her lips and her wet little tongue teasing the tip. Her tight little cunt wrapped around me is going to feel amazing. I'm dizzy with thoughts of all the lessons I plan to teach her.

Or maybe it's all the blood rushing to my groin. "I'm close," I warn her.

I expect her to stop, maybe run into the kitchen to grab a towel so I can finish myself off, but she only releases me long enough to whip her shirt over her head and drape it over the cushion.

She wants me to nut in her shirt? "Uh—"

"I don't care," she whispers breathlessly, wrapping her hands around me again. "I want to make you come. Please?"

Not going to argue with that.

She licks her hand again, then resumes pumping like she never stopped. My eyes squeeze shut as she returns to the perfect pressure and pace. Stroking in rhythm to my heartbeat. How the fuck could anyone tell her she's bad at this?

My toes curl. Tingles race along my spine.

"Coming," I warn.

"Yes," she whispers.

"Fuuuck." My legs go numb as I release. I reach down and grab the shirt, spilling into it. She slows her pumping and loosens her grip but keeps her hands on me.

"Good girl," I breathe out.

I groan through the orgasm, my whole body shaking.

Then it's too much. My body jerks as she grazes the tip of my cock. I let out a wild shout of laughter that pushes me out of her grasp.

"Sensitive after," I say to stop the worry spreading across her face. "That was...so good." I actually don't remember the last time a simple hand job felt so fucking amazing.

Is it the way she's so fucking eager to please me? Or did I just let go and enjoy it because there's no greedy rush to the next event? It's obvious we're not going any farther tonight.

My tongue almost falls out of my mouth when I lower my gaze to her chest.

All she was wearing under that shirt was a completely sheer, pale pink bra that barely contains her ample breasts. Stiff, rosy nipples stab against the flimsy material, threatening to slice right through.

My mouth waters, eager to suck on the pink buds. She notices my stare and quickly jumps up, grabbing the cum-soaked shirt and hurrying out of the room.

Jesus Christ, at this rate, I'll have a PhD in patience when our lessons are finished.

The rush of running water comes from somewhere deeper in the apartment, then the bang of metal on metal. I tuck myself away and drag my body out of the chair. No sign of Margot yet. I walk over to the counter and finish my bottle of water.

"Did I do okay?" Margot returns wearing a rainbow-striped T-shirt.

I can't stop picturing what's underneath.

My brain processes her question. "Gold star. A-plus."

Her whole face lights up and she presses her palms together. She glides over the hardwood floor almost like a ballerina. When she's close enough, I pull her against me, wrapping my arms around her waist and settling my hands over the generous curve of her ass.

"You are really fucking good at that." I lean down and kiss her forehead. "Except for the part where you ran away at the end."

Her face falls.

Shit, I can't stand her making her unhappy for even a second.

Tentatively, she lifts her head, meeting my eyes. "I thought I should clean up. What should I have done instead?"

"Kiss me." I lean down and seal my mouth over hers. She squeaks in surprise then moans and drapes her arms around my neck.

After a minute, she pulls back. "Will you teach me to do that for you with my mouth, next?"

I groan with anticipation. "Fuck yes."

A shy frown creases her face. "I don't know if I can swallow, though."

"Jesus Christ," I groan. "Are you trying to get me hard again?"

"Is that possible?" She pulls back even farther to stare at my crotch.

"With you, yes." I place a finger under her chin, tipping her head up. "Eyes up here."

"So, I did okay? Nothing you think I should improve?" she asks.

Only because tonight's made me realize how sensitive she is, do I put a muzzle on my inner sarcastic asshole and answer in an even tone. "Why, do you want to take notes?"

"Should I?"

Emptiness spreads through my chest. She's only asking because she wants to wrap those perfect little hands around someone else's dick in the future.

Who cares? I fuck women all the time who plan to fuck another member of my club as soon as they're finished with me. Plenty of them badger me for a performance evaluation as they're walking out the door, too. Why does it bug me so much coming from Margot? Especially when that was the entire point of tonight?

She steps back and twists her fingers together. "Can we talk about a few parameters for our lessons?"

Yes, by all means, let's drive home the point that this is temporary. "Such as?"

"Um, I know this probably isn't fair and I do understand that men have needs, but could you not...you know...*sleep* with anyone else while our class is in session?"

Should I be offended, amused, flattered, or irritated by her request? "That depends."

"On what?"

I land on irritated, because I've been fucking my hand while thinking about Margot for weeks now. Not that I'd ever admit it to anyone. "How often are we having lessons?"

"Uh, as often as you think I need them? My schedule can be kind of hectic, then other times it's *dead*." A sly smile creeps across her lips.

I chuckle at the pun. "Funny girl."

"I'll defer to *your* schedule."

"It changes from week to week. Really, I go where the club tells me

I'm needed. Next week's probably the laundromat down in Union. This weekend's Crystal Ball to help out Dex."

She frowns slightly at Crystal Ball.

Is she fucking serious? "What, you don't want me to *see* other naked women during our arrangement either?"

"I didn't say that."

"I don't fuck the club's employees if it makes you feel better," I say with every bit of sarcasm in me this time.

"Okay." She stares at me, waiting for an answer to her original question.

No more fucking muffler bunnies at the clubhouse. No more blow jobs in the back room of the laundromat. No more...*fuck it*. None of that appeals to me right now anyway. Not when I want to teach the woman standing in front of me how to fuck like the queen she is. "Yeah, okay."

"Yeah, okay, what?" she presses.

Oh, you're gonna make me say it, huh? "I won't sleep with anyone else while we're," I wag one finger between the two of us, "doing whatever we're doing here."

"Thank you."

"Can I ask you something, though?"

"Sure."

"Is it a health thing or a jealousy thing." I'm such a dick for asking but I'm really curious about her answer.

Her eyes widen like a deer in the headlights, and she twists her fingers together. "Will you be mad if I say a little of both?"

"Why would that make me mad?"

"Well, you said you don't do relationships. Admitting it might make me jealous if you're..." She swallows hard like she can't even say the words. "That might tread into relationship-y territory." She slowly lifts her shoulders in an apologetic shrug.

Honesty. Margot couldn't lie if I pointed a gun at her. I like that in people. Brave too. She knew there was a chance I'd say fuck no to the whole arrangement, but she asked anyway. "I'm not mad."

She flicks her gaze to the kitchen behind me, like all this eye contact and honesty is too much to handle. "Do you want anything to drink?"

"No, I better get going."

She stares at me.

I'm not staying over unless she asks.

And she doesn't ask.

CHAPTER SEVENTEEN

Jigsaw

As I step into the downstate clubhouse the next day, a sense of wrongness washes over me. This doesn't feel like the club's home anymore. Not since we were raided and had the place turned upside down.

Sure, months have gone by. We've put all the furnishings back together, replaced couches, patched holes in walls, but the security I used to feel here hasn't returned.

Since the raid, I haven't bothered keeping more than a change of clothes, a box of condoms, and a toothbrush in my room. Anything personal resides at my cozy apartment at Rooster and Shelby's place.

Still have to check in with Z and Grinder to see what needs to be done. Z always says I can stop by his house but the uppity suburban neighborhood full of hideously oversized McMansions makes my skin crawl.

Z's office is the second door on my left. I stop there first and tap my knuckles against the wood.

"Come in."

"What's up, Prez."

"Look who it is." He stands and rounds the desk to pull me in for a slap on the back.

"You act like I've been gone for a month."

"Where *have* you been hiding?"

"Nowhere." I've been in plain sight. Except for that detour to Margot's place.

"You covering the laundromat this week?"

I hook my thumbs in my pockets. "If Suds is still on the road, I kinda have to, don't I?"

"No, not if you've got something else going on," Z answers.

Our last president didn't give a fuck what we might be doing in our personal lives. Z's a lot more respectful about giving us a choice. I need to show him the same respect. "I don't mind. I can bring my laptop and get my shit done for Rooster while I'm there."

He snorts. "You better make sure some little tweaker doesn't steal your laptop."

"No shit." The last one who tried learned the hard way not to fuck with the Lost Kings.

"If you don't mind, Eazy's planning to stick around for a while. Would you show him the ropes there? That way, I can start freeing you up for other things."

Hell yeah. Please let those assignments be closer to Pine Hollow. "Like what?"

"Rock and I would like you working with Dex on the support club."

Fuck yes. This keeps getting better. Johnsonville's *much* closer to Margot's place.

"And Teller's going to be wrist-deep in diapers when the twins get here." A quick frown settles over Z's expression, then disappears. "So if you can help out at the funeral home as needed, that would be a relief."

I'm helping out there more than you know, Prez.

"None of the financial stuff," Z hurries to add.

I snort a laugh. "Yeah, no shit, Teller's not letting anyone look at his books."

"Right." Z chuckles, then turns serious. "But stay away from the daughter."

My jaw tightens. *Too late.*

Z scowls at the hard look on my face. "I'm serious. That place is gonna be a gold mine for the club. Don't fuck it up for us."

Openly lying to my president isn't my style—so I say nothing. Instead, I cross my arms over my chest and nod once to acknowledge the message was received—even if it's too late to follow the order.

My non-answer seems to satisfy Z for now. "I know you've been picking up a lot of shifts at Crystal Ball to help out Dex," he continues. "Upstate appreciates that a lot. You're doing more than your fair share for the club. I told Hustler to bump up your pay."

"Appreciate that, but it's not necessary."

"We got you running all over New York, brother."

"Prez," I say in a *let's not fool ourselves* tone, "I'm basically riding to one place, sitting on my ass, then riding elsewhere, playing with cars at the track, riding some more to watch ladies dance naked and if I get lucky, punch a few guys who don't understand the *no touching* policy. None of that's a hardship, I swear." Still leaves me plenty of time to do whatever the fuck I want, and that's all I care about. *Freedom.*

"Don't downplay your role. You do more than that." He closes his eyes for a second. "Just you and Rooster taking over the porn business and making sure I don't have to deal with Stella has been a *huge* relief."

Yeah, I bet it is.

"Again, I'm not as *hands on* with Stella as you were." I smirk at him and he rolls his eyes. "I'm doing the work from my computer. So it's not hard." Was it a dick move to remind him of his involvement with a club asset? Yup. Do I care? Nope.

"It's bringing the most money into the club right now, so it matters." His lips curl into a sarcastic smirk. "Isn't that supposed to be the goal—work smarter, not harder?"

"That's what I've heard."

"All right, so walk Eazy through the laundromat stuff for me. Let me know if you have any issues with him."

"Like what?"

He shrugs. "Whatever."

Great. Is Eazy going to act like a little cuntwaffle who's too good to scrape lint traps and mop the floors? I haven't seen much of him over the last two years, maybe he came home with an attitude.

"Anything else?" I ask.

"Nope. Grinder's home with Serena. I think Lincoln's gonna be here any day now."

Zero interest in that, thank you very much. "Uh, that's good." I jerk my thumb over my shoulder. "I'm just gonna stop by my room, then head home. I'm beat."

"Later." He waves his hand at me.

There's no point stopping by my room. I really just want to go home. Crashing at the new clubhouse upstate had been noisy as fuck last night. Barely got any sleep.

I take the back roads from our downstate clubhouse to Rooster and Shelby's place. The ride takes almost an hour. Tomorrow, I'll be back in Union. With all the zigzagging around I'm doing lately, I might as well join the Nomad squad.

But it's good that I saw Z. Now I've got a plan for the week. Handing off my hours at the laundromat to Eazy will be a relief and free me up for more important pursuits—like "educating" Margot on every sexual skill my deviant mind can fathom.

I can't wait to get my hands on her again. That quick glimpse of her sweet pink nipples drove me insane. Lesson number two needs to be clothes *off* for her.

I turn onto the little dirt road that leads to Rooster's place, then the driveway, and roll right into my spot near the garage.

Rooster and Shelby are outside, switching out the lights on the thirty-foot skeleton I erected in their front yard. I knew it'd grow on them.

I walk around the side of the house to join them, but Rooster meets me halfway with Shelby not far behind.

"Are you okay?" Rooster stops and stares at me like I've lost my mind.

"Yeah, why?"

He studies my face so intently, the urge to punch him curls my fingers. "You've been smiling non-stop since you got off your bike."

I flatten my lips into a line. "So what?"

Rooster strokes his beard and stares at me like he's a hawk fixating on a field mouse. "It's unnatural."

"Stop it." Shelby slaps Rooster's chest and grins at me. "You're even more handsome when ya smile. That's what Rooster was tryin' to say."

Rooster shakes his head but his mouth quivers like the fucker's trying not to laugh. "It really wasn't."

"Where ya been?" Shelby asks me. "I was gettin' worried."

I touch my fingers to my throat and cock my head. "Aww, you were worried about me, songbird? I'm touched."

"Yes." She crosses her arms over her chest. "I was fixing to call Heidi to see if you were upstate."

"I knew you couldn't live without your daily dose of my charm and wit." I ruffle my hand over the top of her head, and she rolls her eyes. You'd think I'd be annoyed with my best friend's girlfriend grilling me on my whereabouts, but her concern wraps around my cold, black heart and squeezes in a sprinkle of warmth.

Rooster cups his hand over his ear. "Daily dose of bullshit? Yeah, sounds about right."

"I stayed upstate last night. Just came from our clubhouse. Had a sit-down with Z." I aim a dickish grin at Rooster. "He patted my head and told me how pretty I am."

Rooster rubs his hand over his throat, up to his chin. "Wish I'd never told him how much you've been helping me out," he mutters. "I knew it'd go straight to your head."

I've been enough of a dick, now it's time to be serious. "He's plannin' to give me a raise, so if you want to charge me more rent—"

"Get the fuck outta here with that." Rooster scoffs. "I'm only taking your money now because you're a pain in the ass about it."

"That's all *you*, boys." Shelby raises her hands in the air and slowly backs away. "Jigsaw, I'm happy you're home."

"Thank you." I point at Shelby and cock my head Rooster's way. "See, that's how you greet someone."

Once she's in the house, Rooster crosses his arms over his chest and lifts his chin. "So, where were you?"

I mirror his pose. "None of your business."

He strokes a hand over his beard. "Uh-huh. Why were you at a car show out in Johnsonville?"

Christ, how'd he figure it out? A picture of Rooster sitting at his laptop searching Google Maps to match up the background in the photo I sent him forms in my head.

"I googled the diner in the background, dipshit," he confirms.

I tug on the collar of my shirt. "This feels kinda stalkerish, brother."

He continues staring at me but doesn't apologize or explain himself. "You thinkin' about getting another cage?"

I glance over my shoulder at my old, beat-up Toyota 4-Runner that I only drive when the weather forces me to. Margot doesn't ride. If I ever want to pick her up, I should probably get something a little nicer to take her out in...

Take her out? What the fuck? Where did that come from?

We're not dating.

Rooster waves his big hand in front of my face. I shake myself out of whatever fevered daydream took over my brain there for a second.

"Yeah, maybe," I finally answer. "But I saw that truck and it made me think of Uncle Boone, that's why I sent it to you, not so you could grill me on my whereabouts."

His harsh expression fades. "Yeah, that was way too pretty for Uncle Boone, though."

"That's what I said too." I cough and look away.

The back door squeaks open. "Jiggy, you want steak fajitas?" Shelby calls out. "Rooster said he'd fire up the grill tonight."

My mouth waters. Whatever mystery southern spices she uses on the meat always tickles my taste buds. "Hell, yes, I do."

"Got it!" She raises one hand in the air in a half wave and disappears inside the house again.

"Hey, instead of grilling *me*, how about you get that grill going, brother?" I jerk my head toward the far end of the patio where Rooster has a Weber three-burner grill stationed. "I'm ready for some steak."

THE NEXT DAY, I'm at the laundromat, watching Eazy pull apart and clean the lint traps and vents. So far, I've had him mop liquid detergent a screaming kid spilled all over the floor, and wipe the tables, chairs, and doorknobs with disinfectant—twice. He hasn't complained about the manual labor, and he's done a thorough job. Could be he has a good work ethic or that he knows Z's gonna ask me for a report later.

My phone buzzes. Expecting it to be Rooster or Dex, I pull it out of my pocket.

Little Lady Death.

Much better than the *Last Responder* name I'd originally listed her under.

A picture appears. A close up of Margot from her mouth down to her chest. My cock pulses like he wants to immediately hunt her down and impale her. I recognize her because I've spent so much time studying those pouty lips that I'm dying to shove my cock between. *Next lesson.*

My gaze drifts lower. A hint of the swell of her breast peeks through the V-neck. I didn't look at her gorgeous tits nearly long enough the other night. Maybe I should break oral into two lessons. First, I'll teach her the joy of having her tits covered in cum. Then, a lesson on how to swallow every drop.

I may have missed my calling as a professor.

I can't stop staring at the photo. It's not racy compared to the pictures most women send me. But I can't stop staring at it. Is she wearing the gray shirt she finished me off with the other day?

Me: That cleaned up nice.

Little Lady Death: I'm going to think of you every time I wear it.

Fuuuck, that's fucking hot.

Good to know maybe this relationship—no, arrangement—will last as long as the life of a shirt.

Me: You're hot as fuck. No, that sounds fucking juvenile. I erase it.

Me: Your lips will look so good around my cock. Christ, that's even worse. I delete that too.

Me: I can't wait to see you again.

Little Lady Death: Looking forward to our next lesson.

I can't believe I'm willingly doing this, but I open my camera app and hold my phone out to take a selfie, making sure to capture the rows of washing machines in the background. Am I really turning into a guy who sends pictures of himself to chicks?

Send.

Apparently, I am.

Little Lady Death: You really are at a laundromat.

Did she think I was lying to her?

Me: Not a titty in sight. Nope. Delete that. No reason to remind her I'll be working shifts at a strip club later this week.

"What's with the goofy look on your face?" Eazy steps next to me and tries to peer at my phone. "You've been staring at your screen for like ten minutes."

I click it off. "No, I haven't."

"Were you watching porn?"

"What? No, you fuckin' creep."

"Were you talking to that hottie from the wedding? Margaret?"

I don't bother correcting him. No reason for him to know her name.

"Nope, not Margaret." There, now I didn't lie to a brother. I don't even know a Margaret. *Heh.*

"You done with those lint traps?" I ask.

He holds up a fluffy tumbleweed-sized ball of gray, black, and white lint. "Want me to knit you a sweater with it?"

"Fucking throw it in the garbage, dumbass."

The bell over the door jingles and I groan when I see the tall, slender brunette walking through with her little sack of laundry.

"Hey, Jigsaw." She wiggles her fingers at me. "I didn't know you'd be here today."

As if you didn't notice my bike parked right outside. "Hey, Tara."

She's not exactly a muffler bunny but if she blows another couple of brothers in the back room, she might as well be.

While she makes a show of bending over to toss her dainties in the washer one by one, I stay behind the counter, pretending to be completely fascinated by a three-day-old copy of the *Union Reporter*.

Rare virus found in horses in Union Point.

Scintillating stuff.

"Who the fuck still reads newspapers?" Eazy rips the paper out of my hands. "Ooo, better stop fucking horses, the article says humans can catch this virus."

I side-eye him. "You have something you need to share, brother?"

"It's in the article," he protests.

"It doesn't say a damn thing about fucking horses."

"Hey, Jigsaw." Tara's soft voice interrupts us. "Could you break this for me?" She holds out a twenty.

We have a perfectly good change machine bolted to the back wall. This is her polite way of asking if I'd like a blow job in the back room today.

I point to the machine but don't want to make her look stupid in front of Eazy. "It's working today."

"Oh." Disappointment turns her pretty mouth down.

I *could* sneak in the back with her. Brush up on my *receiving* skills before my oral lessons with Margot. What's stopping me? A promise I made to Margot? I only promised not to *sleep* with anyone else. A quick blow job doesn't count as sleeping with someone, does it? It's a giant, gaping loophole in our agreement.

How would she ever know?

I'd know.

Honor isn't the only thing stopping me. My desire for anyone else is gone. *Poof.* Up in smoke. One lesson—one *very* chaste lesson by my standards—and I'm totally consumed by thoughts of one woman. All I can think about is Margot's cute, bouncy blonde curls, her quirky humor, and her wicked little smile. The way she's shy but still curious and eager to learn. Never mind, I'd rather have Margot's pink pouty lips wrapped around me a week from now than have anyone else's right this second.

"Tara, this is my brother, Eazy." I slap his back. "He's been out on the road for a while and finally home. He'll be happy to help you out with whatever you need."

Eazy may not know how to read a newspaper, but he can read a woman like a traffic signal. He works a sleazy smile onto his clean-cut face. "How are you doing, darlin'?"

Her eyes sparkle as she looks him up and down. He skirts around the counter, drops his arm over her shoulders and steers her to the cash machine.

Well, aren't I fucking cupid.

I glance at the big clock above the entrance. Feels like way too many hours until I can get my hands on Margot again.

CHAPTER EIGHTEEN

Margot

THIS HAS BEEN THE LONGEST WEEK. ONE OF THOSE WEEKS WHEN IT'S impossible to find a shred of goodness in people. Death either brings out the worst in people or the best and this week, it's been the worst.

Acknowledge the tragedy, ingest it, respect it, and continue serving the family. That's what we do.

But some weeks it's harder to do than others.

The doorbell chimes for the front door. Exhaustion slows my mind and movements as I open it and find yesterday's client. Her tragedy wrapped around me like poisoned tentacles burrowing into my heart and hasn't let go yet.

"Ms. Cedarwood, can we talk for a minute?" she asks, timid as a mouse.

"Of course." I pull the heavy door open wider and step back for her to enter. "You can call me Margot. How are you doing, Laurel?"

She pokes her head inside, quickly jerking it around, reminding me of a delicate songbird checking the surroundings to make sure they're clear of predators. Her face is still covered in bruises. The artist in me wants to run upstairs and grab my makeup for the living and help her cover them. But that goes way beyond the scope of my responsibilities here. I don't want to offend her or do anything to add to her pain, either.

"Do you want me to get my father?"

"No," she answers quickly. "I want to talk to you."

Emotional pain surrounds her. So deep it's almost tangible. Our conversation shouldn't be in the office. I lead her into the parlor where Jigsaw and I sat the night he brought me home. The furnishings might be outdated, but overall it's cozy.

"Sit anywhere," I offer.

Her gaze darts around the long room, from the baby grand piano and bench in one corner, to the table with four chairs by the bay window, to the couch and chairs in the center of the room, to another table and chair set near the kitchen door.

She perches on one end of the couch, and I take the armchair closest, so I'm facing her at an angle but not crowding her.

A red, quilted tote bag rests on her lap and her fingers keep fiddling with the straps.

"How are you doing?" I ask.

"Better. I can't stay long but I wanted to ask if you can do something for me?"

I've been thinking of many things I'd like to do to help her. "Sure."

She reaches in the bag and pulls out a small hand-knitted pink and mint green blanket. "It's not much but I can't stand thinking of Ashley wearing nothing—"

"Oh, no, Laurel. When we took her into our care from the hospital, she was swaddled in a blanket." Emotion threatens to choke off my words. *Stay calm.*

She blows out a slow, relieved breath. "Oh, that's good. Still, I'd like her to have something I made with my own hands. I was making this for her before...and I want her to have it." She passes the blanket to me. "Will you please wrap her in this?"

A deep pang of sorrow tugs on my heart. "Absolutely." With reverence, I accept the soft, small bundle. "Yes, of course, I will. We'll take good care of her. I promise."

"Thank you." She sniffles and dabs her cheeks.

178

I grab a tissue from the box on the end table and hand it to her. She bursts into tears. I move to the couch to sit next to her. Years of practice have forced me to balance professionalism with empathy, but I still struggle.

"They're letting Patrick out on bail," she sobs into the tissue.

A shock of disbelief shoots through me, followed by a rush of protectiveness.

"Do you have somewhere you can go?" Her husband already tried to kill her once, causing their baby to be stillborn. Now that he's out, he might try to finish the job. I've seen it happen before. Dealt with the aftermath. How could they let that man out after what he did?

"I have a restraining order. And they're going to make him wear an ankle monitor. He can't come near me."

That isn't reassuring but I don't want to scare her.

"He'll be at the Horizon Inn," she sneers as if she knows the drill from years of practice. "Knowing him, he'll be ordering takeout and hookers while living like a slob. Not caring at all about what he did."

Horizon Inn, takeout, and hookers, huh?

"You shouldn't be alone, though," I insist.

"My mother and sister are going to stay with me for a while."

"That's good." I rest my hand over hers. "You can call me if you need to. If you have any questions at all."

A soft creak comes from the hallway, only noticeable to me because over the years I've cataloged every sound this house makes. I flick my gaze up to my father in the doorway. He tips his head in a quick nod of approval and silently slips away.

Laurel grabs another tissue and blows her nose. "She'll be cremated in her casket by herself, right?"

"Yes, of course." I squeeze the blanket. "Wrapped in this and anything else you'd like me to place with her."

"Good." She frowns. "Does that cost extra?"

"What? No. Don't worry about any of that. Everything has been taken care of for you."

She blinks and wipes tears away. "Really?"

"Yes.

More tears flow over her cheeks. "Thank you for everything. Both you and your father."

You're welcome sounds painfully inadequate. "Of course. I meant what I said, if you have any questions, no matter how small, you can call me at any time."

"This is what kept me awake." She pats the blanket affectionately.

After she leaves, I honor my promise.

I'm finishing up when my father joins me.

"Horrible, horrible thing." He rests his hand on my shoulder. "Are you okay?"

I start to nod but end up shaking my head. "No. I'm angry. That man shouldn't be granted bail. But it looks like he'll get out."

My father nods in agreement. "I was hoping he'd get served inmate justice, but he won't even be in there long enough. Hopefully, he's convicted and gets sent to prison."

Hopefully. Too many variables. Too many what-ifs.

Where's the justice?

"Babies and children are always the hardest." My father's voice cracks. He touches the edge of the blanket. "This is a beautiful way to make sure she's wrapped up in her mother's love."

"I thought so too," I whisper.

He focuses on me with concern in his eyes. "I heard you singing to the baby earlier."

I nod. We always take special care with children and babies.

"Your mother used to do that too." His voice turns distant but full of affection.

I swallow hard. My memories of my mother are few but the ones I have are of her warmth and gentleness. Tears prick at the corners of my eyes. Dad rarely brings her up—it still hurts too much even after all these years. Hearing him mention her now, in the context of my work, stirs something deep inside me.

"I don't remember her doing that," I admit, my voice clogged with emotion. "But it feels like the right thing to do."

My father's hand tightens on my shoulder, a small gesture of support. "She was always so gentle with them," he says, his voice low and filled with sadness. "She loved you very much. She'd be so proud of you."

I blink back the tears, trying to keep my composure. "Thank you."

"Set your anger aside. Our job is to give her peace and help her say goodbye in the most loving way possible."

"I know." A tear slips down my cheek and I brush it away. "I wish I could do more."

He pulls me into a rare hug. "You're doing more than enough."

"Thanks," I say against his sweater.

He gently nudges me toward the door. "I'll finish this."

He may have said my concern for the babies who come into our care was passed from my mother. But it came from *him*. I've watched him read to children, leave lights on for them, and tuck stuffed animals into their caskets since I was little. Although he seems cold at times, now that I've been doing the job myself for a couple of years, I understand why.

Alone in the hallway, I put my back to the wall and close my eyes.

How to fix this? How, how, how?

Where is the closest Horizon Inn?

My mind races with possibilities, dark thoughts I pull closer and examine. Doing nothing, letting that monster get away, gnaws at me. I see so many awful things, but some are just too much.

A rumble from outside intrudes on my murderous musings. Is that Jigsaw?

My heart trips over itself. I push away from the wall and hurry toward the back door.

It *is* him. Standing at the bottom of the porch steps. He smiles as soon as he sees me, crinkles forming at the corners of his eyes.

He's the first good thing in days.

"Hi." I hurry to the next to last step which almost puts us at eye-level. "What are you doing here?"

He focuses his smoldering gaze on me. "I thought we had a *lesson* tonight." He lifts an eyebrow.

Oh my God. The last forty-eight hours have been such a stressful whirlwind of sadness and work, I forgot all about our date—err, lesson.

"It's been a rough couple of days." My voice breaks and my eyes fill with tears that I somehow hang onto. "I don't think I'm up for a lesson. I'm sorry you came all the way out here." I turn to run inside and bury myself under my pillows, but Jigsaw catches my hand, thwarting my escape. "Hey, hey, what happened?"

I shake my head, unable to share details. "Just work stuff."

"Okay. Come here." He pulls me against his chest and rubs his gloved hand over my back. "No lesson, then. Have you eaten?"

Have I? If I did, it was a while ago. "No," I mumble pitifully.

He releases me but keeps his hands on my shoulders. "Let's go somewhere and get dinner, then. You don't have to talk about it if you don't want to but let's get you out of here for a little while."

I blink up at him and study his serious face. "You…you want to do that?"

"Yeah. Come on." He steps away and gestures toward his bike parked up against the side of the house.

"I don't—"

"Right. Right. Sorry." He squeezes his eyes shut for a second. "We'll take your car."

"I have to go inside and get my keys."

"Okay." He follows me up the stairs into the house, where we promptly run into my father and my cousin.

My father's eyes widen when Jigsaw steps in behind me. Then, a faint smile crosses his face.

"Jensen, how are you?"

"Evening, Mr. Cedarwood." He shakes my father's hand quickly.

"Jensen, this is my nephew, Paul."

They do their introduction handshake thing. How much has my father told Paul about his arrangement with the motorcycle club?

"I was in the neighborhood and thought I'd swing by and see if you needed help with anything," Jigsaw lies smoothly. "I ran into Margot in the parking lot. She said it's been a rough day, so I thought I'd take her out to grab some dinner."

"That's a great idea." My father looks at me with relief.

Here I thought he'd flip at the idea of me spending time with any of the bikers.

"Your dad filled me in on the case, Margot," Paul says with sympathy shining in his eyes. Children always get to him too. "You should get out for a bit. I'll handle the callbacks you're waiting for."

"My notes are on the desk in Dad's office." I glance at the staircase. "I need to run up and grab my car keys."

Dad frowns in confusion.

"I only brought my bike." Jigsaw hikes his thumb over his shoulder.

The expression on Dad's face slips into respectful gratitude. He knows how I feel about motorcycles. He must be pleased Jigsaw doesn't expect me to ride on one.

"Here." Dad slips his hand into his pocket. "Take my car." He gives Jigsaw a once-over. "You can't have enough legroom in the Thunderbird."

My eyes widen so far, it's amazing they don't fall out of my head. Dad's never let *me* drive his precious Cadillac.

Jigsaw clasps the keys. "Thanks."

"You're road captain, right?" Dad nods to the patch on Jigsaw's leather vest. "That means you're in charge of the safety of the club out on the road?"

"Yes, sir. Planning the trips and maintaining vehicles too."

"All right then."

We say a round of goodbyes and Jigsaw walks me back outside.

"What just happened?" I mutter.

"Ready?" Jigsaw settles his hand at the small of my back and steers me toward the garage.

Jigsaw

Old man Cedarwood might not be as uptight as I originally thought. I didn't expect him to be okay with me taking Margot out for dinner. Never in a hundred years did I expect him to hand me his car keys and send us off with his blessing.

The garage door next to Margot's rolls up, revealing a shiny black Cadillac CT5. Not my style but a nice car. Exactly what I'd expect Cedarwood to drive.

I don't know what to do for Margot. She seemed so...drained when she stepped outside. Pale as a ghost and so damn sad. Fuck our sex lessons, I wanted to wrap her up in my arms and stab whoever put that dull listlessness in her eyes and stole the joy from her expression.

Since she doesn't want to talk about it, the next best thing I can do is feed her and get her away from this place for a couple of hours.

She's quiet while I guide the car to the road. When I glance over, she's staring out the window.

"You never know what you're going to get, do you?" I ask. How has this *just* occurred to me? What she does isn't a regular nine-to-five. It's unpredictable. And some cases are probably horrible.

"Sometimes," she whispers. "Hospice gives us a heads-up. Or the hospital does. But other times it's the worst kind of surprise."

Hearing her voice, as sad as she sounds, loosens the knot of tension in my gut. But a relentless need to do *something* to cheer her up continues to bug me.

Remy's Tavern is the only place I can think of to take Margot. It's quiet, he won't ask questions or make her uncomfortable. And the food's decent.

As usual, it's not that busy. I don't know how the fuck he's going to stay in business at this rate. Since my club uses the place quite a bit, we should do more to boost business. Teller was supposed to be working on that but seems to have put some projects on the back burner now that Charlotte's due date is getting closer.

I park at the front of the building and hurry to Margot's side to open her door. She blinks up at me and a faint smile crosses her lips. A big improvement.

"Have you ever been here?" I ask.

"Once or twice."

"A friend of the club owns it."

The corners of her mouth twitch with amusement. "You're taking care of all the friends of the club tonight, huh?"

What? Does she think that's the only reason I offered to take her out?

I pull her out of the car and close the door. "I think you should know by now my club has *nothing* to do with what goes on between us." If anything, I'm heading for an ass-kicking if I keep seeing her behind the club's back.

It's only temporary.

And Rock *did* tell me to keep her happy. Never mind that my own president told me not to mess around with her.

"We wouldn't have met otherwise," she says.

"I don't know about that. I'm spending more and more time out this way. We might have run into each other."

She stares up at me with a serious, almost sad expression. "You wouldn't have given me a second look."

"No, I would've given you a third, fourth, and fifth." I slide my hand over her ass and squeeze.

Stop it. Cheer her up, don't feel her up.

"If we met some other way, I never would've had the courage to make my indecent proposal to you." Her brow furrows like she's still shocked she did it at all.

"Well, thank fuck for pot brownies, then."

She titters with laughter. A quick burst of amusement that warms me down to my toes. Cheering her up feels like my new life's purpose.

I hold the door open for her and follow her inside.

Remy's behind the bar. His gaze goes to Margot first and he flashes a quick, warm smile. Then, his attention shifts to me. It's almost comical the way his eyes bug out. I've gone a few rounds in his underground fighting ring, and he's seen me carve up a body or two, so I get that he's shocked to see me escorting little miss wholesome to dinner.

"Jigsaw, what's up, brother?" He holds out his hand and I clasp it quickly.

Z wants me to help mentor the support club—which includes Remy—so I allow the "brother" greeting. "Just stopped by for dinner."

"Yeah, you got it." His gaze strays to Margot and I reluctantly make the introductions.

Remy nods slowly. "Yeah, your dad took good care of my grandparents. How are you, Margot?"

Christ, this is a small world.

"Remy...Holt, right?" she asks. "How's your sister?"

"Graduating from high school soon."

Margot smiles wider. "That's wonderful. It's good to see you."

He waves his hand toward the seating area where most of the tables are open. "Sit anywhere you like. I'll send Lynette over to take care of you."

"Thanks." I dip my chin at him and curl my arm around Margot's shoulders. "You have a preference?" I ask her.

"A booth, maybe?"

We take one in the back corner. I don't love putting my back to the rest of the bar, but I want to tuck Margot away from the world and keep her safe.

Lynette stops at the edge of our table, hands us menus, and smiles down at us. As the only full-time waitress working here, I recognize her right away.

"How you doing?" I ask.

"Not bad, Jigsaw." She beams a sweet, motherly smile at me and shifts her gaze to Margot, like she's happy to see me out with a nice girl. "What are you in the mood for?"

I shoot a glance at Margot. She shakes her head and sets the menu down. "I trust you."

Every time she says she trusts me, guilt or disbelief punches me in the gut. What'd I ever do to earn this woman's trust?

"Pizza and wings." I hand the menus back to Lynette.

"Ginger ale?" Margot asks.

"Sure thing."

Lynette hurries away and I focus my attention on Margot.

"Tell me about *your* week," she says.

"Uh, nothing interesting." I flash a quick grin. "Trained one of the guys on laundromat maintenance." *Avoided some blow jobs.*

Her lips tilt into a sly smile. "Did you show him how to clean up his act?"

A sharp bite of laughter bursts out of me. "Cute."

She tilts her head and lifts one shoulder.

"Sounds like your week was rougher. You want to talk about it?"

"No." She reaches across the table and slides her warm hands over mine. "But being with you has already lifted some of the darkness."

Usually I bring the darkness wherever I go. How did taking her out make things better? Fuck it, the warmth in my chest doesn't care.

I stare into her pained eyes. "Babies and kids." She takes a deep breath and blows it out slowly. "They're the hardest. When bad things happen to innocent people..." Her voice trails off and she drops her gaze to the table.

The pain in her voice is real and I don't know what to do to make it better.

"Whatever happened," I say, "I hope karma deals with them accordingly."

A slightly unhinged smile curves Margot's lips for the briefest second. "Karma takes too long for my taste, sometimes."

If I didn't know how sweet she is, that statement might be unsettling.

Margot

Being with Jigsaw tonight feels like holding open a curtain that keeps the light pouring in, so I can't drown in the darkness of the week.

My murderous plans come to me in bits and fragments in between our conversation. It has to be quick and unfortunately somewhat painless. It can't be bloody.

By the time we finish our pizza and wings, I think I have a plan.

Jigsaw swipes his napkin over his mouth. "You good?"

When I nod, he collects our plates and pizza tray. "I need to talk to Remy for a minute. Are you all right here?"

"Sure." I frown at him. "Are you clearing the table?"

He shrugs. "I'm going that way, anyway. Might as well save Lynette the trouble."

How can he look so scary on the outside but be so thoughtful? Not only to me but others as well.

What does this outing mean? We were only supposed to be about sex. Well, teaching *me* about sex. As soon as I told him I wasn't up for it tonight, I expected him to leave. Not be mean about it, but I certainly didn't think he'd stick around. That's not what our relationship is about, so I wouldn't have been mad. But he took me out for dinner and light conversation instead.

Lynette swings by our table and sets a white box in the middle. "Some cookies to go. Dark chocolate chip, and white chocolate chip pecan."

"Oh, wow. Those sound amazing." I pull my purse into my lap. "Do you have our check?"

She waves her hand through the air like it was a silly question. "He already took care of it." She leans down and whispers in my ear, "He's a keeper, honey."

My body freezes, except my mouth, which twitches into a hesitant smile. She winks and heads for the kitchen.

He's a keeper.

Why do I suddenly wish that were true? When I know it can't be.

He made it clear from the beginning that he wasn't mine to keep.

CHAPTER NINETEEN

Jigsaw

DENYING MY NEED TO SEE MARGOT FEELS LIKE RIDING THROUGH THE desert and refusing the most basic urge to stop and quench my thirst.

I don't need anyone. Never have. Never will.

All I need is my bike, my club, and a full tank of gas.

But I *really* want to see her.

For our second lesson, of course.

So when she sends me a *how are you* text, I take it as a sign she's ready for our next lesson and can't get my horny ass there soon enough.

She greets me at the back door of the funeral home, looking sinfully cute in a bright yellow T-shirt, bright green terry cloth shorts, and fluffy blue booties. Her blonde curls are brushed into a high ponytail but little damp frizzies stick out around her ears—like she just stepped out of the shower. Except for slightly glossy lips, she's makeup-free, her eyes sparkling under the soft golden lighting.

"Hey," she says softly. "It's been a while. I wasn't sure if you were—"

I flick a quick glance down the hallway. We seem to be alone, the house still, lights low. I lean down and kiss her cheek. "Been a lot of stuff going on, but I was happy to hear from you."

Pink floods her cheeks. She holds out her hand to me. "Come on up."

"Seems quiet here tonight," I say, curling my fingers around hers and following her up the stairs.

"A merciful break from the madness."

Having her lush ass right in front of my face as we ascend the stairs is hell on my restraint. The little shorts show off a lot of her thick thighs that I've been dying to have wrapped around my head.

I want her so much, there's a void in my chest and I'm afraid she's the only woman who can fill it.

Once we pass the second floor, I squeeze her ass.

She squeals and runs faster up the stairs.

"Where do you think you're going?" I rush after her.

The door's not closed all the way. She pushes right into her apartment with me close behind her.

"What're you doing teasing me with these sexy little shorts?" I pull her into my arms.

"These?" She frowns and tries to glance down but I have her pressed to me tight. "Here I was worried you'd be insulted I was so casual."

"Not at all." I lean down and press my lips to hers.

She slips her arms around my neck and squirms against my body. I lift her higher, and she wraps her legs around me.

"Yeah, that's it." I palm her ass, sliding my fingers under her shorts. "You need a review of lesson one or are you ready to dive into lesson number two?" I don't even care about the answer, as long as I get my mouth and hands on her naked body tonight.

"I wouldn't mind a quick review of our previous lesson." She tilts her head, a smile threatening to break free on her face. "Just to make sure all the information stuck."

"Excellent." I spin us toward her lounge chair, but she leans in, kissing along my jaw.

"My bedroom's that way," she whispers in my ear.

"Fuck, yes." I assume she's pointing in the opposite direction, so that's where I go.

Tonight, the door's open. I don't take much time looking at the details, other than the queen-sized bed neatly made up with a colorful floral quilt and dozens of fluffy pillows.

I set her on the bed, and she scoots into the center and leans back on her elbows.

"Casual." I scoff as I slip my cut off my shoulders and set it on top of the nightstand, never taking my eyes off of her. "You're way too sexy for any outfit to ever be *casual*."

"Thank you," she whispers.

I rest my knee on the edge of the bed and stretch out next to her. "Come here."

She rolls to her side and inches closer to me until she's pressed tight to my front, her mouth on mine in pure need. I groan with a deep satisfaction that echoes in my chest as she hikes her leg over mine, opening herself up with not much between us but those dangerously loose shorts.

"I like kissing you," she whispers against my lips. "You make it delightful."

So simple, so sweet. How does that one declaration punch through my chest and squeeze my heart? How can I express that I never even *liked* kissing before her?

I can't think of any words, so I mash our lips together, slipping the tip of my tongue over hers. I brush one hand along her ribcage, walking my fingers to the hem of her shirt and tugging it up. Tonight, she's not as shy. She allows me to strip it up over her head, leaving her in another sheer, nipple-baring bra. Tonight, it's blue.

Then she presses her hands over her breasts, blocking them from my view.

"What are you doing?" I carefully pry one hand off her breast and guide it into my outstretched palm, holding it above her head.

"Hey," she protests and twists her head to stare at our linked hands.

"Margot, I've been dreaming about your breasts. Please don't disappoint me." It's cruel to guilt her when she's so eager to please. I dip down and suck her nipple into my mouth through the material of her bra.

She gasps and wiggles.

I release her nipple, leaving a nice wet spot on the cup of her bra. I blow a stream of air on the stiff tip, watching with fascination as it pokes against the sheer material. "Like that?"

"Yes," she whispers.

"Good, then show me." I nod to the hand still covering her other breast.

Her body quivers as she bares herself. Then she goes beyond what I asked, slowly raising her hand to where I'm still holding her other wrist hostage.

My heart kicks as she lets me gather both wrists in my hand, pinning her in place. "Yes." I kiss her cheek. "Good girl."

I run my hand along the length of her body, stopping to cup her breast. I tease my thumb over the hard ball of her nipple and she arches into my hand. Leaning back, I take a breath and a moment to absorb every inch of her. Skin—pale, smooth, and perfect. Body—plush, curvy and soft in all the right spots.

"Can we take this off?" I hook my finger under the center of her bra.

She nods quickly. I release her hands and help her turn to the side where I quickly unhook her bra. I trace my fingers along her spine, then tug her down again.

I bite my lip, then blow out a slow breath while I take her in. Margot's so timid, she'd probably die if I told her she has the kind of tits men spend a lot of money jacking off to. Pretty dark-pink areolas lead to prominent tips that respond so beautifully to every touch and lick. Between the strip club and the MC's porn empire, I've seen my fair share and hers are spectacular. Since she's feeling vulnerable right now, reminding her that I'm an expert in this field seems like a bad idea. But *damn*.

I pull her closer and feast, rolling my tongue over one nipple, then the other. Christ, I could play with her forever and never get enough.

"Oh!" She lets out a sharp cry and teases her fingers through my hair.

"You like that?" I swirl my tongue around one rosy tip.

"I do. I never...I never thought..." She arches her back and shifts her legs.

I haven't touched her below the waist since we climbed into bed, but she sounds like she's already halfway to orgasm.

"When do I..." She sneaks her fingers under my T-shirt. "When do I make *you* feel good?"

How do I explain that all of her genuine reactions, every soft sigh and whimper, already make me feel like a fucking king? Her delicate fingers trace over my skin, shooting fire through my veins. I'm balancing on a knife's edge, so close to stripping down for her and baring my scars.

But the thought of her reaction stops me cold.

What if the warmth in her eyes flips to pity or horror. Or worse, what if she seeks answers I don't want to share? I don't want to take her out of the moment or have her look at me in a different way.

"A man likes to take care of his woman first, Margot." I slide my hand down her body and tease my fingers along the edge of the waistband of her shorts, then keep moving lower, cupping her hot center. I groan with satisfaction. "Your little shorts are wet."

"What?" She struggles to sit up.

"No." I slip my arm under her and hold her against me. "We covered this in our last lesson. It's a good thing. Your body likes what we're doing."

She stares into my eyes. "I do."

"Good, then let me continue."

My world's rocked sideways as she presses her heels into the mattress, lifts her hips, and slowly pushes her shorts down. That's more than I expected. I want to praise the hell out of her, but *good girl* feels inadequate as fuck.

"You want help with those?" I ask instead.

She nods quickly and I drag them down her legs the rest of the way, tossing them at the end of the bed. "You're incredible."

I stand and unbuckle my belt, shoving my jeans off.

Her eyes widen. "God, you have really sexy legs." She reaches out and squeezes my thigh. "Your quads are like rocks."

That's not the only thing rock hard on me.

"I never skip leg day." I wink at her and climb back into bed, covering her with my body.

"I could do leg day all day every day and never look like that." She pokes a finger into her thigh.

"You're not supposed to." I swat her hand away and kiss where she just jabbed her skin.

Digging my fingers into her flesh, I grab her hip and gently squeeze. "I like how soft you are."

I kiss her sternum and down to her belly.

Her body tenses.

"Relax." I stop and stare at her sheer blue panties. "These are cute. I like."

"I thought you might."

"Yeah?" I trace my finger along the crease of her thigh. "You were thinking about me when you put them on?"

"I was thinking of you when I *bought* them." She waves her hand toward her closet door. "All my other underwear is much more sensible."

My tongue freezes at her sweet admission. She's buying underwear to please me, now? Christ, that tickles some happy center in my brain I didn't even know I had. "Sensible is overrated."

As sexy as they are, the panties are blocking the next objective of our lesson. I tug on the thin straps at her hips.

"Don't," Margot whispers, squeezing her thighs together.

I trace my fingertips over her knee. "Why?"

"I don't...like *that*. It doesn't do anything for me."

Her tentative, vague expressions are cute but I enjoy plainer, descriptive words. "You don't like a man between your thighs, French-kissing your pussy? Licking your swollen little clit?" I stick the tip of my tongue out and wiggle it, demonstrating exactly what I'm dying to do.

She gasps and red floods her cheeks.

My lips twist into a wicked line. "You don't think you can come that way?"

Her eyelashes flutter rapidly as if she's scandalized by the idea of coming in any way, shape or form. Even though I already know how easy it is to unravel her.

"Margot." I use my sternest voice. "Were you a virgin before I got my hands on you?"

"No." Her forehead wrinkles.

"Had you *ever* had an orgasm?"

Even the tip of her nose turns red when she's embarrassed. "Not as good as the ones you gave me."

I groan. This assignment is going to be more involved than I expected. Thankfully I'm up for the job. *Very, very* up. "So, no."

"I think I did. I mean, it felt good but..." Her nose scrunches. "It wasn't like earth-shattering or anything."

So her boyfriends have been two-pump chumps who rammed their fingers in her, probably slurped at her pussy a few times, and called it good. Bet none of them ever found her clit.

Fuck, this is exciting. Nothing excites me more than exploring uncharted territory. Discovering all the different ways to make Margot orgasm is like finding a pot of gold at the end of a rainbow.

"Can we compromise?" I raise my eyebrows, pretending to be a reasonable man. "Give me fifteen minutes—"

"I'd like you to spend the night this time," she protests.

Ignoring that, I continue. "Give me fifteen minutes with my head buried between your thighs. If you *really* don't like it and if I can't make you come by the time time's up, we'll move on to the next lesson."

"Fifteen minutes? That's...forever." Her gaze drops to my dick, straining against my boxer-briefs. "I'm willing to...you know...instead."

"What?" I widen my eyes to a dickish degree. "Wrap your sweet lips around my cock first?"

She blushes and glances away.

"Are you blushing at the word *cock*, Margot?" I can't help teasing her. She's the best mix of adorable and sexy.

"No one's ever said it to me like that before."

Fuck me. Is she lying to me about not being a virgin?

"You want to learn to suck my cock?"

Her chest rises and falls faster. "Yes."

"Glad to hear it." I trace my finger along her jaw. Too bad she only wants to learn how to do this to eventually please someone else. Suddenly, I wish it was all for my benefit. "But I'm not into taking without giving. And you shouldn't accept anything less."

"Really?"

What the fuck kind of guys has she dated?

Who cares?

She's mine for now.

She reaches for the waistband of my briefs, and I brush her hand away.

"Stop trying to distract me. We'll get there." I gesture to my cock. "I promise."

"Well, the whole point of this was to teach *me* to be better at sex. So, shouldn't we focus on *you*?"

There it is again. She wants me to teach her how to be good so she can fuck someone else. A perverse thrill runs through me. I'll teach her so fucking well, I'll ruin her for every man she meets for the rest of her life. Every time her body gets near another dick, she'll be thinking of mine and all the ways I pleasured her.

"Knowing what you like and enjoy *will* make you better at sex. You're not a blow-up doll. If a guy isn't interested in pleasing you too, don't waste your time with him."

"How will I know?"

Sounds to me like that's the *only* kind of guy she's ever dated. "Guys who try to talk you into something before you're ready. Up here." I tap the side of her head. "And down here." I cup her pussy through her thin underwear. She's hot and the material's soaked. *Fuuuck.* Nervous or not, she's really into this.

She inhales an adorably long breath—like she needs to work up the courage. Even that dials up my need for her. She's scared but wants me bad enough to push through her fear.

I'm desperate to please her in every way possible. Need to taste her, feel her quiver against my tongue—we might need to spend more than one night on oral lessons.

"First, these need to go." I tease one finger along the edge of blue lace. She yanks her legs together, blocking herself from view.

"What are you doing?"

"I want to eat your pussy, not your panties."

She gasps, then laughs. "You have a really filthy mouth."

"I know, and I want to kiss your pussy with it."

More giggles and while she's still shaking with laughter, she hooks her thumbs in her underwear and lifts her hips.

"Yes," I groan. "Pull them down for me slowly."

She shimmies and slides the material down a few inches. My patience snaps and I take over, ripping them down her legs and tossing them aside.

She slams her knees together.

"Margot," I warn, running my hand over her calf. "What're you doing?"

"It's really bright in here."

I've pushed her a lot in the short amount of time I've been here, I can give her this. "I like looking at you, though." I push myself up and brush a kiss against her knee. "But if it bugs you, I'll turn the overhead light off."

She nods quickly and points to a small lamp on the nightstand and one floor lamp in the corner.

"Done." I bounce off the bed and turn on the lamp by the bed first, then find the switch by the door and flip the ceiling light off. "Better?"

A soft "yes" comes out of her mouth, but her knees stay pressed together.

One day, when she's more confident, I want to drag this out. Torture her. Have her begging me to let her come, then beg me to make it stop. But not today. I want to help her discover what she likes, and I want to learn everything about her body.

She's teaching me as much as I'm teaching her.

CHAPTER TWENTY

Margot

IT'S NOT EASY TO MEET JIGSAW'S INTENSE STARE BUT I CAN'T CLOSE MY eyes either. He's impressive in his intensity—chest heaving, cheeks flushed, dark gaze focused on my face.

He kneels on the bed in front of me and lazily drags his fingers up and down my calves. Like he's trying to soothe a skittish rabbit. His eyes never leave my face, though. Constantly observing my reactions.

He presses a kiss to one knee, then traces his tongue along the ticklish crease.

"That tickles." I shake with laughter, my legs falling apart a few inches.

"Mmm." He licks and nibbles along the inside of my knee and up my thigh. "Open for me."

His low voice and gentle but insistent touch shoot a surge of lust straight to my center, shoving my shyness out of the way. My knees fall open.

He sucks in a sharp breath and stares for so long, I squeeze my eyes shut. "You're beautiful," he breathes out. Rough, warm hands skate along my inner thighs. "Eyes open, Margot."

"So, what do I do?" Weird how I sound so breezy and confident when my insides are fluttering and churning.

"What do you mean?" He casually rests his palms on my legs, his thumbs tracing the crease of my thighs, sharpening my desire.

"To be good at receiving?" I ask, my heart jumping like a frog in a frying pan. It's so embarrassing that I have to ask.

"Whatever feels good to you."

"That's not helpful."

He blows out a frustrated breath, the air caressing my skin. "If it feels good, say so. If you like something say, 'give me more.'" He flashes a wicked grin. "If it feels so good you can't form any words, tug on my hair." His expression smooths into something more serious. "If you don't like something, tell me to stop. Or smack my head."

My eyes widen in horror. "I'm not going to *smack* you."

His lips quirk at the corners. "Just give me some signals." His eyebrows dip like he just had a revelation. "There's no *wrong* way to enjoy yourself, Margot."

That message finally sinks in. I stare into his eyes and only find the desire to please. "Fifteen minutes?"

"You're not setting a timer, are you?" Both exasperation and humor color the question.

I turn my head and glance at the small digital clock on my nightstand. "Nine-fifteen."

"You won't be able to form the words *nine-thirty* once I get my mouth on you," he mutters, clearly seeing this as a challenge.

A challenge I really want him to win. He's so confident I'll love his mouth exploring my most intimate places, I don't want to disappoint him.

"Most importantly," he says. "Don't fake anything with me. I'd rather have you tell me something isn't working for you, than have you lie."

"I won't," I whisper.

"Good girl." He pushes himself up and leans over my body. "Now, come here and kiss me."

I meet him halfway. Our lips fusing together for a few delicious seconds.

Then he reaches behind me and grabs a pillow. "Lift up for me."

"What? Why?" I ask, even as I dig my heels into the bed and raise my hips.

He methodically pushes the pillow under me, adjusting it until it's even under my hips. "It'll be more comfortable for both of us."

Heat from both embarrassment and desire licks over my skin as I lower myself to the pillow. The awestruck expression on his face—like he's extremely pleased with what's exposed to him—allows desire to drown out my discomfort.

He stretches out on his stomach and hooks his arms under my legs, dragging me closer.

The first brush of his tongue against my skin sends an electric jolt up my spine. I let out a moan of appreciation.

"Good girl." His low, gravelly voice whispering words of praise sends another shiver of pleasure through me. Warm breath pulses against my skin. He dips his head and licks in slow, soft strokes that leave me squirming with desire.

"I...I like that," I whisper in shaky, halting breaths.

He does it again. And again. Until I'm quivering all over. His fingers are firm but gentle as he brushes against my skin and peels my lips apart. A hot flush of shyness travels over my skin. I've never felt so exposed or vulnerable.

Then he moves higher, circling my clit with his tongue, taking his time, applying the lightest of pressure. My mind crackles with how damn good it feels.

Was Daniel the problem all along? He went at my lady bits like a sloppy dog trying to launch a tennis ball with his tongue. No matter how many times I asked him to slow down or use a lighter touch, he always reverted to an eager puppy slurp during his five minutes of giving oral.

Jigsaw doesn't need guidance. And he seems to have infinite patience. He's slow and gentle, only increasing pressure or speed in response to my movements or the sounds spilling from my lips.

He's vocal too, like he's really, *really* enjoying himself. Not treating it as a chore to finish so he can move on to the main event. He's definitely not acting like he's counting to three hundred using the one-Mississippi method in his head, either.

He lifts his head and desire hits me in waves at the sight of his glossy lips and intense stare. "How do you feel about this now? Need a time check?" he asks with a cocky gleam in his eyes.

Time? I couldn't take my eyes off of him if my life depended on it.

"Keep going?"

"Yes, please," I beg.

His lips twist into a wickedly pleased-with-himself grin.

As sexy as that is, I can't help responding with a teasing scold. "A good coach isn't smug when he chooses the right play."

He grins even wider, then dives in, bringing his mouth against me in a hot, open-mouthed kiss. He licks and flutters his tongue against me in the most satisfying ways.

I let out a sharp cry and spear my fingers through his hair.

He groans, the sound vibrating against me and licks harder.

My hips rock against him, offering myself. He growls his approval and flicks his tongue against me faster. With a sharp tug on my clit as he sucks and teases, a sweet, pulsing release spirals through me. He maintains the steady rhythm and pressure until I burst into a million pieces.

Panting hard and overwhelmed with the sensations that go on and on, I squirm away, then struggle to get closer. My body jerks as it becomes too much, and Jigsaw reluctantly backs off. His hands stay pressed to my thighs, thumbs kneading my flesh. He lightly swipes his tongue against my clit, and I jump.

"I can't get enough of you," he whispers more to himself than to me.

I'm too numb to speak yet. My brain hasn't re-entered my head. He drags the pillow out from under me and settles himself against my side. I'm too spent to turn toward him. I focus my fuzzy gaze on the ceiling. "Thank you for being so patient with me."

"My pleasure." The bed shifts as he rolls on top of me. "Are you okay?"

"I'm divine." I reach up and run my fingers through his hair. "I didn't hurt you, did I?"

His fierce expression softens. "No. You can't hurt me, little lady death."

Oh, but he could hurt me.

I never knew sexual experiences could be *this* good. My mind's blown at all I've been missing. Besides the core-melting orgasms, I like *him* so much.

"Was I okay at that?" That's what he's here for, to teach me. I have to stop forgetting that part.

"Magnificent. A-plus for my star student."

Glowing from the compliment, I run my fingers through his soft, thick hair again. He's such a beautiful man. Inside and outside. How did he get to his age and never have a girlfriend? Never ever? Or did the relationship end so badly, he doesn't like to talk about it?

"You've really never dated anyone seriously?"

His shoulders jerk. "Does it matter?"

"No, I guess not."

He dips down and catches my lips in a kiss. I wrinkle my nose at my scent all over him and he laughs against my mouth. "Kiss me."

That seems so intimate for our arrangement, but I can't resist his plea. I hook one arm behind his neck and drag him closer. While our lips slide together and our tongues collide, I slip my hand under his shirt, daring to sneak over his abdominals.

"Can you?" I tug on the shirt. "Take this off?"

A bolt of alarm darts across his face, so fast I might have imagined it. Then his expression settles into languid arrogance. "You haven't earned it yet."

He doesn't want to get too comfortable here. Got it.

I said I wanted him to stay the night but now I'm not sure if that's safe. I don't want to get used to this. To us. To him being here in my bed and never anything more than that.

Jigsaw

Something in Margot's mood has shifted. More than a post-orgasmic haze is keeping her quiet. First the relationship question. Then asking me to undress.

I study her face. Glossy eyes staring up at the ceiling, rapidly blinking like she's trying not to cry.

Danger.

What the hell am I doing? This wasn't supposed to get complicated. I knew this was a mistake. I've been way too casual and familiar with her. Kissing her every chance I get, talking to her like a boyfriend instead of a coach. Insisting on only focusing on her pleasure because I don't *want* to teach her all the tricks to get a man off just so she can use them on someone else who isn't me. The thought of her with some other guy twists a hot knife of jealousy in my chest.

I've violated all of my own rules with her.

I want to honor our agreement and give her everything she needs. But first I need some distance. Clarity.

A distinct buzzing comes from the floor.

Margot turns her head and frowns.

"Fuck, that's mine. I thought I shut it off." I sit up and grab my jeans off the floor, searching for my phone.

Rooster flashes on the screen.

I stand and answer the call. "What's going on?"

"Where are you?"

"Why are you answering a question with a question?" I open the bedroom door and step into the hallway.

He sighs into the phone. Fucking with him when I can't see the exasperation on his big, bearded face just isn't as much fun. "I'm listening."

"Laundromat got broken into."

"Are you serious? What'd they go after, the dryer sheets?"

He snorts. "No, they beat the hell out of the change machine and a couple of washers before giving up and just taking what was in the register."

"Fucking assholes." I tuck my phone between my cheek and shoulder and hop into my jeans, jerking them up my legs.

"Yeah, the worst of it is the front window. Shattered the whole thing to break in."

"Are you shitting me?"

"Nope. Huge fucking mess. Eazy and Z are down there dealing with the cops now."

I flick my gaze toward Margot's bedroom door. Rooster just handed me an excuse to escape. "I'll be home in a couple of hours."

"Where are you?"

"None of your business. Tell Z I'm on my way."

"You don't *have* to leave now." He blows out an exasperated breath. "We have enough people to cover it."

"No, it's fine. You at the house?"

"Yeah, someone hacked into Stella's site, so I'm dealing with that."

"Shit. That's bad, isn't it?"

"It's not great."

"Maybe give Upstate a call and let them know the moon's in retrograde or whatever."

He snorts a laugh. "Yeah, I was going to call Murphy after I got off the phone with you. I'll be sure to tell him that."

"Later." We end the call.

I shove my phone in my pocket and return to the bedroom. Margot's sitting on the edge of the bed, wearing an oversized T-shirt and a sad expression that gives me pause.

Rooster said he doesn't need me.

I don't *want* to leave.

I really should though. Things were getting too cozy before. Too relationship-y.

"I'm sorry, babe. I gotta go." I grab my cut off the nightstand.

She blinks up at me. "We never got to the pleasuring *you* part of the lesson."

I'm painfully aware of that fact.

"I know. We will." I give her a cocky wink even though I'm feeling

more unsettled than anything right now. "That's a lesson all on its own." I force a grin, trying to keep the mood light. My mind's already back on my bike speeding away from the reality that I'm in deeper than I intended.

Cupping the back of her head, I lean down and press a quick kiss to her lips. The way she melts into me and twists her fingers in my shirt has me questioning everything. I want to stay. I'm aching to climb into bed and stay the night. Pretend we're more.

"I'm sorry I gotta go," I whisper against her lips before pulling away.

Without taking my eyes off of her, I slip my cut on, the weight of it grounding me, reminding me of who I am. What I do and what I *don't* do.

"Sure." She tucks her legs up underneath the long T-shirt, the fabric swallowing her small frame. "Is everything okay?"

"Just some club stuff." Her concern only makes me feel worse. This is exactly what I didn't want. Feelings. Regret. I like my freedom. Don't want to feel tethered to another person.

At least I didn't want that kind of connection before I met her.

Now, I don't know what I want.

"See you soon?" She won't even look at me.

"I'll text you." I don't know if that's a promise.

Or a lie.

CHAPTER TWENTY-ONE

Jigsaw

AVOIDING MARGOT IS LIKE NAILING BOARDS OVER THE WINDOWS ON A sunny day. The sun's out. I've seen the big orange ball in the sky. Felt its warmth. I can bask in it and enjoy the benefits like a normal human. But I'd rather deny myself and stay in the dark. I've denied myself her warmth for weeks. Physically, anyway. Mentally, she's burrowed into my fucking brain. I like her too damn much, which means I should stay the fuck away from her.

My longing for her grates on my nerves.

Being with her makes me a hypocrite, though—something I hate in other people. I'm supposed to teach Margot to open up and connect with someone on a physical level and I can't even do it myself. Well, no, physically, our connection is incendiary. It's all the other connections I want to make with her, *outside* of the bedroom, that are a problem.

She helps families navigate grief and loss. I help bury and burn bodies.

She has enough darkness in her life. I have no business bringing more into it.

The club's been a grind. Fixing the damage from the break-in.

Helping Rooster re-upload dozens of videos to the websites we maintain, sorting through a mess of digital chaos.

Serena has baby Lincoln and a few of the guys take a trip upstate to Empire Med to congratulate Grinder and Serena.

Tonight, I'm at the clubhouse when some of the guys get back. They threw this party, to "celebrate" Lincoln's birth, but it's the farthest thing from a wholesome celebration of new life.

A year ago, I would've been right in the thick of things, loving every disgusting minute. Tonight, it makes my skin crawl. I don't think I could get it up for anyone else, even if I wanted to.

All I want is Margot. Her scent surrounding me. Her silky hair brushing my skin. Her voice saying my name. All of her.

I'm really regretting leaving the way I did and I'm not sure how to make it right, or if I should even try.

Our downstate clubhouse, with couples furtively fucking in the corners and openly fucking on the pool table, would scandalize Margot.

After so many years, it's boring to me.

All I want is the shy girl who tends to the dead and asked me to teach her about sex.

I could never bring her here. Within five minutes, she'd run into girls I've fucked who'd be more than happy to give her salacious details just for shits and giggles.

And how the fuck is Margot ever going to tell her dad about us? He might have let me drive his car to take her to dinner but he's never going to be okay with me dating Margot. Marrying her.

Fuck me to hell. *Do I want to marry her?*

"We're back, Jiggy!" a sweet, southern voice behind me announces.

My mouth curves into a genuine smile for the first time in days. I turn around and Shelby's standing there in a loose floral blouse, jeans, and one of the many pairs of cowboy boots Rooster's bought her since they got together. Rooster's standing right behind her, hands on her shoulders, gaze shifting left and right, making sure no one bothers his girl.

But she's only looking up at me right now. "Did you miss us?"

"Always. How'd it go?"

"We couldn't stay long. Serena is beat."

"Yeah, I bet."

"But lil' Lincoln is so cute and squishable." She presses her fists together in front of her face and squeezes her eyes shut for a second.

My lips tilt into a smirk. I shoot Rooster a quick look. "Make you think about having one of your own?"

Rooster gags at the same time Shelby yelps, "Hell, no! I'm happy being the cool aunt right now."

At least they're on the same page.

"What happened to your vow to mind your own business when it came to your friends' reproductive plans?" Rooster scolds.

I scratch the side of my head. "Did I say that?"

"Ya sure did. I heard it," Shelby says.

"I think I was talking about Wrath and Trinity because I get tired of listening to people bug them about it." I flick my hand at them. "You two are still brand new."

Shelby rolls her eyes, but she's trying to contain her laughter, I can tell.

"I'm gonna give you a *brand-new* ass-kicking." Rooster half-shoves me.

"Aww, don't be mean." Shelby teasingly swats at Rooster, but five seconds later, he captures her in his arms, and she leans up to kiss his cheek. They're so disgustingly in love, my heart aches and I have to tear my gaze away.

I've never wanted that playful, lovey-dovey, gotta have her near me all the time, relationship.

Now it's all I want.

But only with Margot.

Another wave of people push through the front doors, including Eazy who heads straight for me.

"Hey, Horsefucker," I greet him with a grin. "How's it going?"

Rooster bursts out laughing. "The fuck?"

Shelby cringes with disgust. "I don't wanna know, do I?"

Eazy rolls his eyes but slaps my outstretched hand and pulls me in for a shoulder bump. "Gee, I'm so thrilled you've been around more lately." Then he turns and gives Rooster the same greeting.

Shelby cocks her head, studying me intently. "You *have* been home more lately."

"Is that a problem?"

"No." But she still keeps looking at me with that curious tilt to her head.

The moaning around us increases in volume as the party dives deeper into degeneracy.

"We really are a bunch of heathens, huh?" I grumble.

Eazy grins and rubs his hands together like a racoon in a henhouse, proving my point. "Yes, sir, we are."

Shelby wrinkles her nose and sweeps her gaze around the room. "No other ol' ladies here tonight, huh?"

"Lilly's still upstate," I remind her.

Rooster leans down and whispers something in her ear. By the blush spreading over her cheeks, it's something filthy. I flick my gaze to the ceiling. They really never get bored with each other, do they?

I glance around the room again. I haven't even slept with Margot yet. How can I be this infatuated with her?

"We'll be back," Rooster says, pushing Shelby ahead of him.

"Sure you will, motherclucker." I slap Rooster's shoulder as he passes me. They head for the hallway, navigating the crowd. Fed up, Rooster finally picks Shelby up and carries her.

"They're cute," Eazy says, following my gaze. "Never thought we'd see Rooster settle down before forty."

My body tenses, waiting for him to make some crack about my best friend or his girl. But after a few beats, nothing comes out. He's too busy staring at the front door. "I invited that Tara chick to come by. You haven't seen her yet, have you?" he asks.

That's the last thing I expected to come out of his mouth. Shit, I really am cupid. "No, brother. Why invite her to this?" I circle my finger in the air.

He shrugs. "Rather be upfront from the beginning, you know?"

What a novel approach. "So go pick her up."

"Nah, I think she'd rather have her own car." A smirk slips over his face. "In case she wants to make an escape."

"Smart girl."

"Hey, Jiggy," someone says behind me. "Where've you been lately?" Bonnie drags her fingers over my shoulder and steps in front of me, her hand lingering on my arm. If she ever bothered to pay attention, she'd know how much I hate that.

I'm way too grumpy for this bullshit tonight. I brush her off. "None of your business."

She glances at Eazy and raises a come-hither eyebrow.

"No thanks, darlin'."

She huffs and walks away.

"No thanks, darlin'," I mimic in a high-pitched voice.

"Oh, sorry, we can't all be a grouchy dick like you."

Lala runs up and stops in front of me. "Hi, Jigsaw." She gives me a cute wiggly finger-wave instead of trying to touch me.

"Hey, sweetheart." I lift my chin. "How you've been?"

"Good." She glances shyly over at the bar. "I brought my friend Kristen with me tonight."

I follow her line of sight and a pretty blonde in a white dress smiles at us. Lala waves her over.

"I thought the three of us..." Lala lets the idea hang in the air. When I don't pick up the thread, she flutters her lashes a few times. "Could have *fun* together."

"No thanks."

Her face falls.

"I just came to talk to Hustler," I say as nicely as I'm capable. It must still sound hostile because her eyes gloss over with tears.

"Okay." She sniffles and shuffles away.

"Why are you here for ten seconds and already making bunnies cry?" Grip walks up and claps a heavy hand on my shoulder.

"Fuck off." I'm not in the mood for his shit tonight, either.

"That girl Kristen's really sweet." He makes this disgusting chef's kiss gesture, complete with lip-smacking. "You see her giant tits?"

"Well, have at it. Lala's looking for a three-way with her."

His eyebrows shoot up with interest. "You're sure?"

"I'm positive. Godspeed, brother."

The noise around me rises to an intolerable level. I bump Eazy's arm. "I'm gonna grab a drink."

He follows me to the bar. A girl I don't recognize is handing out beer and sodas. None of the fancy cocktails with cutesy names Serena used to make when she helped out here—before she met Grinder.

I flick my gaze to the rows of liquor bottles lining the back wall of the bar area and the mirror behind them. Through the sketchy lighting I catch a glimpse of a man I barely recognize. Unshaven, grim face. Eyes dark with regret I can't shake.

Bonnie braces her hands against the bar and leans over. "What do you need, Jiggy?"

Nothing behind that bar. "A Coke is fine, hon. Thanks."

A few seconds later, she passes me a red can. I take a sip, still rooted in place, staring at my reflection like it'll give me answers.

All I see is a man surrounded by the life he knows who wants a woman that makes him question everything.

CHAPTER TWENTY-TWO

Margot

It's been weeks since my last "class" with Jigsaw. *Ugh.* It feels stupid and desperate that I'm actually calling it that. Especially after he couldn't get away from me fast enough. I've been tiptoeing around my own thoughts so I don't dwell on why he's been so distant. Anything to avoid triggering an avalanche of insecurities.

Why did I have to start feeling something for him—thinking it could be more than physical?

He's sent me a few texts here and there—short, casual, meaningless. Like he's sending them to some random woman he's trying to let down easy. Nothing suggests he's thinking about our lessons. It's like he dropped me at the curb, and I'm getting more and more distant in his rearview mirror.

Am I overthinking things? Overreacting? I'm the one who asked for the lessons. Is he waiting for me to tell him I'm ready for another one?

Damn. Why is this so difficult?

Imagine how awful it'd be if this had been a genuine relationship.

I'm actually out of the house for once. On my way to meet my friend April to attend a class on *The Modern Cremation Customer*. Not exactly enthralling stuff, but necessary to keep my license. Except for the annual convention held at a casino a few hours west of us, my father prefers to do as many of these courses as he's allowed online. I still prefer in-person lectures whenever I can. Who knows, maybe I'll meet an under-thirty-five single guy while I'm there.

I spot April as soon as I pull into the parking lot. In her bright, butter-yellow dress, she's hard to miss standing on the sidewalk in front of the entrance.

"Hi!" she shrieks and runs over the pavement to greet me as I step out of the car, holding my purse and a bag of supplies to get me through the morning. "I feel like I haven't seen you in forever." Her body collides with mine in an exuberant hug, a wash of gardenia and something earthier filling my nose as I return the embrace.

She holds me at arm's length. "You look so adorable. I love the pink dress." She fingers the collar of my black cardigan with pink edging. "This is too cute." A bright grin breaks out over her face as her gaze lands on my tiny black-and-gold *All men are cremated equal* pin. "Stop it!" she squeals. "Oh my God, that's hilarious for this class."

"I know, right?" I return the grin, lock my door and slam it shut. "I love the dress." I nod at her sleeveless cotton poplin dress with thick straps and a modest, square neckline. "Aren't you worried you'll be cold in there, though?"

She holds up a white-and-yellow tote bag. "I have a sweater in here."

As soon as we step into the large lecture room, we stand out. Almost all our peers are twenty or more years older and dressed in professional attire at the darker end of the spectrum. April and I circulate around the room for a few minutes, saying hello to colleagues. Most people know my father and ask how he's doing. We run into a few of our college classmates and after they share a few horror stories about job-hunting, guilt settles over me. I never had to worry about resumes and interviews.

"You okay?" April touches my shoulder.

"Oh, yes." I force a bright smile. "I think my dad's tough on me until I hear what everyone else is going through."

"Yeah, I think I got lucky too. I love my place. They're actually open to new suggestions and moving forward."

We find seats in the last row at the back of the room. The lights dim and I bend down to pull a small notepad and a pen out of my tote bag.

"Really?" April tips her head toward the paper.

"I need to do something with my hands."

The president of the Empire Funeral Directors Association steps up to the podium to welcome everyone. "Good morning…" I tune out until he gets to our speaker's bio. "…a third-generation funeral director…"

Just like me. My grandparents, my parents, and now me. It sounds so *weighty*. How did this guy transition into giving lectures instead?

"According to our industry's comprehensive cremation statistics," the lecturer's face shifts into a devilishly comedic smile, "cremation is the *burning desire* of a growing portion of our consumers."

The room vibrates with groans and chuckles. Tittering with my own laughter, I roll my eyes April's way. Her shoulders shake and she gestures toward the front of the room.

"We paid two hundred bucks for this," she whispers.

Two hours later, I'm dizzy with statistics and ideas for ways to offset the revenue losses from more people choosing cremation over casket burials.

"What'd you think?" April asks as we walk out to our cars.

"I wanted to ask if that shift is true in rural areas or just urban. His numbers didn't break it down."

"You're not seeing more cremations?"

Yes, but not legal ones.

That's not true. Besides the bikers' late-night usage of our crematorium, a lot of our customers have chosen that path lately. "There's been an uptick in clients choosing it but not the seismic shift he's talking about."

She shrugs. "You're probably right about the shift being slower in rural areas. I'm more interested in some of the green alternatives being developed. He didn't spend a lot of time on that. Just how to boost revenue for the industry."

"Well, yeah." There's one part of the business I'm more intimately acquainted with than April would be.

"What else have you been up to?" April asks with a saucy eyebrow lift. "Seeing anyone?"

I've never been the kind of girly-girl to talk about relationships with my friends or, God forbid, sex. Probably because none of them had been worth talking about. "Not really."

She leans closer. "Margot." Her stern friend voice rings loud and clear. "You're blushing. Who is it?"

"Just a guy." I give her a teasing push away. "But we don't really have anything in common."

"Is he hot?"

Burn down a barn hot. Why is my mouth twitching into a smile? "Yeah, kinda."

"So, who cares. Opposites attract, right?"

"Maybe. It was just…"

"Were you using him for sex?"

She's teasing, but the question stops me cold.

"Oh my God, were you?" she asks in an interested whisper.

Yes, I was. Holy shit, that's awful. No wonder Jigsaw decided he'd had enough.

"No. It's nothing." I squeeze her arm. "I really have to get back."

I take a short detour home, cruising by the Horizon Inn. What a shabby looking motel. I stop across the street and study the parking lot for a few minutes.

On the way home, my mind returns to Jigsaw. He said he didn't do relationships. Claimed he liked me and found me attractive for some reason. Gave me high marks in all of our lessons. So, was I really *using* him? Or was he using me? He promised to help me, then bailed. I was so stupid for asking him to do that in the first place. Who does that?

I pass the restaurant he took me to the night I was so distraught about Laurel, and it only makes me feel worse about the situation.

"Oh, Margot, I'm glad you're home." Dad steps out of his office to greet me as I come in the back door.

His urgent tone promptly drags my mind away from my Jigsaw dilemma.

I set my purse and tote bag on the bench by the door, and hurry toward Dad's office. "What do you need?"

"Can you give the bikers a call?" he asks. "We need that oversized casket brought upstairs. Paul's busy." Dad rests his hands on his lower back. "And I tweaked my back. I have a family coming by today and from what they said on the phone, I'll need to show them that one."

"Uh, I can move it," I offer, not sure how the heck I'll accomplish that all by myself. "No reason to make them ride all the way out here."

"Margot, it's heavy and awkward. You might get it on the gurney but guiding it into the elevator by yourself? No. Call them. Marcel said he'd make himself available to us as needed."

"All right."

"How was the lecture?" he asks.

"Interesting. The speaker had a lot of out of the box thinking and integrated some interesting ideas into his family's business."

A flicker of annoyance crosses my father's expression. "You'll have to tell me about it later."

"Oh, and Justin Packer says hello and said to give him a call."

He nods quickly. "That's good. I'm glad you spoke to some people there. How's April?"

"Good. Still likes her organization."

"That's good to hear." He winces. "I'm going to ice my back before the family gets here."

"Do you need help?"

"No. Just make that call for me." Still clutching his back, he walks by me, heading for the kitchen.

My stomach flips at the thought of reaching out to the club. At least I'm calling Teller and not Jigsaw. Based on all the people I saw at Teller's wedding, there are a *lot* of bikers in his club. What are the odds Jigsaw's the one sent here? The way I understood it, Jigsaw's home club is all the way down in Union. He's not the one who'd be sent here to do a favor for my dad, right?

Still, the thought nags at me. I don't want to face Jigsaw again when I have all these weird, unresolved feelings strangling my heart.

A deeper part of me, that I'd rather ignore, desperately wants to see him.

There's no getting out of this. Dad's right, we need to move that heavy casket and no one else on our team can do it right now. I sit behind my father's desk and reach for the phone, mentally preparing myself for whoever shows up and knocks on our door.

CHAPTER TWENTY-THREE

Jigsaw

RIDING NORMALLY HELPS CLEAR MY HEAD. WIND IN MY FACE, concentrating on the road. Always outrunning my past, though. Never moving *toward* something. The way I like it.

Or I used to.

Today, I'm riding to the upstate clubhouse. Their garages are bigger than what we have downstate. Stocked with more tools too. It's a better place to work on my bike, that's all. Nothing to do with its closer proximity to Pine Hollow.

First, I gotta pay my respects to the first Upstate brother I find in the clubhouse. I stomp up the steps and open the screen door. It's quiet. Not a soul in sight. Still feels like more of a home than Downstate has lately. That probably has something to do with the fuzzy blanket, carefully folded over the back of the leather sectional that takes up one entire corner of the large living room. Or the cozy, cutesy throw pillows tossed into the corners. Downstate, we have a jizz-covered pool table, buckets of condoms on the end tables, and our "art" consists of "humorous" signs reminding you to "wrap your banana" nailed to the wall.

Low voices murmur from one of the closed doors on my right. I step up to the first one and cock my head, concentrating on the voices. Murphy?

I tap my knuckles against the wood.

A second later the door swings open. Murphy grins at me.

"What's up, brother?" He holds out his hand. I clasp it and he pulls me toward him. "Good to see you."

He steps aside. Rock and Teller are also in the office. Rock nods at me. Teller reaches out for a handshake but neither of them get up. The office is big but not big enough for the four of us to be throwing our arms around each other.

"What brings you by?" Rock asks.

"Uh, I was hoping you wouldn't mind if I borrowed the garage to do a little work."

Rock pulls a face like it's an absurd request. "Of course you can. You don't have to ask."

"Thanks."

"You need help with anything?" Murphy asks.

"You miss being road captain that much?" I ask.

He throws a quick glance at Rock. "I'm gonna plead the fifth on that one."

"Yeah, yeah." Rock flicks his gaze to the ceiling. "I'm *so* hard on them." He circles one finger in Teller and Murphy's general direction. "Yet, somehow they always come find me."

It's said with more affection than annoyance. Still, Teller groans and shakes his head.

"It's all right, Rock." My lips curl into a smirk. "You're just like the big lion that all the other cubs want to frolic around."

Murphy pats his chest. "Who are you calling a cub?"

"Speaking of lions." Teller sits up, his chair creaking from the sudden movement. "Did you ever talk to Eraser and find out why Quill's been out at Zips so much lately?"

Fuck. No, I haven't. I've been too busy pining over Margot and taking care of my Downstate responsibilities.

"No, I didn't have a chance yet. But I can head out there now."

"Maybe Quill just needs friends." Murphy shrugs. "I don't see the big deal."

"It's not a problem unless he's gambling with fake cash there," Teller says. "The kids don't need that kind of attention on them."

Inside, I'm laughing at Teller referring to Griff, Remy, and Eraser as "kids." He really does sound like Rock's mini-me. Outside, I keep my face blank.

Rock tilts his head to look at me. "Sit. Take Wrath's chair." He points to the desk opposite his.

"Uh—"

"He's at Furious, he'll never know your butt cheeks touched the leather," Murphy jokes, correctly reading my hesitation.

"Touch this." I flip him off and drop into the seat, stretching out my legs.

Murphy throws himself into his chair and spins it in a half circle like he's five.

Rock pins me with a hard stare. "Don't worry about Quill now. Let's focus on getting everyone to Digger's memorial and home, then we'll worry about whatever fuckery is going on out there."

"Club first," I say.

A savage smile crosses Rock's face. "Right."

Teller slides his gaze to Murphy. "Don't get your briefs in a knot—"

"I'm not wearing briefs." Murphy rubs his hand over his crotch. "Heidi says it could inhibit sperm production."

I burst out laughing. Rock groans. Teller just glares at Murphy.

"What?" Murphy's eyes widen like he's the poster boy for innocence. "She wants to try for a boy next."

"Christ, don't you have enough kids, yet?" I ask.

Murphy side-eyes me. "No."

Ignoring the spermicidal detour, Rock focuses on Teller. "What were you going to say?"

"What if Eraser is working *with* Quill? Griff and Remy said there haven't been any issues but what if it's because they all know what Quill's up to."

"No. Griff wouldn't have lied right to my face about it." Murphy shakes his head. "Remy wouldn't either."

"Griff said Quill's out there to race, that's it," I say. "Doesn't party with them or anything. Remy says Quill always wins his races." I flick my gaze to Teller. "So if he's trying to wash his fake cash through Zips, it's a shitty way to do it. The couple of bucks he pays for the entrance fees isn't going to move the amount of paper his family's operation is known for."

Rock stares at me for so long, I wonder if I should've kept my mouth shut.

"Good point," he finally says. "You think he's looking to earn their respect."

"Yes." I nod quickly. "But why?"

"Yeah, I don't see a city boy like Quill caring about the opinions of a bunch of hillbilly fighters racing cars in the backwoods of New York," Murphy says.

"Who are you calling a hillbilly?" I ask.

Murphy touches both hands to his chest. "Myself too. I'm just sayin', that's how he probably sees all of us up here."

"You might be right. But he thought enough of us to give up one of his crew to set things right with Grinder," Rock says. "And to ask permission to go through our territory."

"Well, Chaser made him do *that*," Teller says. "But he was supposed to be running his product into Montreal. Johnsonville's a bit of a detour."

"Not if he's running out to visit Chaser," I point out. "Doing some brotherly bonding and getting some racing in on the way home?"

"That's possible." Rock glances at Teller, then Murphy, but I don't think he's looking for them to add to the conversation. "Let's circle back to this after the Deadbranch run."

Great, can't wait to go stick my nose in some wannabe cartel kingpin's business.

The phone on Teller's desk buzzes. Teller grabs it, glancing at the screen then relaxing. "It's Cedarwood."

My skin prickles.

"Take it," Rock says.

"Hello?" Teller answers. "Hey, Margot."

My heart thunders. *Fuck.* Staying away from her hasn't made me want her any less. My entire body's strung tight just knowing she's on the other end of that phone call.

"Not a problem, darlin'."

The urge to punch Teller for calling her darlin' like he's talking to a random club whore takes control of my fist. I sit forward, straining to hear her voice through the phone.

"Bro, you good?" Murphy frowns at me.

"Huh? Yeah." I force myself to relax.

"Give me two hours," Teller says. "Yeah, okay. See you in a bit."

"What's wrong?" I ask with way too much eagerness in my voice.

Rock and Teller share a look. Christ, could I be more obvious?

"Nothing. She said they need some help moving stuff. Her dad hurt his back. Needs it done today—"

"I'll go with you," I offer.

Murphy snickers into his fist.

"Yeaaah..." Teller draws out the word like he's not sure if he wants me to tag along. "Okay."

His phone goes off again. This time it plays the notes of "You Are My Sunshine." Christ, he's a sappy bastard. "It's Charlotte," Teller says as he answers the call.

"Hey, Sunshine, what's—"

The three of us stare at Teller. Still listening to whatever Charlotte's saying on the other end, he jumps out of his chair.

"Okay. I'm on my way home now. Yup. Did you call your doctor's office?"

Rock and Murphy both stand too, crowding Teller, trying to listen in on the conversation.

Teller ends the call, stuffing his phone in his pocket. "I gotta go."

"What's wrong?" Rock asks.

"She's not...feeling right." Teller shakes his head. "It's too early for her to be in labor." He glances at me. "Can you take care of whatever Margot needs?"

Already taken care of quite a few of her needs, mini-Rock.

"Yeah. No problem." My humor won't be appreciated here, and I don't want to risk Rock asking someone else to go. "I'll see if Dex can come with me."

Teller blows out a breath. "Thanks."

"Go take care of your family." I slap his back. "I got this."

The three of them take off together. Poor Charlotte, she's not just getting her husband, she'll have two other bossy bikers hovering around her too.

And I'm going to see Margot.

Hopefully she won't kick me in the balls for keeping my distance.

CHAPTER TWENTY-FOUR

Margot

TELLER SAID HE'D BE HERE IN TWO HOURS. TWO HOURS TO FRET OVER whether or not I'm going to see Jigsaw.

Just in case he *is* one of the bikers who shows up, I run upstairs and add another pin to my sweater. To anyone else, they'll either seem odd or won't even be noticed.

But Jigsaw *will* notice and get the message.

The deafening roar of more than one motorcycle riding through the neighborhood twists my stomach in knots. It's a rare sound in our area. Most likely the Lost Kings are here.

I hurry downstairs, my hand gripping the banister the whole way. The fluttering in my stomach won't stop. The rumbling engines seem to cease at the front of the house. Good. That must mean it's not Jigsaw. He always parks in the back.

But when I finally reach the first floor, voices and footsteps over the back porch indicate we have company.

I swing the door open before either of them knocks or rings the bell.

The tall, older biker, Dex I think is his name, has his hand poised to ring the doorbell. His jaw drops for a second, then he smiles.

Jigsaw's leaner frame peeks out from behind Dex's bulkier one. His heated gaze travels over me so fast, my skin tingles.

I force the warmest, fakest smile possible and hold the screen door open wider. "Afternoon, gentlemen. Thank you so much for coming over."

Dex sweeps his gaze over me, not in a gross way, like most men, just observing. His eyes land on my pins. The corner of his mouth curls up and he snorts.

Our eyes meet and I wink at him. Looks like Jigsaw isn't the only man who gets my sense of humor.

"Come in." I wave them over the threshold, although I'd really rather slam the door in Jigsaw's face.

He stares at the pins and frowns. *Ha! Good.*

I spin away from them, leading them down the long hallway to our left and the door to our storage and initial prep room downstairs.

Damn, I'm being rude. They *did* ride a long way to do a pretty basic chore for my family *and* arrived in under two hours. I shouldn't let Jigsaw's behavior get under my skin.

This is what he meant by our involvement leading to trouble, isn't it?

I face Dex and give him a more sincere smile.

"Thank you so much for coming all the way out here. I know it's a long ride for you both."

"Not a problem, darlin'," Jigsaw drawls in the most obnoxious way possible and slaps his hand on Dex's shoulder.

Dex flicks an irritated glare at his brother.

"Margot, you remember my brother, Dex, right?"

Two can play the obnoxious game.

"Oh *yes.* Dex," I coo, drawing his name out in a way that I hope sounds seductive but probably comes out a bit unhinged. "Of course. I'd *never* forget such a handsome face with such excellent bone structure." I reach up and cup his bristly chin. "Just excellent."

Dex stares at me like I've lost my mind. Maybe I have.

"Yeah." Jigsaw nudges Dex with his elbow. "My brother's very vain. He's had a lot of plastic surgery and Botox."

Oh my God. Is he really that jealous of some harmless flirting? He's the one who's ghosted *me.*

"I can tell that's not true. Don't be jealous." I reach up and pat his cheek like he's nothing more than an annoyance. "Your bone structure is *lovely* too."

Dex has had enough of our back and forth. "Lovely." He snorts. "Clearly you haven't spent a lot of time with him."

Not lately.

Jigsaw

Punishment has never been my kink. Taking Margot's verbal barbs, though, is kinda fucking hot. She's pissed. As she should be. But she's still polite for Dex's sake. I think if I'd come alone, she would've slammed the door in my face.

My greedy gaze sucks her in. She's so fucking perfect. She's even wearing some of her cute little pins today.

One looks like a bottle of glass cleaner? That's odd.

I squint at it, trying to read the tiny print. *Fuckboi repellent.*

The fuck?

She trots down the stairs ahead of us. I grab Dex to stop him.

"What's wrong?" Dex asks.

"Did one of those pins on her collar say *fuckboy repellent?*" I whisper.

His lips twist into a smirk. "Yeah, she must've worn it just for you."

How dare she. I told her from the beginning I didn't do relationships. What exactly did she think that meant? "I'm not a fuckboy."

Dex scowls like he can't believe we're having this conversation. "You're the literal definition of a fuckboy." He shoves me through the doorway.

"Nooo," I protest, loud enough for Margot to hear me. "A fuckboy is self-absorbed and even though he has lots of sex, he's *bad* at it. And, this part's important, he also fucks with a woman's emotions." I start down the stairs but glance over my shoulder to make sure Dex is listening. "I'm sensitive to a woman's needs, *stellar* in bed, and always honest about my intentions…to never see them again."

I jump off the last step, startling Margot who's waiting for us with an irritated expression wrinkling her pretty face.

She glares at me.

I glare right back.

Fuckboy, huh? I shift my gaze to the pin again. Actually, it reads *Fuckboi repellent*, which is even worse. It's offensive to me *and* the English language.

I resent the fuck out of *this* little inside joke. And I have no doubt she wore it for my benefit. She's way too professional to wear that at work for funsies.

Dex groans. "With the amount of brainpower you've spent on this, you could've ended world hunger, Father Fuckboy."

"Your dissertation on fuckboys was enlightening." She taps the pin on her collar and gives us a smug chin lift, like she's accomplished her mission. "I'm pleased one of my pins sparked such a *fascinating* discussion."

I bet you are.

I glance at the other pin. *All men are cremated equal.* Which is probably her way of saying she'd like to toss me in the retort and roast me alive.

"Come on." She waves her hand over her shoulder and marches forward. Lights blink on as we walk through the cavernous storage area. Just how big is this fucking house?

"Back here," she calls out.

We find her standing next to a huge black-and-silver casket.

"Now, *that's* a biker's casket." I nod at the big, fancy tomb. "If I didn't want to be cremated and tossed in the ocean, I'd want my carcass to spend eternity in something like *this*," I joke.

Margot suddenly looks like she's going to cry. "Don't say that."

I'm sorry.

I really wish Dex wasn't here.

"Anyway." Her back-to-business tone buries the awkward moment. "Would you mind moving this upstairs for me?"

She leads us to the freight elevator. How the fuck does this house have a fucking *freight elevator* in it? My stomach churns. I hate elevators. Especially ancient rickety ones in creepy, surprisingly large, old houses.

She rolls over a trolley for us to set the casket on.

Dex lifts his chin at me, indicating he wants me to pick a side.

"Yeah, I got this end." The casket has big silver handles on it, and even though it seems abnormally large, it's easier to lift than I expected. "Why is this so big?"

"It's an over-sized one for our larger customers," Margot explains like a perfect salesperson. "They're becoming more and more popular."

Oversized caskets? Seriously? "They make special caskets for big bastards?" I blurt.

"Please don't speak like that," Margot scolds. "We treat all of our customers with dignity and respect."

Fuck. I know how damn serious she takes all of this. "Sorry," I mumble. *For so many things.* "Just took me by surprise."

We ease the trolley and the casket into the elevator which is bigger than it looks but still a steel death-box as far as I'm concerned. It's not even well lit. Dex ends up pressed against the back wall. Better him than me.

Reluctantly, I step over the threshold. My hip bumps into the edge of the casket and I wince. Then a worse thought occurs to me than being trapped in an elevator.

Bring trapped in an elevator with a dead body.

The doors slowly slide closed. "Wait." I slap my hand against the door, holding it in place. "There isn't a body in here, right?" I point to the casket.

The smile Margot gives me is downright evil. "Maybe, maybe not."

The door slides shut, almost snapping my arm in half.

This is my worst nightmare.

Margot

The stark-naked fear on Jigsaw's face when the elevator doors close sends guilt arrowing straight through my heart. I shouldn't have teased him about the casket having a body in it. That was rude and unprofessional.

Maybe he's claustrophobic? Lord knows, I've had a couple of experiences with that elevator, including getting stuck in it when I was a kid. To this day, I use it as little as possible.

I pull the door next to the elevator open and jog up the narrow stairway. The elevator isn't soundproof, so bits of Dex and Jigsaw's conversation follow me up the stairs.

"Bro, if I tell you something, you promise not to laugh?" Jigsaw's strained voice sounds like it's coming from inside a tin can.

"I'll do my best." Dex's tired annoyance comes through his voice.

"And if you bring it up once we're outside this box, I'll fuckin' punch you," Jigsaw warns. So low I barely make out the words, he adds, "This is my absolute worst nightmare."

How could I do this to him?

It would've taken me five seconds to reassure him it was a brand-new, *empty* casket.

Dex seems to calm him with some deep-breathing exercises. That doesn't alleviate my guilt, though.

I'm standing in front of the elevator doors when they finally open. "We're going that way," I say a bit more professionally.

I lead them to the showroom that's full of other caskets and urns. Jigsaw casts a look around and shivers.

He's probably thinking he dodged a bullet by shaking me loose now. I just wish he'd told me he didn't want to see me anymore. Ended things cleanly. At least that would've made *this* situation a lot less awkward.

"What do you do for fun, Margot?" Jigsaw asks.

None of your business. I'm not his problem anymore. "Go to bars, pick up strange men, and bring them here for sex." I wave my hand toward a white casket with pink lining. "The lucky ones get to go home when I'm done with them."

Count your lucky stars, fucker.

I spin on my heel and walk out of the room. The guys follow me to the front of the house. I open the door wide, indicating I'm not in the mood for chitchat.

Manners. "Oh! I need to pay you something. I'm so sorry." I should've stopped by my father's office to grab some cash instead of letting Jigsaw's presence work me into a snit.

"We're not taking money from you." Dex holds up his hands.

"But it was a long drive."

"Ride," Jigsaw corrects. "And we're good. Thanks for the offer, though."

I open my mouth to protest but they slip past me. Jigsaw slows his steps, his arm brushing against my side. He gives me a look that's full of longing or sorrow, I can't tell.

Or maybe it's just my wishful thinking.

I quietly close the door. For reasons that have nothing to do with being professional, I can't bring myself to slam it in his handsome face.

CHAPTER TWENTY-FIVE

Jigsaw

MY SASSY LITTLE LADY DEATH WITH HER OH-SO-FUNNY FUCKBOY JOKES.

I can't wait to get my hands on her again.

Fuckboy. I should've been insulted that she implied I've been out fucking everything in sight. But I like the way her husky voice tickles my ears too much. Even when she's making fun of me and bestowing compliments on Dex. Fine bone structure my ass.

I definitely need to go back and see her. Try to make things right.

What's the point?

The club's riding to Deadbranch soon. I'll be gone for at least a week. Why start something up and then leave her again?

The entire way back to the clubhouse I'm at war with myself. Dex and I take over the empty war room for a while to go over the route we'll take to Deadbranch for Digger's memorial service.

After we wrap that up, it's still early. Dex heads back to Crystal Ball.

I consider working in the garage, like I'd originally planned to do this afternoon. But I can't stop thinking about Margot. She needed us to move that big-ass casket upstairs. She must be busy with work.

I shouldn't bother her. Not when she basically just accused me of being a fuckboy. And tried to make me jealous by implying she's fucking randoms now. Which I know she absolutely isn't doing. We only made it through half of lesson two.

Before I know it, I'm back on my bike headed to Pine Hollow for the second time today. At least all this extra riding will prepare me for the long ride to Deadbranch.

Shit, I need to warn Margot we're all going to be away.

If that's all I'm going to say to her, I can send it in a text. Or remind Teller to do it. Shit, I should've texted him to let him know everything was fine at Margot's and ask how Charlotte's doing.

The exit for Slater's rapidly approaching.

Get off, or keep riding?

I veer onto the off-ramp. Christ, I hate it out here. So many twisty, narrow roads full of cars half-assedly parked at the curb before the wider rural roads leading out to Pine Hollow and Margot's neighborhood.

Four cars I don't recognize are in the parking lot when I arrive. I tuck my bike in a nook against the house and jog up the porch steps.

The screen door opens with a screech. I pause with my hand wrapped around the brass knob of the inner door. Loud argumentative voices seep outside.

I cock my head, trying to make out any words.

Shrill screams rise above the other noise.

"Fuck this." I twist the knob and enter the house as silently as possible.

"Dad wanted to be cremated!" a woman screams. "He would not stand for this! He would hate this!"

"He's not here!" a man roars. "We need to honor him."

Two more people add their grievances.

Holy shit, is this the kind of fuckery Margot deals with on the regular?

Her soft voice murmurs soothing words I can't make out from here. Is she alone with these crazy people? I creep along the hallway toward her father's office where the voices are coming from.

Mr. Cedarwood's calm, authoritative tone rises above the rest of

the chatter. I slow my steps. Thank fuck Margot's not dealing with that by herself.

Still, I continue until I'm right outside Cedarwood's office. The door's open and I quickly walk past, sneaking a look inside. Margot's on the small couch holding the hand of a sobbing woman. She looks up and our eyes meet. Her jaw drops, then she quickly composes herself and returns her attention to the woman. Three other people are either sitting on chairs or standing.

Margot's okay. That's all I care about.

"Can you go see who that is, Margot?" Cedarwood says. "Were we expecting someone else?"

"Ah, sure." Margot murmurs something I can't make out and a few seconds later steps into the hallway.

Her flaming eyes land on me and she marches my way. God damn she's cute when she's riled.

"What are you doing here?" She grabs my arm and pushes me toward a large room with a hideous patterned rug and lots of chairs.

She reaches behind her and slides a pocket door shut.

"Why did you come back?" She crosses her arms over her chest and glares. "I'm with a family."

"I heard." My gaze skims over her, noting she removed her clever little pins. "Where's your fuckboy repellent?" I flick my finger against the collar of her pink-and-black cardigan.

She lifts her chin. "I didn't need it for *this* consultation. Why are you here?"

Because I think I'm falling in love with you, you adorably bonkers woman. "I want to talk to you."

"So. Use. The. Phone." She enunciates each word slowly, like she's speaking to a toddler.

"You know I only said that shit before so Dex wouldn't think anything's going on between us."

"*Nothing's* been going on between us for weeks." She lifts her chin and huffs. "But you're right. You were honest from the beginning that you don't do relationships. I'm sorry if something I did made you feel like I wanted you to be my boyfriend."

Boyfriend. My entire body cringes. I'm not boyfriend material.

But I want her so fucking much.

A spark of mischief lights up her eyes and tilts her lips to the side. "Your little fuckboy dissertation was flawed, though."

"Is that right?" I take a step closer, staring down at her, closing in like a predator. "How so?"

"'Stellar in bed' means you would've left me *satisfied*, and, well..." She raises a mocking eyebrow and shrugs.

"The fuck I didn't." I lean down and whisper in her ear, "Last time I left here, my chin was dripping with your scent, you little liar."

Her chest rises and falls faster, and she braces her hand against my chest, as if she wants to push me away but can't find the strength.

After a few seconds, she lifts her head and glares into my eyes. "You should've warned me you don't honor your commitments."

That's right, you know I left you satisfied. Wait, commitments? "Honor my...*what*?"

"Our *lessons*." She practically snarls the word. "We weren't finished."

Never had someone so angry they didn't get to suck my dick.

The corners of my mouth turn up. "You still *want* your lessons?"

She lets out an indignant sniff. "No."

Yes, she does. Or she would've kicked me out by now. Can I do this? Be her actual fuckboy? Teach her everything she wants to learn, knowing we're never going to be more?

"You didn't find anyone else to teach you?" I rest my hands on her shoulders as if my touch can act as some sort of human lie detector.

She shrugs me off and glances away. "I haven't had the time."

Bullshit. She doesn't *want* anyone else.

Keen awareness that there's an office full of people less than a hundred feet away waiting for her to return slaps me into reality. "Can we talk when you're done?"

Her gaze strays to the closed door. "I don't know how long this is going to take."

"I'll wait."

She glances around the room, then sighs. "Okay. You can wait upstairs. Keep Gretel company for a while."

I chuckle. Is the cat pissed at me too? "How do I get in? I thought it was a biometric lock?"

She clenches her jaw. "There's a button on the side. If you press it, a keypad pops up. The code is," she leans closer and whispers, "sixty-five-ninety-eight."

Who is she worried about overhearing us? The ghosts?

"Got it."

"You don't want to write it on your hand or something?" she sneers.

I flick my gaze to hers and add some frost to my answer. "No."

"I have to get back." She grips my arm, just a slight, friendly amount of pressure. But fuck, I've missed her hands on me. "It really might take a while." She gestures toward her dad's office. "It's kind of messy."

"Sounds like it. You need me to stay down here for protection?"

She seems to consider it for a few seconds. "No. It'll be okay."

"Want me to run out and get something for dinner?"

"You don't have to." She shrugs, then brightens. "There's only one place that delivers pizza out here. We have a menu in the kitchen down the hall."

I wanted to do something nicer than pizza, but it'll have to do. "Okay. Any requests?"

"They make really good calzones. Just ask for extra sauce. They have a sausage and peppers pizza that's good too."

"You go there a lot?"

"At least once a week."

"Okay."

I want to lean down and kiss her, but she still looks prickly. Instead, I nod and take a step back, giving her space. "You finish with the Jerry Springer bunch, and I'll order some food."

She flicks her gaze to the ceiling. "This is one of the ones where... ugh!" She squeezes her hands together in front of her face like she's choking someone.

"You sure you don't want me to stay down here? In case you need me to escort someone out?"

It must be bad because she considers the offer a bit longer this time.

"No, it'll be too hard to explain why you're here to my dad."

God forbid you tell him we're—yeah, I get why she wouldn't want to tell him we're fuck buddies.

"If you need me, text."

She seems to relax a fraction, a hint of the Margot I've missed making an appearance. "Thank you." She steps closer and rests her hand on my arm. "I'm glad you're here."

Why is it so easy for her to say how she feels when I couldn't do it if I had a gun to my head?

After she returns to the appointment, I slip into the parlor across the hall so I don't have to pass Cedarwood's office again. I push through the swinging door and search the kitchen for the pizza place menu.

Calzones. Chicken wings. Pizza. *Fuck it.* I order a bunch of stuff, give them my card number, then head upstairs.

The code works on her door, and I push my way inside.

Gretel's sitting by the entry closet, flicking her tail as if she's annoyed no one's been around to entertain her.

"Hey, girl," I murmur, crouching down to pet her. "Miss me?"

She stares at me, allows me to stroke my hand over her back once, then turns around and walks away, tail held high in the air.

"I guess I deserve that." I shrug off my cut and hang it in the closet.

It's weird to be in Margot's space without her. That she trusts me enough to leave me alone in her apartment when she's not here feels like we're already building back our relation—whatever this is.

Or she didn't want you to wait downstairs where her father might see you.

I take off my boots and leave them near the closet, then pad into the kitchen. Good thing I ordered so much food, her fridge is full of sparkling water, eggs, and not much else.

I grab a bottle of water, unscrew it and take a quick sip. My gaze lands on the lounge chair. The place of our first "lesson." Maybe I'll strip down, pose on the lounger, and greet her like something out of a bad porno when she gets back.

Nah, too soon.

There really isn't anywhere else to sit, though.

I sink into the chair. Margot's scent is all around me—a mixture of something floral and crisp. Underneath that, a faint pungent scent like vinegar lingers. Chemicals from her job? I've never noticed it before. Gretel jumps up and curls herself into a ball next to me. I absently stroke my fingers over her fur. After a while, her purring kicks into high gear.

I pull out my phone and check the restaurant app. The food hasn't even left the place yet. Then I send Teller a text letting him know things are okay here and ask if Charlotte's okay.

A few seconds later, he responds.

Teller: We're good. Thx for taking care of that.

The stack of books on the table next to me grabs my attention and I set my phone down.

Deadly Women Throughout History, Encyclopedia of Serial Killers, Handbook of Crime Scene Forensics, Investigation of Death, and *History of Poison.*

What the ever-loving fuck is she into?

None of those are light, fluffy books to unwind with after a long day of caring for dead people. They're death-adjacent but not quite related to her work.

Curious, I pull myself out of the chair and walk over to the bookcases. More non-fiction on these shelves. Lots and lots of true crime books, chemistry books, some books on burial customs and funeral rites. At least they all sound like normal titles for someone in her profession. Further down, she has a collection of romance novels. I pull out a few titles to see if Trinity has designed any of the covers or if I recognize the models. One copyright page lists Trinity H. Ramsey as the photographer and designer. And even though the bulky, muscled and oiled model on the front is only pictured from chin to abs, I'd bet my Harley it's Wrath.

I grab my phone, take a quick picture, and send it to Rooster.

Me: Found one in the wild. Should I send to Wrath?

Rooster responds with a row of laughing face emojis.

Instead of antagonizing Wrath, I send the photo to Trinity with the same "found in the wild" caption, knowing how excited she'll be to see her work on someone's shelf.

Two texts come in at the same time.

Rooster: Where are you?

Trinity: OMG! Where?

That was a mistake. I don't bother answering either one.

The door clicks open behind me.

I shove the book back on the shelf and jam my phone in my pocket.

Margot steps inside. The fiery edge she had earlier seems to have disappeared, replaced with something more vulnerable and *tired*. Tired of the world and tired of bullshit. Probably my bullshit in particular.

"Hey, that was quicker than I expected," I greet her. "The food isn't here yet."

She closes her door and rubs her temples. "They finally settled on the casket you guys brought upstairs for us," she rasps. "So, thank you again for doing that."

I want to go to her and wrap her up in my arms, but I also want her to come to me to look for comfort. "Not a problem."

Gretel runs to Margot and twirls around her legs for a few seconds, then runs away again.

My phone buzzes and I pull it out. "Food's on its way. I'm going to run downstairs." I pause. "That okay or am I going to run into your dad?"

"No, he went home. Paul's around though, but he won't mind if you're here." She tugs her cardigan off. "I'm going to change."

"Okay." I meet her by the door. She stares up at me, expecting what?

Fuck it. I need her body against mine. I pull her into my arms. At first, she's stiff and resistant. But then she softens and slides her arms around my waist.

The hard knot of tension in my chest finally loosens. I've missed having her in my arms.

"I'm sorry I called you a fuckboy," she murmurs against my chest.

Deep, rumbling laughter eases out of me. I kiss the top of her head. "I'm sorry I've been acting like one."

Margot

Danger. I shouldn't trust Jigsaw again. But he's here now. He came back. That's enough. I'm a big girl. It's not his responsibility to protect my heart.

Hugging him, being held against his body feels too good. Familiar, comfortable, exciting. A spark I haven't felt since the last time I saw him lights me up inside.

His phone dings.

I pull away as he grabs it and checks the screen. "Food's here." He squeezes my shoulder. "I'll be right back."

"Okay." I hurry into my bedroom and strip off my dress, hanging it on a hook by my closet. I slip into a loose pair of soft, stretchy pants and a T-shirt.

For several stomach-churning moments, I stand frozen in my bedroom. Should I have put on something nicer? Sexier?

What are we going to talk about?

I'm in the kitchen gathering dishes and silverware when Jigsaw returns, holding a stack of white cardboard boxes and a grease-stained white paper bag. "How much did you order?"

He sets the pile on my counter and rubs his fingers over his chest. "A little bit of everything."

I pull down my prettiest plates. Cream stoneware with black leaves and acorns around the edges. I've only had a chance to use them once since I bought them. Did he get drinks too? I pluck my tall black beaded glass tumblers down, setting them on the counter with a *thud*.

Jigsaw comes up behind me and slides his hands over my hips, pressing himself against my back. Warmth pulses against my exposed shoulder and neck as he leans over and drags his lips against my sensitive skin. Sensation shoots straight to my nipples and I sigh, leaning against him.

"Is this lesson number three?" I ask between shaky breaths.

He withdraws his hands and cold air rushes in to replace his warmth. "Dinnertime." He pats my behind and reaches past me to grab the plates.

What just happened?

I take the glasses and follow him to the other side of the counter. "I'm sorry I don't have a proper dining table. I never bothered—"

"It's fine." He eases onto one of the high stools and pats his hand on the other one. "Come sit next to me."

"Of course." I hop up, twisting the swiveling seat so our knees touch. "Show me what you got."

He flicks open one of the smaller boxes. "Calzone. You didn't specify what fillings you like, so I just got plain cheese and ricotta."

My mouth waters. "That's my favorite. I usually only eat half, though."

"Good to know." He sets the calzone on my plate, then locates a small container of sauce and sets it in front of me.

"I feel like nothing else will be as exciting now," he teases, opening up a white plastic container. "Hot wings. Pepperoni pizza. I'm a pretty basic fella."

"I like basic." I tap the perfectly golden crust of my calzone. "This is really just a big pizza pocket."

I cut the calzone in half and twirl my fork in the gooey cheese that oozes out. "Do you want half?"

"I'll try a piece."

I cut one piece into half and use my fork to set it on his plate.

"Thanks."

I thought I'd be nervous sharing a meal with him in my house but it's easy and cozy. From going out before, I already know he never comments or criticizes what or how much I eat.

Dinner isn't completely anxiety free. I only end up eating a quarter of my calzone and barely taste any of it. What we're hopefully going to do afterward has me bubbling over with excitement and a bit of fear. It should be my turn to go down on *him*.

I'm going to suck—*ha!*—at it and need a lot of instruction. Shame beats against me. He's probably had, I don't even want to think of how many women, do this for him who knew what they were doing. How's he supposed to relax and actually enjoy it if he has to stop and give me pointers every few seconds?

"You're not hungry?" he asks.

"I am." I slant a look at him. "For something off-menu."

He drops the half-eaten slice of pizza on his plate, grabs his drink and takes a long swallow. "Let's go."

Giddy and a little nervous, I take his hand and lead him into my bedroom. He closes the door behind us, then uses his bigger body to press me against the wall.

"What do you want tonight?" he asks, staring down at me.

"To make you feel good."

"I always feel good around you. What else?"

I blink, letting his first statement sink in. "I want to learn how to make you come with my mouth." I stick my tongue out at him in case that wasn't clear enough.

"Don't worry. You're going to put that fucking tongue to work." He tilts my head and seals his lips over mine. Our tongues clash and slide together. He snakes his hand under my shirt and pulls it up over my head, unhooking my bra before I've caught my breath.

I work at his belt buckle but still can't figure it out. His lips curl with amusement and he finally takes over. As soon as it's out of my way, I unbutton his jeans and carefully tug his zipper down. He strips his jeans off and kicks them toward my bed.

"Please?" I slide my hand under his T-shirt.

He stares at me for a long moment, then grips my shoulders and turns us so he's the one leaning against the wall. "Pants off." He nods to me.

I quickly shimmy out of them and fall to my knees. Like I stumbled into the sexiest underwear commercial ever, he crosses his arms and grips the hem of his shirt, slowly dragging it up and over his head.

Dear lord, he's a perfect masterpiece of muscle and tattooed skin. I kneel up and slide my fingertips over ridges of defined muscle then trace the strip of hair that runs from his belly button underneath his boxer-briefs. His stomach muscles flex and ripple quicker as my finger stops at the waistband.

"I'll have to do this more than once, you know." I slide my hands over his thighs—so firm and strong.

"Yeah?" He reaches down and cups my chin, rubbing his thumb against my bottom lip. "Why's that?"

"Once to train me—"

A sharp scowl crosses his face. "You're not a *dog*."

"To *teach* me how to do it right," I continue. "And then again so you can actually enjoy it."

His eyes close for a second. "Margot, please believe me when I say, if your mouth is wrapped around my cock, I'm going to be enjoying the fuck out of it."

"Oh."

"You're overthinking this." He cups my face, gently caressing my cheek. "Unless you try to bite my dick off, there really isn't a wrong way."

I blink, unsure of how to respond to that or the image his words bring to mind.

"Go ahead." His eyes darken as I curl my fingers under the waistband and tug his boxer-briefs.

Impatient or wanting to demonstrate, he pushes the briefs down and withdraws his hard length. Up close like this, he seems bigger, more of a challenge. My mouth waters and I yank his briefs all the way down his legs.

"Something about them offend you?" he asks, wrapping his fingers around himself and slowly stroking up and down.

"I want to admire your legs." I lean in and brush a kiss against the inside of his knee, then higher.

His body trembles as I slowly kiss my way to him. He's watching me with an unreadable expression that makes my stomach lurch.

"Did I do something wrong?" I ask. He kissed and teased my legs and I loved it. Maybe men don't like that.

"Not at all." He reaches for me. "Come here."

"But." I tease the tip of my tongue against the head of his cock. "I'm right *here* and you're—"

"Not like this. Come here," he says in a firmer tone.

"But I thought that's what men prefer."

He squeezes his eyes closed for a second. "Some do. I don't. I told you you'll have to ask...communicate. . .come *here*." Frustration burns through his command.

I take his hand and he yanks me up and into his arms. Unable to help myself, I wrap my hand around his cock, stroking him.

He sucks in a quick breath and maneuvers us toward the bed. Dropping down on the edge, he leans over and grabs one of my pillows, tossing it on the floor at his feet.

I kneel on it and look him in the eye. "Is this better?"

He grabs my face and smashes his lips to mine, kissing me deeply before breaking away. "Yes. I needed to kiss you."

"Oh." Heat fans across my skin.

I shuffle closer, my breasts grazing his thighs. He leans back on his hands and lifts his chin. I'm distracted by his ab muscles rippling as he casually waits.

"Go ahead. I'll give you instructions as needed."

"Hmmm." I wrap my hands around him. "But I requested formal training, Professor Orgasm."

He lets out a low, rough laugh. "What?"

"You heard me." I increase the pressure and he hisses.

"Use your tongue," he urges.

"Where?" I sneak down and tease the tip of my tongue against his thigh. "Here?" I dart a quick lick against his other one.

His stomach muscles flex and ripple as he struggles between laughing and panting. "No."

I catch his eye and stick my tongue out, taking a long, slow, deliberate lick along the underside of his cock, from root to tip.

"Oh, fuck," he groans and closes his eyes.

"Here?" I ask innocently.

His eyes slowly open and he stares down at me. "Now you've got it."

I tease my tongue over him again, then suck him into my mouth.

"Yes," he groans and rests one hand on my shoulder. "That's my girl."

Encouraged, I take more and more of him, until I cough and gag, then retreat.

"Easy." He reaches for my breast, teasing and lightly pinching my nipple.

I alternate between sucking and licking. Taking as much of him as I can then only concentrating on the head of his cock and the very sensitive spot at the tip. His shaky breathing and rocking hips give me all the instruction I need.

He snakes his other arm between us and kneads my breasts. Bolts of pleasure dance from my nipples to my clit. Between his attention to my body and his whispered affirmations of "just like that" and "good girl" my body's humming with need.

I slip one hand between my legs and touch myself.

"Fuck yes," he whispers excitedly. "Play with your clit for me. Do you like sucking my cock?"

I try to nod but end up whimpering something I hope he understands as *very much.*

His body pulls tight and his hips move faster. Is he close? A flutter of nerves skitters over me. I don't want to choke if he comes in my mouth. Suddenly, that's all I can think about. My hand between my legs stops moving. The one on his cock slows.

"Keep rubbing your clit," he whispers urgently. "Make yourself come for me. Please."

Oh my God, how does *please* sound like a demand coming from his mouth? Now I have to do what he asks.

"Good girl." He plumps my breasts and presses them together. "I love your fucking breasts. So beautiful. Will you let me come on them?"

My eyes pop open.

"Yeah." He nods quickly, his face flushed, eyes feral with need. "Come closer. Give me those tits."

A hot shock of desire drowns out all sound for a moment. I swirl my tongue down his length once more, then release him and press myself closer.

"Ah, fuck." He squeezes my breasts together as hot semen splashes against my skin. He uses one hand to guide himself and ends up painting more than my chest with his release.

Unsure of what to do, I brace my hands on his knees, so we're at least connected in some way.

"Are you okay?" he asks, brushing my hair off my shoulder.

My heart's pounding wildly and I'm a little in shock. Satisfaction drowns out my surprise, when I see the content smile on his lips.

I did that.

I made him lose control. I flick a glance down at my cum-coated skin.

"I'm fine."

"Look at the mess I made of you." He brushes his knuckles against my chin. "Thank you." He leans down and kisses my forehead. "Let me clean you up."

He stands, then helps me off the pillow. "You made my legs all shaky, woman," he teases.

"I did?"

"You see anyone else around? Come here." He slides an arm behind my back and one under my legs and scoops me into his arms.

"What are you doing?" I squeal, flapping my hands in the air as he cradles me to his chest. "You can't carry me."

He snorts like he's insulted. "Margot, I lift heavier things than you in the gym every day."

"Really?"

"Yes, really," he says in a mocking tone as he carries me out of the bedroom and down the hallway to the bathroom.

He sets me on the tile and grabs a towel, quickly wiping most of the mess from my chest and stomach.

"Come on." He slips his arm around my shoulders and pulls me close to his side. I push the shower door open. After he studies the complicated faucet system I had installed, he flips and twists the nozzles. "Fancy setup," he says.

"I like my showers long and hot." I poke him in the side. "Like my men."

His eyes crinkle at the corners. "Yeah, how many men you let in that shower?"

That erases the smile from my lips. "You'll be the first."

"I'm honored." He leans down and presses his lips to mine. "Thank you."

He backs up to the wall and sticks his hand under the spray. "It's getting there." After stepping into the shower, he holds out his hand to me. "Come on."

My skin's barely wet when he leans down and kisses me. As he pulls away, I sigh.

"Was that…good?" I risk looking up at him. "Did I do it right?"

He clenches his jaw tight and turns his head toward my built-in shelf full of hair and bath products. As if he needs a moment to compose himself.

After studying the products for a few seconds, he picks up a purple bottle of black orchid and patchouli bodywash and clicks the cap open. He sniffs it, then pours a generous amount in his hand. "Little lady death, you're killing me."

With his eyes focused on my chest, he slides his foamy hands over my skin. "You're covered in my cum from neck to nipples, and you're still asking me if you gave me a good blow job?"

His low voice echoes in the shower all around me.

I don't have an answer.

"Yes, you blew my fucking mind. Literally." He tweaks one nipple.

Laughter bubbles out of me. "I can't help it."

Placing his hands on my shoulders, he turns me to face one of the shower heads, set at a height to hit my body. Once he's rinsed me clean, he bands one arm under my breasts and slides his free hand over my stomach.

"I don't think you came, though," he whispers against my ear.

"I was close," I admit.

He releases a growly sound of approval that rumbles against my back. "You liked sucking my cock?"

I tip my head back so I can see his face. "Yes."

His hand slides between my thighs. "Spread your legs for me."

Carefully, I inch my feet apart.

My body jolts as his fingers sweep over my clit. He slowly starts working them in a quick, focused circle. "You were so good," he rasps. "I didn't get to slide my dick between your beautiful tits the way I wanted."

"Oh," I squeak.

"Yup, that's gonna be another lesson," he murmurs, continuing the relentless grinding in just the right spot. "You're really close, aren't you?"

I grip the arm holding me with both hands and lean against him.

"That's it. Close your eyes." He somehow knows better than I do the exact pressure and pattern to use on my body. Within minutes, I'm shaking and close to shattering. "Let go," he urges.

A sharp scream rips from my throat as bolts of pleasure spark throughout my body. My eyes snap open. "Jensen."

His dark eyes glitter with longing. "I've got you."

When I can breathe again, he's watching me with a slight tilt to his lips.

"Thanks." I let out a nervous laugh, suddenly self-conscious again.

"My pleasure." He reaches behind me and a sharp sting cracks against my butt.

Laughing, I fall forward, sliding against his slick skin. "Hey!"

"Go ahead and dry off. I'll be out in a minute," he says.

"Okay. I'll get a towel for you."

"Thanks."

I slide the door open and step onto my bath mat. My regular towel's on a hook by the shower and I wrap it around myself. On my

way to my laundry room/linen closet, I snag the hand towel off the floor.

When I return, he's still in the shower.

"Leaving a towel on the hook right outside," I call out.

"Okay!"

Still tingling from my first shower orgasm, I head to my room to get dressed.

Is he going to stay this time? Do I want him to? Are we going to do more tonight?

In my bedroom, I pick up his clothes from the floor and set them on the bed. I wander into my closet, searching for something sexier than a T-shirt and shorts to sleep in. In a basket on a shelf, I find a sleep set I bought on a whim a few years ago. Tiny white shorts dotted with blue flowers. It has ruffles on the legs and a matching tank top that buttons halfway down. It always seems too impractical to sleep in but it's the cutest thing I have, so I slip it on, pleased it's a little looser on me than when I bought it.

"Margot?" The closet door opens wider, light spilling in from the bedroom. "Oh shit. What is this?"

"My closet." I pick up the basket and put it back on the shelf.

"This house is wild," he says as I snap off the light and close the door behind me.

"Did you ever hear about the Winchester house?"

"The mystery house in San Jose? Yeah. Rooster and I talked his aunt into taking us there for Halloween one year."

"You're kidding!" I squeal. "I'm so jealous. When I was growing up, I thought this house was like that." I wave my hands around. "Because it seemed like every time I went exploring, I found something new. And it was part business, part private home, you know?"

"Yeah, that must've been weird."

With disappointment, I notice he's put his shorts and shirt back on. "I was hoping to study your eight-pack abs one of these lessons, you know."

His lips curl in a tight smile. "I don't want to distract you from getting some sleep."

"Does that mean you're staying?"

"Yeah. That all right?"

"Sure." I turn my head and give him a sly smile. "I hope you like cold pizza for breakfast."

"Love it." He chuckles.

"Let me go do my rounds."

"Rounds?"

"Check on Gretel. Make sure the door is locked. That kind of stuff."

"Have at it." He picks up his phone. "Going to set my alarm."

My rounds are quick tonight. Gretel's curled up on top of her cat perch in the next room and barely glances at me as I pop in to check on her. I put the rest of the food in the fridge, and the dishes in the sink.

Jigsaw's tucked into the side closest to the door when I return. His big frame looks awfully good taking up so much space in my bed. I close the bedroom door and turn off the lights.

"How do you know that's not my side?" I tease as I walk around to the other edge of the bed.

"Maybe I wanted you to crawl over me." He flips the covers back and I climb in, kneeling beside him.

His gaze travels over me, lingering on my chest then skips lower. He reaches over and slides his hand along my thigh. "This is cute." His hand travels higher, under the leg of my shorts. "Like these a lot."

"Well, I'm glad I found them, then." I stretch out beside him and pull the covers up.

"Come here." He holds out his arm and I eagerly scoot closer, resting my head on his chest.

For a while, I bask in the happiness of having him actually stay. Listening to his breathing and the slow, steady rhythm of his heart.

"You still awake?" Jigsaw's low rumble pulls me from the well of contentment I'd been drifting toward.

"Sort of."

He hugs me to his chest. "I gotta tell you something."

I knew it. I knew something would ruin this moment. Fully awake now, I press my hand to his chest and sit up. "What?"

"Nothing bad. Well, that depends on your perspective, I guess."

"We're done with our lessons?"

A sharp frown creases his brow and he almost seems...disappointed?

"No." He pulls me down next to him again but I keep some distance so I can see his face. "I'm going to be away for a week or two. The whole club's going to be away, actually. Well, except Teller. So if you need something, call him. He's sticking around because his wife's going to give birth to those twins any day now."

"Awww." My stomach flutters. "How sweet. Are they excited?"

"Yeah, I think so. Teller's more...anxious. Constantly fussing over Charlotte."

"I can understand that. She must be so uncomfortable. Then when they get here, twins will be a handful. Do they have help?"

He snorts, his lips curling into an affectionate smile. "Yeah, whole club will be helping them out. Probably won't leave them alone. Grinder and Serena have had Lilly at their house practically every day since baby Lincoln got here."

"That's really sweet."

He lifts one shoulder.

I bite my lip, hesitating before I tentatively rub my hand over his chest. "So, what's this big club trip for?"

"Uh, the old president of another charter passed away." He shifts his gaze, as if the topic weighs heavily on him. "He'd been a member for a long time."

Working in the death business hasn't made me immune to grief yet and sympathy tugs on me. "I'm so sorry."

Jigsaw doesn't offer any stories about the man, or even his name. The silence that follows suggests this visit is more about club protocol than true mourning.

My concern grows and my hand rubs faster against his shirt. "Will you be safe?"

He studies me with an intensity that quickens my pulse. "Yeah. Dex and I mapped out our route. It'll be a couple of days of long, hard riding but it'll be good for the club to be out on the road together. We're meeting up with our Virginia charter, so we'll get to catch up with those guys too."

Just how many charters of his club are there? All the googling in the world wouldn't provide those kinds of details about the Lost Kings MC. "Are your...the ol' ladies of the club going too?"

"No." He shakes his head, his expression turning serious. "Lot of different clubs and some tension in that area. Everyone thought it was safer to have them stay home."

"So, you came over to give me one last lesson before you hit the road?" I try to keep my tone light, but fear that we're done drags my voice down.

"Not at all." He rests his hand over mine, stopping my restless movements. "I'll be back. I'm not planning to stay and party. Just paying my respects and coming home as soon as my prez gives me the all-clear. Dex will want to get home to see his girl, too, so I'll probably end up riding back with him."

My breath catches. Does he realize what he just said? Dex will want to see *his girl too*. Does that mean Jigsaw considers *me* his girl that he'd want to hurry home to see?

I swallow hard, the question dancing on the tip of my tongue. *No, do not ask him that*. Not after the way I seemed to spook him last time.

Instead, I snuggle closer. "I'll miss you." The words slip out before I can stop them.

The hand over mine travels up my arm, his touch firm and reassuring. "I'll miss you too," he rasps, like he's admitting something he isn't ready to say.

Sleep tugs at the edges of my consciousness again, even though my mind's racing with my plans for the next few weeks. It feels more urgent to make my move now.

"I'll be back before you know it," he whispers, breaking the silence.

"We'll continue our lessons, right?" I ask, hating the pathetic hopefulness in my voice.

His body stills and he's silent for a beat too long. "Yeah," he answers slowly, his tone now smooth and casual. "We'll pick up where we left off."

"Was this lesson two-b? Or lesson three?"

He lets out a rough laugh. "I don't fucking know."

Doubt coils around my heart. I should've kept that question to myself. He leans over and presses a quick kiss to my forehead, lingering for a moment like he's inhaling me. "Get some sleep."

CHAPTER TWENTY-SIX

Jigsaw

TWO GLOWING GREEN EYES GREET ME THE NEXT MORNING. STARING down at me from the top of the headboard.

"How'd you get in here?" I whisper to Gretel.

"Mrrraor." She leaps onto my chest.

"You're graceful but not light." I scoop her into my arms and sit up. Her body vibrates and she butts my chin with her head, purring like the engine of a Honda Rebel.

I glance over at Margot. Sound asleep.

"Don't wake her," I whisper to Gretel.

"Mrrrp." She purrs even louder and adds a sharp chittering noise.

Still holding the cat, I slide out of bed and walk to the door. It's open just enough for Gretel to slip through. I know Margot closed it last night.

"Did you do that?" I ask the cat. Apparently, I'm a person who talks to cats now.

Gretel tilts her head and purrs louder. If a cat can look smug, it's this one.

"You'd be terrifying if you had thumbs." I tuck her under one arm and step out of the bedroom, quietly closing the door so Gretel doesn't return to wake Margot.

I set the cat on the floor outside the bedroom, and she streaks down the hallway to the bathroom. "That's where I'm headed, you little demon."

She's perched on the sink when I get there.

"I'm not a fan of having an audience." I pick her up and set her outside the door, then close it in her face.

"Mrrraor." *Scratch. Scratch.*

Christ, I haven't felt this much pressure to pee as fast as possible since I was a kid at summer camp.

Mid-stream, the door clicks open. Gretel leaps onto the edge of the counter and stares at me.

I side-eye her. "You're very rude."

When I'm finished, I turn the tap on to wash my hands, but Gretel sticks her face under the stream instead.

"Is that what you wanted? You're thirsty?"

She continues slurping at the water. After a few seconds, I nudge her out of the way and wash my hands. She flicks her paw through the water, batting droplets at me.

"I thought cats didn't like water?" I shut off the tap and pick her up off the sink, tucking her under one arm again. She doesn't seem to mind being carried around like a sack of apples.

As we approach the room next to Margot's bedroom, Gretel wriggles and I set her down. The door's ajar and she streaks through the narrow opening. I step inside. It's shadowy, so I search for a switch and find a complicated panel near the door.

Bright, white light floods the room. The walls and ceiling are a soothing, dark charcoal gray—almost black with white trim. A gray built-in unit lines one wall. The front seems to have one large door with a handle at the bottom. On each side there are tall shelves with glass doors. The bottom has several rows of drawers. I step closer to the shelves. DVDs. Ah, an entertainment center. She does have a television after all. I touch the handle of the center door and pull. It slowly and silently slides upward, kind of like a garage door. A large, flat-screen television fills most of the space. Underneath, different electronic equipment.

"Mrrrawr."

I flick my gaze to Gretel who's strutting along a wide, padded window ledge like she's showing me her favorite feature of the room. Obviously, it was made for her to look outside. Black blinds are rolled all the way to the top so as not to obstruct Gretel's view. Under the ledge, there's a feeding station and one of those kitty water-fountain things.

"You have your own water fountain, and you still followed me into the bathroom?" I run my hand over Gretel's back and rub my fingers behind her ears.

She purrs and dances back and forth, rubbing her face on my hand over and over. When she's done marking me, she sprints along the ledge like it's an airplane runway and leaps into the air. My gaze follows as she lands on the high platform of a carpeted cat tower in the corner, next to a black, leather love seat. Margot's created quite a little theater room /cat habitat. No wonder Gretel spends so much time in here.

"I thought you'd left." Margot's morning-husky voice stirs my dick.

I turn and she's still wearing that adorably sexy sleep set. "Nope. Ms. Stealthy up there broke into the bedroom. I woke up to her staring down at me like a little gargoyle."

"Oh. She knows how to pop the doors open." She laughs, making her braless tits jiggle. "Sorry."

My mouth waters.

"Mrrrawr." Gretel leaps onto the couch, then the floor, where she scurries over to Margot and twirls around her legs—in what I'm starting to think is her "feed me" dance.

"I, uh, overslept a little." She gestures toward her bedroom. "I need to get dressed. I have a family coming in at nine."

Damn. I had a few other things in mind. "Yeah, okay. I gotta get downstate and start packing."

"How much can you really take on your bike?"

"You'd be surprised. But someone will be driving a van or a truck to haul extra shit."

Her eyes spark with interest. "Who drives it?"

I need to get closer to her. "A prospect usually or someone else affiliated with the club. If it's a big family run, the girls will sometimes take an SUV with the kids."

"So the old ladies don't always have to ride on the back?"

Why's she asking? My chest tightens. Is she asking because she thinks that because *she* doesn't ride, that's a deal-breaker for me?

"No one has to do anything they don't want to. Most of them do, though." I snort with laughter. "Heidi says after a few hours in the car with the kids, she's ready to ride. So, they'll take turns and stuff. Or we went down to Virginia last Christmas and the girls rode in Trinity's Jeep the whole way—Shelby said it was too cold to ride." I shrug. "We make it work."

I want to ask her why she's so curious, why it matters so much to her.

But I'm also afraid of the answer.

CHAPTER TWENTY-SEVEN

Jigsaw

DIGGER'S MEMORIAL HAS BEEN A SHITSHOW WASTE OF OUR TIME. COPS canceled the memorial, so all the charters came to Deadbranch for one big circle jerk at the clubhouse before we all head to a local hotel for the night. The next morning, we're all meeting in Rock's room before our big sit-down with our national prez, when I get a text from Jezzie.

Princess PITA: Stuck in Bridlewood, PA. Can you pick me up?

What the fuck? Why is my sister in fucking Pennsylvania when she's supposed to be in class? I pull up the town on my maps app, it's not even close to our aunt's house but it *is* close to the New York border.

Who the fuck am I gonna call to go get her?

Me: I'm down in Tennessee. Are you okay?

She takes way too fucking long to answer for my sanity. Thumbs frantically flicking against my screen, I open up the "where's my phone" app, where the little dot indicates she is indeed somewhere in bumfuck Pennsylvania.

Still no answer.

"What's wrong?" Rooster whispers to me.

"I might need to bounce ASAP. Jezzie needs me."

"Fuck, brother." He runs his hands through his hair and flicks a glance at the door. "Priest sent me a message earlier. He needs me to stick around after the meeting."

"Fucking hell, why?"

"Don't know. But I don't want you riding alone."

"Thanks, Dad, but I think I'll be fine."

My phone buzzes again.

Princess PITA: I'm fine. I'll find a ride.

I scowl at the message. Now, I won't be able to stop worrying about her.

The meeting with Priest takes shitshow to a whole new level. An asshole of a brother from my original charter in Washington challenges Priest. He loses—badly—and hightails it the fuck out of there.

After the meeting, Rock's busy making the rounds with the national officers. Z jerks his head to the side, indicating he wants his officers to follow him. I tap Rooster's shoulder.

"Let's go."

Z opens a door downstairs and holds it wide for us to enter.

Rooster leans against the wall and I stand next to him. Grinder takes up a position next to the door.

"We're waiting for Hustler," Z says, glancing into the hallway. "Actually, I don't need him right now. I'd rather keep this circle small."

"What's on your mind, Prez?" Rooster asks.

"I'm guessing that whole shitshow that went down at the table," I say.

"I'm sure we'll all discuss this once we get home and get Upstate and Downstate in the war room." Z nods. "But we all saw what happened out there, right?"

"Acorn showed his entire ass to every charter in the organization?" Rooster deadpans. "Yeah, Prez, we all saw it."

Z glares at his VP, then looks at Grinder, and me. "You all see where this is going, right? Rock might want to keep living in denial about it, but Priest *will* eventually step down. And he'll want to do it when he has enough power to name his successor."

"How's that make sense?" I ask. "It's farther for everyone."

"Not really." Z shrugs. "Only Washington and no offense since I know that's your original charter, but I don't see them lasting much longer if Pony can't keep control over his crew."

"That was ugly," Rooster mutters. "Fucking embarrassing. Don't be surprised if Priest's Nomad crew wipes Washington off the map sometime soon."

Z's sharp blue gaze lands on Rooster. "First thing Rock will need to do is disband the Nomad charter."

Rooster shrugs. "You're getting way ahead of things, Prez."

Z's not finished, though. "Squiggy ain't gonna be able to handle the Prez position for long. I'll bet Priest wants you to stick around to ask you about running this charter."

Rooster's eyes widen and my stomach plunges into my boots. "Yeah, that's a no from me," Rooster says. But I know my brother too well. He'll consider the offer. It would make his and Shelby's lives a lot easier if she was in Tennessee, closer to the heart of the country music scene.

Rooster catches my eye and I shrug.

"I go where you go, brother." An edge of doubt creeps into my mind as the words leave my mouth. A year ago, that would've been one-hundred percent true. Now? I just moved Jezzie to New York so she could be closer to me. And I have Margot. The thought of leaving her jabs me in the ribs in an unfamiliar way.

Except, I don't exactly *have* her. We talked about getting together for more *lessons* when I return. Nothing more.

She's already told me the job market in her field is tight. She won't want to leave her family business and start over in a whole new state where she'll have to get licensed again.

Rooster—perceptive bastard that he is—is still giving me that questioning face. I pull a *what the fuck* look at him and he finally takes his attention elsewhere.

"All right." Z claps his hands. "We're not going to solve this today. Let's say our goodbyes and meet with Upstate out front. I know Dex, Sparky, Stash, and Murphy want to head home." Z points at me. "You're rolling out too?"

"My sister said she's good, but I haven't heard back from her whether she's made it home or not yet. But I can stay if you want me to."

"No, check on your sister," Z says. "I wanna get the hell out of here too but I'm not leaving without my VP."

Rooster's cheeks lift. "Aw, thanks Prez. Appreciate you not abandoning me here."

"G, you wanna head home?" Z asks.

"I'll wait to ride with you and Rock." He claps his hands together. "Been fifteen or sixteen years since we all rode together."

"I know, brother."

Fuck, I feel like a baby next to them now. Rooster and I were still in high school when Grinder went to prison. I slide my gaze Rooster's way, and he gives me a look like he's having the same thought.

"All right, let's go." Z waves his arm in the air and opens the door.

Z and Grinder step into the hallway.

Rooster tips his head to the side, silently asking me to hang back.

"Yesss?" I ask as dickishly as possible. "What's up, *Prez*?"

"Shut the fuck up. That's not even funny. Christ, you heard Z. They'd been patched into the club for years. Fuck, Grinder was an officer before we had hair on our balls. I ain't ready to wear the president's patch."

I reach down and scratch my crotch. "Speak for yourself. I was born with hair on my balls."

He closes his eyes and blows out a long, slow, irritated breath. "Keep laughing. You'll be my VP, and I'll have all sorts of bitchwork for you."

"VP? Not SAA?"

He blinks a few times. "Figure I get a two-for-one deal that way, 'cause I know you always have my back."

"Fuck yeah, I do." I tilt my head and squint at him. "For someone who said he wouldn't take the job, you sure have given it a lot of thought."

Rooster doesn't have a comeback and that almost unnerves me more than anything else that's happened on this trip.

CHAPTER TWENTY-EIGHT

Margot

IF GOD EXISTS, HE WATCHES OVER THE MISCHIEVOUS WITH AFFECTION. At least that's what I tell myself on these missions. Somehow, I haven't been caught yet. Maybe it's because I choose my targets carefully and for just reasons.

No one probably works all that hard to find the killer of child molesters, wife-beaters, and baby killers.

It's still risky. I could get caught. I could get *killed*. These are, after all, dangerous men that I hunt. I'm not like Jigsaw and his biker brothers, with their muscles and strength. I have to pick and choose my targets carefully and work out a solid plan.

I check the mirror of my rental car and adjust my short, black wig. Pin-straight, chin-length bob with heavy bangs that end right below my eyebrows. I even put in brown contacts. Tight black leggings and sleek, black high-top sneakers hopefully give me the illusion of a little more height. A padded butt enhancer and thin shoulder pads under my black long-sleeved cropped jacket alter my shape just a little. It's all about perception and illusion. If anyone remembers seeing a woman at Patrick's door, none of the characteristics someone might mention to the police have anything to do with me—shy, blonde Margot Cedarwood from Pine Hollow.

Little Lady Death. Jigsaw has no idea how on the nose that nickname is.

Thinking of him brings on a wave of longing. I miss him. He's sent me a bunch of texts since he left for Tennessee, but I still have no idea when he'll be back in New York.

I wish I could tell him about my favorite side hobby.

I've been watching the Horizon Inn motel for days. Every day since Jigsaw left on his trip to be precise.

Every night around seven p.m. a delivery driver shows up with food. Always a different driver. Sometimes it's bags of groceries, other times a pizza, or even just a plain brown bag covered in grease stains.

Once I knew his room number, I placed a small camera on the balcony across from his door, so I can monitor him throughout the day. He never leaves the motel room. Never lets a maid in either. Laurel was wrong about the hookers; so far, I've only seen food arrive at Patrick's door. This might be my easiest kill yet.

A car swoops into the parking lot. Music, loud and thumping. The car slows to a crawl as the driver reads the room number signs.

Perfect.

I turn off the dome light in my car and step out.

Here's the riskiest part of my plan. Running along the side of the building, I pop out near the bottom of the stairs leading to the second floor and scurry up a few steps. Large, unkempt shrubbery obscures the bottom half of the staircase, making it dark and shadowy. A perfect temporary hiding spot.

A few seconds later, the delivery driver approaches the stairs.

Please let this be the right one.

I grab the banister and act like I'm running down to meet him. "Oh, hey. Is that for Room 242?"

He squints at me, then smiles. "Yup."

I hold out my hand for the bag. "Thanks."

A frown creases his forehead. "Patrick…?"

"Larsen, yup," I confirm, giving him the correct last name.

"Excellent. Thanks."

"No, thank you." I hand him a folded-up twenty-dollar bill, hoping

surprise at the amount of the tip will override any other details about our encounter, like the black latex gloves I'm wearing.

"Whoa, thanks ma'am." He grabs the bill and unfolds it, his attention not lingering on my hand. "You sure?"

"Yeah, I think he always forgets to tip in the app, you know?"

"Glad I didn't spit in his chili now." He laughs and darts away.

Gross. I sigh. If that guy's my undoing, then I deserve to be caught.

The hard part isn't over for me yet. I'm exposed outside. It's dark but anyone could walk up on me at any time. The motel isn't exactly deserted. I drop my butt to the stairs and plop the bag between my feet. To anyone observing, I could just be checking to make sure my whole order's here. Totally normal, right?

The syringe I pull out of my sweatshirt pocket isn't at all normal, though.

Chili, the kid said, right? I pull the two twine handles apart and peer into the bag. Chips, what looks—and smells—like several wrapped hot dogs, a tall white cup with a clear dome-shaped cover with swirls of whipped cream underneath, and finally a wide, white cup with a plastic lid—complete with ventilation holes—in the corner. Perfect, I don't even have to puncture anything. I uncap the syringe and plunge the tip into one of the holes in the chili container and slowly empty about half of it.

Enough odorless, tasteless fentanyl to kill a football team slips into the hot, smelly cup. Just in case, I pluck a napkin from the bag, wipe the tip of the needle and empty the rest of it into the milkshake. The perfectly swirled whipped cream at the top deflates a little but that shouldn't look too strange. It's sitting in a bag with a bunch of hot food, after all. Even if he decides not to drink the milkshake, hopefully he doesn't skip the chili.

I tuck the empty syringe and the dirty napkin in my pocket and stand. A quick scan of the immediate area shows it's still empty.

Time to make my delivery.

I hurry up the steps and walk down the long corridor, trying to stay in the shadows. I stop outside his room and crouch down to grab my small camera. No reason to leave evidence that could lead straight back to me.

Once I unfasten the camera and stick it in my pocket, I tap my knuckles against the door. My heart pounds wildly and an invisible band of fear tightens around my forehead—or maybe my wig's too tight. Sweat breaks out on the back of my neck.

"Just leave it!" someone barks from inside.

I pitch my voice into something worthy of a helium-drunk cartoon character and garble a few nonsense words.

"What?" The door flies open.

Face-to-face with evil, he's not all that impressive. Just another pathetic excuse for a human who enjoys taking out his anger on those who are weaker than him.

"Patrick?" I ask sweetly, holding up the bag.

His hostile attitude switches to interest as his gaze lands and stays on my chest.

"That's me." He opens the door wider. "Come on in."

"Oh, we're not allowed to." I giggle like an airhead.

"Aww, come on, you can break the rules for a minute." He snatches the bag out of my hand and peers inside, then back at me. "I just gotta grab my wallet for a tip."

A ditzy, and possibly deranged, smile spreads over my face, "Sure, okay, then."

I follow him inside, stopping to wad a piece of napkin into the lock so the door doesn't close all the way.

The room's disgusting—dirty clothes strewn everywhere, overflowing trash can of takeout bags, boxes, and wrappers—but Patrick seems to have no shame about inviting a stranger inside.

He sets the bag on a round table next to the curtained window and pulls out the milkshake.

My breathing freezes. Blood pounds through my ears in a steady, terrified rhythm.

He doesn't so much as frown at the wilted whipped cream.

Come on, fucker. Take a sip.

He pokes a straw into the hole at the top of the dome and sucks a long, frosty pull from the cup.

A slow exhale passes my lips.

Fentanyl is an extremely potent opioid. With the amount swirling around in that cup, he should feel it soon.

He smacks his lips and sets the cup down. "What'd you say your name was?" he asks.

"Ashley." I wait for his reaction.

A flicker of recognition at the name his wife chose for their daughter crosses his face, then disappears with a shrug of his shoulders.

Not one fuck given.

A wallet rests in the center of the table. He picks it up, flips it open and pulls out two dollar bills.

Really, you brought me in the room for two dollars?

He drops the wallet on the table and picks up the milkshake again.

Giddiness surges through me as he takes another long sip.

Lap it up, scumbag.

Still holding the cup, he approaches me with his arm outstretched, pushing the money at my face.

I swipe the dollars out of his grasp.

His gaze narrows on my gloved hand and his forehead wrinkles.

"What're you..." He blinks rapidly and sways on his feet.

"Thanks for the tip." I stuff it in my pocket.

As if he'd downed a case of beer, he staggers to the messy, rumpled bed and drops onto the edge. He sucks on the straw again.

The sugar rush isn't going to clear your head. A giggle slips past my lips, and he frowns in confusion.

"What's..." He clutches his stomach and the cup tips precariously to the side.

"Whoa, mister." I grab the cup. No reason to spill potential evidence all over the place. "Maybe we should get some food in you instead of all that sugar?"

"Yeah...gimme one dem hot dogs," he slurs and vaguely points toward the table.

"Sure thing." Keeping as much distance between us as I can in the small room, I scurry to the table, set down the cup and unwrap one of the hot dogs.

"Here ya go." I press the revolting onion-smothered hot dog to his lips.

His eyelids droop but he opens his mouth and takes a bite, sloppily chewing.

"How's that?" I ask, peering into his eyes. "Better?"

"No." He clutches his stomach and stretches his mouth into a wide yawn, like he can't draw in enough air.

"Want some chili?" I ask.

"N…no." He waves his hand through the air frantically.

I set the hot dog back on the table and stand with my back to the window, watching him struggle to breathe.

"Help…me…"

"No thank you," I say sweetly.

Wretched choking sounds tear at his throat. He slides off the bed, hitting the floor with his knees and flopping over on his side.

I approach slowly, still wary he might be onto me and faking.

"This death is too good for you," I whisper, staring down at him.

I'd rather wale on him with a baseball bat. Replicate the same bruises on his face that he left on Laurel's. But that would leave too many obvious clues. Police would be looking for a suspect. There'd be a chance I'd leave DNA behind. Hell, there'd be a chance he would've overpowered me and *I'd* be the one to die.

So, this way is smarter.

Cleaner.

And solves the problem. For good.

Vomit bubbles out of his mouth and his entire body spasms.

Almost time to go.

I pull a plastic baggie from my pocket and a small pair of scissors, then crouch next to him.

"Don't mind me. I need a little souvenir for my collection." I ruthlessly grab his thick, greasy black hair and clip a handful. "Be thankful I'm not taking one of your eyeballs. That'd be my preference, but it would raise too many questions."

His eyes bulge, as if daring me to scoop one out. The temptation gnaws at me, but I resist the urge. A missing eyeball would scream murder, not accidental overdose.

He tries to twist away, his torso contorting weakly, but he's too far gone to escape my grasp.

I sprinkle the hair into my bag. Without the root it'll be hard to get DNA from it. Besides, by tomorrow night, it'll be encased in a little resin ornament that I'll hang next to my others.

CHAPTER TWENTY-NINE

Jigsaw

My obsession and need to see Margot fuels my ride home. We meet with Upstate outside and everyone goes through another recap of events. I'm antsy as fuck to get on the road.

"Before we go," Rock says, holding out his hands to stop us from getting on our bikes, "I want to commend everyone for the way you handled today. No one expected to see Priest challenged. The situation could've quickly gone south."

A smirk spreads across Murphy's face. "I think we were all too stunned to speak."

"Even so," Z throws an appreciative look at every brother in our circle, "thanks for not making a bad situation worse."

Finally, Rock gives us the all-clear to leave.

"Some of us are sticking around to have a few conversations," he says. "Everyone else is free to stay, go home, or go wherever you want. No one rides alone, though."

Hallelujah, praise Satan, let's ride.

It takes another round of backslapping and goodbyes—as if we're not all going to see each other at the clubhouse in a couple of days to discuss this fuckery again—before we actually leave.

"Let's get the fuck outta here," Sparky grumbles as he straps on his helmet. "I warned you this was gonna be nothing but dark energy."

Dex bites his lip, trying not to laugh. "Yeah, you did, brother."

I straddle my bike, so fucking happy to be heading home, and grin at Sparky. "Remember to air out your boys, brother!"

He shakes his head and laughs. Brother bitched all the way down that his balls ached.

Some of the brothers from our Virginia charter join our pack. Dex and I will take the lead. Murphy and the VP from Virginia are right behind us. Sparky, Stash, and Ravage fall somewhere in the middle. The road captain of Virginia pulls up the rear. When we split from Virginia, we'll probably shuffle our positions.

I raise my fist in the air. "Tuck in your dicks and cushion your balls, boys!"

Dex shakes his head and fires up his bike to drown me out. I laugh and start mine. Everyone behind us revs their engines.

The first leg of our run is smooth. Around Philadelphia, we stop again.

"You still riding to see your sister?" Murphy asks.

"Not sure." Somewhere along the way, she'd sent me a text saying she was fine and home.

"I wanna goooooo!" Sparky shouts.

"Jesus Christ, chill," Dex mutters.

"Bro, go on ahead." Distracted by searching my phone for an app, I wave my hand. "I'll either head out to see Jezzie or I'll catch up with you."

Dex eyeballs Sparky's fidgety ass. Stash keeps trying to calm him down, but it doesn't seem to be helping. "You sure?" Dex asks.

"Yeah."

"I'll stick with Jiggy," Murphy says.

"All right." Dex gives me a fist bump. "Hope everything's okay with Jezzie. You gonna bring her around to visit soon?"

"I was thinking of bringing her out to Zips since it's closer to her place?"

"Yeah, that sounds like a plan." Dex taps knuckles with Murphy, then the guys head north.

Once I finally pull up the "track my phone" app, I verify Jezzie's at home.

She keeps saying she's an adult and I don't need to pester her. But she *did* ask for my help.

I'll call her tomorrow. Maybe visit her this week.

Right now, I want to see Margot.

I've never wanted to get home to a woman before in my life. But my need to see her drowns out everything else.

Shame pops like bubbles over my skin as I fire up my bike and continue northwest. I can't stop feeling like I'm choosing my own selfish desires over family again.

CHAPTER THIRTY

Margot

Jigsaw: Back in NY. Can be at your place in an hour.

Me: I'll buzz you in.

Frantic and so eager to see him, I hurry into the shower. I carefully shave my legs and smooth oil all over my skin.

After I'm finished, I take my time carefully drying my curls so they're smooth and bouncy.

Then, I pull out the sheer, steel-blue camisole I bought, hoping to wear it for Jigsaw once he got back. It came with matching shiny satin shorts, and I slip those on too. Just in case I have to run downstairs, I pull on a white-and-blue striped, long-sleeved button-up shirt.

My phone buzzes again.

Jigsaw: Here.

Butterflies flip and flutter in my stomach as I race to the intercom. I don't think I've ever missed someone this fiercely or been bubbling over with so much excitement to see them again.

Impatient, I jab the button that will unlock the downstairs back door, then open mine. Jigsaw's heavy boots thump against the stairs.

As he reaches the top, he slows his steps.

His arms are tanner than when he left but not his face. Our eyes lock and a slow smile spreads over his face.

"Aw, fuck." He stops and braces one arm against the doorframe. "Look at you." His words are low and hungry. He runs his free hand over his chin like he's contemplating his next meal. "How are you even prettier than when I left?"

"Is it this?" I tease the hem of my shorts higher.

His greedy eyes roam over every inch of me. "It doesn't hurt."

I curl my fingers at him. "Come in."

"Babe, I've been riding hard for almost two days."

"I don't care." I tilt my head. "You didn't stop home at all?"

"Nope." He hesitates, crosses the threshold and closes the door behind him. "Came straight here from Deadbranch." He cocks his head. "Some guys were as eager to get home so we rode together most of the way."

"I'm glad you weren't riding alone."

He holds out his hand. "Come shower with me."

"I just got *out* of the shower."

His lips tip into the cocky smile I missed. "Come with me anyway."

I can't take my eyes off of him as he unlaces his boots and leaves them by the door. While he shrugs off his cut and hangs it in the closet, I start unbuttoning my shirt.

"Whoa, what're you doing there, little lady?" He prowls closer and takes over the unbuttoning. He slides the shirt off my shoulders, revealing the sheer camisole.

He lets out a low whistle of appreciation. "Wow. I can see right through that."

"That was kind of the point."

"You get this for me?"

"Yes," I whisper.

"I like. A lot."

I've reduced him to one-syllable words.

Empowered like never before, I take his hand. "Come on. Take your shower. Give me your clothes, and I'll throw them in the wash."

"But then I'll be naked."

I glance over my shoulder. "Yes, I know."

"I like coming home to this," he says so low, I almost miss it.

Could he ever consider this his home? Here with me?

I stop at the laundry room, open the door, and grab some towels. Jigsaw moves on ahead of me, into the bathroom. When I join him, he already has the shower running. He faces me and peels off his dark blue T-shirt.

I hold out my hands for it.

He hesitates and lets out a sigh. "You don't have to do my laundry, Margot."

"Well, you said you were riding hard the last two days." I make a big show of pretending to search the bathroom. "I don't see any other clothes with you, so…"

He tosses me the shirt. "My saddlebag's on my bike. Got my stuff in there."

"You want me to go down and get it?"

He sweeps his gaze over me again. "Not dressed like that, I don't."

"Well, yeah." I roll my eyes.

"Nah, nothing in there's clean, either." He works his belt loose.

"You can bring it up later."

He nods and empties his pockets—phone, wallet, keys, some change and a crumpled dollar bill—then cocks an eyebrow and lifts his gaze to me. "You plannin' to watch me undress?"

There's a cocky challenge to his question that sends a shiver over my skin. "Oh, yes."

His shoulders shake as he pushes his jeans down, then his briefs.

"Wow," I breathe out.

Chuckling, he balls up his clothes and holds them in front of him.

"Give them to me." I hold out my hands. "I handle bodily fluids all day. Your sweaty jeans don't scare me."

He fake-retches to the side but hands me his clothes.

"Thank you." I turn to leave. "Have you eaten?"

"No but we can do that later." The shower door softly rattles as he slides it open.

I hurry into the laundry and toss his stuff into the washer. Running it while he's in the shower will probably cut his water pressure in half, but I'm hoping he doesn't plan to be in there long.

Once his clothes are churning, I run to the kitchen and grab a bottle of water.

By the time I return, he's stepping out of the shower.

I lean against the door and watch him rough a towel over his hair. Every movement he makes intoxicates me with his virility and strength. He wraps the other towel around his waist. His gaze lands on me as he's tying a knot at his hip.

"You watching me, little creeper?"

"Definitely."

In two slow steps, he's standing in front of me. Water drips from the ends of his hair, running down his chest. I reach up, running my fingers through the thick, damp strands. "Your hair's longer."

"I haven't had a chance to get it cut."

"I like it," I whisper.

His mouth turns up at the corners. "Then maybe I won't bother."

"I can cut it." That's weird, isn't it? He's going to think I'm nuts. "If you wanted me to."

He seizes my wrist and brings it to his lips, brushing a kiss against my pulse point. "I'd like that."

I hold up the bottle of water. "I don't want you to get dehydrated."

Accepting it with a smirk, he twists the cap off, tips the bottle to his lips and takes several long swallows without taking his eyes off me.

He sets the bottle on the counter.

I reach up and trace a crown tattoo on his shoulder—very similar to a patch on his cut. "Your club's important to you."

"They're my family." He hooks two fingers under the straps of my camisole and drags them down my shoulders. "But family vacation time is over. Class is in session."

A thrill runs through me, followed by a pang of sadness. *What if I want this to be more?*

The thin material falls away from my chest, and cool air drifts over my skin. My breasts tingle as the air rushes over the tips.

He sucks in an appreciative breath. "Fuuuck."

"Welcome home, Professor Orgasms."

He squeezes his eyes shut and shakes with silent laughter. "I missed you."

"I missed you too." More than I'd ever want to admit.

"I like this a lot." He cups my breasts, rubbing his thumbs over my nipples. I shrug myself free of the camisole and it falls to the floor in a whisper.

Our eyes meet. "You plannin' to give me a proper welcome home kiss?"

In my excitement to see him, how did I not do that already? I jump and loop my arms around his neck. "Yes."

He bends his knees and gently lifts me, my naked skin rubbing against his damp skin and the roughness of the towel.

"Wrap your legs around me," he urges.

I press my lips to his first.

Jigsaw

Fire licks over my skin. Not from the blistering hot shower I just took. From Margot. This is what it's like to have someone waiting at home for you after being on the road? Someone who's excited to see *me*. Not a club girl hanging around to welcome *all* the brothers home, who will stumble into a bedroom with any patched brother who picks her. Just for me.

Gripping her thighs, I press her back against the bathroom door and lean into the kiss. She doesn't hold back or hesitate. Our lips slide and crash together in a sloppy, frenzied rush of longing. Her palms press against my cheeks and she pulls back, staring at my face like she can't get enough.

The feeling's mutual. From the cute outfit to her shiny blonde curls, she obviously took time getting ready for me. "Your hair looks really pretty," I say. It's inadequate, but the best I can come up with.

"I did my whole curl routine after my shower."

Guilt spreads over my chest. "Wish you'd waited." I pull her away from the door, grab a better hold of her, and head down the hallway.

Her eyebrows pinch together as if she's worried she did something wrong. "Why?"

"Because I'm about to mess it all up."

She laughs softly and strokes my cheek. "I don't mind."

Ah, fuck. The one thing I need, I left in the pocket of my cut. I can't let go of her, though.

"Where are you going?" she laughs as I carry her into the living room.

"Need something." Keeping one arm around her, I press her to the wall next to the closet. Her thighs tighten around my waist, and she loops her arms around my shoulders again. Where the fuck did I put them? Trying to search with one hand sends frustration burning through me. Finally, my fingers fumble over the small square box. I yank it out, put it between my teeth, and hoist Margot into both arms again.

She pries the box from my mouth and quickly scans the front.

"Just in case you're ready for lesson four." *Please be ready.*

She shakes the box. "Only three?"

I snort with laughter, almost dropping her as I cross the threshold into her bedroom. "Best I could do on the road."

I shove the door closed behind me, hoping we're not interrupted by a certain nosy kitty.

She unwinds herself from my body, stretching her legs to the floor. I set her down and she practically skips to her nightstand, rolling open the top drawer. With a triumphant smile, she pulls out a box eight times the size of mine.

Jesus Christ, I don't even know what to say. What a way to show me she's ready for her next lesson.

Her lips curl devilishly. "I've got you covered." She winks. "So to speak."

Awkward laughter eases out of me. It's a fucking box of condoms, not a key to her apartment. Wait—she gave me the combination to her keypad, so technically I *do* have the key to her place.

"Twenty-four? That's a lot of lessons," I tease, picking up the box.

"Well, I know you're a *thorough* teacher."

That I am. I scan the box again. "Elite large, huh?" She bought them all for me. Not someone else.

"For the longer and wider man." She stretches her hands in front of her like she's measuring a wooden beam, not a dick.

I capture her around the waist and boost her onto the bed, so she's standing in front of me, nipples almost level with my mouth. I seal my lips over one and suck hard.

"Oh!" she gasps and digs her fingers into my shoulder, the sharp pressure easing knots of tension from riding for so long.

I release her nipple and stare up at her face. "Your hands feel good on me."

"I like touching you." She tips her head down, a slight frown creasing her brow. Can she see my back from that angle? Do I even care anymore? I think I could talk about my scars with her if she asks.

"Margot?" I run my hands underneath her shorts, up silky-smooth thighs. "I'm dying to kiss your sweet pussy."

She drags her fingers through my hair, sending pleasure skittering over my scalp. "You're supposed to be teaching *me* to be good at sex."

"This is all part of the lesson." I tug on the sides of her slippery little shorts and slide them down her legs, hissing in a breath when I encounter nothing underneath. "Fuuuck," I groan at the sight of her.

She shifts, trying to cover her pussy with her hands.

"No." I capture her wrists and pin them to her sides. "Don't you dare try to hide. You're beautiful. I want to *see* all of you. I've fucking missed you. Been thinking about you non-stop."

"Really?" she whispers.

"Yes, look." I hold up my right hand for her inspection. "I've got callouses on my hand from jerking off every time I think about you coming on my tongue."

"What?" She giggles and grabs my hand as if she believes every word. I'm not exaggerating by much. Mostly, I'm trying to tell her there wasn't anyone else while I was on the road. I've only been thinking about her.

"Don't deny me." I lean in and kiss her belly. "I can't wait to touch, lick, taste, and *look* at every inch of your body tonight."

Why am I revealing so much about myself when she still wants me to get her primed to find another dude to fuck?

As happy as she is to see me and all the care she took before I got here, I don't think her objective has changed. "Any man worth your time..." I quickly clear my throat. "Any man you want to *keep*, should want to worship your body, Margot. You're the prize. Don't forget that."

I pull her shorts off the rest of the way, bending to untangle them from her feet, and her scent washes over me like a baptism—ocean air and honey.

Sliding my hand up her inner thigh, I reach her center and feather one finger along her slit. She gasps and clutches my shoulders for support as her legs tremble.

"Come on." I guide her to the edge of the bed. "Lie back for me." I kneel and slide her butt right to the edge, then hook her thighs over my shoulders.

I brush my nose against her inner thigh, inhaling her scent. She wriggles closer.

"Yes," I encourage, pleased she seems so relaxed this time. I still don't want to hurry. Pressing kisses to her thighs, I stop and run my tongue along her crease, enjoying the way she squirms. I sweep my knuckles against her slit and hum a satisfied noise. "You're so wet for me."

"I have been ever since your text came through."

"Really?" Using my thumbs, I spread her and flatten my tongue against her slit. "Did you know how much I wanted to do this?" I drag my tongue against her in several long, deep licks.

Her shaky breaths and little whimpers are all the answers I need. My cock's throbbing, desperate to finally be inside her. I reach down and tug the towel off and wrap my hand around my cock, squeezing hard at the base.

"You're so sweet," I whisper against her skin. "Been wanting to do this again."

Her legs tighten over my shoulders like she's trying too hard not to move.

"Work yourself against my face, I don't mind."

"I want...I want..." She balls her fists in the blanket.

"What?" I flick my tongue around her clit. "This?" I lick directly over it and her body jerks. "Mmm, okay." I suck her clit between my lips and slide two fingers inside her.

"Oh God!" Her hips shoot up, but she'd need a crowbar to pry me off her. I work my fingers in and out, groaning at her taste flooding my mouth.

Her hand grapples with my hair, finally pressing at the back of my head, holding me to her. Fuck yes. Hips bucking wildly, she explodes while I keep working her through the orgasm.

The need to fill her descends on me like a violent storm that I keep riding into even as electricity crackles over my skin. I need her clenching around my cock, the way she's squeezing my fingers.

She whimpers as I withdraw and reach for the box on the nightstand. While I was busy reading the stupid box before, I should've fucking *opened* it.

While I'm tearing through surprisingly sturdy cardboard, she moves to the edge of the bed on hands and knees. Her fingers curl around my cock. I gasp and my head falls back as she seals her lips over me.

"Fuck." My hands curl into fists, crumpling the box. Her tongue licks and flutters all along my length while I finally tear the box apart, strips of condoms flying everywhere. "Keep doing that," I rasp, grabbing one of the foil squares and ripping it open.

Pressure builds at the base of my spine.

No fucking way. As much as I'm dying to come on her tits again or down her throat, I've been waiting way too long to get to this lesson.

I gather her hair in one hand and gently tug. "Stop, baby. Please."

She drags the back of her hand against her shiny lips and stares at me with bright eyes. I work the condom on fast, then hug her to me and roll us onto the bed, landing on top of her.

"How do you want me?" I'm shaking with the desire to squeeze inside her but torturing both of us is fun too. I slide my cock back and forth through her soaked lips, groaning at how slick and ready she is.

She struggles and writhes under me. "Just...normal."

My lips twist with amusement. "What do you consider normal?"

Her face screws into a mask of frustration. "I don't know. Like this. You over me."

"Missionary." What a terrible name for such an intimate position. "Or man on top."

"What do most men like?"

Fucking hell, if I wasn't so goddamn desperate to finally fuck her, the reminder that this is nothing more than a sex lesson might kill my hard-on. "I haven't taken a survey."

"What do *you* usually prefer?"

No other woman exists for me right now. I can't think of anyone else when I'm with her.

And I don't think she'll find ass up, face down so there's no eye-contact all that charming.

"Just shut up and pay attention." I try to say it playfully, but it comes out more of a raspy growl.

Her eyes widen, but she doesn't look away. She drags her fingers along my sides, to my ass and back, like she can't get enough of touching me. "I think I'm nervous," she whispers.

God damn, that fucks me up.

I gather her in my arms and press kisses to her cheeks and lips. "I'm nervous too."

"What, why?"

My lips curl into a smirk and I roll my hips, sliding through her wetness again. "I've been wanting to do this since we met." I dip down and kiss her over and over. "Been waiting so long. Afraid I won't last long enough for you."

She runs her fingers through my hair and her lips curve into the sweetest smile. "I'm happy to do this as many times as we need to until you're fully satisfied."

Never. "Careful, you don't know what you're asking."

Margot

Finally, finally, finally. My heart pounds with anticipation.

Jigsaw's big body settles over mine. His chest pressing against my breasts, arms braced by my head, keeping most of his weight off me. His hard length prods my entrance and gradually pushes inside. My breath catches at the sensual stretching and filling sensation. It doesn't hurt or pinch or feel like being stabbed with a blunt instrument.

It's pure pleasure.

Unlike anything I've ever experienced.

"Are you okay?" His voice, rough with restraint, adds to the sounds of our bodies sliding together.

"Yes." I loop my arms around his neck and peer up into his eyes. "You're perfect inside me."

He dips down and kisses my cheek, then my lips. "Want more?"

"Yes." I tighten my arms around his neck, holding him to me, and kiss him back.

He presses forward, filling me completely, then gathers me closer, our skin brushing together. My nipples grazing his chest. His cock stretching me open. He withdraws, then slowly thrusts back inside, working up to a steady rhythm.

Flames lick beneath my skin, spreading through my body in waves. I arch and move against him, lifting my legs higher, hooking my feet at his back, drawing him closer.

"Good girl," he whispers, kissing my neck. "You want me in deep, don't you?"

"Yes, God. You already are. But I can't get enough."

He growls and grinds into me harder. I don't know if it's the determination in his eyes or the angle and spot he's hitting, but a harsh wave, frightening in its intensity, spreads over my body. "Oh my God," I choke, clutching his shoulders. "Jensen."

"That's right," he rasps. "Don't you ever forget who makes you come this hard."

I couldn't if I wanted to. I can't force my voice to form any words. Just moans, whimpers, and breathy cries. The pounding of my heart drowns out all other sounds.

"Yes." Jigsaw's pleased groans fill my ears as he lowers my legs and covers my body with his. He drives into me with slower, deeper thrusts. "Your pussy's so fucking tight. Your face so pretty while you're coming on my cock for me."

His lips graze my neck, and he sucks. The way he treats me is almost like this is real. Not a lesson. He captures my lips and brushes his tongue against mine, groaning with pleasure into my mouth as he finishes.

"Little lady death," he whispers through panting breaths, brushing kisses against my forehead, cheeks, and mouth. "I'm so glad you bought that bigger box."

I slide my hands over his back, touching rougher, bumpier skin than the smoothness of his glorious legs and stomach. His body freezes. I stroke my hands along his sides instead and he shakes with silent laughter.

"That tickles, you little devil." He leans down and scrapes his teeth over my nipple.

"Give me a second." He kisses my cheek again, then pulls away, our sweaty limbs sliding against each other. "I'll be right back."

I sit up and kiss his shoulder. "Thank you."

He slips out of the bedroom, and I melt into the mattress in a boneless, sweaty pile of satisfied flesh.

Based on my previous relationships, I assumed sex was something I wasn't built to understand or enjoy. It had been gross, uncomfortable, and left me feeling bottled up and sad, not euphoric and satisfied.

My body's still tingling. Little electrical zaps running up and down my legs. Sweat mists my skin and I'm not even self-conscious about being completely nude with the lights on. Jigsaw seems to love everything about my body. Never stops praising and touching me everywhere. Even my rounded tummy that never seems to go away, no matter how many calories I restrict or times I run up and down the stairs. Daniel had always been disgusted by my stomach and every other jiggly part of my body. He preferred me to leave on a T-shirt when we had sex. Slowly, Jigsaw's burning away all of those bad memories and replacing them with good ones I'll remember forever.

The door opens and clicks shut. I lift one eyelid.

Jigsaw stops at the side of the bed, naked and absolutely stunning. *There's* something I never appreciated in bed before, how exquisite a man's body can be.

"Look at you," he rasps, an appreciative gleam shining in his eyes. He stands by the edge of the bed and absently rubs his hand over his collarbone, staring at me like I'm a buffet and he can't decide what he wants to feast on first.

He dives into the bed, sliding his arms under my body and pulling me closer. "How do you feel?"

"Electric," I whisper, stroking my fingers over his chest. "I like your tattoos."

"Thank you." He kisses my forehead. His hand strays to my breasts, cupping one and gently rubbing his thumb over the tip.

My back arches into his touch.

"Your breasts are beautiful." He dips down to suck my nipple into his mouth. A thousand arrows of pleasure shoot straight to my center. How does he do that?

I gasp and spear my fingers through his hair.

He releases my nipple and rolls me onto my back, aiming for my other breast.

I was too anxious to ever ask before, but now I'm loose and lust-drunk. "They're not too...big or jiggly?"

He frowns in confusion and stares at me like I asked to chew on his penis like a piece of bubblegum. "What?"

I tilt my head, angling my chin toward my chest.

"There's no such thing as too big." He cups my breasts with both hands. "Fit my hands perfectly."

Even in his firm grip, they wobble. "But—"

He lightly pinches my nipples. "They're not basketballs, they're supposed to jiggle." A wicked gleam enters his eyes. "Do I need to gag you?"

My lips push into a pout. "How am I going to learn if I don't ask questions?"

"The lessons don't seem to be sticking, though." He sits up and strokes his hand over his hardening length. "You seem to be a learning by doing type." He reaches for a condom on the nightstand and drops it on the pillow by my head.

A full-body shiver of excitement ripples over me. He wants to have sex again? "Is that normal?"

"What?"

I lower my gaze to his erection, growing larger with each passing second. "I mean, we just finished. Can all men do that? More than once a day?"

He chokes on a laugh. "I can't speak for all men." He flops next to me and strokes his knuckles over the tops of my breasts. "I'm sure with the right motivation, plenty of men can."

"What's *your* motivation?"

"You." He slides his hand between my breasts, down my belly, and nudges my thighs apart. "Naked and next to me. I don't need much more motivation than that."

I let out a sharp gasp as he slides one finger along my seam and over my clit.

"Fuck, you're drenched," he says like it's the best thing ever.

"I like when you're playing with my breasts." I lift my hands and squeeze them.

A feral expression plays over his face. "Yeah? What else do you like?"

My breath hitches. "When you touch me down there."

He slips his finger inside me, then slides out and teases my clit. "Where? Be more specific."

I can't look away from his intense eyes. Am I really saying these things out loud? "When you rub over my…clit."

"Like this?" He brings two fingers to the exact spot and slowly circles them.

"Oh God, yes." I squeeze my eyes shut and lift my hips.

"Mmm." He lets out a satisfied hum. "I like that too." With agonizing slowness, he builds the pressure and speed, massaging the same spot over and over like he has all the time in the world. My skin burns as my body winds tighter and tighter.

Needy whimpers spill from my lips and Jigsaw leans in to catch them with kisses. "That's it," he encourages. "Come for me. Then I'm going to teach you how to ride me." He brushes kisses over my cheeks and forehead. "Should have started there. You're going to look so fucking sexy grinding yourself on my cock."

A clear image of exactly that flashes in my mind. I want that so badly. *Right now.*

The tension breaks, sweet release washing over me.

He withdraws his hand. My heart's still wildly dancing in my chest. The mattress shifts.

Jigsaw's hand squeezes my thigh. "Up."

"I don't think I can move."

"You don't want to fail this lesson, do you?" he teases with a rough chuckle.

The competitive side of me forces my eyes open. He's stretched out on his back, rubbing the base of his condom-covered cock. "Come on."

I roll to my knees. The urge to cover myself wars with my love of the way he looks at my body with so much appreciation.

"How?"

His lips tilt into an amused smirk. "First of all, come closer. Throw one leg over me."

I straddle his hips. His cock slides along my cheeks and I glance over my shoulder. "I don't think that's where it's supposed to go."

Another cocky smile. "That's advanced coursework. We're not there yet." With his free hand, he motions me forward.

I brace myself on his shoulder and he guides himself to my entrance. He hisses as I slowly lower myself.

Oh my God, I almost cry from how amazing he feels at this angle. How is he so much bigger than anyone else I've ever been with, but it doesn't hurt at all?

"Now what?"

"Do what feels good." He rests his hands on my waist.

"*You* feel fantastic." I press my hand to his chest and slowly rock back and forth. "Amazing."

His lips kick into a teasing smile. "Are you sure you're bad at sex?"

"What?" I stop moving. "Why?"

"Because so far you're really good at it." He squeezes my hips, encouraging me to continue rocking back and forth. "Keep moving. Trust yourself. Let me see."

But the question threw me and now I've lost my momentum. He lazily sucks his thumb into his mouth and brings it between my legs. "Lean back a little."

I brace my hands on his thighs, arching my back.

"Fuck yeah." He rubs around my clit in small circular motions until I can't help but move myself against him. "There you go," he encourages.

"Oh." I gasp and throw my head back, moving my hips faster and faster. Pleasure sneaks up and explodes through me as my body pulses with glorious wave after wave.

I haven't even caught my breath when Jigsaw's rough hands dig into my hips, holding me in place for him to thrust up into me over and over. The quick strokes extend my own pleasure and I grip his forearms to hang on.

He shouts and throws his head back. Every muscle in his body strains through his release. Finally, he roughly yanks me down over him, hugging me to his chest, kissing the side of my head. He slides one hand down and pats my behind. "You're so fucking good. So fucking good," he repeats.

Glowing with pride that I've made him so happy, I kiss along his jaw and neck. His shoulder jerks and he laughs. "You're tickling me again."

Jigsaw

"I think I'm still coming," she pants against my neck.

Too drained to speak, I grin from ear to ear.

"That was…that was so amazing." She sits up and shakes her head, messy curls sliding over her shoulders. "No, amazing isn't strong enough."

She blinks at me in wonder, eyes sparkling. Cheeks and chest flushed and rosy from orgasm.

A possessive desire punches me in the chest. I'm the first one who did this to her. The *only one*. And I want it to stay that way. I want all of her orgasms to belong to me from now on.

"Come here," I hold out my arm and she eagerly squirms close, resting her head on my chest. Blonde curls, soft as silk, slide over my skin. Something smoky and seductive—incense, maybe—tickles my nose.

The guy who told this woman she's boring in bed needs a slap in the face—with a hammer. Or maybe I should thank him. Otherwise, by now, she probably would've been married to some boring twatwaffle who would never appreciate the explosive passion that simmers underneath Margot's prim exterior.

Like I suspected, she responds best to gentle touches and slowly working her up to a frenzy. She really goes wild when I whisper all sorts of dirty things in her ear. And she absolutely thrives when I praise her, which I end up doing a lot because she's *so* fucking good at everything.

"Is it always that...intense?" she whispers, tracing a restless pattern over my chest.

I capture her hand and bring her fingers to her mouth, kissing each one. "No, it's not," I answer honestly.

The irony of her blowing my mind when she's the one who asked *me* to help her improve her sex game isn't lost on me.

Plenty of women have told me I'm good at getting them off, but something's different with Margot. Like she was made for me to unlock and discover. And she's uncovered something different in *me*.

Even if we're not fucking like the fate of the world depends on our orgasms, I enjoy being with her. Her oddball humor mirrors my own. Even the silence is nice. She doesn't seem to feel the need to fill every blank space with meaningless chatter.

"Are you staying?" she asks, with the most hesitant tremor in her voice.

"Yeah." I stroke my hand over her arm.

She snuggles close. Her breasts are pressed against my side, leg thrown over mine. Instead of panic, I feel peace.

I have no business getting used to this. Our arrangement's temporary. Fuck, I should give her a final report card now—A-plus straight down the line—before I do something dumb like get attached to her, or worse, fall in love with her. Since I'm fairly certain I'm not capable of love, it's the attachment thing that keeps me from falling asleep.

I like the weight of her soft little body next to me way too much. Her slow breaths, the rise and fall of her chest, the way she purses her lips in her sleep.

Cuddling—when I'm the one who warned her not to catch feelings —seems like a bad idea. But I can't exactly grab my jeans and hit the road. Well, I could. I can do any fucking thing I want.

And for the rest of the night, I want to hold Margot in my arms and smell her hair, apparently.

CHAPTER THIRTY-ONE

Margot

I'm not sure how much later it is when I wake again. My room's darker.

Jigsaw's still holding me. I lift my head and find him watching me.

"Did you sleep?"

"Can't."

"Why?" I roll away from him. "Is your arm numb from holding me? You should've just told me to move."

He stretches and flexes his arm. "But I like holding you."

"I like being held by you." My cheeks warm and I have to look away.

"Hey." He rolls closer and grips my chin, turning me to face him. "Are you okay? Hurt anywhere? That was a lot...if it had been a while..." His voice trails off, but his serious eyes never leave my face.

I close my eyes for a second, checking in with my body. "No, I feel spectacular."

Relieved, he blows out a breath and pulls me closer, draping his arm over my waist.

"Can I ask you something without you making fun of me?" I drag my fingers over his shoulder and down the arm resting on my body. "It's a bit strange."

"I love strange." He props his head up on his hand and waits. "Hit me."

Heat slides over my skin. Am I really asking this? I'm pretty sure I already know the answer. "How come, and please don't let this go to your head, you're, um, a lot *bigger* than any other *experience* I've ever had. But it doesn't hurt?"

Instead of the laughter I expected, dead silence fills the space after my question.

Finally, he takes a deep breath and asks in a much calmer than he looks voice, "Did any of those other *experiences* ever bother to warm you up?"

"Not the way you do," I admit.

He slides his fingers over my shoulder and down my arm. "Your body needs to be ready." His hand slips between my legs and he groans. "You don't have any problem getting wet. I'm guessing whoever you were with didn't bother with foreplay."

Now that I know the difference, I can say, no, there was never real foreplay.

"Your mind's important too." He strokes his fingers through my hair. "If you're anxious or worried it's hard for your body to get excited."

I squirm closer and rest my hand on his chest. "Are you always so considerate and patient? Or am I receiving such a robust education because you want to be a good teacher?"

The tenderness in his expression vanishes. He rolls to his back and throws his arm over his forehead. "Fuuuck me," he mutters.

"What?"

"Nothing." He stares at the ceiling for so long fear prickles over my skin. Is he mad at me?

"Thank you."

He flicks his gaze to me. "For?"

"Being such an excellent teacher and letting me ask weird questions. Even if I annoy you."

He sighs and pulls me closer. "You don't annoy me." He glances over. "Now will you tell me what your asshole ex said that made you think you're not good at sex?"

"No. It's too embarrassing." I lift my chin. "Besides, it doesn't matter anymore. You've proved him wrong." When he doesn't answer right away, panic claws at me. "Right? You think I'm good?"

"I think you're perfect." His gaze shifts to the ceiling again. "And I hope to fuck you won't try to waste your time winning him back."

"What?" I push up. "Why would you think...that's not what this is about."

His jaw clenches tight. "Isn't it?"

"No. Look, just say it if you want to. We're done with lessons. You're done." I choke on a sob. "With me now."

"What? No." He sits up and pulls me against him. "Why would you even say that?"

"Because we had sex. It was amazing. You don't have anything else to teach me."

He rumbles with laughter, but there's a hard edge to it that leaves me uneasy. "How wrong you are, little one."

Tingles of desire push my concern and exhaustion away. "Oh."

"I told you I was happy you bought that big box of condoms." His fingers trace a lazy path between my breasts to my stomach. "There are still many, many things left to teach you."

Jigsaw

"I'm looking forward to learning them." Margot seems less hesitant.

Fuck, for a minute there, I was going to agree with her and say, yeah, let's call this good.

But I can't fucking do it.

"Did you say something about food before?" I pat my stomach. "I'm starving now."

"Yes." She sits up quickly, like she's worried she hasn't been a good hostess. "I made a baked sausage and cheese rigatoni earlier. I was planning to freeze it and have it throughout the week."

"That sounds good."

She blows out a relieved breath. What'd she think I was going to do, reject a home-cooked meal?

Being with her is so comfortable, I sit up without thinking and swing my legs over the edge of the bed, tapping the lamp by her bed on.

Behind me, she gasps and moves closer, her knees rubbing against my hip.

"Who did this to you?" Her feathery touch against the ancient scars crisscrossing my back sends a shiver down my spine. Why does this one tiny woman have the power to make me tremble?

Who did this to you? Not *what did you do?* Most people assume it was an accident or even that the scars were self-inflicted. The ink I tried to cover it with didn't quite get the job done.

"My father." None of the shame I usually feel from admitting my own flesh and blood enjoyed whipping me to shreds comes with the admission. The twisted glee I sometimes get from shocking people with the truth is absent too. Understanding. That's all I want from her.

"Your father?" Her voice soft and pained.

Unable to speak, I nod.

Light, feathery sensation slides over my skin. "Does this hurt?"

"No. It feels…weird, like, less sensation in spots. But it doesn't hurt anymore."

Heat from her soft naked body. Something wet splashes against my skin.

Having her at my back, touching me but not looking directly at me, makes it easier to say, "He was a mean fucker."

"What about your mother?"

"She 'disappeared' when Jezzie was four or five."

"Your little sister?"

"Yeah." My lips curve, remembering her as a kid. Always too serious for her age.

"What do you mean your mom *disappeared*?"

"My father said she died but we never had a burial or anything." The more I talk, the easier it is for the words to come out. "As a kid, I accepted his word. Didn't have much choice. But as I got older, I started to wonder if he killed her or she ran away."

"Where is he now?" She shifts her body so she's sitting next to me, one leg tucked under her. She winds her arms around my bicep, pressing her breasts against me, and rests her chin on my shoulder. As if she senses the physical contact helps me explain.

"He'll never hurt another woman or kid again." I flash what some have called my serial killer smile. "That's all I can say for certain."

Margot's stare burns into the side of my face. I turn and her lips curve into a sinister smile. "Good."

Her approval pushes me to confess something only Rooster and a handful of brothers know. "I scattered pieces of his body from Oregon to Maine. It would take years and a lot of people to put him back together. That's how I got the road name Jigsaw."

She blinks. "So when you joke that your name comes from collecting the body parts from your enemies, you're *not* kidding."

"Sometimes, if you say the unhinged stuff with a straight face people assume you're fucking with them."

"I'll have to try that." A pained expression crosses her face. "Is that why you didn't want to take your shirt off the first couple of times we…"

I nod slowly and try to give her the truth. "I didn't want to ruin the moment. Or have you ask me questions—"

"I'm sorry, I —"

"No, it's fine. I'm glad you asked." I rest my hand on her knee. Thoughts I can't form into words bubble up.

I've never told all of that to anyone before…

…You're not just some sex project to me…

But I can't seem to line them up the right way.

Instead, I do what I'm good at. Crack a joke. "You think my clothes are dry yet? I don't want to drape my balls all over your furniture while you're feeding me."

Margot doesn't laugh. She leans in and presses the softest kiss to my cheek. "I'll go check."

CHAPTER THIRTY-TWO

Margot

"So are you allowed to tell me about your trip?" I ask once we're seated at the kitchen counter with steaming plates of rigatoni.

"Yeah, it was a shitshow from start to finish, really." He stabs into the pasta and spears a chunk of sausage.

"Why?" I hesitate. Bikers are so damn secretive. "Am I allowed to ask?"

"You can ask. I might not share all the details, but I don't care if you ask." He pops more pasta in his mouth and chews slowly, closing his eyes. "This is so good. Thank you."

"Thanks for having dinner with me."

He rests his hand on my leg and flexes his fingers.

"So, the shitshow?" I prompt.

"Ah, yeah. The memorial was canceled before we even got there."

"Why?"

"Long story. Nothing to do with us, really." He pokes one tine of his fork into a piece of sausage over and over. "Before we left, we had a big meeting since brothers from all our charters were there."

"Seems prudent."

"Yeah. This asshole from my original charter tried to challenge our national prez. That was the shitshow part."

"Oh wow. That sounds...rather daring. Kind of stupid if he didn't shore up alliances beforehand."

"Exactly!" He sets his fork down. "Well, he didn't. I'm not even sure he ran it by his president before he opened his big yap."

"So, what happened?"

He watches me for a few seconds before answering. "We voted it down."

"Did he burn rubber out of there when the meeting was adjourned?" I snicker.

Jigsaw laughs with me. "Sure did."

He finishes his plate and sips his ginger ale.

"So, that sounds exciting."

"Yeah, real exciting." He flashes a teasing smile. "Then before we left, my sister reached out. Said she needed me to pick her up somewhere she wasn't even supposed to be." His jaw clenches and he rolls his eyes. "So I split from the guys outside Philly. Then she calls to tell me everything's fine and she's home. So, I'm probably gonna ride out to her place this week to check on her."

I swallow hard. His sister's important to him. His only blood relative. But he still came to see me first? "Are you sure you don't want to check on her now?"

He taps his phone, sitting on the counter next to his glass. "She was telling me the truth. Tracked her phone right back to her apartment."

It takes me longer than it should to puzzle that out. "You track your sister's phone?"

"Of course I do," he scoffs.

"Does she know?"

"Yeah," he answers slowly. "It's one of the conditions of me paying for all her shit." His lips curl into a frightening smile. "What she *doesn't* know is that I have a backup app installed. So if she shuts off the main one, I'll still be able to find her."

"Wow, you are...sneaky."

"No, kids are sneaky. I'm just smarter." He shrugs. "She's a good egg. Hasn't tampered with it yet."

I cock my head and study him for a moment. "Do you have access to *everything* on her phone?"

"Are you asking if I spy on my sister? Read her texts?"

"Yes."

His lips twist, like he's debating if he should lie to me or not. "Yes, I have access. No, I don't *spy* on her. Unless I have to." He blows out a breath. "Trust me, I don't have time to waste reading all her back and forths with her friends about what time they're meeting at Panera and what kind of mac and cheese is superior."

I press my hand to my lips and snicker. "Sounds like you snoop a little."

Jigsaw smirks, his eyes narrowing slightly. "Maybe just a tad," he admits, his tone playful. "But only to make sure she's not getting into anything too crazy. She's a good kid but she's gone through a wild phase or two."

"She's lucky to have you looking out for her," I say softly, feeling a twinge of envy for the closeness they seem to share. My own older brothers have certainly never been so concerned about me. "How big is the gap between you two?"

"About eight years."

"Ah, both of my brothers are a lot older. They were teenagers when I was born, and I think resented my presence."

"Really? They didn't look out for you? Protect their baby sister?"

I snort and shake my head with disbelief. "No."

"Shit, Teller has ten years on his sister, and he's always looked out for her the best he could."

"I'm close to my cousin. He's only a few years older than me. He'd protect me in school, but he got picked on too, so..." Why am I talking about any of this like it still matters?

"Actually, I don't know why I'm surprised." He hesitates as if he's not sure he wants to continue. "I had older brothers too, but they took off when they turned eighteen. Didn't give a fuck about me or Jezzie."

"Are they...have you ever tried to find them?"

He pauses for an even longer time before answering. "Yeah, once or twice."

I swallow hard, afraid to ask my next question, but unable to stop myself. "You said it's possible your dad may have killed your mom...is it possible he...?"

"It's possible." He reaches for his glass and spins it in a slow circle. "I've thought of that too. It was one of his 'wives' who helped me escape—"

"Wait, *one of his wives?*"

He shoots a sharp look at me that snaps my mouth shut. "I don't know what else to call them. He had a bunch of women around we were supposed to call 'Momma this or that.' He'd refer to them as his wives. But there were other 'elder' type men around who had leadership roles too and other kids who came with their families."

"So, do you have more siblings out there?"

"Probably," he answers slowly, still turning the glass around and around. "Don't really want to find out, honestly."

"I don't blame you." Should I continue or drop it? He doesn't seem happy talking about this. "You said one of them helped you escape?"

"Yeah." He curls his fingers over his shoulder, tapping his back. "The last whipping I took was so bad, she was afraid he'd kill me." A pained smile crosses his face. "She was a nice girl. Took a big risk to give me a few things so I could leave." He shrugs. "Didn't matter. I got to school and passed out from an infection. People found out what happened to me—"

"Was your father arrested?"

"Nope." His tone's laced with a dull bitterness.

"What about Jezzie?"

"Didn't have a mark on her."

"How'd *you* escape, then?"

"Rooster's aunt and uncle came and got me."

His playful, confident demeanor has changed so drastically over the course of this conversation. His answers dwindling down to just the basics when there must be more to it. I'm used to counseling people in one specific area of tragedy. Grief and loss. This is so much more complex. What should I say?

Joining a motorcycle club makes sense. The complete opposite of the religious oppression he grew up in but also a somewhat strict and orderly organization where they dress similarly and have to attend mandatory meetings. Although, the intent with a cult is to control the person by restricting their thoughts and access to information, while the motorcycle club doesn't restrict anything unless it could potentially harm the *whole* club.

Okay, definitely don't point out the similarities—or differences—between a cult and an MC. He won't appreciate that.

"*Mrrrar.*" Gretel twines her body around the legs of Jigsaw's stool, then mine.

"Hey, girl." Jigsaw leans down and scoops Gretel into one hand, lifting her into his lap. "I was wondering when you might make an appearance."

I'm so charmed by the way he lets her rub herself all over his chin and the gentle way he pets her, I don't have the heart to tell him I don't allow her near the kitchen counters. As if she senses me watching, she ignores our plates and the counter, and curls up in Jigsaw's lap instead.

"She *really* likes you," I say.

He smiles and keeps petting her.

Maybe it's a good thing she distracted us from the heavy conversation. I reach over and rub behind her ear and scratch her chin.

After a few minutes, Gretel's had her quota of affection. She hops off Jigsaw's lap onto the floor, meows at us, and saunters away.

Jigsaw's shaking with laughter. "She has a lot of personality packed into such a tiny body."

"She does."

He reaches over, settling his hand on my bare knee. "Hey, thanks for listening. I didn't mean to get too heavy."

I slide my fingers over his knuckles. Large hands—scarred and rough—that aren't afraid to get dirty or defend himself, but are also so gentle when he touches me. "It's okay. I want to know more about you." My voice breaks a little. "I hate that you suffered so much as a child, though." I don't want him to think I feel sorry for him. If anything, I admire the strength it took to become the opposite of what his father was.

His expression softens and he gently squeezes my leg before removing his hand. "I don't talk about it much. It's over. Seems pointless to dwell on the past."

"I can understand that." It's more than that, though. The reasons he "doesn't do relationships" seem clearer now. Whether he realizes it or not, he's carefully built walls around himself.

I'm lucky he let me have a glimpse inside.

And wonder if he'll ever allow more than that.

CHAPTER THIRTY-THREE

Jigsaw

UNEASE CURLS IN MY STOMACH. I REVEALED AN AWFUL LOT TO MARGOT while we had dinner. Things I've never told another woman. She deals with enough grief and sadness. I shouldn't dump my ancient baggage on her.

She slides off her stool and presses the softest kiss against my cheek. "Are you still hungry?" She nods to the glass dish still half-full of baked pasta.

I could probably finish the whole thing, but I don't want to eat all of her food. "I'm good."

"I only have fruit for dessert." She lifts her chin toward a bowl on the counter full of red apples and a few ripening bananas.

"You mind if I run downstairs and grab my stuff?" I don't want her to think I'm trying to move in, but I'd like to get my toothbrush and a couple other items.

She grabs our plates. "Not at all."

"I'll help you with that." I stand and try to take the plates from her hands.

"I've got it. Go get your things." She points toward the hallway. "The laundry's right next to the bathroom. Wash whatever you want."

I lean down and press a quick kiss to her forehead. "Be right back."

Am I really doing this? Staying over at a woman's place? Wanting to stay. It's not because Rooster's still in Tennessee and the house will be empty. If I'm lonely, I could go to the clubhouse and hang with the guys who came back with me. If I just need a warm body to fuck, I can easily ride down to Crystal Ball and sweet-talk one of the dancers into spending the night with me at the clubhouse next door.

But I specifically want to be *here*. In a house I find a little bit creepy, with a woman I can't seem to get enough of.

By the time I return, she's cleaned the kitchen. She's bending over, sliding something into the fridge. Now that one hunger's been satisfied, another appears with a vengeance.

I drop my bag by the door and stride into the kitchen. She closes the fridge at the same time I reach her. I grip her hips and pull her to me.

"Miss me?" I breathe against her neck.

A soft, gasping laugh flows past her lips. "I did."

Sliding my hands from her hips to the buttons of her shirt, I quickly work them loose, pleased she didn't bother putting anything else on underneath. She leans against me, bracing her hands on my thighs and arching her back, giving me better access to the buttons.

"You don't mind me stripping you down in the kitchen, right?"

She shakes her head.

"Good." I cup one breast, lightly pinching her nipple. "Are you game for another lesson?"

"Yes."

I drag the shirt down her arms and toss it on the counter. "Come here." Grabbing her by the hips again, I push her closer to the counter. "Brace your hands against the edge."

She gets where I'm going with this immediately, bending at the waist to press her palms to the curved edge. "Like this?" She tilts her hips, tipping her ass up.

"Exactly." I run my fingers down her spine, loving the way she trembles under my touch. "These shorts are cute, but they have to go."

"Okay." She twitches her hips from side to side as if asking me to hurry.

I drag them down her legs, stopping to kiss the backs of her thighs and sink my teeth in one round butt cheek. She hunches her back like she's trying to hide. "No." I tap her butt. "Arch your back for me."

A hesitant grunt catches in her throat. I think I understand the problem. "Margot. I love your ass." I trace my fingers over one cheek and down the back of her leg. "That night when we were all here." I don't remind her *why* we were here. "When you bent over in the kitchen downstairs to get that case of water, I had to work so hard to control myself." I rise and, holding onto her hips, drag her back against me so she can feel how hard I am for her behind my fly. "I wanted to strip you out of that cute little bank robber outfit you were wearing and do exactly this."

Short, nervous laughter bursts out of her. "You remember what I was wearing?"

"Yeah, you were fucking adorable." Since that night I've been consumed by her but it seems like too much to admit. I wedge my hand between her thighs. "Spread your legs for me."

She inches her feet apart.

I groan as I cup her bare pussy, sliding a finger between her lips. Anxious or not, she's into this. "You're so wet." I tease her clit until she's rocking against my hand.

She reaches one hand back, clutching at my jeans.

"No." I place her hand back on the counter.

She turns her head and glares. "Why are your pants still on?"

I dip one finger inside her and groan when she closes her eyes and drops her head. Breathless and arching into my hand, she lets out a frustrated whine.

"Give me a minute." I drag her wetness to her clit, slowly circling and teasing until I find the right motion that strings her body tight. I work my jeans loose with one hand and pull the condom I'd stashed in my pocket earlier free.

She moans and bucks against me as I fumble with the fucking rubber. "Hold on."

Growling with annoyance, I have to stop touching her so I can use both hands to roll the condom down my dick.

She arches and wiggles. Raises up on her tiptoes, then down again. Eagerly waiting. I grab her hips. I have to bend at the knees to line us up but finally I'm sliding into her, fighting the urge to slam in one thrust.

"Yes," she whispers, pressing back against me. She squeaks and retreats.

"Too much?" I ask, stopping my movements.

"No…just different."

"Different good?" I squeeze her hips. "You move. Work yourself on my cock. Show me how much you need."

She's hesitant at first, then moves in unhurried, languid movements. I sink my teeth into my lip, pushing away my desire to bang away at her with quick, deep thrusts.

Her raspy moans echo around us. "Jensen," she breathes.

"I've got you." I push forward again, filling her with slow, even strokes.

"Oh God yes," she whimpers.

Her body trembles and tightens. She clutches the counter, hanging on as I increase my pace.

Fuck. I want her mouth on mine. Her breasts mashed up against me. Visually, this is hot as fuck, but I suddenly need more. She's building toward another orgasm when I pull out of her.

"Jigsaw?" she yelps.

I grab her around the waist and boost her onto the counter, dragging her to the edge and wedging my body between her spread thighs. I crash my lips against hers and swallow her moans of pleasure. She circles her arms around my neck and drags her fingers through my hair.

This angle sucks. The counter's too high or she's not close enough to the edge. Whatever the physics of it is, my knee keeps hitting something, throwing off my rhythm.

"Come here." I lift her off the counter, impaling her.

"Oh!" she gasps and giggles, then wraps her legs around me. Using her hands on my shoulders for leverage, she starts working herself up and down.

"Fuck." I squeeze my eyes shut. "You're a natural at this."

My frantic gaze ping-pongs around the apartment for a suitable surface. Can I make it into the bedroom?

Chair. It's closest. Pants falling down my legs and Margot distracting me with her movements, I shuffle to the chair and gently lay her in it. I have to slip out of her for a moment. She threads her fingers through my hair and pulls me down for a kiss as I fill her again. In a hard, frenzied rush I pound into her. She lifts up, pressing her mouth to mine, opening so I can sweep my tongue against hers.

This woman has me absolutely turned inside out. The sounds of our bodies sliding together mingle with her breathy whimpers. She hooks her arm around my neck and whispers against my ear, "Your cock feels so fucking good filling me."

Demons below, those filthy words coming from Margot set me off. I sink deep inside her, spilling into the condom. Completely spent, I rest my head on her chest. Her heartbeat's wild against my ear. She threads her fingers through my hair and brushes kisses against my sweaty forehead.

If I'm not careful, I could get addicted to this.

Margot

After we peel ourselves out of the lounge chair, Jigsaw kicks off his jeans.

"Felt like I had a lot of things working against me there." He lets out a wild bit of laughter and runs his hands through his hair.

"I couldn't tell." Everything we did was electrifying. Except maybe when he pulled me to the edge of the counter and we couldn't make that angle work.

He decides to worry about doing his laundry later and we end up in my bed. I'm spent but restless.

Words I want to say bubble up, then pop. Questions I want to ask but shouldn't.

He holds out his arm, inviting me closer. Tentatively, I inch my body next to his until our legs are touching. His skin's so warm, his body so solid and brimming with life even though his eyelids droop as if he's on the verge of sleep.

I rest my head on his chest. He runs his fingers over my hair. "I didn't mess it up too bad, considering." His voice and laughter rumble against my cheek.

He seems to be twirling locks of my hair around his finger. It's soothing and I'm almost drifting into sleep when his chest ripples under me.

"You can knock kitchen counter sex and standing doggy off your list now, but I think you're going to need a shorter guy for the counter sex."

My heart stops. *Shorter guy?* List? I don't want anyone else.

This is still nothing more than some casual lessons for him.

I sit up, fear beating a steady drum in my chest.

"What's wrong?" Concern edges into his voice.

"I made a mistake."

He sits up, resting his hand on my back. "About?"

"This."

"It's the feel-good chemicals from all the orgasms." He rubs his hand over my back and kisses my shoulder. "Give me a few minutes and we can try some other positions."

"You're awfully cocky," I grumble.

Maybe he's right. I'm still riding a wave of euphoria that's only making me think this has turned into something else. It obviously doesn't mean anything more than that to him.

He said he missed me while he was away. I know I missed him something awful. My heart's breaking but I don't know what to say or what questions to ask.

He's opened up to me about his scars, his childhood. That means something, doesn't it?

Apparently not.

We're just sex. That's it. No one was supposed to catch feelings.

That's what we agreed to.

I don't think that's enough anymore.

CHAPTER THIRTY-FOUR

Jigsaw

I SPENT THE LAST FEW DAYS AT MARGOT'S. DIDN'T MEAN TO STAY THAT long, but I couldn't find the desire to leave. I helped her check more positions off her list, and when she had to work, I kept myself busy. Either I rode to a friend's gym and worked out, stopped by Remy's bar to annoy him, or hung out at the racetrack with Eraser. At least that way, I could reasonably claim I was doing *something* for the club like Z asked me to. Sort of.

But when Rooster sends me a text saying he, and the rest of the club, are almost home, it's time to go.

Unfortunately, Margot's with a family. I end up leaving her a note.

M-

Need to run home.

Had a good time.

See you soon.

J

I stare at my chicken-y scribble. *Had a good time*—understatement. *Hope you enjoyed the orgasms* sounds cocky. I don't want to leave anything too X-rated in case, for some reason, her father comes up here and sees it. This doesn't feel right either, though.

I'll text her later. Hopefully, by then I'll have come up with something better. Maybe Rooster can give me some advice. He's always sending sappy shit to Shelby.

No. They're engaged. Margot and I are just...fuck buddies? Teacher and student? I grab the note and add *"A++"* at the bottom.

The ride downstate gives me time to think about my time with Margot. Several times, I have the urge to turn around, go back to her place, and rip up that note.

But I keep riding.

I arrive at the downstate clubhouse a few minutes before Z, Butcher, Grip, and Suds pull in.

Z's busy on his phone as he approaches the clubhouse.

"Where's Rooster at?" I ask.

He scowls, finishes whatever he was doing, and glances up. "Hello to you too."

"Hey, Prez," I say with a bit more respect. "How was the ride?"

"Fine. As for Rooster, aren't *you* usually the keeper of his whereabouts?"

"He rode home with you guys, right?" I ask, ignoring the whole keeper thing.

"Yeah," he answers with obvious irritation in his tone. "Grinder and Rooster kept riding straight to their houses." He glances at his phone. "I assume Rooster is 'reuniting' with Shelby by now."

"We're not sitting at the table?" I ask.

"No. I'm just here to drop off something. I have my own *reuniting* with my woman I want to do."

Jamming my hands in my pockets, I stare down at my boots and laugh. "Gotcha, Prez." I open the clubhouse door for him. "After you."

"Gee, thanks." Z pats my cheek, then stops and glances back at my bike. Fuck, all my gear from the trip is still strapped to it.

He shifts his gaze from the bike to me one more time, then steps inside the clubhouse.

Phew.

I lift my chin at Butcher and Grip. "How'd it go?"

"You missed a good time," Grip says, slapping my shoulder. "Those

southern muffler bunnies suck cock like it's their mission in life, brother."

I roll my eyes skyward. "Good to know. Thought it was a muffler bunny-free zone for the memorial?"

Grip shrugs. "Memorial was over."

Butcher lifts his chin at the clubhouse. "Z's been grumpy the whole way home."

"Poor Lilly." Grip lets out a dirty chuckle. "Z's probably gonna fuck her through a wall when he gets his hands on her."

"Z's gonna put your face through a wall if he hears you talking about his ol' lady like that," I warn, although I've had my own impure thoughts about Lilly once or twice. I wouldn't say them out loud, though.

I follow them inside. Eazy, Suds, and a few other brothers are at the bar, rehashing the trip. Lala's got her friend Kristen behind the bar with her serving drinks.

The noise and chatter of the clubhouse grates on me after a while. I stay to bullshit with the guys a bit longer, then check the time. Rooster and Shelby should be taking a break from their "reuniting" by now.

As much as I enjoy the camaraderie with my brothers, my mind's somewhere else. With a certain someone whose soft curves, blonde hair, and wicked sense of humor constantly hover in my mind.

After a quick nod to the guys, I slip out the front door and head home.

Rooster's in the kitchen, shirtless and guzzling water from a gallon jug.

So many jokes come to mind. My eyes are about to pop out of my head with the effort of holding them in.

"I so badly want to make a joke about your ol' lady draining you dry but I feel like it's disrespectful to Shelby," I finally blurt out.

Eh, I tried.

Rooster blows out a slow, irritated breath, sets the jug on the counter and turns around. "And yet, you said it anyway. Hello to you too, cock-knocker. Where've you been?"

"Clubhouse. Figured we were all meeting there, but everyone went home to fuck instead."

He shakes his head, but the corners of his mouth twitch with amusement.

I glance at the hallway leading to the back staircase and up to their bedroom. "I assume Shelby will be unconscious for a few minutes. Can I talk to you for a sec?"

He stares at me, then must decide I'm not yanking his chain, and nods. "You want coffee? Shelby made a huge batch of kitchen sink cookies." He nods to a long blue-and-pink tray loaded with cookies sitting in the middle of the table.

"What the fuck are kitchen sink cookies?" I ask, although I'm intrigued and already on my way to grab one.

"Uh, chocolate chunk, pecans, coconut." He shrugs. "They're good."

I take a small bite of one. "Sweet Jesus, you should go away more often."

His mouth twists into an annoyed smirk and he rolls his eyes. "So, yes to coffee?"

"Yeff," I mumble around a mouthful of sweet chocolate-coconutty goodness.

While the coffee's brewing, he leans against the counter and crosses his arms over his chest. "Why do you look like you're about to explode and splatter Jigsaw particles all over my kitchen?"

"What?" But he described how I feel accurately. I stay by the table and grab another cookie. While I'm munching on it, working out what I want to say, he crosses to the fridge and pulls out a carton of half-n-half and a carton of milk. At the counter, he grabs a glass, pours milk into it, then hands it to me.

"Thanks," I mumble, swallowing the rest of the cookie. I drink half the glass, then set it on the table.

Just say it. "Don't get mad." I hold my arms out straight in front of me in a *don't kill me* meets *calm down* gesture.

Rooster groans. "Always a good conversation opener."

"When you and Shelby first hooked up, it was only supposed to be a vacation thing, right?"

As I knew they would, Rooster's eyes narrow at *hooked up.* At least he let me spit out the whole question.

He growls a noise that's neither a yes nor a no.

Not put off by the warning growl, I persist. "When did you know it was more than a vacation fling?"

"Jesus." He rakes his fingers through his hair and stares at the floor for a few seconds. "So many times. But I guess the first time it really hit me was the night I brought her up to Blaise's ranch."

"That's when we were still in Texas." Is he serious? "You barely knew her."

He shrugs. "What can I say? I just fucking *knew* I wouldn't be able to let her go."

"But you did." He'd been one unpleasant motherclucker on the ride from Texas to New York too.

"Yeah, club had to ride home. But she and I kept in touch." He hesitates, then twists his face into a *fuck it* expression. "I woke up thinking about her every day."

"Woke up *alone*, if I remember right. We all thought you'd lost your mind, leaving parties early." I shake my head like I'm deeply disappointed, but really, I'd been impressed with his restraint. "Turning down porn stars."

He sends me a withering glare. "Your attention to where my dick goes is disturbing."

"I'm just saying. It's not like Shelby would've known the difference."

"*I* would've known the difference." He lifts his shoulders. "What would've been the point, anyway? I wanted her. No one else could make me happy."

"Happy? Bro, lots of women would be thrilled to make you *happy*."

"Not happy in my pants, you degenerate." He lets out a disgusted snort. "Happy in *here*." He pounds on his chest.

More obnoxious words roll onto my tongue, but something clicks in my own chest that makes me swallow the joke.

The coffee maker chimes, and Rooster pours the dark, steaming brew into two mugs and brings them to the table, setting them down with a *thunk*. I grab the half-n-half and pour some into my mug and use half a cookie to stir it around. *Cookies and cream in my coffee.* I reach for the sugar bowl and dump in two spoons worth.

"Then when she came to New York," Rooster continues, dropping into the chair at the head of the table, "seeing her again. *Nothing* had changed for me. I still wanted to be with her just as much."

I nod slowly and take a cautious sip of coffee. The hot liquid sears my tongue and I set the mug down. Everything he's saying finally makes sense to me. "I remember how bummed you were when you two said goodbye in Kodiak."

"Awww, that's the sweetest thing I ever heard." Shelby's bare feet whisper over the tile floor as she shuffles up behind Rooster, wraps her arms around his neck, and peppers the side of his face with kisses. "I hated leavin' you then and I hate it when we're apart now."

His cheeks lift and he pats her arm, then pulls her around into his lap. "Were you spying on us, chickadee?"

"Nope. Y'all sounded so serious. I was worried it might be club business and didn't want to interrupt." She glances over at me and reaches out, touching my arm. "You sound like you have something on your mind. Everything okay?"

Damn, I love this girl.

Rooster's instincts about Shelby were on target from the beginning. Why am I so convinced my own instincts about Margot are wrong?

"Yeah. I'm good, songbird."

"He's being a nosy little goblin is what he is," Rooster grumbles.

"Hush your mouth." Shelby scolds him with a smile on her lips, then returns her attention to me. "You want me to do a reading? I'll take out the fancy cards Rooster gave me."

Rooster stretches his neck and stares up at the ceiling. "Does he really deserve a reading with the *fancy* cards?"

Shelby elbows him. "Yes."

I smirk at Rooster. "I think Shelby loves me more than you do. You keep it up with that attitude and she's going to replace you as my best friend."

He rumbles with laughter. "All right, all right. I'm sorry. Yes, get the fancy tarot cards out."

Shelby doesn't move. She stares at me intently. "Are you seein' someone, Jigsaw?"

Jesus, maybe she *is* psychic.

"'Cause it didn't look like you ever came home after Tennessee. Where ya been?"

"I thought you were upstate hanging with the girls while we were gone?"

"I was but Lilly and I came home yesterday." She loops her arms around Rooster's neck and kisses his cheek again. "When we knew our men were headed back."

Rooster's smile morphs into a frown.

"And then when I realized no one was here," Shelby continues, "I went and stayed at Lilly's 'cause I'm still too chicken to stay in my own home alone."

Well, fuck if that doesn't lay a ton of guilt on me. "Why didn't you call me?"

"Figured you were busy." She shrugs.

Now I feel like I owe her an explanation for not being around when she needed someone. "Can this stay here?" I knock my knuckles against the table. "I have a reputation to maintain."

Rooster rolls his eyes, but Shelby raises her right hand. "I won't breathe a word. Not to anyone." She glances at Rooster. "He's the only one I'd share secrets with, anyway. And he's sittin' right here."

I blow out a breath. If I share this with them, then it's real. No going back. Damn, I want it to be real. "Yes, I'm kind of seeing someone."

"Define 'kinda,'" Shelby says.

"It started out as…one thing. But now I think it's a lot more."

"Awww!" Shelby coos and slides out of Rooster's lap to throw her arms around my neck. "Who is she?" she squeals against my ear.

"Thaaat's not important."

"Uh-oh." Shelby retreats to the chair on the opposite side of the table. "Don't tell me it's that heifer Stella. I will *not* go on double dates with that bag of hair. She's mean and snotty as heck."

I choke on a laugh. "No, it's not one of the club's porn princesses. Or a stripper."

Shelby opens her mouth.

"Not a club girl either," I say, cutting off her question.

Rooster sits forward, staring at me like he can peer inside my head and uncover the information he wants. "But it *is* someone affiliated with the club, isn't it?"

Fuuuck. He's doing the math. There aren't many single women affiliated with the club who aren't porn stars, strippers, or muffler bunnies. He's gonna come up with Margot's name really fast.

"As long as it ain't my momma, I'm all for it," Shelby mutters.

"It's not Angelina," Rooster says slowly. "Dawson's been making progress with her."

Shelby titters with laughter.

"It's not Heidi's friend Dawn. She's got a kid, and you're morally opposed to raising crotch goblins."

"Yes, I am." I nod.

Shelby shakes her head. "Rude. But also, same."

"It's not Shadow's wife, Myra, because that'd be really fucked up, even for you," Rooster says, still drilling twin holes into my forehead.

"Look, stop trying to guess." I pull a helpless puppy face. "And give me some advice."

"What advice do you need?" Rooster's tone is so serious, I almost believe he's not fucking with me.

"Did I catch monogamy from you two? Or did I get hexed from, you know, being with her too many times in a row?"

"Jiggy!" Shelby slaps her hand against the table. "What in the hell's wrong with you?"

Rooster narrows his gaze, his face getting all pinched like it does when he's thinking really hard. "He's being obnoxious to mask his real feelings. Because feelings make him uncomfortable."

"Look who woke up thinking he's Sigmund Freud today," I quip.

"Is that true, Jiggy?" Shelby asks.

"No, I'm a naturally gifted comedian," I answer in a *this should be obvious* tone.

"You're really not," Rooster says.

Shelby stands. "All right, I'm getting my cards. The universe will help us get to the bottom of this." She points a sassy finger at me. "Don't move."

"Yes, songbird."

As soon as she clears the room, Rooster leans forward. "It's Margot, isn't it?"

I tilt my head and blink at him.

"Don't try that I'm-so-innocent face on me," he warns. "Teller's gonna kill you if you fuck stuff up with our access to the oven."

"No shit." I take a breath. "She and I already talked about that before anything..." I shake off that train of thought. "Nothing's getting fucked up." Then, in the most serious tone I've probably used with Rooster since his uncle died, I admit, "I think I'm falling in love with her."

Holy shit. Did I just really say that?

He opens his mouth.

I hold my hands in the air. "I know. I always said I'm incapable of that. My heart's still black and shriveled but she seems to like it that way."

He chuckles, then takes a big breath, like he's relieved. "Good. You deserve someone who appreciates you. You're too unique to be wasted on someone boring."

"Hah, so you admit I'm special."

"Definitely special." He wipes the sarcastic expression off his face. "So that's why the twenty questions about Shelby and me?"

"Yeah. It started out like a friendly arrangement situation." I'll go to my grave before I'd betray Margot and share that she asked me to help her get better at sex. Not even with Rooster. "But now I just want to... see her all the time. Be around her." *Smell her hair.* "Do stuff with her —*outside* of the bedroom. Although, that's usually where we end up."

"So what's the problem?"

"Is that normal?"

"Yes, it's normal," he says with more patience than I'd expect when I'm asking such a dumb question.

"Since we were really clear in the beginning that it was strictly…" *for educational purposes.*

"Sex?" Rooster answers for me. "Use your big boy words."

"Yes," I grit my teeth. "*I* warned her multiple times not to catch feelings…and that I don't do relationships."

"Jesus Christ." He glares at me. "She was really okay with that?"

"Yes. You might think I'm an asshole, but I'm always honest."

"I don't think you're an asshole. I think you're a horndog." He sighs. "So, what's got you so stressed?"

"We had an arrangement. That was working fine." I blow out an annoyed breath. "And now *I'm* the one who caught feelings, okay. Are you happy now?"

Rooster bellows loud enough to shake the fucking house. "Oh, man. This is good. I believe this is what they call *karma.*"

"Only if she doesn't feel the same way," Shelby says, returning to her chair across from me.

"You heard all of that?" I ask.

She flicks her hand in the air like she's swatting a fly. "Just the highlights." She meets my eyes. "I missed the big reveal of *who* it is, though. I *know* you told Logan."

I sigh. "If I tell you, can you please keep it to yourself for a little bit? Don't share with Serena. Or Heidi. Or Trinity. Or Lilly. None of the girls. *No one.*"

"My lips are sealed." She pulls a black box out of a black velvet satchel. "You said I'm your best friend now. And I would *never* break a bestie's trust."

"It's Margot." I wait for Shelby's reaction.

Her eyes light up. "Oh, the pretty little mortician?"

"She's actually the mortuary cosmetologist. But she has her funeral director license…you know what, I don't quite understand all of their roles." I wave it off, not the point. "She tends to dead people and their families, yes."

"Cool job," Shelby says. "Must be real sad, though, sometimes." She casts a quick glance at Rooster. "Not everyone's death is a relief. She must see some of the worst humans do to one another."

"Yeah. It's rough on her some days. And there's certain stuff she won't do because she's seen a lot of consequences," I say carefully.

"She doesn't ride," Rooster guesses immediately.

"Don't make a big deal—"

He holds his hands up. "No judgment. As long as she's not gonna try to make *you* stop riding."

"Never even hinted at it." I drill Rooster with a look. "And I won't try to talk her into it either."

"Fair enough." Rooster nods.

"Daaang." Shelby whistles and somehow even her whistle sounds Southern. "Y'all worship at the altar of Harley-Davidson. You *must* be head over boots for her."

"We don't…never mind." Nah, she's got a point.

Rooster drums his fingers against the tabletop. "So, did you ride home from Deadbranch and go straight to her place?"

"Uh." I scratch the side of my head. "Yeah. I only planned to see her and say hi, you know. But then one day turned into two and…" I shrug.

"How'd you leave things?" Rooster asks. "You know, when you finally left?"

I curl my fingers around my mug and stare at a few rogue cookie crumbs floating at the top. "She was working, so I left her a note."

"A note?" Shelby scowls at me. "What'd it say?"

Not enough.

"That's personal, songbird."

She and Rooster share a look.

"Do you think she feels the same way?" Shelby asks.

"Sometimes. I don't know." My jaw clenches as I think over our "semester." "She kinda asked about my 'no relationships' stance once and I bailed for a bit," I admit, feeling like an asshole.

Shelby rolls her eyes but holds her tongue.

"She expressed some strong opinions about my behavior."

Rooster shakes with the effort of holding in his laughter.

I squint at the wall above Shelby's shoulder. "And she might've indirectly called me a fuckboy."

Rooster loses it, clutching the edge of the table and laughing his big, bearded face off.

Shelby wrinkles her nose. "Yeah, truth hurts, don't it?"

"I'm not…never mind." I wave my hand at the cards. "Are we doing this?"

She clutches the cards in both hands. "Are you going to take it seriously?"

I side-eye Rooster. "Well, he hasn't been very helpful, so maybe the cards can provide some answers."

"What do I need to be helpful about?" Rooster throws his hands up. "You haven't asked a serious question, yet."

"Yes, he did," Shelby says quietly.

Rooster finally works the smirk off his face.

Shelby starts shuffling the cards. "Clear your mind," she instructs. "Focus on what you want to ask the universe."

Am I boyfriend material or destined to be a fuckboy forever?

Jesus Christ, is that what I'm really asking the universe? But now that the question's formed in my mind, I can't stop it from repeating over and over.

She sets the deck in front of me. "Cut it."

The cards are smoother than I thought. They slide when I pick them up and I almost spill them all over.

"Relax," Shelby says. "This is just a tool to get you thinking about your life."

"You're going to need more than one deck," Rooster says.

"Logan!" Shelby shakes her head.

He runs his fingers over his lips as if he's capable of keeping his mouth shut.

"All right. Focus on your question, Jensen. We're going to do a five-card relationship spread and see what we can figure out."

"You're birth-naming me. Now, I'm scared."

"I don't want the universe to get confused," she explains. "Okay, pull the first card for me. Don't look at it, though. Just set it down."

I don't even believe in this shit. Why's it freaking me out so much?

Nothing happens when I pull the first card and set it on the table.

Without touching my card, Shelby pulls another one and lays it a card's width away from the first one, then a third one at the top, one in the middle, and the final one at the bottom, forming a crude cross.

"The first card represents your role in the relationship. The second, Margot's. Third is your past foundation." She taps each card as she explains their role in the reading. "Fourth is the current state of things. Fifth is your future."

Do I really want to do this? My father considered any of this spiritual stuff devil magic. Even though I don't believe that, an echo of unease from my past creeps over me.

She flips over the first card and bites her lip.

"What?" I lean over the table, trying to see the card better. An image of a muscled-warrior type dude with long hair, wielding a sword and shield while wearing a loincloth is in the center of the card. *Knight of Wands.* I flick my gaze to her face again. "Why are you laughing?"

"I'm not!" She covers her mouth with her hand.

"Yes you are."

She flaps her hand at me. "Stop."

She flips the second card and a little furrow forms between her brows. *The Hermit.* All it looks like to me is a woman hiding her face under the hood of a long robe, with one shapely leg peeking out.

"Awww," Shelby breathes out.

The third card is a naked goddess with long hair mostly covering her bits, floating in the stars with what looks like eight sticks. *Eight of Wands.* A knowing smile spreads over Shelby's face.

The fourth card is a skeleton rowing a boat under a glittering night sky. *Death.*

"The Death card isn't bad," Shelby warns.

The fifth and final card she turns over has a man and woman toasting two chalices together with vibrant roses blooming and intertwining with the stems of the chalices.

Shelby rests her elbows on the table and studies the cards. Her mouth's tilted up and she seems happy…almost smug with the cards in front of her.

"Okay," she finally says. "The first one. This represents you. I laughed because sometimes people joke that the *Knight of Wands* has big fuckboy energy."

Several slow, sarcastic huffs of laughter pop out of Rooster. Shelby and I ignore him.

"Jesus Christ. I can't believe I told you that," I grumble.

"No. No. It's more than that," she insists. "He also symbolizes fiery passion, stamina, that you're flirty, you have great chemistry, but a bit reckless or impulsive at times. It can mean a lot of passionate flings and fear of commitment."

"Ding, ding, ding," Rooster says.

I mean, the card's not entirely wrong.

"Now, your partner's card, *The Hermit,* can also have several meanings."

"They *all, always,* have several meanings," Rooster says.

"Your snark is not appreciated at this time, brother." I throw my palm in front of his face. "Continue, please, songbird," I say to Shelby.

She flicks a glance at both of us. "In a reading like this, it could be she's gone through a hermit phase to learn more about herself and find healing. Someone who isn't comfortable with, or wants to learn about, their sexuality, or has trouble with body image." She points to the card. "See how she hides under the robe? But it could also mean she's assumed the hermit role to take time to heal from past bad relationships?"

All of the above. "Yeah." I'm too stunned to say more than that. The accuracy is freaky as fuck. The whole reason we started our fling was because some asshole ex of Margot's made her feel so bad about herself.

"And that could mean she's ready for something new," Shelby concludes.

"That's good, right?"

"I think so." She taps the card of the woman and the eight sticks. "The third one is about the past foundation of your relationship—"

I frown and lean closer to the cards. "Are you sure it's not a gang bang card?"

Rooster snickers.

Shelby shoots a glare at both of us. "No."

"I'm just saying, it looks like she's floating in the air with eight dicks."

"Do you want me to finish or not?"

"Yes." I pull a contrite face.

"So, the *Eight of Wands* can signify explosive chemistry and a quick, passionate attraction to each other."

"Got that right," I mutter.

The *Death* card's still sitting there staring me in the face. "Does the next one mean we're going to fuck ourselves to death with all that explosive chemistry?"

"No," Shelby says with impressive patience. "The *Death* card can be about changes, and rebirth. The end of one thing and the beginning of something new."

"She's a mortician and lives in a funeral home," I point out. "Couldn't it just be about her job?"

Shelby blinks at the cards. "I guess."

My lips quirk. "I call her 'little lady death' sometimes."

"Charming," Rooster mutters. Shelby brushes his arm with the back of her hand.

"So, the card isn't magic," Shelby explains. "This is more to help you think about your life. What makes you feel truly alive and what makes you feel dead inside?"

Margot. Not being with Margot.

"Or, what's ending?" Shelby adds.

"His carefree fuckboy days," Rooster says.

"Logan," Shelby warns. "Stop pushing negative energy into my reading."

"No, he's right," I admit. "I never saw myself wanting to be with one person long-term."

"So that image that you have of yourself as the carefree, flirty playboy might be what's dying and he's being replaced by a mature man who's ready to be a suitable partner."

"With explosive chemistry," I add.

"Yes." Shelby closes her eyes for a second, like she's asking the moon goddess for some extra patience. "This final one, the *Two of Cups*, signifies mutual love and balance. High levels of intimacy and big feelings. Extreme sexual compatibility and physical attraction. It's one of the best relationship cards." She happily taps the card. "This is where you're headed."

I stare at the cards and a flicker of hope flares in my chest. "Are you sure you're not bullshitting me?" I wave my hand over the cards. "This sounds...almost too perfect." *Except for that* Hermit *card.* I didn't tell Shelby any of those details about Margot.

"Well, it's not exact," Shelby says. "It's all up for interpretation. You can study the cards and reflect on your question and how the images apply to it."

"Can I take a picture of it?"

"Sure! I do that when I have a good reading."

I stand and hold my phone over the table, getting all five cards in the frame and snap a picture.

"Thanks."

I sit back down and stare at the cards. *Death. Change. Passion.* It's all there. I want to believe in the cards and how Shelby interpreted them.

But the old me doesn't want to let go, yet.

Something whispers *it's too good to be true.*

CHAPTER THIRTY-FIVE

Margot

M—
NEED TO RUN
HOME.
HAD A GOOD TIME.
SEE YOU SOON.
        J
            A++

IS HE FUCKING KIDDING? HAD A GOOD TIME? A LETTER GRADE HASTILY scribbled in the corner?

I'm numb from the day, and coming home to the pathetic Post-it Note on my kitchen counter is like finding a spider floating in my coffee cup. I crumple it in my fist and throw it in the trash.

My happy oasis, my bright cheery apartment, feels tainted with memories of Jigsaw now. I don't bother to change out of my black pantsuit and emerald blouse. I grab my purse and head downstairs.

Outside, the cool evening air slides over my skin, refreshing me, encouraging me to go somewhere. Do *something* besides sit home and think about Jigsaw.

I drive around aimlessly for a while. Well, maybe not that aimless. I'm heading toward Johnsonville.

Faint lights glow from a side road. That's Remy's place, right? Maybe I'll stop there. Lynette was nice. And I'd love to get my hands on more of those dark chocolate chip cookies she gave me the last time.

The parking lot's more crowded this time. A few classic cars like mine, an SUV, and two motorcycles. My heart stops. I'd never looked at Jigsaw's close enough to know if one of these belongs to him.

The green flames on one catch my eye as I pass it. Pretty. Still looks like a death rocket, though.

"Hey, Margot, what're you doing here?" Remy grins at me from behind the bar and sets down whatever he was working on back there.

The tavern's kinda dark but clean and sort of vintage looking. The booth in the back Jigsaw and I had sat in is occupied with three larger guys in flannels or hoodies. No black leather vests with back patches.

I quicken my steps and sit on the stool in front of Remy.

"Hi. I was passing by, and I thought I'd stop in for something to eat."

He flashes a devastatingly handsome smile. "Welcome."

"Jigsaw said the buffalo chicken sandwich is good here." Mentioning his name sends a shooting stab of pain through my chest.

His smile fades and he lifts his eyebrows. "He did, huh? Here I thought he only liked stopping by to glower and threaten to stab me."

My jaw drops. "He does what?"

"I think it's because he likes me so much. Violence is his love language." The corners of his mouth curl. "You can tell him I said that, too."

"Sure." *I'll make that my priority.* "Are you working by yourself?"

"No." He sets a glass of ice water in front of me. "Lynette's here. Buffalo chicken, right?"

I nod quickly. "And extra blue cheese."

"You got it."

He slips out from behind the counter and strides down the short corridor. Such broad shoulders and good posture. Jigsaw says Remy's some kind of MMA fighter. He must be quite lethal. Too young for me, though.

And I don't *want* anyone else. Obviously, I can't tell *Mr. Had a Nice Time* that, though. Why did I have to ask him to teach me about sex? And why do I wish it could turn into something more?

He was honest that it wouldn't ever be a real relationship. At first, that was fine. But staying at my house for the last few days sure made it seem like it was heading in that direction.

Behind me, the door opens and closes, bringing in a cool swirl of night air. I don't bother turning around to see who it is. It's unlikely I know them, anyway.

A guy walks up to the counter. Tall, but not as tall as Jigsaw. Lean and fit but not as muscled as—*stop it.* His head's covered with shockingly orange spiky hair. He glances down the hallway, taps his fingers against the bar.

"Remy should be right back," I say.

He turns and his eyes widen for a second. Then a broad smile spreads over his face. "Hello," he says smoothly. "You look familiar."

I take a sip of my water and flash a quick, polite smile. "Do I?"

He arches an eyebrow, his grin broadening. "Yeah, I'm pretty sure I've seen you around."

"Margot."

"Torch," he introduces, his voice smooth. "I'm a friend of Remy's." He glances down the hallway briefly before his focus returns to me, a playful glint in his eyes. "You here alone tonight?"

"Just grabbing something to eat." I aim for a casual tone, but I'm still anxious talking to this stranger.

Torch leans his elbow on the bar, his posture relaxed. "Mind if I keep you company while you wait?"

"Not at all." *Why not?* Jigsaw isn't interested in me. I wanted experience so I'd be comfortable dating someone else, right? He gave me what I asked for. Now it's time to move on. I glance at Torch again. He's shorter than Jigsaw. Isn't that what Jigsaw suggested, that I find someone shorter to try kitchen-counter sex with?

My stomach turns. That one had really hurt.

Remy returns with my sandwich, his attention shifting between Torch and me. "Here you go, Margot." He sets the plate down, then reaches over the counter to shake Torch's hand. "What's up, brother?"

The door behind us opens again, excited female voices chattering away.

"Hey, girls," Remy greets, and gestures toward the booths.

Torch turns and points at one of the women. "Ella, you owe me another race."

"In your dreams." A tiny pixie of a woman runs over and gives Torch a quick hug. "I'll smoke your ass every day of the week and you know it. What're you doing over here?"

Torch reaches over and touches my sleeve. "Talking to Margot. Margot, this is my cousin-in-law, Ella."

"Hi." She sweeps her hand in a quick wave. "Is the Thunderbird out there yours?"

"Uh, yeah."

At my confused face, she touches her hand to her chest. "Oh, sorry! That probably sounded creepy, huh?"

"No, no," I protest. *Odd, yes, not quite creepy.*

"I recognized all the other cars but that one. It's sweet."

"Thanks."

She lifts her hand and waves to someone behind me. "My man's getting impatient over there." She laughs and punches Torch's arm. "Are you joining us?"

"I'll be over."

The girls cross the bar, squealing and hugging two of the guys at the table. The third stands to make room and our eyes meet. *I know him.* Griff smiles and nods at me. He leans over and says something to his friends, then crosses the bar, coming straight toward me.

Good grief, this is a small town.

"Hey, Margot," Griff's warm, rich voice greets me. "What're you doing here?"

"A friend brought me by the other day. I fell in love with Lynette's dark chocolate chip cookies, so I thought I'd stop in again."

"I think they're walnut chocolate chip today," Remy says. "But I'll grab a few for you now. Before these clowns eat all of them." He teasingly jabs a finger toward Griff, then Torch.

"Why you throwing shade at your brother-in-law, Remy?" Torch asks with a smirk.

"Nice to hear you admit you're a clown." Griff reaches over and claps Torch on the back, then laughs.

Torch doesn't seem insulted. If anything, it seems like their verbal jabs are a regular occurrence.

"How's it going?" I ask Griff.

"Good, thanks. I wanted to say thanks for sending that guy with the '67 Mustang Fastback my way."

"Oh, he actually came to see you? That's great!" I smile, happy I could help.

Griff nods and glances at the table in the back where the two couples are laughing and sharing a pizza. "You're welcome to join us if you want."

"Uh, I'm good, thanks." I gesture to my sandwich, though I'm suddenly too nervous to eat in front of everyone.

"All right, well, glad I ran into you." He gives Torch one last hard look before heading back to his table.

Torch has moved down a few seats to talk to Remy. I take a quick bite of my sandwich, savoring the spicy sauce, then lift the bun and drizzle the cup of blue cheese over the whole thing.

I glance at the guys in the corner. Griff nods at me. Not in a flirty way, more like a subtle sense that he's looking out for me.

I hurry to finish my sandwich, taking sips of water to quell the spiciness.

I'm dipping a piece of celery in some stray blue cheese dressing when Torch returns. I quickly swipe my napkin over my mouth.

"So, Margot, do you ever go to the drive-in out on Route 50?"

"Oh, wow. Not in years. My parents used to take me there when I was a kid." Until my mom passed away and we stopped leaving the house all that much.

"Well, they're still open. Wanna go Friday night?"

As of right now, I have Friday off, but that can always change. I hate to make plans and then break them, but I'd also like to go out and do something fun. Torch seems safe. Remy knows him. Griff knows him. That woman, Ella, seemed comfortable around him. "Sure," I finally answer.

"Great." He pulls out his phone. "Give me your number. I'll pick you up—"

"I live all the way out in Pine Hollow." I smile apologetically. "And my job's kind of unpredictable. I might get called in." Shoot, why'd I mention my job? *Please don't ask what I do.*

He stares at me for a few seconds. Probably trying to decide if I'm giving an excuse.

"Really," I say.

"Okay. You want to meet here first? Have dinner and then go?"

"Sure."

"If you get called in or something, I can bring you right back."

"Okay."

A pleased smile spreads over his face. "Good." I hand him my phone and he punches his number in. When his screen lights up, he answers, then disconnects.

"I'll call Friday afternoon to make sure we're still on," he suggests. "That okay?"

"Yeah, that works."

"Great. I'll see you then." He nods at me, then walks over to Griff's table.

A refreshing wave of confidence washes over me, like I'm in control of my life again.

Torch might not end up being anything serious, but maybe that's exactly what I need. Because for a few seconds, he actually helped me forget about my Jigsaw problem.

CHAPTER THIRTY-SIX

Jigsaw

MARGOT HASN'T ANSWERED ANY OF MY TEXTS.

Maybe that's for the best.

I'm guessing she didn't find my *had a great time* Post-it Note flattering.

I can't stop thinking about Shelby's card reading, though. Kill the old me so something new can grow. It's harder than it sounds.

Tonight, I'm headed in the direction of her place, but take a detour to Remy's bar instead. I haven't harassed him in a few days. He probably misses me.

And I'm hungry. It's got nothing to do with avoiding Margot at all.

The place is the busiest I've seen it in a while. And for once, I don't think it's only Remy's buddies taking up the spots.

Remy's behind the bar and grins as soon as his gaze lands on me. "My favorite serial killer. How are you?"

I bare my teeth at him and drape myself over a seat at the bar.

He rests his elbows on the counter and leans over, getting too close to my face. "Interesting you chose that seat. That's where your friend Margot sat when she stopped in last night."

"Oh, yeah?" I ask, faking indifference.

"How in the hell do you two know each other again?"

"None of your business." I point to the beer tap. "You want to take my order or are you just back there as decoration?"

He grabs a glass and pulls the beer, then sets it in front of me. I take a slow sip and try not to cringe at the bitterness of the cheap swill.

I don't want to give Remy the green light to pry into my life, but I'm curious about why Margot stopped in here. Was she looking for me? Did she ask Remy if I'd been in? Fuck, was she hoping to hook up with Remy? He'll nail anyone with two sets of lips, so it wouldn't take much effort to capture his attention. "So why was she here?"

"For cookies." He shrugs. "And she said you told her we have the best buffalo chicken sandwich."

I nod and take another sip. "I did say that. I forgot to remind her how annoying the owner is, though."

Remy laughs it off, not insulted. "Do you want something to eat?"

"Gee, could ya?" I cock my head, being as dickish as possible. "The buffalo chicken."

"Coming up."

While he's gone, I turn on my stool and survey the room. A couple of old guys who look like they spent the afternoon golfing are in a booth by the back. Another younger couple that look like they stopped here on their way home from work. A rowdier group of what could be frat bros, although there aren't any colleges nearby.

"Looking busier," I say when Remy returns with my plate.

"Yeah. Teller's been helping me with some advertising and stuff."

"Good."

He drifts away to take care of other patrons. I'm almost done when he returns. "So, you never said how you know Margot. You two related?"

I huff out a laugh. "No."

"Well, I know she's not your ol' lady."

I narrow my eyes. "How's that?"

His lips twitch, like he's having trouble keeping that smug smirk off his pretty face. "Torch asked her out and she said yes."

The last bit of sandwich I'd been holding crumples to mush in my fist. Bread, sauce, lettuce, and chicken ooze between my fingers. "What?"

In full smirk mode now, Remy stares at the bar top and wipes a rag against the same spot over and over. "Yeah, they got to talking. Something about going to the drive-in Friday."

The fuck they are. "Thanks for the information." I grab the towel out of his hand and clean the chicken off my fingers.

"Don't kill Torch," he warns me. "He's Eraser's cousin."

"I know who he is."

"And," he continues as if I hadn't said anything, "we're looking at him for treasurer of the support club. I also need him to help me run this place while Griff's away this summer."

"I'm not killing anyone. Like you said, she's not my ol' lady. She can go out with whoever she wants." My stomach twists at the thought, threatening to reunite me with my chicken dinner for speaking such blasphemy.

I pull out my wallet and throw enough cash on the bar to cover the food and then some.

"Wait a second." He scoops up the money. "You need change?"

"No," I growl.

Out in the parking lot, I stare at the road that leads into Johnsonville. It'll take longer to get to Margot's place if I take that route. I could use the time to cool off.

She said *yes* to a date. Must be ready to try out all those new skills I've been helping her learn.

Fuck, that hurts more than getting my dick caught in my zipper.

What did I expect? I keep reminding her we're not dating. The last time she hinted at having feelings, I ghosted her. She somehow took me back and I'm still keeping things "sex only." I left her a fucking *note* instead of calling her or, I don't know, sending her flowers or some shit. Jesus, fuck, why didn't that occur to me?

See, I knew I wasn't cut out to be her boyfriend. "Sex only" works for us. Why mess with it? If she wants to start fucking Torch, then I'm free to return to my parade of muffler bunnies and randoms.

Except, I don't want to.

The weight of years of one-night stands and meaningless encounters crawls over my skin. Margot and I are more than that, aren't we? We talk a lot. Christ, I've never loved listening to a woman's voice as much as I love Margot's.

Sex? *Best I've ever had.* Because I've trained her to my liking or just because we're so compatible?

How the fuck would I know? Best is the best. Does it matter why?

I never take her anywhere or do anything fun with her. Mostly because I like the peace and quiet at her place. Just being in her presence. Does she *want* to do shit like go to the drive-in?

She does have that big DVD collection and a whole theater room. She must like movies. Maybe if I spent more time getting to *know* her instead of trying to discover all the various ways I can make her orgasm, I'd know the answer to such a simple question.

I'm in a worse mood by the time I finally approach her house. She must've heard me coming. I've just finished backing my bike into the spot I like to leave it when she steps into the parking lot in pajamas and bare feet.

"What are you doing here?" she asks.

"We need to talk." I storm across the pavement toward her, my boots scraping over the asphalt.

"Uh, okay." She hurries up the back steps and into the house. "Come on in. Why are you so...?" She whirls her hands around in front of her face. "So flurried?"

I stop and close the door behind me. "Flurried?"

"Flustered, hurried, angry...I don't know!" She plucks her fingers in the air. "Your energy seems hostile."

In an instant, my annoyance evaporates. This woman fucking slays me.

"I'm not angry or hostile," I say.

She waves her hands in front of my body. "Sure, you're the picture of tranquility."

Damn right I'm not tranquil. I point to the staircase. "Get up those stairs."

Fury flares in her eyes. "Excuse me?"

"We need to talk, and I don't think you want anyone to overhear this conversation."

She throws her arms out wide but backs up toward the staircase. "There's no one else here."

"I'm not fucking around, Margot."

Still facing me, she works her way up the first flight of stairs backwards while I stalk her every step.

At the landing, she turns and sprints.

"That's better," I grumble, matching her pace.

She slams her palms against her door. I press my body against hers.

"You trying to outrun me, little lady death?"

"As if I could with your long, mountain man legs." She fumbles her hand on the tap pad and the door finally clicks open.

I take my weight off of her so we don't fall into the apartment, but move fast in case she's thinking of slamming the door in my face.

"Are we having a lesson on primal hunter/prey kinks that I don't know about?" she asks.

Primal. That's how I feel. Like someone tried to touch my mate and I need to reassert my position in her life.

I advance and she steps back.

"Are you going out with Torch this weekend?"

Guilt creeps into her eyes and she takes another step away. "Nuh… not…who told you that?"

"Fuck." I stab my fingers through my hair. "No. That's the only acceptable answer."

Her eyes widen and she sucks in a sharp breath. "Why would I say that?"

"You're *not* going out with him." In case she thinks this is personal against Torch, I add, "Or anyone else."

She crosses her arms over her chest, drawing my attention to her plump tits trying to pop out of the low V of her shirt.

Focus. Answers now. Tits later.

"Says who?" she asks in a low, deadly whisper.

"Says *me*."

"And who are you to me?"

Danger. Fuuuck. I stomped right into this minefield.

"Because the last time I checked," she continues, still in that gravely pissed-off tone, "you warned me not to 'catch *feelings.*'" Her lips curl into a sneer on the last word.

Man, I'll never live that one down, will I?

"And, you keep reminding me this is temporary." She points to the kitchen. "Remember when you told me I should find someone shorter if I wanted to try counter sex again?"

I wince. I *did* say that, didn't I? I really am a dick.

"And now you have the audacity to come in here like some snarling beast, mad at me because someone else asked me out?" she shouts. "Are you kidding?"

"We *also* said we weren't going to fuck other people," I remind her. "While classes are in session."

"Who said I wanted to fuck anyone!" she yells, jabbing her finger in the air toward my face. "It's a date. What fucked-up world do you live in that a simple date automatically equals sex?"

I've never heard Margot drop so many *fucks* at once. It's fucking hot. I grab her wrists and drive her against the wall, pinning her next to her closet door.

Her eyes widen and she glares up at me. "Let go of me!"

I release her wrists but keep her pinned with my body. "I don't want you to go out with him."

"Why?" she demands.

Breathing hard, I stare down into her defiant eyes but can't force out the reason.

"You said you don't have relationships. You don't want a girlfriend or an ol' lady." She draws out the word in a mocking tone. "So why do you care who I non-sexually date?"

I snort and take a step back. "Does *he* know it's non-sexual?" Something worse occurs to me. "How long do you think it will stay non-sexual? Wasn't that the whole point of what *we're* doing?"

"Yes. You've been a fantastic tutor." Her voice drops to a kitten-like purr that irritates the ever-loving shit out of me for reasons I don't want to examine. "Maybe I'm ready to test my new skills with someone else."

"The fuck you are."

"Why? What else could you possibly have left to teach me?"

My jaw clenches. Whip-fast, I grab her ponytail and wrap it around my fist, tilting her head back. "You still need to learn what happens to bratty little girls who misbehave."

Her eyes flare with indignation, but her lips twitch with amusement. "Oh, really?"

"Tell him no," I demand.

She flashes a wicked grin. "Or what?"

"Break the date, Margot."

"Why? You haven't given me a good enough reason."

"You need a reason?"

"A *good* one."

She's infuriating and *fuck it;* I want her so much. "You're mine."

"I'm your *what?*"

"Mine," I growl, slamming my lips over hers to stop her from making me say it.

She hooks one arm around my neck. I release her hair and slide my hands down, lifting her and pressing her against the wall.

"What am I to you?" she whispers, pressing her hand to my chest in an attempt to hold me back. "Tell me."

"I told you. You're mine."

"What does that mean?" she insists.

I blow out an annoyed breath. "You need a title? My woman. My *girlfriend.*"

"You want me to be your girlfriend?"

"Why is that so hard to believe?"

"Because you told me, rather explicitly, that you don't have relationships."

"Well, now I want to."

"Why?"

"Why *what?*" I said it. What more does she want from me?

"Why do you want me to be your girlfriend? Because someone else asked me out?"

"No. I *like* you. Every little fucking thing about you. Your sense of humor, and all the quirky challenges that come out of your mouth. I like the way you care so much about what you do. How you try to protect and honor dead people you didn't even know in life."

Her eyebrows squinch together.

"You need me to continue?" When she doesn't answer, I keep spilling all the thoughts that have been taking up space in my head for months. "I respect the way you don't let people talk you into things. Even me. You're hotter than fuck. You wear the cutest outfits." I squeeze my eyes shut for a second. "But I really like you naked best. Your body drives me insane."

I usually know where things are going every time I'm with a woman—nowhere. I should've let it stay that way. I don't think I can go back to nowhere. Not when I want to be *somewhere* with this woman.

"Do you really mean all of that?" she asks.

"Every word."

She cups my cheek. "I'll tell him I can't make it."

"Good."

She wiggles her body like she's trying to get free from my iron grip. "Uh, let me go so I can get my phone."

"Now?" I slip my hand under her shirt and cup her breast. No bra in my way. *Fuck, yes.* I rub my thumb around the hard bud of her nipple. "He can wait."

"You chased me up the stairs…barged in here." She gasps as I close two fingers over her nipple and squeeze. "And…and…"

"And what?" I tug her shirt up and free one arm. Can't be bothered getting it all the way off. I dip my head and suck her nipple into my mouth, swirling my tongue around the tip.

"Ah…nothing. I don't know." She rakes her fingers through my hair. "I'll do it later."

"Yes, you will." I boost her into my arms again, sliding my palms under her ass, and holding her against my body.

She quickly locks her arms around my neck and glances at the floor. "Don't let go of me."

I've never been good at holding onto anyone. Never wanted to before.

But I never want to let her go.

CHAPTER THIRTY-SEVEN

Margot

I CAN'T THINK. I CAN BARELY BREATHE. JIGSAW WANTS TO BE WITH ME. Wants me as his girlfriend. Not his student that he's throwing a few pity sex lessons.

The man who said he doesn't do relationships now wants to be in a relationship. With me.

He kisses my neck, my cheeks, and aims for my lips but I pull away.

"So this is a relationship, now?" I ask.

He groans. "I already said yes."

"No more crappy Post-it Note messages?"

He closes his eyes. "I didn't know what else to say. I'm not good at…I'm not good at putting feelings and shit into words."

I cock my head. "Is this just because someone else asked me out? You're jealous? But a few weeks from now you'll disappear on me again?"

"No. I've wanted to tell you…for a while." He closes his eyes and looks so miserable, I have a twinge of regret about pressing him. "I just don't know how."

Tears blur my eyes. "I don't either, you know. I've never felt like this before. I don't know if it's the amazing sex or something more."

His eyes search my face. Is he hurt? Shocked? "Why can't it be both?"

"I want it to be." I press my hands to his cheeks, burning every inch of his face into my memory. My thighs tremble, and I hitch them higher around his hips, locking my ankles together behind his back. "I like you too, you know. I like your sense of humor. I love your loyalty to your brothers and your club. I like that you're scary on the outside but so sweet to me. I like that you're protective over me but not suffocating. I love that you don't try to talk me into things I don't want to do." I mash my lips against his. "I love how hard your body is but how gently you handle me."

"Little lady death, why are you trying to kill me?"

"What?"

"Thank you." He kisses my cheeks and then my lips. "For understanding me. Accepting me for who I am but still somehow changing me into something better."

I think that's what love is? I think I love you.

No. I can't say that. Not yet.

"I don't want to change you," I whisper.

"But you are. For the better. And I want to."

"Okay." I yank my shirt off the rest of the way, letting it fall to the floor.

His gaze drops to my breasts.

I lean closer, capturing his lips with mine. It's more than a kiss. It's full of excitement about all the new possibilities we've opened. After a few long, warm collisions our sweet kiss flips into something more frantic and needy. I'm tugging at his shirt, but it's trapped against my body and our lips are still fused together. I'm so busy trying to thwart the laws of physics, I don't realize he's heading for my bedroom until the door slams shut behind us.

Still clinging to his wide shoulders, my heart swoops as he gently lays me on the bed. I shove my pants down over my hips, while he shrugs off his cut and rips his T-shirt over his head.

"Show me." He lifts his chin as he works his belt loose.

Flushed with excitement, I don't need to ask. I press my feet flat into the mattress and slowly inch them apart.

"Fuck," he grumbles with annoyance, while he struggles to get his boots and jeans off. "Touch yourself for me."

I slide my hand down. My body jerks as I massage two fingers over my clit.

"Good girl," he rasps. He wraps one hand around his cock, pumping a few times before reaching for my nightstand.

Prickles of pleasure fan over my thighs. My teeth dig into my bottom lip as he smooths the latex down his shaft.

"Please hurry." I hold out my hand for him.

Hi gaze slides between my face and the hand between my legs.

"I want you inside me. Now."

He unleashes a feral growl and climbs over me. I cup his cheek and stroke my thumb against his bristly chin. He shifts his hand between us and I gasp as his cock grazes my entrance. I lift and wrap my legs around him.

We both groan as he slowly sinks inside.

"You okay?" Eyes burning, he studies my face.

Need forces me to shift my legs higher, gasping at the friction against my clit. "Yes. Please move."

Laughing, he slips his arms underneath me and licks the side of my neck. He slowly draws back, then presses inside, working to a quick, steady rhythm.

"Better." He kisses and sucks at my neck. "You're all wet and ready for me? Liked me chasing you up the stairs?"

I dig my fingers into his biceps, amazed at his strength and control. "Maybe. I don't like fighting with you, though."

"Not a fight," he says through heavy breaths. "A passionate discussion."

"I like that better."

"Good." He straightens, pulling me up with him.

"What are you doing?" I gasp at the change in angle and friction.

"Need you to do some work but I like your tits mashed up against me." He yanks my hips closer, coaxing me to ride up and down his cock. I wrap my arms around him tighter and bury my face against his neck. Mouth open, I moan into his ear. Kiss and suck at his neck. My thighs flex, rolling my hips, finding more of that delicious friction right where I need it.

"You feel so good." He presses kisses to my cheek and neck. "Born to ride my dick, baby." He gathers my hair in one hand and tugs, forcing me to meet his lust-glazed eyes. His other arm curled around my back keeps me anchored to him. Rough, calloused fingers dig into my butt and hips, turning me even more frantic.

He squeezes his eyes shut, the cords of his neck tightening with the tension of holding on. That's what pushes me over the edge. Me. My body. How we fit so well together. I have the power to take him to the edge and push him right over.

My body seizes, stealing my breath. He seals his mouth over mine, swallowing my little cries. Pleasure showers over me, my thighs shake, toes curl as our sweaty skin slides together.

"Fuck." Jigsaw releases my hair and squeezes my ass, pushing me impossibly closer to him, setting off more fireworks.

The intensity forces a scream out of my throat.

My world spins sideways. He drops me on the bed, pushes my legs up to my chest, and slides right back inside me. "Holy shit!" My eyes pop from the force of sensation at the new angle.

"Okay?"

"Yes. Good. Harder."

His hips slam into me at a rapid pace, jiggling my breasts. The hot feral gleam in his eyes tips me into another orgasm, sharper in its intensity.

"Coming," he rasps, jerking inside me, his body tight. He groans and slows into a deep grinding swivel of his hips.

We collapse in a sweaty tangle of arms and legs. He pulls my limp body half on top of him with my head resting on his chest. His heart thunders beneath my ear.

"I can't move," I whisper.

"Same." He flexes his fingers over my hair, affectionately massaging my scalp.

"I don't want anyone else." I lift my head and kiss his chest, wishing I also had the courage to give him the three words burning in my heart.

CHAPTER THIRTY-EIGHT

Jigsaw

A SACK OF POTATOES LANDS ON MY CHEST THE NEXT MORNING, WAKING me with a startle.

No. Not a sack of potatoes. A cat. More specifically, a cat's *ass* in my face.

"*Mrrrar.*" Gretel turns around, her tiny paws like needles poking into my chest and rubs her head on my chin.

"You're cute, so I'll forgive the rude wake-up call." I run my hand over her back. Her motorboat purrs rev into high gear and she curls herself into a circle on my chest.

"She really likes you," Margot whispers.

"I like her too." I tilt my head to see her better. "But her morning greeting needs improvement."

She laughs softly. Careful not to disturb the cat, Margot lifts herself so we're face to face. "Morning."

"Morning."

"I'm glad you're still here."

Did she think I was going to bail? After I told her I was in this for good?

Gretel stretches one leg and gently swats at Margot's hair with her paw.

"Oh, I'm sorry." Margot laughs, scooping Gretel into her arms. "Do you want some alone time with *my* man?" She sets the cat on the bed and Gretel jumps off and slowly leaves the room. "That's right, keep going, you little hussy."

I pull her down and roll on top of her, pinning her underneath me. "I like hearing you call me your man." My lips quirk. "Even if it is to the cat."

"You do?"

"Yes." I kiss her neck. "I like waking up with you. Even if I have to endure fifteen pounds of fur landing on my chest first thing in the morning." Is that who I am now? A man who has a girlfriend with a cat?

She cringes and laughs at the same time. "I'm sorry."

"It's okay." I kiss her cheek, then roll to the side.

She reaches over to the nightstand and picks up her phone. "Shoot. I have to get ready."

"We're not staying in bed today?"

"I would love that." She rests her hand on my chest. "But I have to prep for back-to-back funerals tomorrow."

That's a mood killer.

"Sorry." I sit up.

"One was a very long consult yesterday before you showed up. That's why I was headed to bed so early."

Shit. I was so worried about my ego and getting my dick in her I never asked her something as simple as *how was your day*. I'm already sucking at this boyfriend thing. "Sorry I messed up your night."

A quick burst of apology widens her eyes. "You didn't mess up my night." She tilts her head to the side, her hair covering her face, reminding me of *The Hermit* card in my reading. "You were the best part of my whole day."

Maybe I'm not fucking up the boyfriend gig yet.

She rolls out of bed. "But I really do have to get ready." Her expression softens. "You can stay here if you want."

"I have a few things I need to do today."

A hesitant cloud of doubt dulls her expression. Can't blame her. "I'll come back tonight. If you want me to."

"I do," she whispers. "Is that okay?"

Instead of answering, I stand and kiss her, letting the warmth of my lips on hers show her how much I want to be with her. "It's more than okay." I pull back enough to see her face. "But I'll head out early tomorrow, though. Sounds like you'll be busy here and I'm supposed to ride out to see my sister."

Her eyes brighten. "Oh, good. Is she okay?"

Warmth that she seems to care about my relationship with my sister spreads over me.

"Yeah." I rake my hands through my hair. "I still want to go see her. Might take her to my buddy's racetrack for the day."

"That sounds like fun."

I open my mouth to ask if she wants to join us, then stop myself, and not only because I know some of my club brothers will be there and find out about us. "How long does the funeral go?"

"Hours." She takes a deep breath like she's fortifying herself for a grueling day. "Then there's all the cleanup here. And the first family, well…they're difficult. I'm sure there will be issues."

"You need me to stick around? I can go see Jezzie day after tomorrow instead."

"No, we're used to it. If they're too belligerent, Paul and Henry handle it or we call the sheriff's office."

Grief makes people do crazy shit. For the first time, I wonder how safe Margot is living here. "Well, if you need me, please call. Zips isn't that far from here. I'll come over and bring a few guys with me."

Her lips curve and the tension in her shoulders seems to ease. "That would be quite a sight. All these handsome men on Harleys roaring into our parking lot to calm the angry mourners."

"I'll make sure to bring my ugliest brothers then."

She leans up and kisses my cheek. "Haven't met one yet. You're each beautiful in your own ways."

While she's getting ready for the day, I go into the kitchen to make her breakfast. If Rooster could see me now. The number of times I've given him shit for fetching Shelby tea and stuff backstage at her concerts, and here I am watching a YouTube video on my phone to figure out how to make my scrambled eggs fluffy enough.

Margot enters the kitchen while I'm at the stove using a spatula to scrape the egg mixture into long ribbons in my pan. Her gaze dances to the banana that's propping up my phone on the counter to the toast popping out of the toaster, the coffee brewing, and finally the stove.

"No one's ever made me breakfast before." Her voice holds a note of awe. She looks so damn happy, I almost forget to give the eggs another swirl.

Guess I'm good for more than orgasms after all.

"Well, it seems like you have a busy day." A smirk tugs at my lips. "And you already got a late start because of me." I wave the spatula in my hand toward the counter. "Sit."

The eggs won't win any awards for presentation but they look edible and I didn't burn the toast.

Margot sticks a forkful of eggs in her mouth and hums with happiness. "They're perfect."

I reach behind me and hit my phone to stop the *Perfect Fluffy Scrambled Eggs Every Time* video from playing.

Margot's lips curve with amusement, but she doesn't say anything.

I set water and coffee next to her plate. "I'll clean all this up." I wave a hand toward the sink. "I won't leave a mess for you."

"Thank you." She flicks her gaze to the stove. "Aren't you going to eat?"

I'd been too focused on getting her food right to worry about it. Besides, I have more time than she does this morning.

"I'll eat after I hit the gym."

She raises her eyebrows and makes this sexy humming sound.

"When will you be done with work today?"

"Late, probably seven or eight. There's always a lot of last-minute stuff." She rolls her eyes. "Especially with a family as difficult as this one."

"That's not the same one with the jumbo casket, is it?"

"Gosh no." She squints. That must've been a dumb question. "They make that family look like perfect customers."

"So if I come back at nine, does that work?"

"Yes."

"And you need me to clear out early tomorrow?"

"Clear out makes it sounds so nefarious. But I have a meeting with the priest at eight." She chuckles, then sips her coffee. "So maybe."

I smirk, resisting the urge to make the obvious joke about how much sinning we've been doing.

"All right." She sighs and slides off the stool, taking her plate to the sink. "I better go before Dad starts hitting the buzzer."

"Does he really do that?"

"Sometimes."

"Well, let's get you downstairs, then."

She pushes out her bottom lip into the cutest little pout. "But I don't want to leave you."

I pull her into my arms, holding her close, not wanting to admit I don't want her to leave, either. "I'll be back tonight."

CHAPTER THIRTY-NINE

Jigsaw

THE RIDE OUT TO JEZZIE'S APARTMENT WAS PEACEFUL. THE RIDE TO ZIPS was not.

First, Jezzie complains about my bike. Then she squirms and moves around so much behind me, it fucks with the bike's stability. I have to work hard to control the steering and not overcorrect to compensate for all the shifts in her weight.

By the time we finally roll into Zips, every muscle in my body screams from the constant battle to keep us upright.

"I'm not getting back on that thing. So either you find a normal vehicle," she huffs, glaring at the cracked pavement as if blaming it for the ride, "or I live here now."

I point to the back of the bleachers. "You can find shelter there. I'm sure it'll be cozy."

"Ugh." She stomps ahead of me.

I raise my hands to the sky and tip my head back. *What the fuck did I do to deserve this?*

"Slow down." I jog to catch up with her, while pulling out my phone to check my texts.

Rooster: When are you getting here? Dex's about to throw down with Torch.

Fucking Torch. I better not see that orange-haired prick, or I'll knock him out myself.

Did Margot ever break that date?

Me: We're here. Dealing with a Jezzie tantrum.

Rooster: What'd you do to her?

Exist? I don't fucking know.

I tap out a text to Margot.

Me: You cancel that date with Torch?

Then I erase it. She's busy working a double funeral today. She doesn't have time for my jealous antics.

We're approaching the track when I spot Dex and Emily by the bleachers in a heated conversation. Not sure how I feel about her yet, or if she's ol' lady material. But Dex is into her. Never seen him so fucked up over anyone before.

Torch is nowhere in sight. Smart guy.

I nudge Jezzie's elbow. "That's one of my brothers. I want to introduce you."

"Gee," she says with exaggerated, wide eyes. "I never would've guessed, with the matching outfits and all, brother dear."

"What crawled up your butt today?"

She blows out an annoyed breath. "Nothing. I'm hungry."

"We'll get some food in a minute."

We stop in front of Dex and I grin at him. "Hey, happy campers. What'd my boy do now, Emily?"

"*Boy*." She flashes an amused grin at me. "Isn't he older than you?"

"So he says." I pat Jezzie's back. "This is my sister Jezzie. Jezzie, this is my brother Dex and his girl, Emily."

Emily half-lunges forward like she's going to hug Jezzie hello. My sister's face must be in full prickly hedgehog mode, though. Emily stumbles and puts her arms down.

"It's nice to meet you," she says.

"Hi," Jezzie says in a small voice. What is she, suddenly shy? She glances at Dex. "Club brother."

I elbow her.

"My brother promised me food and race cars." Jezzie lets out a

dramatic sigh, as if she has the worst brother in the world. "Yet, I see neither."

According to Dex, Emily's used to dealing with her own little sister's antics. Her face breaks into a big sisterly smile. "Food I can help you with. It's around the corner," Emily says.

"Thanks, Em," I say. As soon as they're out of earshot, I shove my hands in my pocket and rock back on my heels. "Whatcha been doing?" I ask in the most obnoxious way possible.

He blows out an irritated breath.

"Rooster told me to hurry up and get my ass here because you were ready to give some guy a beatdown."

Dex rolls his eyes. "Rooster should mind his business."

"I don't know," I sing in a high-pitched voice designed for maximum annoyingness. "You and Emily looked pretty intense. Someone try to rub up on your girl?"

"We're always intense." Dex turns toward the track. "Let's go get some food. If you're gonna be busting my balls, at least let me eat a burger while you're doing it."

We haven't cleared the bleachers yet when Dex asks, "So you're finally bringing your sister around to meet us?"

"Yes, I thought this would be better than having her at the clubhouse." We're on the asphalt that runs in front of the bleachers. Jezzie's forgotten all about food. She's talking to Griff and Remy, but she's twirling a lock of her colorful hair around her finger, eyes locked on Remy like he's the most fascinating thing she's seen all day. Emily's nowhere in sight. "That might've been a miscalculation."

"I don't think you have anything to worry about with Griff."

"Hmph."

I spend a few minutes bullshitting with Dex while keeping my eye on Jezzie smiling and laughing at whatever dumb shit Remy's saying. Griff keeps looking over his shoulder, like he wants to bounce.

She's an adult. She's allowed to have friends.

Just not *this* friend.

"This motherfucker," I growl as Remy flashes one of his panty-dropping smiles at my sister. I shove Dex out of my way and storm over the blacktop.

"No. No. Nope." I slam my arm between Remy and Jezzie and chest-bump him back a few inches. "Not happening."

Griff moves next to his buddy. And I sense Dex come up on my side.

Remy blinks and stares at me and then my arm blocking him from my sister. "The fuck?"

"Jensen!" Jezzie all but stomps her foot on the ground. "Stop." Her little hands fly into my chest with all the force of a dragonfly.

"Stay. Away. From. My. Little. Sister," I warn Remy.

Griff bursts into laughter.

"She's your *sister*?" Remy asks, slowly clicking the pieces of the puzzle into place. His gaze slides to Jezzie and then to me.

"So, this is awkward as fuck." Griff jerks his thumb over his shoulder and laughs. "I'm gonna go be literally anywhere else."

"Thanks a lot, bro," Remy calls after him. "You're a big help!"

I'm glad he's finding this so funny. "You better settle the fuck down."

Dex's heavy hand lands on my shoulder and squeezes. "Remy was being polite to a guest. That's all, *riiight*?" He draws out the last word to make it clear to Remy the only answer that will stop me from gutting him with my hunting knife is "yes."

"I've seen his version of polite," I say without taking my eyes off Remy. "Not this time. Not this girl."

"Fuckmuppet." Jezzie lets out an exasperated huff. "Let me go find a club so you all can beat each other over the heads." She turns and stalks away toward the picnic tables where Emily's sitting with her little sister Libby, and Shelby.

Thanks a lot Emily. You couldn't walk my sister the extra five hundred feet?

Who am I kidding. I know better than anyone how hard it is to make Jezzie do anything.

"Jiggy, I didn't know she was your sister," Remy says. "She was with

Emily, so I figured she was with Lost Kings. I was trying to be polite. Like Dex said. That's all." He holds up his hands.

Fuck, yeah. I shouldn't be getting this worked up over it. Jezzie's off at college, talking to whoever the hell she wants when I'm not around. It's just…Remy. *Fuck no.*

"Trust me, I get it," Remy adds. "Off-limits. Message received."

My gaze strays to the track where Griff has Remy's little sister in a clinch next to his car. *Heh.* Hello, instant karma, my old friend.

Remy walks off, and Dex jabs his finger into my chest. "The fuck, bro?"

I rub my chest and scowl at Dex. "You really giving me shit after you just did the same thing five minutes ago?"

"One, no I didn't. Two, you weren't even here for it, so shut your mouth. Three, it's different. I don't know the dude who was rubbin' up on my girl and trying to look down her dress. And we're not trying to patch *him* into our support club. We *know* Remy and he's done a lot to help out our club." He stops his insane countdown and lowers his voice. "Including helping us bury bodies."

Remy *has* come through for the club a lot. We've used his bar for sit-downs with rival clubs and gangs. We used his downstairs murder room to dismember a body. He's let me take last-minute fights at his underground fighting ring when I needed some extra cash. Pays me to work as a bouncer at the fights sometimes too. And he rarely asks for anything in return. I'm not ready to admit Dex is right, though. "My reaction woulda been the same if Rav or Hustler or anyone wearing the blue and gray had been all up in her business."

"Bro, they were standing like two feet away from each other," Dex says.

Whatever. If Margot were here, her calm, reasonable manner would soothe this storm brewing in my chest with just a look. It's a beautiful day too. And she's stuck dealing with crazy families, overseeing not one, but two funerals. "You think we should invite Margot out here one of these days?"

Dex stares at me like I chopped off my dick and dropped it at his feet. "Why?"

Why the fuck did I have to say that? "Funeral home's another club business. Pine Hollow isn't actually that far from here."

"So you've given this a lot of thought?"

Only thinking about her every minute of every day.

"No, I just understand how maps work," I answer in the most dickish way possible. "She's always cooped up with dead folks. Might be good for her to hang with people her age who are still breathing."

"How altruistic of you." Dex frowns at me. "You're not going to try to hook Margot and Remy up to keep him away from your sister, are you?"

"What?" My shout echoes off the bleachers. "Fuck no."

Dex flicks his gaze to something behind me. I brace myself, expecting one of my asshole brothers—most likely Rooster—to grab me.

Sure enough, I glimpse a big hairy forearm coming down on me two seconds before I'm yanked against the hard wall of Rooster's chest. "Whatcha doin' cock-knocker?" Rooster's disgusting hot dog breath fans over the side of my face. "Causing trouble?"

"Get off me, motherclucker." I laugh and use an evasion move, ironically learned from Remy, to escape Rooster's sloppy rear naked chokehold.

"What'd you do to poor lil' Jezzie?" Shelby stomps up next to Rooster. "She's hella riled up."

She's so cute. She almost looks like one of the flamingos she loves so much when she stomps her foot like that. Not the intimidating girl power vibe I think she's going for. I adjust my cut and stare at her. "What I *do*, songbird."

"Tag!" Dex punches Rooster's shoulder as if he's passing off the responsibility of looking after me to Rooster.

Rooster cocks his head, while Shelby's glare could burn a hole through my forehead.

"What'd you do, big brother?" Rooster makes a goofy pouty face at me.

"Nothing." I fling my arm toward the picnic benches where she's sulking. "She's been pissy with me since I picked her up. Couldn't sit still on the bike, I almost fuckin' dropped it like ten times. And I gotta find a cage or she's apparently living at Zips, now."

"I'll get my hands on a car for you," Rooster promises.

Shelby's concerned eyes ping-pong between Rooster and me. "Awww, dang it." She glances over her shoulder.

"What?"

Shelby's mouth twists. "If I tell you, you can't say anything. I'm breaking girl code here."

Even more confused now, I shake my head.

She wags a finger between us. "We're besties now, remember? I keep your secrets, you keep mine." She tilts her head as if she's asking if I get her meaning.

"Yeah, okay."

She side-eyes Rooster, then leans up on tiptoes. I still have to bend down so she can whisper in my ear. "First thing Jezzie did when she joined us, was ask if any of us had a tampon," she whispers.

I blink and pull away as cold understanding settles over me. "Well, fuck. Why didn't she tell me? I would've pulled over and bought her whatever she needed."

Shelby stares at me. "Off the top of my head, I'm guessin' she didn't wanna go tampon shopping with her big brother."

Rooster snort-chokes into his fist.

I shoot a glare at him.

"She okay now?" I ask Shelby.

"Yeah, Heidi got her sorted with some girly products and Advil. Turns out, she's the only one of us ladies prepared for *all* emergencies at all times."

A laugh bursts out of me. I'm sure being a young mom taught Heidi all about the art of being prepared.

"Don't go fussin' over Jezzie," Shelby warns. "Then she'll know I told you and she'll hate me."

"I won't say a word, songbird."

Later, after many hamburgers have been consumed and a few scuffles have broken out, the lights over the track blink on, chasing away all the shadows.

People rev engines, run practice laps, line up their cars, and place bets.

Dex took Emily and Libby home. Griff gave Molly a ride home, which Remy didn't even blink at. Murphy and Heidi had to pick up their kids from Wrath and Trinity's place.

Most of the people remaining I trust. Jezzie's been hanging out with Shelby and two of the wives from our would-be support club—Ella and Juliet.

"She seems to be having fun, now," Rooster says, watching the girls.

"Yeah, I know. It's me. I'm the problem," I grumble.

He blows out a breath. "I didn't say that."

I tap my phone and check the time. Margot should be done or close to it by now. I meant what I said to Dex earlier. She could use a fun night out. "When are the races starting?" I ask.

"Any time now."

I pull myself out of the picnic bench. "Will you keep an eye on Jezzie?"

"You know it."

"I'll be right back."

I walk out to the parking lot in the hope that it'll be quieter. It's not. More people are still arriving. I wave hello to a few guys I know, but keep moving until I get to my bike.

Margot answers right away. "Hi, Jigsaw."

Satan help me. The way she says my name in that breathy little voice grabs me by the balls. "I miss you."

She sighs into the phone. "I miss you too. How's it going?"

"How'd *your* day go?" I ask instead.

"Long. Depressing. But we're almost done with the cleanup here."

"Do you need help?"

"No. You're with your sister." She pauses. "You *are* with her, right?"

"Yeah, but she's been pissy with me all day."

"Why? What'd you do?"

This woman knows me too well already. "Now, why do you assume *I'm* the problem."

She's silent.

"Well, I picked her up on my bike and we rode here," I answer, trying to picture Margot's face. "She wasn't comfortable. Said she's never ridden that long before which I know isn't true. But she's refusing to ride home." I'm not going to get into what Shelby told me over the phone.

Margot laughs for several long seconds. "Do you want to borrow my car?"

"I can get my hands on a car." I want to see Margot. Be with her. Introduce her to my sister. Not borrow her damn car. "That's not why I called."

"I don't mind."

"Why don't you come to Zips with me?"

"You want to leave your bike here and take my car?"

Shit, yeah, I guess I have to. "That's fine."

"All right. I'll get ready."

Margot

Jigsaw: On my way.

I'm tired and need a shower but I can't stop smiling at my phone.

Me: About to get in the shower. I'll be ready when you get here.

He responds with a devil-face emoji.

Laughing, I enter my apartment.

"Gretel, I'm home."

She's nowhere in sight. I guess if I want someone to greet me at the door, I need to get a dog.

I hurry through my shower, washing the grief and sadness off my skin.

What do people wear to clandestine racetracks in the middle of the night? I wander through my closet, running my fingers over different outfits, and finally land on a pair of jeans. I swipe through my T-shirts and find a black one with an image of a tarot card design of a skeleton holding a black cat. I shove my feet into my favorite blue-and-pink Adidas Gazelles platform sneakers, so I don't feel so short around all of Jigsaw's giant friends.

Nerves flutter in my stomach. He's really introducing me to his sister already? And his friends. What we have is getting more and more real every day.

I grab my keys and my purse and head down to the first floor, bumping into Paul, still wearing the suit he wore for the services today, coming up the stairs.

"Where you off to?" He gives me a tired smile.

"Just out. Meeting some people."

His lips curl into a teasing smirk. "You're going out with that biker guy, aren't you?"

Heat sears my cheeks.

As if the Harley pipes were designed to rat me out, the rumble of Jigsaw's bike thunders out on the street.

Paul bursts out laughing. "That thing isn't exactly quiet. I know he's been here a lot lately."

"I like him," I whisper.

"Good." He squeezes my arm. "Have fun."

I give him a quick, impulsive hug. "Thanks."

The engine cuts off near the side of the house and I hurry down the rest of the way.

Jigsaw's stepping onto the back porch when I open the door. "Hey."

"Hi, gorgeous." A broad smile stretches across his face. "You look cute." He nods to my shirt. "Is *The Cat Lady* an official tarot card?"

"No. But I thought it was cute." I close the door behind me and join him outside.

He pulls me into his arms and leans down, brushing his lips over mine. "You're cute."

I curl my fingers in his shirt, holding him to me for a few extra seconds. "I'm happy you called."

"I missed you." He wraps his gloved hand around mine and we cross the parking lot to the garages.

The cool air coasting over my bare arms feels nice after being in my stuffy blazer all day.

"Shelby will love the shirt," Jigsaw says as the garage door rolls up. "She's into reading tarot cards."

"Really? Is she good at it?"

He glances down at me, an affectionate smile twitching at the corners of his mouth. "Yeah, I think so."

"How have I lived here my whole life and never known this place existed?"

Jigsaw glances at the overgrown grass and weathered, barely legible sign for Zips racetrack. "It probably hasn't been popular since before you had your license. All kinds of people race and gamble here now. They do theme nights sometimes. Drag racers, street legal, import only, American, whatever."

He steers my car around the outside of the racing area, following a smaller dirt road into the closed track area. He effortlessly backs my car into a spot at the end of a lot of other done up cars lined up along a fence.

"I think your car will be safer here than out in the lot," he explains.

"Thanks."

He takes my hand and we walk through the grass, passing little white buildings with long, sliding windows in the front—like the kind of place you'd buy cotton candy and hot dogs from at a fair.

"In the summer, they'll have fried dough and stuff in some of these booths," Jigsaw explains.

"Oh, yum. I haven't had fried dough in years."

Hard boots slap over the packed dirt path, running up behind us.

Jigsaw swears under his breath and turns around. "Don't do it, fucker."

Grinning like a fool, Rooster slows his steps. "So close." His gaze drops to me. "Hey, Margot."

"Is this your way of watching my sister?" Jigsaw asks.

"She's right there." He points straight ahead to a group of girls standing around a red 90s Ford Mustang with bold white stripes painted down the hood. Two of them are about my height. For once, I won't feel like the shortest one in the group.

The place is lit up with floodlights. Engines roar, exhaust fumes tickle my nose, and plumes of smoke billow in the air.

"For an illicit racing ring, there sure are a lot of cars here," I say to Jigsaw.

"Shit, half of them probably belong to Remy's crew," Rooster says. He slaps Jigsaw's shoulder and jogs ahead of us.

"Remy's here?" I say to Jigsaw.

"Yeah, he's here all right," he grumbles. One corner of his mouth kicks up. "Your *friend* Torch is here too."

I roll my eyes skyward. "I sent him my *sorry I can't make it* text yesterday, so I don't know why you're still bent out of shape."

He rumbles with laughter and pulls me closer, kissing the top of my head.

"What's so funny?"

"I like when you call me out. Wish you'd been here earlier."

"You didn't gloat to Torch, did you?"

"Fuck no. I didn't even talk to him today. Dex almost kicked his ass for chatting up *his* girlfriend."

"Gee, Torch sure gets around," I mutter.

"Is my lady death jealous?" he whispers in my ear.

"No." I turn my head quickly and kiss his cheek.

"What's that for?"

"I'm happy to be here with you tonight."

The serious lines of his face melt into a genuine smile. "Come on, I want you to meet my sister."

One of the young women by the Mustang breaks from the pack and strolls toward us.

"There she is." Jigsaw beams. "Apologies in advance," he mutters under his breath.

On edge after the warning, a shaky smile spreads over my lips to greet her.

When she's close enough, Jigsaw wraps his arm around her shoulders and pulls her to his side. Annoyed with him or not, she tips her head back and looks at him with affection in her eyes.

"Margot, this is my sister, Jezzie."

I'm so nervous to meet his only relative that my hand shakes as I reach for hers. She holds it for a few seconds. Staring at my face for so long, I fight the urge to twitch and yank my hand back.

Shaking off Jigsaw's arm, she leans closer and stage-whispers, "Blink twice if you're being held hostage."

"What?" I let out a nervous laugh and pull away.

"Knock it off," Jigsaw groans.

"No, no, no. You're too pretty and wholesome for my brother." She lowers her voice. "Did he hypnotize you?"

"Only with his charm." *And his big dick, but I don't think you want to have that conversation.* I smile up at Jigsaw and take his hand.

"Huh, I haven't met that version of him, yet. He sounds swell, though." Jezzie grins and throws a light punch at his shoulder.

He pretends to flinch. "Har. Har. You're hilarious. Really."

"Sorry, Margot." Jezzie turns more serious eyes on me. "He embarrassed me earlier, but I shouldn't take it out on you."

"Why'd you do that?" I ask him.

He widens his eyes and presses his free hand to his chest like I've mortally wounded him. "Why do you automatically assume she's telling the truth?"

"Because I have older brothers too."

He chuckles. "I didn't *embarrass* her. I just shooed away a certain hound dog."

I roll my eyes at his innocent explanation.

Jezzie grins. "I talk to boys at school all the time and you never know about it." Her smile fades. "Don't ask me to hang out with your friends if I'm not allowed to talk to them."

"I can't win," Jigsaw mutters. "Whatever. You're a big girl. Do whatever you want. When he breaks your heart, I'll have to kill him. Then I'll be in prison, so please promise to bring me a cake with a nail file baked in it."

"What if I break *his* heart?"

"I'm fine with that."

Jezzie leans up and throws her arms around her brother's neck and pops a quick kiss on his cheek. "Aww, I love you."

"Have you been drinking?" he asks.

"Ugh." She lets out a disgusted snort and backs away from him. "I can't even say anything nice, now?"

"I'm just not used to it." A playful grin twitches at the corner of his mouth. "It's confusing."

He's left shaking his head while Jezzie skips back to the other women.

"You two are covering up a lot of pain with all those 'jokes,' aren't you?" I peer up at him and tilt my head.

His lips pinch together. "Pain, resentment, guilt. All those good, healthy emotions."

I shake my head. "That's not healthy at all. She seems like she can handle herself pretty well." I don't want to say *for someone who grew up in a cult*, because that sounds terrible, but I think he senses it.

He pulls me off the dirt path into the shadows between two of the buildings. "I don't want to be like our dad, trying to control her every decision." I can barely see his expression in the weak, hazy moonlight, but the pain in his voice is clear. "But I also can't stand the thought of anyone ever hurting her again." He drops his gaze. "And I think there's some resentment on her end."

"Why?"

He blows out a long breath. "Because when I got her away from our father, I sent her to live with our aunt. She was a safe place for Jezzie. But I think Jezzie thought she was going to come live with *me*. And I didn't really have the right living arrangements for that."

"Did your aunt take care of her?"

"Yeah, they're really close now. But at the time, I was basically leaving her with a stranger." He shrugs. "I'd probably do things a little differently now. But you can't change the past, right?"

"Very true." I study him for a few seconds, not sure if he'll be receptive to what I want to say. "Maybe you can tell *her* that?"

"Admit I was wrong?" His eyes widen in jovial surprise. "What kind of big brother do you think I am?"

Laughing, I shake my head. "I don't actually think you were wrong. You said it yourself, your aunt was a safe environment. I think you made the smartest decision you could, under the circumstances. But you can tell her you have regrets too and that you wish things could've been different. Or maybe just listen to her?"

"But we do the barb and banter thing so well."

I've said enough. "Yes, you do."

He squeezes my hand. "Thank you. I'll have to think about it. Maybe I'll ride out to campus and take her out for dinner or something one night so we can talk."

"That's a great idea."

"Do you want to come and be referee?"

I think he's testing the water with his teasing tone, but underneath it, he's serious. "I will if you want me to, but I think it's better if it's just the two of you."

"Maybe you're right." He smirks, a shadow of his usual cockiness returning. "I'll do my best to keep it civil but no promises."

I blow out an exasperated breath and try to hide my laughter.

"Come on." He curls his hand around mine again. "I want you to meet Shelby when you're not riding a pot brownie high."

"Oh my God." I press my hand to my forehead. "I'll never live that down, will I?"

Shelby runs up to us. "Hi, Margot! Oh my God, I love your shirt! Did Jiggy tell you we—"

"*Bestie*," Jigsaw draws out the word in a low, warning tone.

I flick my gaze between the two of them. "You what?"

"Nothin'. Come here, so you can meet everyone." Shelby threads her elbow through mine and pulls me toward the Mustang. "I'm so happy you joined us tonight!"

"Thanks." Her enthusiasm is infectious and she seems so genuine. I already like her. We stop in front of two women who I recognize from the night at Remy's bar.

"Margot!" Ella shouts, sliding off the back of the car and landing on the ground with a muted thump from her heavy Dr. Martens boots. Her gaze shoots to something—or someone—behind me. "I, uh, didn't realize you were with Jigsaw."

She shakes that off and drags the redhead by her side closer.

Shelby pats the woman on the shoulder. "This is Dex's niece, Juliet."

I turn, seeking Jigsaw's attention. Isn't he worried it will get back to Dex or his other club brothers that we were out together?

He steps up next to me and slips his arm around my shoulders in a possessive way that makes it obvious we're *together*.

Apparently, he's not worried about his club finding out.

"Ladies, how many races did you win tonight?" he asks.

Ella ripples with laughter. "None. This car's a dog. Eraser wants to strip it for parts."

"I thought you never lose?" Jigsaw teases.

"I blame the car." She pats the side panel.

While Ella, Shelby, and the others talk about the car, I pull Jigsaw aside.

"You're not worried Juliet will tell Dex about us?"

His jovial expression slides into a serious, but affectionate one. "No, I'm not worried about it." He tips his head back and stares at the night sky for a few beats. "I think I'm going to tell them myself."

A surge of excitement and anxiety tangles in my chest. We've admitted to ourselves that what we have is no longer just a fling. But if he's ready to tell his club, it's not just real—it's everything.

CHAPTER FORTY

Jigsaw

LAST CHURCH, WE SPENT MOST OF THE TIME REHASHING THE SHIT THAT went down in Deadbranch. Then Dex told everyone he wanted to bring Emily and Libby up to the clubhouse.

Didn't seem like the right time to make *my* announcement.

But today, I'm doing it.

Personal shit usually goes last, although my news kind of blurs the line between business and personal.

Club business is light this week. A lot of logistical stuff about who's working where. This week, I don't volunteer for any shifts at Crystal Ball when Dex says he needs some bodies. If Dex is desperate for help, either Z or Rock will tag me in. But I'm not volunteering any time soon.

"All right." Rock's gaze sweeps up and down the table. "Anything else?"

Nut up. Let's do this. Teller's gonna kill me. I dart a quick glance his way. He lifts one blond eyebrow in a *what the fuck's up* sorta way.

"Ahhh..." I lift my hand in the air to get Rock's attention before he declares church is officially over. "I have a request."

Rock inclines his head my way. I quickly glance down the other end of the table at Z, *my* president. He frowns slightly and leans forward.

"I got you," Rooster says low enough for only me to hear. Under the table, he taps his fist against my leg.

"What do you need, Jigsaw?" Rock asks.

"I'd, uh..." I sit up and clear my throat. Jesus fuck, this shouldn't be that hard. "I'd like to bring Margot up here next Friday for the bonfire."

One corner of Rock's mouth twitches, but otherwise his face remains stone cold.

"Cedarwood's daughter?" Teller asks slowly. "That Margot?"

As if we know any other women named Margot. "That's the one."

Across the table, Dex ducks his head and snickers.

I slouch lower, intent on kicking him, but Wrath's scary gaze narrows on me. I freeze with my foot in mid-kick.

"So, you were told *not* to fuck with a club asset and you decided to, what? Date her?" Wrath's tone lands somewhere between amused and murderous.

Huh. I expected Teller to get more annoyed about my news, since Cedarwood's Funeral Home is action he brought into the club.

"Date's a little..." Fuck it. "Yeah, I'm seeing her. Often. We're together."

"Duuude, are you *that* desperate for pussy?" Ravage moans. "She touches dead people all day."

Stash lifts out of his chair with a full body shiver and a disgusted groan.

I narrow my eyes at Ravage and Stash. "I'm not askin' for any opinions."

"You sure as fuck didn't ask for permission, either," Grinder says.

Great, now *my* sergeant-at-arms is pissed. I slide my gaze between Wrath and Grinder. I'd survive a beating from one of them, but probably not both of them at the same time.

Suddenly all the co-mingling the upstate and downstate charters have been doing since Z took over our club seems like a bad idea.

Rock chuckles and I turn his way again. "This is on me, I guess." He dips his chin. "I asked you to keep an eye on her, didn't I? Keep her out of Teller's way?"

At least one of our presidents is amused. I shrug. "You mentioned something about me being charming."

"Her expectations must be in hell." Hustler smirks at me. "Perfect for you."

"Jesus Christ." Teller shakes his head as if he's finally checked into the conversation. "You fuckin' serious, Jigsaw?"

"I can see it." Murphy chuckles. "They probably make a cute couple." The way he says *cute* sounds more like he means *deranged*.

Dex shoots a quick glare at his VP. "She's actually a nice woman." Dex smirks at me. "Has your quirky humor too."

Pleased someone else noticed, I dip my chin in thanks.

"You know about this, Rooster?" Z asks.

"Ahh, not until recently," Rooster answers slowly, walking a fine line between not lying to our president and not throwing me under the bus. "I knew he'd been gone a lot lately. Didn't realize *who* he was with at first."

Now's probably not a good time to tell anyone she's been to Zips with me.

"Shiiit." Suds punctuates the curse with a shrill whistle. "He must be into her. Jiggy's never officially brought a woman to the club who wasn't free ass."

"Shut the fuck up," I growl.

"You ain't sleepin' with her, are you?" Butcher asks. "I'd be scared she'd try to embalm me in my sleep or somethin'."

"Watch it, asshole," Rooster says.

"No, get all those obvious jokes out now, fuckletoes." I jab my finger in the air toward Butcher. "That right there is why I brought this up today." I slowly slide my gaze up and down the table, looking each of my brothers in the eye. "If anyone cracks corpse jokes, says inappropriate shit to her, or makes her uncomfortable in any way," I slip my knife out of the sheath resting against my leg, hold it up for everyone to see, and tap my finger against the tip. "I'm not gonna take too kindly to it."

"For fuck's sake," Rooster says on an exhale.

"Are you *threatening* your brothers at the table?" Rock asks with the barest hint of amusement lurking in his voice.

"Not a threat." I turn and hold his steady gray stare. "Just sharing information." I let my gaze slide around the table again. "Same as any of my brothers would do for their women."

Bricks lets out a low, shrill whistle of amazement.

Dex nods at me, like he's a proud papa.

"All right." Rock slaps the table to grab everyone's attention and let them know he's about to issue an order that better be followed. "Margot is Jigsaw's guest. She's *also* a club asset. I expect everyone to treat her with respect when she's here."

Wrath picks up Rock's unspoken threat. He stares at Ravage. "Don't make me discipline you in front of everyone on friend and family night."

"Why are you singling me out?" Ravage's overly outraged tone suggests he knows exactly why.

"You gonna make me say it?" Wrath cocks his head. "Really?"

Rav's gaze slides between Wrath and me. "I won't say anything to her."

Wrath turns my way and raises an eyebrow.

"Yeah, okay." I nod.

"Everyone can go," Rock says.

I hop out of my chair and weigh my options. In either direction, I have to pass one of our presidents. Which one's less pissed with me?

"That went better than I expected," Rooster says.

"Yeah, thanks for having my back, dick."

He cocks his head and I swear somewhere under that bushy beard, there's evidence I hurt his feelings. "What exactly did you want me to say?"

"Nah, I appreciate what you said." I resist the urge to glance over Rooster's shoulder. "You know I'm not escaping without gettin' drilled for more info."

He snorts. "Yeah, especially after you pulled out your knife, genius."

The weight of Z's stare pushes against me, but I turn and head toward Rock's end of the table. He's busy talking to Teller. *Perfect.* I slide behind Murphy's big, ginger ass, still planted in his chair. My cut whispers against the wall as I squeeze by.

Almost home free.

As I round the corner of the table, Rock steps in front of me and presses a hand to my chest.

"*You*, stay for a minute."

So close.

Rooster steps next to me, making it clear he's staying too.

Wrath still hasn't left his chair, so I guess he's also sticking around.

Murphy stands and claps a hand on my shoulder. "If she's not comfortable here, you guys can always come over to our place. Or stop by early and Heidi can talk to her." His mouth tilts sideways. "Warn her what to expect."

Warmth replaces my annoyance. I wasn't expecting that from Murphy. He's got enough going on at his house with his kiddos and his endless quest to impregnate his wife again. I nod quickly. "Thanks."

Finally, everyone clears out and it's just Rock, Z, Wrath, Teller, Rooster, Grinder, and me.

"Have a seat." Rock nods at Murphy's now empty chair.

Z moves into the chair next to Wrath. Rooster sits on my left. Teller returns to his chair on my right. Grinder stands behind Z's chair with his arms crossed over his chest.

No escape.

"I take it this is serious?" Z starts the inquisition.

Serious? Do I even know what that means? My shoulders jerk up in answer.

"She's already been vetted," Wrath says. "Because of our relationship to the funeral home."

"She's literally opened up the crematorium for us when we've had bodies to burn," Teller adds. "She can be trusted."

I blow out a relieved breath. *Thank fuck.* Rock's son reminding everyone about that night will go a long way to helping everyone move on to acceptance on this issue.

"What else?" Rock asks. "You seemed concerned about something more than just bringing her to meet everyone as your girl."

I lift my head and meet Z's interested stare across the table. Then Wrath's and Rock's. Should I share this? It's not a big deal.

"Margot's sensitive," I answer slowly. "Doesn't have a lot of people in her life. Growing up in the funeral home, she got bullied a lot as a kid. Even now, people are kinda weird to her when they find out what she does." I shrug again. "I don't want anyone making her feel bad when she's here. It's a really hard job." I absently rub my hand against my chest. "She sees a lot of nasty shit, so people poppin' off dumb jokes just makes it worse."

Understanding, not pity, lights Rock's eyes.

Z hums a sound of what might be approval.

"I shouldn't have said anything." I lift my chin toward the door. "Now that Rav knows it's a sensitive spot, he'll probably razz her more."

"No he won't," Wrath promises.

"Insults are our love language." Z smirks.

"Lilly teach you that, Prez?" I ask.

Teller holds out a hand like he's hitting a Pause button. "We all like ragging on each other but we usually don't give the girls more than they can handle."

"*Usually* is the key word there." Rock shoots a glare at Wrath who grins in response. "*Some* people don't know when to quit."

"What?" Wrath's eyes widen with the realization Rock's talking about *him*. "Hope handled herself just fine." He stabs a finger against the table. "Besides, I had a good reason for trying to scare *her* away."

Z lifts his hands toward the ceiling. "Finally! You admit it."

Rock chuckles.

"Rav gets into it with Charlotte," Teller says. "But—"

"He's showing up to a battle of wits unarmed," Z finishes for him. "That's on him."

Teller laughs. "That's not *quite* what I was going to say."

"I don't know." Rooster bumps my elbow. "You're always teasing Shelby."

I glare at him, but he's grinning at me. "Shelby loves our witty repartee. It's our thing."

"She does," he agrees.

"Don't take this the wrong way," Z says.

The smile slides off my face.

He holds one hand up to go with the warning. "You're smart enough to realize she has an unusual job. No one likes to think about their own mortality. Some people will be naturally curious."

"Curiosity is fine. She doesn't mind answering *normal* questions." I cross my arms over my chest and sit back. "I don't want Ravage asking her if she jerks off the corpses or something."

Everyone groans.

Z shoots a look at Wrath, then Rock. "Let's not act like he wouldn't ask something like that."

"Or *exactly* that," Wrath adds. "Hand gestures and all."

"This is serious, though?" Rock asks. "If you two split, is she still able to keep what she knows to herself?"

"I think so. She's a practical woman. She didn't have a problem doing stuff for the club before we got together. You all saw her the night of Carter's rescue. She didn't hesitate to help us out. Honestly, she's never brought it up to me again, either."

"So you're saying you guys actually talk?" Z asks.

I shoot a glare across the table. "Yes. We talk about stuff."

"Yes, but if she feels betrayed or disrespected in some way, is she still able to be *practical*?" Grinder asks.

I consider his question, what he's really asking. "I'm not planning to fuck this up, G."

Wrath snorts. "She goes to the cops, then she and her father get in trouble too. What's she going to say, 'I've known about some potential crimes that I participated in months ago and I'm just coming forward now?' Cops aren't wasting their time on that."

"Besides." An evil grin spreads over Teller's face. "There's no evidence anything even happened, and she doesn't know who went into those ovens."

"Right," I say. "I really don't think it's an issue."

"Okay. Bring her up," Rock says.

Convincing the club was easier than I expected.

Now I hope my little lady of death is ready to come party in the woods with some bikers.

CHAPTER FORTY-ONE

Jigsaw

As much as I want to go straight to Margot's place and give her the good news that my club's not gonna murder me, she's busy with a service and I can't leave right away after church. Walking out of the war room with Rooster by my side, I nod to the ol' ladies waiting for their men to come out of the chapel.

"Where's Shelby at?" I ask Rooster.

His lips twist into an amused smirk. "She wanted to do sun salutations out at the stone ruins on the property. Trinity joined her."

"What, the champagne room doesn't have the right vibrations for yoga anymore?"

"She's always liked it out there." He shrugs. "You all right with how things went down?"

"Yeah." I nod quickly. "Surprised Wrath stuck up for her so fast. And Teller wasn't as pissed as I expected."

"I think Z's more annoyed than anyone. We're gonna be feeling the heat of that for a while."

Fuck, just what I need. Our prez pissed off at both of us.

"Shelby liked Margot a lot," he says. "Glad you brought her the other night."

"Yeah." I lower my voice. "Thanks for keeping that to yourself in there."

"Surprised you didn't speed out of here to go give her the good news. Did she know you were doing this today?"

"I mentioned it but not today specifically. She's busy with work, anyway."

He stops in the hallway outside the champagne room. Loud chatter from the dining room drifts toward us from one end, and in the living room, the guys and ol' ladies are laughing and talking. But for the moment, Rooster and I are alone.

"Pine Hollow's a bit of a ride, brother. I assume, because of her job, she must be on call a lot and need to stay close to home. You plannin' to transfer to this charter so you're closer?" he asks.

That had never occurred to me. "Are *you* planning to transfer here, brother? Because the rule's always been, I go where you go. That's not changing."

His lips roll into a thoughtful line.

"Besides, your place isn't that far from her. And last I knew, Z wanted me handling more things out that way, anyway."

"Yeah, surprised no one brought up the support club today." He tilts his head toward the dining room and we continue walking. "Noticed you didn't jump up and wave your hand around to get picked for a shift at Crystal Ball this time." He snickers.

"She didn't ask me not to, just so you know." I jam my hands in my pockets. "I can't explain why, I just don't feel like it."

"No, I get it."

"If Dex is really desperate, I'll help out." I elbow his side. "Besides, you haven't been there lately. He hired these two new dancers and one is a creepy little bitch."

"The double-P dancers?" He rolls his eyes. "Rav told me all about it. The one who only whispers?"

"Pepper and Porsche," I confirm.

We push our way into the dining room where brothers are standing around in groups, catching up. The dining table hasn't been set up yet, but club girls and prospects are working fast.

Rooster and I grab cups of coffee at the bar. I'm stirring sugar into mine with my back to the rest of the room when I sense movement behind me.

"Ohhh!" Ravage shouts. "Look who it is! The next member of the pussy-whipped club."

"Jesus Christ," I mutter, turning around to face him.

"You've talked a *lot* of bullshit over the years," Rooster reminds me.

"Yeah, yeah."

Rav's grinning like an asshole, overflowing with jokes, I'm sure.

"You need a hug or a slap?" I whip my hand back and forth in front of Rav's face. "I'm down for either one."

"Brother, are you serious?" Ravage snickers. "No more Crystal Ball. No more muffler bunnies. No more anonymous ass on the road."

Christ, when he puts it that way, it sounds so fucking pathetic, I'm even more confident about my decision.

I bob my head up and down. "Yup, yup. Get it out of your system now." Rooster's right. I've run my mouth a lot. I have this coming, so I'll let them have their fun.

Stash raises his hand like he's waiting for someone to tag him into the conversation. "I thought you enjoyed women of all sizes, shapes, ages—"

"I do." I cut Stash off. "But I'm not afraid to admit that I now see the value in being a one-woman man."

Rooster snorts. "This should be entertaining."

I side-eye him. "You don't have to join in, motherclucker."

"I can think of *one* very important reason. You can have sex whenever you want," Ravage says. "Without having to work for it."

I shoot him a withering glare. "You're confusing *girlfriend* with *blow-up doll*."

"Again," Dex adds. "He always gets those confused."

Rooster chuckles and taps Dex's shoulder. "The fuck you doing here with these clowns?"

"Maybe we should buy Rav a blow-up doll for his birthday," Stash suggests.

"Just say *you* want one," Rav fires back.

"I don't *need* one." A smug smile stretches over Stash's face. "Got all I can handle."

"Only thing you're handling is your dick and a Fleshlight," I mutter, taking a sip of hot, sweet coffee.

Butcher joins our circle. "Bro, you sure about this? What's the upside?" His eyes widen as he seems to notice Rooster and Dex—two happily non-single brothers next to me. "I mean for you, Jiggy."

It's impossible to put it into words for these guys when I barely understand it myself. "I have someone who actually listens to me."

"Poor Margot." Dex snickers. "I don't even want to know what twisted shit you've subjected her to."

"I know, right?" I grin at him. "Her patience has no limits."

"You mean, she laughs at your shit-tastic jokes," Rooster says. "And she's not faking it. She actually thinks you're funny."

"She doesn't fake *anything*." Too late, I realize how dirty that sounded.

"Is she a screamer?" Rav asks. "Because those quiet, nerdy ones are usually some of the dirtiest bitches—"

I lunge for him. My hand's wrapped around Rav's throat before my coffee cup even splatters against the floor. I squeeze and tighten my grip. "The fuck did you say?"

Rav's eyes widen to the size of frisbees. He grabs my wrist, attempting to pry me off of his windpipe. "Not...her...specific—specifically," he sputters.

"All right, Jiggy, ease up." Dex touches my shoulder, pressing gently. "Rav's just dicking around, he wasn't disrespecting her."

I force a crazed grin onto my face and release Rav. He stumbles backward, holding his throat and coughs.

What's happening to me? Rav and I trade way worse insults all the time. I won't apologize, though. Insulting each other is fine; talking about Margot that way is unacceptable.

"Sorry, Jiggy." Rav backs out of grabbing range. "Just messing around like we always do."

"Yeah, I know," I answer with a gruff bite to my tone. It's as close to an apology as he's gonna get.

"You know, when a mosquito lands on your ball sack, that's when you'll understand you can solve problems without violence," Sparky says.

We all turn and stare at him.

He holds up his hands. "I'm just sayin'."

If anyone else said it, we'd be questioning his membership in the club. For Sparky, it's nothing surprising.

"Thank you, Philosopher Pot Plant," Dex says.

Rooster's staring at me with an expression I can't quite read which is insane since I usually know every thought rolling through his head before he does. "What?" I snap.

"Nothing." His mouth slides into a sly grin. "Does this mean I can reassure Shelby that her mother won't be your date to *our* wedding?"

I roll my eyes at him but can't come up with a quippy comeback. Margot broke me. I don't even want to joke about nailing Rooster's soon-to-be mother-in-law just to annoy him. One of my favorite pastimes.

"Wow," Dex says, drawing out the word to a dickish extreme. "Is he speechless or is he having a stroke?"

Rooster waves his hand in front of my face. "Dunno. Hard to tell."

I slap his hand away.

"So I had a thought." A devious grin sneaks across Ravage's mouth.

"Well, that must've been a long and lonely journey inside that dusty brain," Dex mutters.

I bump my fist against Dex's arm. "Good one."

Ignoring us, Rav unleashes his big thought of the day. "Are you planning to give Margot the heads-up that you've nailed Shelby's mom?" Rav grins and squeezes his hands together like an excited five-year-old waiting to be handed a lollipop for being a good boy at the doctor's office. "Since, you know, you're all gonna be in each other's lives forever and all?" He waves his hands between Rooster and me.

Oh, fuck. *Do I need to share that with Margot?*

Is a meteor about to hit the planet? Ravage actually has a point.

Rooster's stare twists into downright hostile.

"Oh, come on," Dex says, slapping Rooster's shoulder. "This isn't news."

I smirk at Rooster, daring him to deny it.

"Asshole," he grumbles.

"Thanks, dick," I grumble at Rav.

"That's what you get for choking me, motherfucker."

I take a quick step toward him and enjoy his flinch.

As the laughter and jabs die down, I catch Rooster watching me again. His eyes narrow like he's puzzling something out. Not a fan of that. "You got something to say?" I snap, more harshly than I intended.

"Nope. Just never thought I'd see this day. I want to soak it all in." He claps my shoulder. "My boy's growing up."

Instead of laughing that off with one of my usual snarky comebacks, I stop and look Rooster dead in the eyes. "Isn't that what Shelby's reading said? The old me has to die to feel truly alive?"

He frowns, as if he can't believe I brought that up. "Cards or no cards, you're headed somewhere good, brother."

His words—and apparent faith in me—plunge deeper than a knife.

CHAPTER FORTY-TWO

Jigsaw

ONCE AGAIN, I'M SNEAKING INTO MARGOT'S PLACE UNDER THE COVER of darkness.

She meets me at the back door, looking absolutely adorable in a black long-sleeved top with white skeletons printed all over it, matching pajama pants, and bright red socks on her feet.

Not caring who might be around tonight, I immediately scoop her into my arms and crush my lips against hers, taking her mouth in a greedy kiss.

"Missed you," I say in between soft licks and tastes of her tongue.

Her fingertips feather against the back of my neck, sending an electric current straight to my dick.

"You're a sight for sore eyes," she whispers.

Her grave tone presses Pause on all the filthy things I want to do to her. "Bad day?"

"Not really. I just missed you."

How do those simple words have the power to sneak into my chest and curl around my heart? I lift her higher in my arms. "Wrap your legs around me."

"Are you going to carry me all the way upstairs?" she asks, while doing exactly what I want.

"I can't let go of you, so yeah."

She tightens her arms around my neck and rests her head on my shoulder, holding on while I slowly navigate the three flights.

At her door, I stop, wanting to press her against it and grind myself into her center but she left it ajar. I kick it closed behind us.

"How do you want me?" I ask.

She tugs the collar of my shirt aside and kisses my neck. "In your lap, like the other day. With you holding me while I rock myself up and down your long, thick—"

I slam us against the wall, using my arms as a buffer so I don't hurt her back and seal my mouth over hers, absorbing her dirty words into my lungs. She tastes like heaven and I'm vibrating with the need to be inside her but also want to take things slow.

"Or, we can do this," she whispers in between kisses, "and do that next."

"Greedy little girl tonight, huh?"

I hate setting her down, but I need a minute. "Get in the bedroom and show me how much you want it."

Interest sparks in her eyes, and she bites her lip. "Okay."

I'm shedding clothes as soon as she steps away. My boots and cut are off and I'm working on my jeans when she calls my name.

I lift my gaze and almost come in my pants. My shy girl, leaning in the doorway, wearing nothing but a *get over here and fuck me* smile, wiggles her finger at me.

"You're so fucking gorgeous." I strip my T-shirt off and close the distance between us. She retreats into the bedroom, triggering my instinct to chase her.

I get my arms around her before she reaches the bed.

"How do you want me?" I growl against her throat.

"On the bed."

I shove my jeans and shorts down my hips and drop onto the edge of the mattress. My gaze lands on a condom ready and waiting for me. "You mean business tonight, huh?" I grin and tear into it.

She stares as I quickly roll it on. Our eyes meet and something both wild and tender passes between us.

"Come here." I curl my hand around her hip, dragging her closer. "You ready?"

"The friction from you carrying me up the stairs almost made me come." She bites her lip, almost like she's frustrated.

"Well, climb up and come get it." I hold my cock steady as she braces herself against my shoulder and boosts herself into my lap. "That's it." I guide myself to her opening as she hovers over me.

"Jensen," she breathes out as she slowly sinks down on me, her nails digging into my shoulder. "Oh God."

"Wrap your legs around me."

She shifts and rocks sideways, trying to get her legs in position. The whole time I'm biting my lip, trying not to blow. She feels so fucking good.

She lets out a deep, satisfied groan when I'm fully inside.

"Do your thing." I keep one arm around her back for support. "Show me."

Holding on to my shoulders, she leans back and rocks her hips against me, then circles, then returns to the slow, maddening, rocking motions.

She hugs me tighter, fusing our bodies together while circling her hips. I touch my lips to hers and she opens for me, kissing me deeply.

"You're so sexy, baby," I whisper in her ear. "Telling me what you want. Taking what you want. You have me so crazed. I'm trying so hard not to come before you."

She answers with a deep, ragged moan. "Feels...so good. Oh!" she gasps and moves faster, grinds into me harder.

Heat pools at the base of my spine. Pleasure circles through my abdomen and down my thighs. I'm not going to make it much longer.

She releases another moan that shoots through my chest. Her body squeezes me so damn tight. She throws her head back, the ends of her hair tickling my legs, adding to the sensations overwhelming me.

"Right there," she gasps.

Thank fuck. Thank fuck. Thank fuck.

Hot, intense waves pulse down my spine as she spasms around me. I finally let go and explode, emptying myself. She sags against me, resting her head on my shoulder. Her tongue darts out, softly flicking over my skin. We stay that way for a few minutes, sweat cooling on our bodies.

Finally, I have to help her off me. I gently set her in the middle of the bed. "I'll be right back."

On the way back from the bathroom, I stop outside her door.

That wasn't fucking. That wasn't a lesson. *We made love.*

She turns her head and smiles as I enter the bedroom and close the door.

I slide in next to her and ease one arm under her body, rolling her toward me. She hitches her leg over mine, just the way I like.

"How was your day? How was church?" she asks, tracing one finger over my cheek like she can't get enough of touching me.

"Told the club about us." I want her to understand how important she is to me.

She pulls back and stares at me. "Is that going to make things complicated?" Sadness or worry clouds her expression.

"No." I run my hand over her hair, twirling her messy curls around my finger. "Club's already vetted you because of the relationship the club has with your dad."

"Vetted me?"

I cock my head. She has to know what I mean by that.

"Oh, they trust me to not ever speak of your nocturnal activities." She tickles her fingers over my chest. "No worries there, I'm an excellent secret keeper."

Of that, I have no doubt. But it suddenly feels like we're talking about different things.

"What does this mean?" she asks. "What's next?"

"I want you to come to the clubhouse with me. Hang out with all my brothers and their ol' ladies."

She ducks and presses her forehead to my chest, her soft, silky hair tickling my skin. "I'm not always good around people. You know, *live* people."

"Hey." I press my fingers to her chin and tip her head back. "That's not true. You counsel people and get them through the worst time in their life. You had fun when we went to Zips, right? My sister loved you. You've already met a lot of my brothers. They all like you."

"Really?" The surprise in her voice squeezes my dark, shriveled heart. "They don't think I'm a weirdo for what I do and where I live?"

"No." *And I made it really fucking clear today that they better not make you uncomfortable.*

"Will Rooster be there?"

I frown at her. "You got a thing for my brother?"

"No," she answers in her even, patient tone. "I know you say they're all your brothers, but he's the one who's closest to you."

"Yeah." I nod.

"And I feel like I know him the best. He's nice to me."

"Teller isn't nice to you?"

"He is. But he's all business."

I snort-laugh. "Yeah, I'm aware. He's even worse now that he's about to be a dad."

"Aww, I'd like to see the twins when they get here," she says.

I study her face. "You like babies?"

She shrugs. "I don't have a ton of experience around them, but yes."

"Well, you'll have more babies and kiddos than you'll know what to do with, then. My brothers seem to be reproducing like rabbits lately."

She laughs softly.

"Dex will be there with his girl, Emily. Her sister, Libby, will probably be there too. Shelby's looking forward to seeing you again."

"Really?"

She sounds so happy and also…surprised.

"Yes. She liked you," I assure her. "The ol' ladies are all good women. They'll love you."

"This is a big deal, isn't it?" she whispers.

"No. It's just a fun night at the clubhouse. They like doing bonfires in the woods upstate. Very casual."

"Oh. Upstate? So not your club?"

"It's still my club. Every charter is open to us. But Downstate and Upstate are basically merging into one club lately." I shrug. "I kinda like being up there better. They have a nicer setup. Private. Peaceful." I

421

squeeze her to my side. "Things I'm starting to appreciate more and more."

She tips her head back and flashes a wicked grin. "Bonfire in the woods, huh? Maybe you can chase me through the forest and if you catch me, we can give standing doggy against a tree a try." She wiggles her butt against my hand.

I rumble and shake with laughter. "Oh, it's on now, little lady death. You better wear something with easy access."

CHAPTER FORTY-THREE

Margot

"So, will I get to see your home club too, then?" I ask Jigsaw after he stops laughing.

"Yeah, of course." He hesitates. "The parties and stuff there aren't always quite as...wholesome, though." His rough voice prickles the hairs on the back of my neck. "Eh, they still get rowdy upstate too but there are dedicated nights to just close friends and family. Plus, they have a second clubhouse now in Empire, right next to Crystal Ball."

A clubhouse next to a strip club? That sounds like a girlfriend's nightmare fuel. "What are you saying?"

"The clubhouse is always, uh, crawling with muffler bunnies looking to take care of the guys. And they're not always shy about when and where they fuck. Or announcing who they've fucked to... um, anyone."

I pull away and frown, suddenly wishing I hadn't been so eager to rub myself all over him earlier. "Muffler bunnies? Is that the term of endearment for biker groupies?"

"Yeah."

"I've read that before, not the term *muffler bunny*, but the rest of it." I wave my hand in the air like it hadn't both intrigued and disgusted me.

"It's always that way," he says without apology. "Usually I'd…" He stares at my face like he's trying to memorize every curve, freckle, and eyelash before he says something that will push me away. "All I've been able to think about since we…" He shakes his head. "All I can ever think about any more is *you*. Your face. Your voice. The way you feel when I sink my cock deep inside you." His eyes gleam with wonder.

I swear my heart stops. "And?"

"I don't want anyone else."

"Don't *want* anyone else or haven't *had* anyone else? I need clarification."

His lips tilt. "You're not finding this flattering, are you?"

"Not really." I tilt my head and study him. "But I'm intrigued, so continue."

"No, I haven't fucked anyone else, Margot. And not only because when we started this I promised you I wouldn't. I didn't *want* to."

"Aw, has that been hard for you?" I tease.

He reaches down and grabs his crotch. "No. That's what I'm trying to explain."

I burst into giggles.

"Poor Jensen." I graze my finger over a ticklish spot along his neck. "Did I break you?"

He lifts his shoulder, trapping my hand and laughs. "I'm not complaining." He squeezes and rubs his big hands over my hips. "Not complaining one bit."

"Why are you telling me this?"

"Because you mentioned visiting Downstate. I don't want you to think I'm hiding anything. I want you to visit there. I just want to warn you what you might encounter."

"Your home charter," I say, the words feeling unnatural on my tongue.

"Yes." He smiles as if he's pleased I remembered that, then his expression turns serious. "Girls like to sometimes…haze ol' ladies? Tell them tales about…"

"Your wild, swinging bachelor days?"

"Yeah."

I work that out in my head for a few seconds. "So, you're trying to politely tell me that if I visit *your* clubhouse, there is a high probability that some random woman—or many random women—will introduce themselves by telling me that they've fucked you at some point? Is that what I'm supposed to infer from this roundabout conversation?"

He bites his lip and nods.

My stomach rolls with disgust. But that's unfair. He's thirty. Of course he's slept with other people. I'm more jealous that they were actually having *good* sex and I didn't know how good it could be until I met Jigsaw.

"Well, I guess I'll have to thank them for teaching you"—I wiggle my fingers in front of his body like I'm weaving a magic spell—"to be so talented at all the sex stuff."

He chokes on a laugh and shakes his head. "I don't know what to say to that. But standing your ground is usually the best approach with them."

"If your club loves and respects ol' ladies as much as you claim, why do you let the...muffler bunnies...harass them?"

"We don't *let* them. If they get caught disrespecting an ol' lady, they usually get tossed out and told not to come back." He shrugs. "But...it's not always that simple."

"Okay." I'm liking the idea of visiting his downstate clubhouse less and less.

"I'm not saying it will happen for sure. I just want to warn you."

"Okay." I sit up and slide to the end of the bed. "Just remember, if anyone messes with me." I glance over my shoulder and catch his eye. "Or if any of those girls try to touch you in front of me." I narrow my eyes so he understands how serious I am. "Don't forget, I'm used to carting dead people around." I flex my arm muscles. "I'm stronger than I look. And I know how to dispose of bodies."

CHAPTER FORTY-FOUR

Jigsaw

Margot is the most exciting and terrifying woman I've ever known. So hesitant and concerned about running into girls from my past one minute. Then stone cold the next, reminding me she knows how to dispose of bodies.

Absolutely intoxicating. My perfect woman.

Adorable too, because I can't picture her hurting a fly. She's too sweet. Too sensitive to ever hurt someone. All that means is I need to keep her close and protected when we're at the clubhouse.

"I'm not taking more shifts at Crystal Ball either," I announce.

She tilts her head and sits on the edge of the bed next to me, tucking her leg up so it grazes my side.

I rest my hand on her knee, sliding my thumb over her satiny skin.

She's quiet, waiting for me to elaborate.

"I'm not saying I'll never have to work there again. But I didn't volunteer this week when Dex asked."

"Why? Don't you lose money then?"

Dex, or the club really, pays me well for those shifts. But I didn't factor that into my decision. "I make money with the club other ways. It's not a big deal."

"I didn't ask you to do that."

"I know."

She bites her lip. "I don't want you to be mad at me later."

"Margot. It's my decision. I just wanted you to know."

Is now a good time to mention one of the other ways I earn with the club is through our porn production company? Probably not. All of that's done electronically. I rarely have to see the girls in person.

"You realize I look at naked bodies all the time too, right?" she asks with a teasing lilt to her lips. "They're just *dead*."

I sit and stare at her, then shudder. "That absolutely never occurred to me until this minute."

She stares at me, waiting for...something. Does she think I'm judging her? Or that I'm going to bail? "I know you treat them with respect and care, Margot."

"Thank you."

"You can always tell me anything."

She glances at her closet door. "Since you've been spending a lot of time here lately, you can leave some things here. If you want."

"Already left my toothbrush in the bathroom."

She winces. "Yeah, I had to get you a new one. I caught Gretel gnawing on yours."

"What?" I laugh for a solid minute. "Glad you caught her before I used it."

"Anyway," she says. "Are you a fold stuff and put it in a dresser guy? Or hang everything up?"

"Uh, both?"

She nods once. "I'll move stuff out of that dresser." She points to a large multi-drawer piece of furniture across from the foot of the bed. "I have more drawers and stuff in my closet. And I can clear a space for you right inside the door."

My heart pumps a little faster. I've never wanted to share closet space—or any space, really—with a woman before.

She pats my thigh. "Come shower with me?"

"Don't have to ask me twice."

Laughing, she hurries out of the bedroom. Maybe she wasn't kidding about wanting me to chase her down.

"Can you bring me a robe?" Margot calls from the hallway.

"You know I prefer you naked." And in the spirit of her beautiful nakedness, I snatch a condom off the nightstand in case I get the urge to nail her to the shower wall with my cock.

"It's in the closet behind the door!" she shouts.

Closet behind the door? My eyes dart to the long, narrow closet she mentioned clearing out for me. I swing the door open, surveying the space, mentally measuring it again.

This house is like a labyrinth, each level occupying space in ways that defy logic, as if the walls themselves are playing tricks. It's even weirder than the eighteenth century homestead of horrors I grew up in.

The closet's a long, dark corridor. Above me, a string dangles, and I pull it. Bright yellow light flares, illuminating the space, chasing away the shadows but not making the closet seem any less strange.

Clothes. So many clothes hang from rods and colorful hangers. Different clothes. Lots of black on one side of the closet. All bright colors on the other. Dresses and cardigans. Leggings and sweatshirts. Like each of Margot's personalities has its own wardrobe. Not sure how she plans to make room for my sad little collection of T-shirts, jeans, sweats, and flannels.

No bathrobe in sight, yet.

I move farther into the long, deep corridor that seems to open up into a wider square at the end. Creating a T-shaped room. What a strange fucking house. No wonder she compared it to the Winchester Mystery House.

Maybe this was originally used as a nursery? A room close to the main bedroom, connected by a hallway, that was then converted into a closet when she had the place remodeled? No, the original builders wouldn't have placed a main bedroom on the third floor. Would they? What do I know? I'm a biker, not a fucking architect.

I pull another string that illuminates the far end of the closet. Shoes. Enough shoes to fill a damn store. Lots of heels. Lots of urban-style sneakers in a variety of colors. My girl really likes bright colors on her feet.

To the right there's a desk with a mirror over it and makeup scattered all over the top. Two big ring lights on either side of the desk probably help brighten the space so she doesn't do her makeup Dr. Frank-N-Furter style. A shelf with a few different styles of wigs. *Huh.* I can't picture Margot wearing a wig. Maybe she's really into dressing up for Halloween?

No dust or cobwebs in here. She uses the space often. I turn to investigate the other end of the T shape. One wall is just a long mirror. Across from it, little pegs and hooks have been affixed to the wall to create a display of hair accessories. Barrettes, bows, scrunchies, clips, all sorts of things I can't even identify. Funny, since so far, I've only seen her use simple elastics and a few fancy hairpins. Under that stands a tall, ornate chest made of cherry wood and brass hardware. A jewelry armoire. Rooster's aunt had a similar piece of furniture where she stored jewelry and other sentimental items.

Above all of that, some sort of rod hangs down from the ceiling. Odd, opaque, marble-like crystals hang like pendants suspended from thin velvet ribbons about eye-level for me. Ornaments?

Wait, is the first one an *eyeball*?

No, that's nuts. It's probably some Halloween decoration from a discount home store. My girlfriend doesn't have an *eyeball* hanging in her closet, for fuck's sake.

She does have access to a lot of bodies.

Jesus Christ, now I'm doing what everyone else has done to her. Assume the worst because of her job. Besides, even if it really is an eyeball, who am I to criticize? I collect pinky fingers from people I've murdered for my club. And I've got a jar full of my father's teeth stored in an old trunk in *my* closet. Maybe Margot collects weird shit. Everyone needs a hobby.

I pluck one of the other ornaments between two fingers and study it. Clear glass, maybe? And what looks like...hair clippings suspended inside? I release it and it sways back and forth. Creepy. I understand why she keeps them hidden here. I grab another ornament, This one's not suspended by velvet. It looks more like a shoelace or more specifically, a round boot lace. Same strange hair clippings inside.

Another one has the hair and what looks like a fucking *tooth* encased in it. This part of the closet dead-ends. Unless I've totally lost my bearings, I think the back of the hall closet must be on the other side of the wall.

Between that and the armoire with the freaky ornament collection, there's a flat space with nothing. Margot has every inch of wall space in this closet covered with *something*. The blank space seems strange. I press my palm flat against the dark-stained wood. The faint edge of a seam scrapes along my fingers and I push.

A piece of the wall swings open. *No, not the wall.* A hidden door. Similar in size to a cupboard. Someone Margot's height can probably stand inside but I'd have to duck.

Keenly aware that I'm naked and exploring hidden compartments in my girlfriend's home, I swing the door shut. Never mind how much I hate small, dark, confined spaces. With my luck, I'll walk through it and somehow end up in her cousin Paul's dining room with a condom in my hand and my dick on display. That's not the impression I want to make on her family.

"Jigsaw?" Margot's voice comes from what seems like miles away. "Where are you? The shower's getting cold."

Keeping my distance from the "ornaments" I return to the long corridor leading back to Margot's bedroom.

And bump right into her.

Hair damp and a plaid flannel bathrobe wrapped around her body, she stares up at me with alarm flashing in her eyes. "What are you doing back here?"

When I don't answer right away, she cocks her head.

"I was looking for your robe," I say.

She turns slowly and points. "It was right inside on that hook by the door. You didn't need to come all the way down here."

Breathing hard, I just stare at her.

Ask about the eyeball? Or pretend I didn't see it?

"This closet is something else. Was it another room or something originally?" I step forward, but she's blocking my path.

Her gaze drops to my fist. "What's in your hand?"

I slowly uncurl my fingers, revealing the crumpled condom packet. "In case we got frisky in the shower." My voice comes out flat and hollow, the furthest thing from *frisky* imaginable.

My heart pounds with the need to get out of the closet. To grab Margot and drag my beautiful, sweet, innocent woman away from whatever's back there in the corner.

No. I can't run. From the day I returned to my father's farm, whipped him raw and slit his throat, I've never hidden from anything. I do whatever my club asks, get bloody when I need to, and protect the people I care about without hesitation.

I back up a few steps. Margot follows.

I reach up and tap a fingernail against the eyeball ornament. "What the fuck is this?"

Please say a cheap ornament from The Dollar Tree. Please don't tell me you keep the eyeballs of your clients.

The unhinged version of Margot who's peeked out from time to time makes a full appearance. "If your eye causes you to sin, pluck it out, right?" She beams wide and bright.

A chill runs over me. Obviously, she's referencing a biblical quote but it doesn't explain why *there's an eyeball in her closet.* And the sin talk reminds me a little too much of my father.

"I'm familiar with the concept," I say slowly. "And all the ways anything from the Bible can be twisted to fit someone's needs. Believe me."

"I believe you." She nods and seems to drift into thought, weighing several explanations. "Remember how you told me your father is scattered across the country? So he can never hurt anyone again?"

A dark cloud of impending doom fills the small space around us.

I claw at my throat while trying to hang onto my sanity. "I told you that because I trust you."

"And I trust *you.*" She tips her head back and studies me. "I struggle with this all the time." She paces in front of the armoire, keeping her eyes fixed on the ornaments above her. "I'm supposed to offer comfort to our clients and their families. I see things no one should ever see. Things bad people do to innocents. I have to sit through sermons all the time. And when someone pulls quotes from Genesis and claims they're about God's love, I want to rip out my hair and scream."

"'Now I know that you fear God, since you have not withheld your son from me.'" The ancient line I couldn't have recited yesterday if someone held a gun to my head suddenly falls from my lips.

"Yes." She whirls around. "What Abraham does is evil. If someone did that today, they'd end up in jail."

I thought being trapped in the elevator with a casket was my worst nightmare. But discussing the Old Testament in a narrow closet with my girlfriend, when *there's an eyeball pendant swinging from the ceiling,* just shot to the top of my *things I never, ever want to do* list.

"Not always," I say.

She stops and a smile worthy of the most unhinged version of Harley Quinn lights up her face. "Exactly."

What the fuck? "Uh, I kind of agree with you but that doesn't explain why you have a fucking *eyeball* pendant in your closet."

"It's from my first kill." Red splotches spread over her cheeks. "My last one was while you were in Tennessee."

Her last one?

How many were there in between?

I stare at her. She's dead fucking serious. This isn't an elaborate prank. My sweet, soft woman who cares so compassionately for the dead, wears quirky pins, asked me to teach her about sex, and looks like innocence personified, is a fucking *serial killer.*

My stomach twists in horror, a cold sweat breaking out across my skin. She's *not* a slightly kooky woman who collects pieces of her clients—that would actually be preferable.

She murders people.

The sledgehammer of truth slams into my body, knocking the air from my lungs.

Shattering everything I thought I knew about my woman into a million pieces.

Jigsaw and Margot's story continues in:
Collect the Pieces (Lost Kings MC #25)

THE LOST KINGS MC® WORLD

by *USA Today* bestselling author
Autumn Jones Lake
This is my suggested
suggested chronological reading order
For all of the books in the Lost Kings MC World

1. Kickstart My Heart (Hollywood Demons #1)
2. Blow My Fuse (Hollywood Demons #2)
3. Wheels of Fire (Hollywood Demons #3)
4. Renegade Path (A Lost Kings MC World Novel)
5. Slow Burn (Lost Kings MC #1)
6. Corrupting Cinderella (Lost Kings MC #2)
7. Three Kings, One Night (Lost Kings MC #2.5)
8. Strength From Loyalty (Lost Kings MC #3)
9. Tattered on My Sleeve (Lost Kings MC #4)
10. White Heat (Lost Kings MC #5)
11. Between Embers (Lost Kings MC #5.5)
12. Bullets & Bonfires (A Lost Kings MC World Novel)
13. More Than Miles (Lost Kings MC #6)
14. Warnings & Wildfires (A Lost Kings MC World Novel)
15. White Knuckles (Lost Kings MC #7)
16. Beyond Reckless (Lost Kings MC #8)
17. Beyond Reason (Lost Kings MC #9)
18. One Empire Night (Lost Kings MC #9.5)
19. After Burn (Lost Kings MC #10)
20. After Glow (Lost Kings MC #11)
21. Zero Hour (Lost Kings MC #11.5)
22. Zero Tolerance (Lost Kings MC #12)
23. Zero Regret (Lost Kings MC #13)
24. Zero Apologies (Lost Kings MC #14)

...and many more to come!

ABOUT THE AUTHOR

Autumn Jones Lake is the *USA Today* and *Wall Street Journal* bestselling author of over twenty novels, including the popular Lost Kings MC series. She believes true love stories never end.

Her past lives include baking cookies, bagging groceries, selling cheap shoes, and practicing law. Playing with her imaginary friends all day is by far her favorite job yet!

Autumn lives in upstate New York with her own alpha hero.

www.autumnjoneslake.com